PAINTED
VESSELS

PAINTED VESSELS

BOOK 1

GINA RENEE FREITAG

This book is dedicated to everyone who is wading through the middle of the unknown. Whether you feel God's presence or not, He will never let go of you. Trust His plan; it is better than anything we can imagine.

For I know the thoughts that I think toward you, says the LORD, thoughts of peace and not of evil, to give you a future and a hope.

Jeremiah 29:11

PART 1

For our light affliction, which is but for a moment, is working for us a far more eternal weight of glory, while we do not look at the things which are seen, but at the things which are not seen. For the things which are seen are temporary, but the things which are not seen are eternal.

2 Corinthians 4:17-18

Chapter 1
ADA

"Wake up, Ada. We can't stay here any longer."

Ada kept her eyes closed, resisting Eli's orders. She needed more sleep. After only a few days of hiding in this old cabin, Ada felt as though the constant chill had finally left her body. The aches and pains caused by long days of trekking through underbrush were starting to feel like a memory. Even her nightmares had slowed, giving her a small hint of peace. She didn't want to get up. She didn't want to leave. And she certainly did not want to think about why it might be necessary.

Her eyes fluttered open, revealing the low morning light. It was almost dawn; the sun hovered on the horizon, unwilling to rise above the trees. Just as unwillingly, Ada sat up.

"Can't we stay?" she asked. "One more day."

"I know you don't want to go," Eli said as he grabbed items from the shelf and stuffed them into his bag. "But I'm worried. They might be closer than we think. We can't let them find us." He buzzed about the room with a determination that made her uneasy.

"How can they find us, Eli? We haven't stopped running since we reached the woods. How do you know they're even following us?"

"Because of this," he said, pulling a leather satchel out of his canvas bag, the one he had taken from that horrible man at the abandoned rock quarry. He placed the satchel in her hands. "I didn't know it was in the bag," he added.

She opened it with trembling fingers, and as she peeked inside, her heart sank. This changed everything. Her eyes darted around the cabin, and a wave of fear crashed over her as the safety of this oasis melted like a mirage in the desert.

They had stumbled upon this mossy old hunting shack four days ago, and it seemed like the perfect place to hide. It had been well stocked despite the layer of grey covering everything. The table and counter, the folded clothes and linens, and the jars of canned food on the shelf had all been coated in a colorless, dusty film. Even now, the beds hadn't lost their extra blanket of ashen drabness.

So what? At least the cabin had beds. Before finding this rundown shack, Eli had made them places to sleep in the woods. But fir boughs stacked upon bumpy tree limbs could never be as comfortable as a real bed, even a dusty one.

The fact that he was able to make beds out of fallen branches was the point she needed to remember, though. He was able to get them off the cold ground at night and made better lean-to shelters than she could, ones that wouldn't leak or fall on them. He could find water, he was good with directions, and he knew how to trap small animals. Eli had kept them safe for this long; she shouldn't question his decisions now.

She knew he was right; he usually was, and she trusted him. She had known Eli all her life, almost fifteen years. He was a year older than her, and his family had lived in the house next to hers for as long as she could remember. Eli Noble and Ada Young were best friends and always had been. They walked to school together, helped each other with their chores, and frequently explored the fringes of the back woods. Even their families—the Nobles and Youngs—ate supper together regularly. At least they used to.

Ada had always stayed home, though, whenever Eli went camping with his dad. It was one of the few things she had never done with him. Instead, the father-son duo would disappear into the wilderness for several nights at a time. Deep in those back woods, Mr. Noble taught his son all the things that were currently keeping Ada alive.

After coming home from those excursions, Eli often took her to the edge of the woods and showed her what he had learned. Last May he had her taste the edible plants he could now recognize. As she nibbled on a dandelion, he told her that when they were married someday, they could explore the woods for days and never go hungry. And when they found the perfect spot, he would build her a house, just like his dad had done for his mom.

But several days ago—almost one year later—Eli's hopes of learning any more skills from his father came to a shocking end, and from that day on, their lives would never be the same. That cold April day, which had dashed Eli's dreams, was also the source of Ada's nightmares. It was a day they both tried not to think about, yet it was constantly on their minds.

Now they desperately needed to hide, but this couldn't be what Eli had imagined when he looked to their future. Surviving in the woods was not the idyllic fairytale Ada thought it would be. Always having to worry about who might be tracking them was distressing. After several days of constantly moving, trying to stay warm, and often failing to find food, she felt broken.

Finally, having no one but themselves and owning nothing but a stolen bag of clothes and a ten-inch Bowie knife, they had chanced upon this refuge against the cold, harsh wilderness. Though faded and crumbling, this little shack offered them a place to rest. In the cabin, they would be warm and dry, maybe even safe. They could stop running and start thinking, for just one moment, about what to do next. But that hope vanished when Eli showed her what was in his bag.

As she closed the satchel's flap, her stomach flipped. The greasy leather smelled like smoke and sweat. Repulsed, Ada shoved it to the bottom of the bag. Now she was motivated to leave, even if it meant returning to those indistinguishable days and nights of trudging through the woods. They would continue to run, always moving forward.

In a daze, she watched Eli stuff old clothes into his bag. Next, a metal bowl and two cups from the cupboard went in. Shaking off her dread, Ada opened a drawer and sifted through its contents. As Eli wrapped a small knife in linens and placed it with the other items, Ada found two candles and some flint and steel, which she packed into the bag as well. Eli discovered a length of rope in a crate by the door. Setting it aside, he rolled the blankets from both beds into a tight bundle. Using one end of the rope to tie up the bundle, he created shoulder straps with the other end.

"Do you mind carrying this?" he asked.

"No, I don't mind," Ada said. She picked up a pot that was sitting on the woodstove. "Should we take this also?"

It would be easier to cook in that pot rather than on a spit made from sticks. Whenever Eli had managed to snare the occasional animal, they cooked it over a fire and ate it with their hands, resulting in burnt, greasy fingers.

"We should look for some utensils," she added.

"Good idea," he agreed. "See if you can tie the pot onto the blankets."

Eli found metal plates and utensils under the counter and tossed them into the bag. He grabbed a cloth from the shelf and tore it into strips.

"Should we take the jars of food?" she asked, nodding toward the shelf.

"Maybe one," he replied, bringing the strips of cloth to her. "Otherwise, they might get too heavy, and I don't want them to knock together and break in the bag. Here, give me your arm."

Ada obeyed, and he pushed her sleeve up and wrapped her forearm in the cloth strips. It was uncomfortable, but she felt safer with her arm covered. After tying the ends together and tucking them under the edge of the wrapping, Eli gave her a half-hearted smile.

"That should work for now," he said. "Could you do mine?"

She nodded and wrapped his arm just like hers. Eli scanned over the room one final time and grabbed a jar of greyish-yellow vegetables from the shelf.

"Okay, let's go," he said.

The two young people abandoned their sanctuary, shouldering their respective loads.

"Which way?" she asked.

Squinting, Eli pointed to the southeast. As they began to walk, the sun finally peeked over the treetops.

Chapter 2

EVELYN

Mrs. Evelyn Russell was East Haven's self-appointed expert in all things domestic, so the prospect of having newlyweds move in next door gave her quite a thrill. She first learned of this possibility while taking a well-deserved break from her own affairs yesterday afternoon. As she sat in her kitchen nook sipping spiced tea, she took a mental inventory of her pantry's stock of canned goods and other various sundries. But the task of reorganizing was forgotten when she noticed David Holden, the town's banker and property holder, escorting a young couple into the old Colebrook house.

That house had been empty for years. Situated on a plot of ten acres, it had once been efficiently kept on the inside by Mrs. Colebrook and smartly maintained on the outside by Mr. Colebrook. It was a sensible three bedroom house with an economic floorplan, neither too big nor too small.

Evelyn had often thought that if the Colebrooks had been a touch more creative and not so thrifty, their home might have been improved upon greatly. It was a sturdy building with abundant potential. In fact, after it had been vacant for only two months, she began to think of it as the perfect house for one of her own daughters to settle into. With Evelyn's influence, it could be a splendid home indeed. Several years later, her dream of beautifying the Colebrook house finally died away when all four daughters had married and moved away. But now, Evelyn felt a small rekindling of an expectation once denied her.

The couple viewing the house seemed young; they couldn't have been married for more than a few months. Due to their simple appearance, they must be starting out their married life with little to no means. They were not a local couple, and given that East Haven was a remote town, the young bride would not have a maternal figure to turn to when facing her daily trials of early marital establishment. Evelyn would be an indispensable help to her new neighbors.

To many of the local townsfolk, Mrs. Russell was considered a know-it-all and a busybody with strong, unbendable opinions. Evelyn, however, saw herself as an experienced homemaker with a burden to help the less enlightened housewives of East Haven. She *must* help them strive toward their own perfection. She wasn't able to admit, or even understand, the true source of her meddling. She was, in fact, a lonely widow, deprived of the opportunity to shape the early years of her own daughters' marriages. Of course, how could they be anything but shining examples of wifely excellence, especially considering the training Evelyn had given them before they moved away?

When it came to her daughters, she believed herself to be an undeniable success at motherhood. Her son, unfortunately, was another story. Adding him into the equation threw off her results, but this was not her fault. Instead of trusting his mother's wisdom, the young man completely ignored what she had taught him and held to a different opinion of what success looked like. When he ran off to pursue his own silly ideas instead of making a mark for himself in East Haven, it was easier for Evelyn to tuck away all mention of him underneath the many proud stories she had of her daughters. She acknowledged her son's existence only when necessary.

To ease the agony caused by the absence of her daughters, Evelyn never allowed the mistakes of a new bride to escape her notice. Young wives continually needed correcting, and she was quick to point out those corrections. She loved to demonstrate her extensive knowledge, and it invigorated her to think that this couple might move into the Colebrook house. She allowed herself to imagine an intimate, parent like mentoring relationship forming between her and the young woman. Helping this fledgling couple would undoubtedly wipe away the ache in Evelyn's heart. And of course, they would be forever grateful for the guidance she planned to give.

Wrapping her shawl around her shoulders, Evelyn dreamed of this perfect scenario. She began scheming as she stepped out her front door, and she had nearly completed an entire domestic lesson plan by the time she marched into town. She must find Mr. Holden and learn all she could about these newlyweds, starting with whether or not they intended to rent the Colebrook house and when she could expect them.

After she returned, she would finish working on her pantry. She had completely forgotten to get back to it yesterday, but she was not to blame. Since it rarely happened, it was always exciting when someone moved into town. Walking contently down the main street of East Haven, Evelyn Russell sifted through her almost forgotten plans to improve the Colebrook house, confident that her summer would be most interesting indeed.

Chapter 3

ELI

Eli dipped his hands and knife into the water and washed away the sticky blood. He was grateful they were able to camp close to a creek. Removing the pelt from a rabbit was messy work. The skin still needed to be scraped clean, but first he cut up the carcass so Ada could make a stew. He detached the sinew from the legs of the rabbit and removed them from their protective sheath. After rinsing the ligaments, he set them aside to dry. He would make them into cord later, which could be used to sew the pelt. He scraped one of the leg bones clean and set it with the sinew. He planned to sharpen it into a tool that could push the cord through the hide as he sewed it into something useful. He then scraped the fat and connective tissue from the skin.

Once finished, Eli washed himself and the rabbit pelt, which he placed on a log to dry. He was hungry. The stew would strengthen them, and he wanted to eat before starting the next unsavory step in the tanning process. Ada glanced up from the bubbling pot and scrunched her nose at him.

"You should change," she said. "It's time for supper."

He glanced down at himself. He was splattered with more blood than he realized.

"Sorry."

He unbuttoned his shirt and set it aside. Though the weather wasn't warm enough for only an undershirt, he didn't want to get a clean shirt yet. He planned on wearing the stained one later while tanning the rabbit skin.

After eating, Eli helped Ada wash the dishes and put their camp in order. He added wood to the fire, knowing he would need the embers. As the fire quickened, he admired their little encampment. This was a comfortable place to stay. They had already been there for a day and a half; he hoped they could remain for at least two more.

"You should sleep," he suggested.

Ada nodded, walked over to the lean-to, and slipped under a blanket. Sometimes it felt like they were playing house, but then reality would set in. This was not a game, and their lives depended on him remembering that. Ada looked better after eating, but Eli was convinced that a strong wind might blow her away. The outline of her collar bone was more defined than it used to be. Food was hard to come by, and they were only able to have meat once every few days. For the rest of their meals, they ate whatever plants they could find.

Eli's dad would have eventually taught him how to trap larger animals, but when they went hunting for deer, they had always brought a rifle. All he had now was the Bowie knife and the small paring knife from the cabin. Perhaps he could make a spear out of the larger blade, but for now, he was working on another project. With warm stew filling his stomach, the spear could wait.

Eli put his shirt on and carried the paring knife, a spoon, and the pot over to the rabbit. It was only the fourth one he had snared since they had been hiding in the woods. Mostly, he caught squirrels, muskrats, and even mice. Not the best for eating, but when the choice was between that or ferns and dandelions, meat always won out.

Using the knife and spoon, he removed the brain and put it into the pot. He added some water, and as he placed the pot among the coals, he thought about his dad. His father often spoke of man's ties to the earth, and because of his deep faith, he seasoned his lessons with his love of God.

"Creation is amazing, Eli. God gave us everything we need to survive right here on His glorious earth. You just have to look around to see how well He provides."

Being in the woods produced a bittersweet ache in Eli's heart. He missed his dad, but the outdoors provided a continued connection to the man. It seemed as though his father was standing beside him, repeating the wisdom he had shared through the years.

"This plant is safe to eat, but stay away from those mushrooms. Mark your snare site so you can find it later. Only take from the earth what you need; never waste any part of an animal. Wasteful people discard the organs,

but our ancestors understood that the heart and liver nourish our bodies better than the flesh. Even the bones can be useful."

There was no limit to the helpful survival tips that William Josiah Noble whispered out from his son's memories.

Eli removed the pot from the coals. He mashed the hot water and brain into an oily tanning mixture. As the liquid cooled, he found a rough rock and buffed the pelt. Once the skin was soft and supple, he slowly rubbed half of the mixture into it. Another coating would be applied in the morning, after it had dried. Eli still had a jar from the cabin; he poured the rest of the liquid into it, screwed the lid on tight, and set it aside. Hoping to keep curious animals away from their camp, he carried the rabbit pelt downstream and hung it over the water between two trees.

Back at camp, Eli changed into clean clothes and gathered their dirty ones. He washed them in the creek and laid them out to dry. As he glanced at the wet clothes, it struck him that they were all men's clothing, even the ones Ada had to wear. He wondered if it bothered her or if she even cared. Either way, he was grateful they had extra layers for warmth.

The clothes he had taken from the cabin were for a smaller man and worked well enough for Ada, even though they hung on her and made her look more petite. But the clothes he had found in the canvas bag were for someone larger. Was that man still alive? Eli remembered how lifeless the man from the quarry had looked as he lay unconscious on the ground.

Right before Eli had crept up and hit him over the head with a metal bar, he watched him stuff food and clothes into the bag. The man had paused to harass Ada, and that was Eli's chance to overtake him. He swung the bar as hard as he could, and the man dropped instantly.

Eli stared at the figure on the ground, forgetting the urgency of their escape, but hearing Ada yell woke him out of his stupor. He grabbed the man's bag, and while searching his pockets for some keys, Eli discovered the Bowie knife that now proved essential for their survival.

"Hurry!" There was a tremor in Ada's voice as she peered around the cavern. Tears streamed down her cheeks.

He found the keys and carefully tossed them to her. While Ada reached through bars to unlock the cage separating them, he took the man's shoes as well. Ada's feet were bare, and she wouldn't get far. But she could manage Eli's boots if he wore the man's larger ones. He knew he was stealing, and it made him feel guilty, but these things would be invaluable in the difficult days ahead.

He didn't like thinking about the rock quarry. Those days were not pleasant. He shook his head as if ridding himself of pests. He wanted the memories to leave him alone, so he forced his mind back to the rabbit pelt. Tomorrow he would finish tanning it and make fur lined socks for Ada. His boots were already old before he gave them to her, but now they had holes in them. The socks would protect her feet and would be thick enough to fill the oversized boots. They would keep her feet from rubbing and prevent further blistering.

As the night grew cold and dark, Eli glance toward the lean-to. If Ada had nightmares again, he wanted to get a few hours of rest before she started screaming. He put out the fire, walked over to their shelter, and wrapped himself in one of the blankets. He pressed his back against hers and savored the heat from her body. She was warm, and her rhythmic breathing was comforting. Maybe she would sleep through the night. Closing his eyes, he soon drifted into a fitful slumber.

~&

Eli watched Ada's back as she poked the fire with a stick. She must be hungry. He hadn't been able to catch any animals for two days. Nevertheless, he was determined not to disappoint her; he had a plan. As quiet as he tried to be, his footsteps gave him away, and she heard him sneaking up behind her.

"There you are," she said as she turned around.

With a proud grin, he placed the metal bowl in her lap. It was full of small, pink raspberries. The smile spreading over Ada's face was the best thing he had seen in days.

"Eli! Where did you find these? I love raspberries." She looked at them with renewed energy. "Oh, I think they might be under ripe," she observed.

"Yeah," he agreed. "It's probably the end of May—maybe."

Concern filled her eyes, but before she could say anything, he continued.

"I found a beehive inside a tree. I put some honey on the berries to make them sweeter. We missed your birthday, Ada. I want to celebrate it today. These berries can be your birthday cake."

He remembered her birthday the night before last, after he had hung the rabbit pelt over the creek. Seeing berry bushes while returning to camp reminded him of the year Ada's mother had made a small raspberry tart for her. Ruth Young was an excellent baker, and the aroma filling their home that day made Eli's mouth water. Ada had loved the tart and, to his delight, shared it with him. Because the Youngs grew them in their hothouse, raspberries were not an uncommon treat, even in early May. Eli wasn't able to make a tart, but they had the berries—and he had a gift for her.

13

"Do you really think it's been that long?" Ada's smile faded. "It was barely April when—" Her voice cut out. She tried to wipe her eyes without him noticing but failed.

"I don't know; it might be May. It doesn't matter, though. Right?" He was hoping to sound indifferent; maybe it would bring back her smile. "Here, this is for you," he added and brought her gift out from behind his back. Earlier, he had wrapped it in a shirt and tied it with a length of vine pulled from a tree.

The gift itself wasn't a surprise; she knew he was making socks for her. Over the past several weeks, she had watched him tan the four rabbit pelts. He then traced her feet and figured out how to shape all the pieces. He couldn't do any of that without her knowing about them. It was the presentation of the gift, however, that became the surprise and caused Ada's smile to return. She unwrapped her present and hugged and petted the socks, cooing over them. She put them on her feet and tested them in the boots.

"They're perfect, Eli. Thank you."

She gave him a hug and asked if they could please eat the berries now. She wanted to hear how he got the honey from the tree without getting stung. As he told her, he showed the sting on his hand that he did get. She rubbed his hand gently and praised his heroic efforts. They carried on in this desperately needed pretend play for the rest of the birthday party. It reminded them of the normal life they yearned for.

They kept the fire stoked, and as the night sky darkened, they nibbled on sweet-tart berries and woody, new-growth fern curls. They laughed and pointed out constellations they knew as well as ones they made up, telling each other stories about the starry pictures in the sky. Eventually, the fire dwindled, and their conversation slowed.

"Tomorrow we should pack up. It's time to move on," Eli said with a sigh.

"Okay," she agreed. "Thank you for remembering my birthday."

Ada gathered a few items together and set them by the lean-to. As Eli spread the embers of the fire and stamped out their glow, he watched her shake out the blankets. This was a good day, even though they didn't have much to eat. But what about tomorrow?

They needed food. They needed to be safe. They needed to find someone they could trust. Eli wasn't sure how much longer he could do this on his own. Failing to keep Ada safe was not an option, and he realized he was going to need help. For now, they would keep going forward because he couldn't think of anything else to do. But there was one thing he did know, one thing he felt certain about—time mattered. They couldn't, or shouldn't,

14

stop moving for too long. Something was pushing Eli, filling him with an urgency that kept him moving. Forward, forward, forward.

Tomorrow they would keep going forward.

Chapter 4

MARCUS

Pastor Marcus Duncan had a routine. Every weekday after lunch, he wandered throughout the town and planned his sermons. On these strolls, he observed all the scenes around East Haven's main street. He would watch his parishioners going about their daily activities and listen for the Holy Spirit's guidance on his upcoming message. He wouldn't put pen to paper until Friday, but by then his sermon had written itself. He simply needed to transcribe the thoughts in his head. It was an effective routine.

Most of the townsfolk knew this was his habit, so between the hours of one o'clock and two thirty, they limited their discourse with him to passing pleasantries. This Tuesday would have been like any other if it weren't for David Holden, who leaned against the wall of his bank and beckoned to Marcus, claiming to have information he would want to know.

"The Colebrook house sold yesterday to a couple from out of town."

"Really? That's great news," Marcus said. "We haven't had a new family move into town for a while. Who are they?"

"Well, their name is Gardner. They're in their early twenties, so just starting out. No children yet." David chuckled. "You remember those days, don't you? Long time ago! It must be an exciting adventure to begin married life in a new town."

"Absolutely," Marcus agreed with a nod. "But I wouldn't want to make a change like that. At least not now, not at my age. It was easier to take risks back then, wasn't it? Can *you* remember that long ago, friend?"

Marcus winked as David rubbed his thinning hair.

"And what brings the Gardners to East Haven? Do they have friends or family here?"

"No," David said. "East Haven was the third town they visited. They didn't find what they were looking for elsewhere." He grabbed the lapels of his jacket proudly. "They fell in love with the Colebrook house and agreed to buy it on the spot. I think they're from Bradford, or maybe the outskirts."

"Bradford? You have a friend from that town, don't you?" Marcus asked.

"Harold Ross," David said with a nod. "He owns the bank, as a matter of fact. He's an honest man and quite organized." David chuckled as he spoke of his colleague. "If I know Harold, he'll have very detailed records regarding Mr. Gardner's account. That will make my paperwork easier, so I'm grateful for it. The Gardners will return a week from Thursday to pick up their house key. I believe you'll like them, Marcus; they're an agreeable couple—and humble." He paused for a moment. "But you might find them a bit different."

"Different?" Marcus was somewhat intrigued. "What do you mean?"

David laughed. "Oh, just something about their style and demeanor. I got the impression they may have lived a more eccentric life than one usually finds in a small town. Don't worry, I'm sure it will be good for us."

"Hmm," Marcus said with a slow nod.

David was correct; the town could benefit from some variety. But as pastor, Marcus would be the one dealing with the gossip, not to mention all the *honest Christian concern* if the Gardners strayed too far from convention.

"You said they'll move in next Thursday?"

"Yes, and I thought it might be nice to have some townsfolk clean the house before they arrive. It's been vacant for several years and could use some attention. Do you think your wife would be willing to head up that project?"

"Grace?" Marcus nodded. "Definitely. I'll talk to her about it this evening. She could ask Hannah Weber to help. I'm sure Hannah would see the opportunity as an excellent way to welcome her new neighbors."

"Perfect. Thank you, Marcus." David clasped his shoulder. "I'll unlock the house next Wednesday. That should be enough time to give it a good wipe down. Speaking of neighbors, here comes Mrs. Russell."

He indicated the widow's approach with an almost indiscernible nod. Marcus turned and saw Evelyn walking briskly toward them, her jaw set with determination.

"Mr. Holden? Mr. Holden. I am so glad I caught you. Oh, hello Pastor Duncan." She nodded at the two men. "Mr. Holden, please tell me about the couple who was with you yesterday. I am so anxious to know everything. Mr. Holden, please tell me. Will they be moving into the Colebrook house?"

"Mrs. Russell, you are going to have to start referring to the old Colebrook house as the new Gardner house," David said with a wink.

Evelyn shook her fists in triumph. "Thank the Lord! That house has been empty for far too long."

"David," Marcus said, inspired by a new thought. "Why don't I talk to Grace about having a warm supper waiting for them next Thursday? I'm sure they'll be tired from their travels and would appreciate not having to cook their own meal."

David nodded his agreement.

"They're moving in next Thursday?" Evelyn asked. "So soon! Supper is an excellent idea, Pastor. I will make dessert for them. The Gardners, you say? What sort of name is that? I imagine they must work the land."

Evelyn chuckled at her own joke. "Well, one can only hope. Seeing some colorful flowers in their yard would improve my view, I should think. So then, a simple cake. That is a most sensible, everyday dessert—not too fancy nor too sweet. It will be just the thing for these Gardners." She readjusted the shawl around her shoulders. "Now, Mr. Holden, what can you tell me about them?"

"They seem young and pleasant, Mrs. Russell. I'm sure they will be good neighbors."

"Young! Well, I could see that from my kitchen. But where did they come from? What type of families do they have? What are their manners like? Are they well brought up and educated? Teachable? Surely, even Pastor Duncan would appreciate knowing that. Come now, are they Christians? Oh, please tell me they aren't heathens from the west. What a shame that would be. How troublesome it is to avoid questionable neighbors."

"I didn't have a chance to get any of that information." David glanced sideways at Marcus. "I'm sorry to say, but the business at hand yesterday was mostly about the house."

"You know, Mrs. Russell," Marcus added, "those of different faiths still need to see Christ's love and charity in their neighbors."

"Yes, yes, of course. All heathens need to hear about Christ, and we must pray diligently for their souls. But sometimes, no matter how hard we pray, a bad apple is just that. You know what they say about a bad apple in a barrel of good apples. Well, it is just as true with a bad soul. Spiritual rot can spread like a disease."

The pious old widow sniffed as she lifted her chin a touch higher. "We Christians can't be too careful. Now, Mr. Holden, are you truly going to make me find out about these people all by myself?"

She stared at the banker, waiting to hear more. David probably knew what the inquisitive woman wanted to know; nevertheless, he only nodded at her.

"Come now, are they as poor and green as they look?" she finally asked. "You must know something that will give me an idea about the kind of neighbors I'm getting."

"Mrs. Russell, I can't tell you anything about their finances," David said, tilting his head. "But their age would imply they are newlyweds. And I believe they've been living in Bradford. Anything more, we will all have to find out in good time."

"Humph! Apparently," she said with a resigned sigh. "Well, I had better go to Johnson's Mercantile and get sugar for the cake. Good day, Mr. Holden. Pastor, please tell your wife I will bake a cake to go with the supper she prepares for the Gardners. Just a simple, unfrosted cake. I would hate to make that poor young wife feel intimidated. We wouldn't want to give the impression that the people of East Haven are too extravagant."

With another nod, she marched toward the general store, calling out to Agnes Miller who was passing by. Evelyn asked if she had heard the news: the Colebrook house had finally been rented. She beseeched Agnes to please pray that the young couple were *not* heathens.

"Rented?" Marcus asked as he glanced at his friend. "I thought they bought the house."

David nodded his head. "They did."

Marcus watched the woman cross the street toward Mrs. Miller and the mercantile. With Evelyn on the job, all of East Haven would soon know everything *she* might imagine about the town's new inhabitants.

"Perhaps it would be an ideal week to give a sermon on loving our neighbors," Marcus said.

"Yes," David agreed with a laugh. "That would be ideal. Thank you again for talking with Grace. I better let you get back to your sermon planning."

He shook Marcus' hand and walked into the bank, continuing to chuckle under his breath.

Marcus pulled a pocket watch out of his vest and looked at the blued hands. A quarter to three already! He turned toward his office and decided to skip his afternoon walk for the rest of the week. This plan would require him to write his sermon while hiding behind his desk, which rarely fostered creativity, but neither did an overly talkative town. At least he had a topic.

Marcus took in a deep breath and enjoyed the sweet smell of spring rain turning into fresh summer flowers. As he walked to the church, the Holy Spirit guided his mind back to his sermon.

Chapter 5
ELI

Eli lay on his stomach, propping himself up with his elbows as he peered at the town below. Ada was next to him, her head resting in the crook of her arm. She had fallen asleep several minutes ago. He glanced at her, trying to decide which he felt more: the longing to be as deeply asleep as she was or the excitement of what the next day would bring. Nervous excitement had won over exhaustion for the moment. He wouldn't be able to sleep anyway.

They had spent the entire day watching this town, trying to determine if it was a good place to execute Eli's plan. Observing the town wasn't particularly thrilling, but the idea of going into those streets was making it hard for him to sit still. Fortunately, they had several things going in their favor, considering their covert needs at present.

It was most likely early summer. Eli had noticed the days getting longer, and the nights were not quite as frigid as they had been. With summer setting in, the rainy days were beginning to spread further apart, and the ground didn't stay wet for long. This allowed them to keep low to the ground. They could watch the comings and goings of the town in relatively dry comfort. Their clothes, which were made up of drab browns and greys, camouflaged them well, and the hill provided a decent vantage point. They could spy on the town without being seen, and the forest was immediately behind them in case they needed to make a hasty retreat.

For several days now, Eli was aware of the fact that they were coming to the end of the big wilderness in which they were hiding. At first, they

21

stumbled upon small farms with fields of young wheat or corn backed up against the edge of the woods. They were able to skirt around their boundaries, and then the trees would stretch out before them again, making it possible to continue moving toward the unknown destination tugging at Eli.

After the farms, small clusters of homes accompanied by a shop or two began to appear. These little communities were easy to circumvent, but larger towns soon sprung up, making it difficult to move forward without being seen.

Sure enough, the landscape had changed. Towns were now the prominent feature with modest areas of wooded land separating them. Eli had suggested they travel these parts only at night. He would guide Ada through the streets, aided by moonlight when the skies were clear or with a candle on cloud covered evenings. This mode of travel was slow, however, and he felt anxious about their pace. Whenever they came to the woods again, he would push on and only allow for short rests until they reached the next town.

If the town was bigger, they might see a few staggering figures in the streets. These men were too intoxicated to care about a couple of kids passing by, but seeing the men still made Eli's heart skip. He would hold his breath and pray that he and Ada were mistaken for mischievous boys who had slipped out of their home to uncover the mysteries of the local saloon. At least, that was his intention when he had cut Ada's hair.

When they had stumbled upon the first of the rolling grain fields several days ago, Eli noticed a few land laborers. Fortunately, these men were too busy eliminating a mole threat to notice the two coming out of the brake. Upon seeing the workers, Eli pulled Ada back into the woods to reassess their next steps. That was when he suggested they disguise her as a boy.

She was already dressed in men's clothing, but they needed to do something about her hair. Without a hat to conceal it, it would have to be cut. Since she wasn't able to brush her hair, she had kept it braided, but it was such a tangled mess by that point, Eli doubted it could ever be unbraided again. Short hair would be easier for her to manage and would help her look less like a girl, which would be safer as the inevitability of running into others quickly approached.

Having Ada's permission, he used the Bowie knife to cut off her braid at the base of her neck. He sawed away chunks of hair around her face and along the back of her head. Her eyes watered and she bit her lower lip. She must have been upset about losing her hair. Eli certainly didn't want to see it go; he had always liked her hair. It was long and thick, and it looked soft and wavy when it wasn't tangled. Before their time in the woods, she would sometimes wear it loose and unbraided. Eli would fight the urge to run his fingers through it.

He tried once when Ada was six years old, but she pushed him down and ran away crying when his sticky fingers caught her hair and pulled harder than intended. After a stern scolding from his father, Eli decided it was better to leave Ada's hair alone and admire it from afar. As he continued cutting her hair, he soon realized that her tears weren't from vanity.

"Ouch!" She tried to pull away.

The blade tore at Ada's hair more than it cut. Eli eased up on the knife, but he felt once again like that clumsy boy yanking at her pretty curls.

"I'm sorry," he kept repeating after every wince.

"It's all right, Eli. It doesn't hurt that much, but please don't take too long. And then give me the knife; I get to cut yours next." She somehow managed to giggle through another wince.

Once Ada was properly disguised, Eli worried less about being close to an increasing population. However, he had still insisted they travel only during the dark hours. But now he was contemplating going into this town during the light of day, and the reason for his plan was tucked safely away in his pocket.

Two towns back, while quietly slipping through its dark streets, Eli thought he had heard someone whisper his name. The voice was an echo-like hint of a sound that had not been produced nor even heard by Ada. His heart leapt into his throat, and he was sure its rapid beating would wake every single home around them. He froze.

Ada stopped walking and turned toward him with a questioning glance. As Eli gained the courage to look for the source of the sound, he convinced himself it was made by a nocturnal animal skittering about in the dark. Then he saw something metallic glinting in the moonlight: a coin! He picked it up, stuffed it in his pocket, and grabbed Ada's hand. Pulling her into a swift jog, he led her toward the end of town. There, they slipped between some trees and lost themselves in the safety of the wooded area behind the last building.

Whether it had been an animal or just his tired mind playing tricks on him, Eli knew he had God to thank for the coin in his pocket. If he hadn't stopped in that exact spot, or if the moon hadn't been shining down at that exact angle, he wouldn't have found it. Those didn't seem like coincidences. And since he had just been pleading with God to help them find food, discovering the coin was an answer to prayer and not just dumb luck.

He had been noticing that as the wilderness decreased, so did his ability to trap animals. It would only be a matter of time before their hunger would

23

force them into the open. But now they could buy food honestly instead of having to risk stealing it in their desperation. All they had to do was find a town big enough to ensure the people in it wouldn't pay them much attention.

When they came upon this town below the hill, Eli was convinced they had found the right place. A small open-air market was located along the street running through its center. The market had six tables of wares set up under stretched oilcloth canopies. From the hilltop, Eli wasn't able to see what was on those tables, but he hoped one of the merchants would be selling some cheese—or some bread at the very least.

His stomach growled as he wondered how much food the coin would buy. A twinge of excitement hinting at a change in their favor danced under that growl, but perhaps it was just the anticipation of tasting something more palatable than squirrel or mouse.

Nevertheless, he wanted to proceed with caution. He insisted they spend the next day watching the market and all of its customers. He wanted to know how long it stayed open, how busy it was, and what type of people came to the tables. And now that he had this information, Eli was confident that the best time to go was first thing in the morning as the market was opening and before it got too busy.

There was a thicket of bushes at the bottom of the hill, just outside the edge of town. From that area, they could safely enter the streets. It was close to the market and would be perfect for gaining quick access to the food they needed. In the morning while it was still dark, they would sneak down and wait in the bushes for the sun to rise. When the market opened, they could casually stroll into town, buy some food, and stroll out of town before most people were finished with their morning chores.

The shadows soon elongated, and the market began to close for the evening. Eli woke Ada and motioned her back under the cover of the trees where they made camp. He told her his plan, and she agreed it sounded promising. Having nothing else to eat but a few rough plants, they decided to go to bed and get as much rest as they could.

Even though they needed the energy for the next day, Eli doubted they would get much sleep. Hunger and nerves were not good sleeping tonics. They wrapped themselves in their blankets and Eli put an arm around Ada, a habit he had formed to help ward off her nightmares and to keep warm. He closed his eyes; the morning couldn't come fast enough.

Chapter 6

MARCUS

Marcus and his wife Grace spent the morning cleaning the vacant home with the help of Isaac and Hannah Weber, who lived on the property next to the old Colebrook house.

No, that was wrong; it was now the Gardner house. That would take a while to sound natural in his mind.

Grace started a fire in the oven's firebox and placed a large pot of stew on the warming surface. While they dusted cobwebs, the house gradually filled with the scent of beef, vegetables, and herbs. To make the meal complete, Hannah had mixed up a batch of corn bread that was now in the oven forming a golden crispy top and emitting its own complimentary aroma throughout the house.

Marcus stood on top of the step stool he had brought from home and wiped the tops of the cupboards with a damp rag. The savory aroma from the stove was torturing his appetite. He considered abandoning his chore while only half done to remove himself from the temptation to dive into the stew. Of course, a quick peek under the lid couldn't hurt. As he climbed down from the stool and reached for the lid, he could hear Grace and Hannah visiting while sweeping the floor in the adjacent room.

Isaac was somewhere in the house, wiping the tops of window frames. Being taller, Marcus and Isaac were assigned with cleaning the top half of the house while the women cleaned the bottom half. They washed windows, swept away cobwebs, dusted base boards, wiped counters and basins, and aired out each room. The industrious men even found a few small repairs needing their attention. By now, the house looked and smelled inviting.

Returning to his task, Marcus finished wiping the cupboard tops, but his eyes kept drifting back to the stove. Perhaps he should try a quick sampling of Grace's stew, just to make sure it was warm enough for the weary travelers. Reluctantly, he decided against it on the assumption that there was stew at home. He hoped she had made extra for them to eat later.

Leaving the kitchen before he could reconsider his dilemma, he thanked the trio, telling them the house couldn't be any cleaner. Agreeing, the group decided to pack up their supplies and take them outside. The house was tidy, the supper was warmed and ready, it was early afternoon, and the young Gardner couple would be arriving at any moment.

Grace swept the porch while the other three waited. Soon they were joined by Evelyn. She marched up the steps of the covered porch, holding her perfectly baked cake.

"Ooh, here they come," she said as she approached the small group of friends.

The five figures all turned toward the direction of downtown. Sure enough, a wagon drove up the lane, sparsely loaded with furniture and a few securely packed crates. It pulled to a stop as it came into view of the house.

Marcus could just make out a young man and woman sitting on the wagon seat, first looking at the cleaning party on the porch and then glancing nervously at each other. He hoped their welcome would not come across as overwhelming to these newcomers. If that were the case, it was too late to change their plans now.

The young man put a hand on the woman's arm and spoke what Marcus assumed was a reassuring word. The woman nodded, the couple smiled at each other, and the man shook the reins again, easing the wagon back into motion. As it approached, Marcus took in a deep breath and looked at the others.

"This is it," he said, smiling at Grace. "It's time to meet the Gardners."

Chapter 7

ADA

A da stood still as Eli scanned her from head to toe, assessing how she looked. To avoid notice, they needed to appear as neat as possible before going into town. He rolled up her sleeves so they wouldn't hang past her fingers; it helped, but her clothes still hung on her.

"Try tucking in your shirt more," he said, "and let me check your arm again. I can wrap the fabric tighter if you need me to."

Earlier that morning, he had inspected the strips of fabric wrapped around her arm to make sure they hadn't shifted while she slept, but now he wanted to check them again. Yes, the strips still covered her lower arm. To be honest, they were tight enough to make her always aware of them. She wanted to rip them off, but she knew that wasn't a good idea. Instead, she tried to ignore them.

"They're fine, Eli," she said, but he insisted she check his arm as well. Again, the wrappings were accomplishing their job. Both of their arms were fully concealed.

He handed Ada a jacket, and after she put it on, he ran his hands over her arms to smooth out the crumpled sleeves. Those stubborn wrinkles wouldn't go away, and he finally gave up.

"You look like a hayseed," he teased. "Try not to trip on your cuffs, okay?"

"Hush up. You're one to talk."

"Here, let me help." He knelt down and rolled up her pant legs. "They'll look better if they don't drag on the ground."

Ada pushed him off balance. "Boys always look like a mess. At least I match you." She hoped she sounded more lighthearted than she felt.

Eli stood and patted down her hair. He pressed his lips together and looked as though he were stifling a smile. Ever since it was cut short, Ada's hair refused to behave. It flipped up in the most unpredictable ways. She knew she looked ridiculous, but most boys were just as rumpled, and looking like a young boy was what she was hoping to accomplish. She was to pose as Eli's younger brother, and if asked any questions, she would shyly look at him to answer so her voice wouldn't give them away.

"Well," Eli said with a sigh, "I guess we're as ready as we'll ever be. Remember, Ada; stay close to me and be ready to run. There's a denser wooded area to the east." He pointed in that direction. "If we need to, we'll head back to this bush and then over to those trees. We can lose someone who's chasing us in there."

Ada nodded and smiled faintly; her hands were shaking. Eli looked calmer than she felt. Was he even worried? Maybe boys knew some secret about looking calm. If so, she hoped she wouldn't attract unwanted attention by not knowing it.

Thankfully, she didn't have to lug around their blankets. Eli put the bundle under a bush and covered it with branches; they would come back for it later. But she noticed he wasn't willing to leave the canvas bag. He cinched it up tight, put an arm through each strap, and cinched those as well. After securing the pack, he placed his hand on her back and guided her out from behind the tall bush and into the town's street. They put their heads down to avoid eye contact and walked toward the end of the road where the market was.

Once on the street, Ada felt exposed. She didn't like it. When she peered at Eli for encouragement, his haggard expression told her something was wrong. Her heart raced as they continued down the street. She looked around and saw that there was no market. No tables, no oilcloth canopies, and definitely no food.

Eli's gaze darted from shop to shop. Now he finally looked nervous. She wondered if he would try to enter one of the stores, but the thought of being trapped behind a closed door caused a hot panic to spread from Ada's stomach to her legs. If they had to run, she might not be able to. She kept her eyes locked on him.

"Hey, you!"

A gruff voice called out from behind, forcing them to spin around. Ada found herself staring into the eyes of a dreadful old man with leathery skin and a stringy mustache. Something about him reminded her of the man from the rock quarry. He grabbed onto Eli's wrist before they had a chance to run. The man's knuckles turned white as his hand tightened into a vice-like grip. His other hand landed on Ada's shoulder.

"What are you boys up to?" he demanded as he sneered at her. "Very bad boys, I'd say. You two better come with me."

Neither of them said a word. The man lifted Eli's wrist upward, twisting his arm at the shoulder, which caused him to grimace with pain. As his arm was pulled, Eli's sleeve pushed back exposing the edge of the fabric strips. The man looked at the bandaged arm and then into Eli's eyes. A smile crept across his face as his rough cheek twitched.

"What happened to your arm?" he asked. Amusement danced behind his eyes. He dug his fingers into Ada's shoulder to let her know he hadn't forgotten about her.

"I—I burned it." Eli stammered.

"Shut up," the man growled, cutting him off. He leaned in and breathed hot, stale breath in their faces. "I know who you are. And I know someone who'd like to see what you have hidden under that bandage. I bet I can guess what he'll find." As he spoke, greed plucked at the corners of his grin. "You're definitely coming with me."

Before Ada could blink, Eli lifted his foot and brought his hard, sturdy boot down on the man's worn-out shoe, crushing the toes within. Simultaneously, his free hand jabbed straight for the man's throat. The momentum of the strike caused the man to stumble back, clutching at his neck and gasping for air as shock leapt across his face.

Eli grabbed Ada's arm, spun her around, and pulled her into a run. They couldn't go back to the woods as they had planned; the man blocked that path. He shook off the effects of Eli's attack and ran after them with renewed anger in his wild eyes.

Tears threatened Ada's vision as they turned right and ran through an alleyway between two shops. The alley dumped them onto another street, and Eli led her to the left. She lost all sense of direction as she was being pulled along. Without Eli, she wouldn't have known where to go or what to do. She never stopped to think that perhaps he was running just as blindly.

Rounding another corner, they sprinted toward a parked caravan of horse drawn carriages resembling tiny houses. Ada recognized a large, pleasant looking woman standing by one of the wagon homes. She was one of the merchants from the market. The woman handed a bag to a man, who then secured it under a canvas tarp that covered the outer storage area of their wagon. The traveling merchants were busy packing up their belongings and didn't notice the two running toward them as they prepared for their departure.

While the merchants were distracted, Eli and Ada ran to the closest wagon. A dog was resting on the ground with his head on his paws. His ears perked up as they neared the wagon. She barely had time to wonder if the dog would bark at them before Eli pulled her up the steps that led to a door. He yanked it open and pushed her inside, climbing in after her. As he shut the door and guided her deeper into the dark, Ada prayed the man hadn't seen them.

She tried to catch her breath, aware that they were both breathing too loudly. She clutched Eli's arms and squeezed her eyes shut, burying her face into his chest.

"What are you two doing in here?" a deep voice boomed out from beside them.

They spun toward the voice, wide-eyed. In the dark, Ada could just make out two silhouettes. Oh no, not again! She held onto Eli tighter.

As her eyes adjusted, Ada noticed that one of the occupants was a woman who did not look unkind, only startled by their sudden appearance; a sympathetic smile spread across her face. But the other was a tall, broad-shouldered man with a shaved head and closely trimmed beard. He wore a sleeveless undershirt and a stern expression.

His arms were crossed in front of his chest and he stood with a wide stance, giving him an even larger and more imposing look. His bare skin was covered in dark lined pictures, implying they had a story to tell. He took a step forward, placing himself between them and the door.

"You boys have some explaining to do. Start talking."

As he glared at them, the dog began to snarl right outside the door.

Chapter 8

MARCUS

Marcus waved at the couple as their wagon approached the house. The young man nodded. He eased the horses to a stop and jumped to the ground as the pastor walked toward him, followed by the others.

"Welcome to East Haven, Mr. Gardner," Marcus said, holding out his hand.

The young man shook it confidently. He looked sturdy, like a man who knows how to work hard.

"I hope you don't mind, but David Holden opened the house so we could clean it before your arrival."

"Thank you; that was thoughtful. David mentioned someone might be doing that."

As he spoke, the young man helped his wife down. She smiled easily at the welcoming party. She was small but did not seem fragile.

"I'm Marcus Duncan; I'm the pastor of the town church. This is my wife Grace."

Grace stepped forward and smiled at the young woman. She held out her hand, which was warmly received. "Mrs. Gardner, I am so glad to meet you. I hope your travels weren't too taxing."

"Thank you; they were fine, but I think I'll sleep well tonight."

Marcus continued the introductions while they each shook hands. "This is Isaac and Hannah Weber. They live in that house with their son Noah," he said, pointing to the left. "Noah is the cutest three-year-old you'll ever meet."

The parents smiled at his comment. Evelyn, however, sniffed and pursed her lips. Marcus should have introduced her first; she was, after all, the elder of the group.

"And this is Mrs. Evelyn Russell, your neighbor to the right. We—"

"It's *wonderful* to meet you," Evelyn said, cutting in. "We've started a fire in your stove; the house will be warm and cozy. We made some supper, which is heating on your stovetop. You will not have to worry about a thing tonight. Here is a cake to enjoy after your meal. It's an old family recipe of mine."

As Evelyn handed the cake to Mrs. Gardner, Marcus witnessed a silent exchange between Hannah and his wife. Hannah mouthed *"we?"* and Grace raised her eyebrows, rolling her eyes. When Grace noticed he was watching, she bit her lip. Marcus winked to let her know he understood her frustration.

Heedless of anything but her own part in the conversation, Evelyn continued. "Come now, Mrs. Gardner, let us women help you unpack your kitchen crates. The men can bring them into the house, and while we unpack, they can unload your furniture and set it in place. That should—Oh. I see," she said, noting how little was in the wagon. "This will take hardly any time at all. Well, it will be better to get it done before the day is over. You may wish to put it off in favor of resting after your journey, but trust me, you will be glad tomorrow. And you can be sure I know how a kitchen ought to be arranged. Listen to me, and your kitchen will only have to be set up once. I will show you how it *must* be done." With a decisive nod, Evelyn marched into the Gardners' home uninvited.

The young Mrs. Gardner turned toward her husband with a silent plea for help, but he only smiled.

"She's right." A glint of laughter flashed in his eyes. "We won't take long." He glanced at the small wagonload and then at Marcus and Isaac. "I appreciate your help. This will go even faster now."

Marcus saw the hint of a smile touching Mrs. Gardner's mouth as she watched her husband move to the back of the wagon. Turning toward the house, she climbed the porch steps, followed by Grace and Hannah. The three women went inside to await Evelyn's instructions on the proper placement of the dishes, while the men began to unload the crates and carry them into the house.

"Mr. Gardner, I hope you and your wife are planning to come to church this Sunday," Isaac said as they each grabbed another load to carry in. "It would be a great way to meet the town; most of East Haven will be there. And Pastor Duncan, here, gives a keen sermon."

"Do you have a building you meet in?" the young man asked.

Marcus thought it was an odd question. "Yes, our meetings are held in the church building at the east end of town. It may be small, and we don't have a bell for our steeple, but it works well for us."

Marcus must have looked surprised by the question, because Mr. Gardner let a quiet chuckle escape under his breath.

"Sorry. Of course you do." He shook his head and added, "We would love to attend. Thank you for the invitation."

Unloading the crates didn't take long to accomplish, and soon Isaac was carrying the last one into the house. Only the furniture remained. As Marcus unstrapped part of the bed frame, Mr. Gardner removed his jacket and rolled up his shirtsleeves twice. Marcus now understood why David thought the young man would stir up talk in town.

"You have, um… that's, uh… that's some interesting artwork. So, those are… you have tattoos." Marcus stumbled over his words as he indicated the young man's arms.

A winding network of thick black vines started at his wrists and branched off as they continued to creep under his sleeves. Mr. Gardner let go of the chair he was about to pick up and straightened to a stand. He looked at Marcus, silent for a moment, as if trying to determine the intention behind his comment.

"Yes, I do," he finally said as he picked up the chair again and jumped to the ground. He placed it in front of him and reached for another.

Marcus realized that his words may have sounded critical, so he abandoned the bed frame for the moment. He handed a third and fourth chair to Mr. Gardner and climbed down from the wagon.

"I meant—they just caught me by surprise, that's all. I don't often see someone with tattoos. I'll be honest, Mr. Gardner; most of the folks in East Haven have probably never seen anyone with tattoos, let alone lived side by side with them or gone to church with them. You shouldn't be surprised if people are apprehensive, at least when first meeting you. But I'm confident it won't take long for my parish to remember that people can sometimes have—well… *interesting* lives before they come to know Christ. I'm sure once they get to know you, they'll accept the fact that you have a past, however rough it might have been. I hope you can be patient with them."

Mr. Gardner listened as Marcus summed up the townsfolk. He nodded and rolled up his sleeves past his elbows.

"And some of us, Pastor, have had an 'interesting' life after knowing Christ."

He turned his arms to Marcus. The vines did indeed continue to spread along his skin, and on the inside of his left arm, two of the thickest branches twisted together to form a cross.

"But I think you and I may have different ideas about what qualifies as interesting—and what a rough past is."

Marcus nodded, acknowledging what the young man had pointed out. "I guess I have a few assumptions of my own that I need to consider. I'm sorry I jumped to conclusions."

Mr. Gardner chuckled, and Marcus knew his apology was accepted.

"I'm aware of the conclusions this town will make about me. I've experienced it before. I try not to worry about another man's judgment; my only concern should be God's opinion." He paused briefly. "And my wife's, of course," he added with a smile.

"I know sailors often use tattoos for identification," Marcus said, "but you don't seem like a seaman to me. So, what inspired you?"

The young man leaned against the wagon and crossed his arms in front of his chest. "As a pastor, you understand that everyone will experience trials at some point in their life. God's Word tells us to expect them. In my twenty-two years, I've already had my share of difficult times, and I expect I'll have more. We don't always get to understand our troubles, but I hope I never forget that God is in control. These tattoos are a testimony to my darkest trials and who it was that brought me through them. They also remind me that God has a plan, and He's refining me for His purpose."

The young man shook his head and sighed.

Marcus put a hand on his shoulder. "I'd like to know your whole story, Mr. Gardner. I think I would enjoy it."

His face relaxed, but his eyes remained serious. "You might hear my story someday, Pastor Duncan, but 'enjoy' is the wrong word."

Marcus was silent for a moment, pondering what he had said. "Fair enough," he finally replied. "How about I say, then, that I believe I would *benefit* from it."

"I can accept that," Mr. Gardner said. "And please, call me Eli."

"All right, Eli. Call me Marcus."

The men shook hands again and sealed their new friendship with a smile. They picked up the four chairs, one in each arm, and carried them into the house.

Chapter 9

JED

"Start talking," Jed repeated over the dog's loud barking.

He had been startled when the two boys burst through the door of his vardo. They stared at him with terrified eyes. The older boy pushed the younger behind him and tried his best to square his shoulders.

"Help us," he pleaded. "Don't let him find us."

These boys were more afraid of the man pursuing them than they were of Jed, and that wasn't something he was used to. As he peered between the window shutters, he recognized the old man. The merchants had been in town for two weeks, and in that time, Jed had seen him frequent both the saloon and the jailhouse. He had a loud, perverse way about him. He was obnoxious and rude to the townsfolk, yet he seemed to have a tight friendship with the local deputy. Something about the man didn't add up.

The intruder shouted at the merchants, demanding to know if they had seen two kids run through their camp. He was angry and didn't like their answers. The dog barked and made lunging motions toward his feet. As the old man kicked at the canine, he attempted to gain access into the wagons but met with resistance from the vardos' owners.

"What does he want with you?" Jed asked the boys.

"Nothing good. Please help us," the older boy begged as his eyes darted toward the door.

The younger boy was trembling, and in that moment, Jed decided to help. After all, these kids had made it past his dog, who chose to bark at their pursuer instead of them.

He heard the old man approach his vardo, yelling at the others to get out of his way. As the handle began to move, Jed thrust open the door, blocking the entrance with his towering frame. He stepped to the ground, letting the door close behind him. He glared at the man. Startled by Jed's sudden appearance, the stranger backed away, nearly falling over the dog and narrowly escaping a sharp nip from his growling, tooth filled mouth.

"You see a couple of kids run through here?" the old man demanded, peering sideways at the mutt.

"These kids belong to our group," Jed said as he gestured toward Sammy and Myra. The two young children stood in the protective grip of their mother Goldie. "And those better not be the kids you're looking for." Jed took a step forward.

Ira, the children's father, positioned himself in front of them, blocking the stranger from his family. The man scanned the merchants, and his scowl melted. They were a small group but outnumbered him eight to one. He backed away.

"No, I'm, uh… looking for two boys. Vagabonds, up to no good."

"Look somewhere else, old man," Jed said as he flashed a warning glance at the other men in his company. Ira, Floyd, and Tony were ready to help send the intruder on his way, by force if needed.

"Well, if you see them, don't trust them. They're troublemakers," the man insisted. "You'd be wise to turn them over to Deputy Wiggins. He'll know what to do with the little thugs. Tell him I was lookin' for them; I'm Rake. Tell the deputy I witnessed their mischief and warned you about them."

Jed took another threatening step toward him. Frowning at the merchants, Rake decided to give up his search.

"I don't have time for this. They're getting away," he grumbled as he stomped off in defeat. Jed's dog followed Rake for several paces, barking aggressive warnings at him.

"Cobra, come!"

Jed joined the men of the caravan as they circled around each other. Cobra jogged up to his master, panting happily.

"That's not good," Ira said, shaking his head. "I don't want anyone snooping around our camp, looking for children. We need to go. Now." He glanced at his wife, who was nodding her agreement as she continued to hold onto their children.

"I'm with Ira," Tony said. "Ashbrook has just run its course in our circuit. This town isn't as welcoming as it used to be. I don't think we should come back next summer."

"Okay. If everyone's ready, let's wrap this up and get going," Jed said as the group all nodded. The men broke away from the circle to finish their last-minute preparations, and Jed motioned to his wife Rosa. "You okay with a couple of stowaways?"

"You bet. That man was up to something, and those boys look like they've been running scared for a while."

"Yeah, that's what I was thinking," he said.

They stepped into their wagon with Cobra. The boys huddled together in the darkest corner. The dog pranced up to them, curiously bumping them with his nose. Rosa pulled a round loaf of bread from the cupboard; tearing it into two pieces, she handed them to the older boy. He gave the larger half to his silent companion, who shoved the bread into his mouth and gulped it down, barely chewing.

"Thanks," he said and took a bite as he held out a hand for Cobra to sniff.

"What are your names?" Jed asked, grabbing a shirt and pulling it over his arms.

The smaller boy's eyes widened, and he looked to the boy who was speaking for both of them.

"I'm... Aaron. And this is my brother Adam," he said.

Jed knew he had just heard a lie. Maybe these boys shared one parent, but they didn't look anything alike. He doubted they were brothers as much as he doubted their names.

"So, *Aaron*, what's your story?" he asked, catching Rosa's eyes with his own. She had been scrutinizing the younger boy as he ate.

"Um... We were living with our grandma in Bluemont, but she died. We're trying to get to Newbay."

Jed studied the boy, who was clearly weaving this tale as it left his lips. Bluemont and Newbay were two large cities far to the east. The boy must have pulled the names of those cities from his last geography lesson, just to fill in his impromptu lie.

"Newbay, huh? What's there?"

"Work," the boy answered without hesitation. "And some distant family. They might take us in."

"You're a bit off course. Those cities are both several hundred miles to the east."

The boy closed his mouth and looked down at his bread. Jed could almost see the wheels turning in the boy's mind as he tried to think of a way to salvage his story. Instead, he changed the subject.

37

"Please, Mister. Some men are bothering us. We just need to hide for a while."

Jed sighed when he saw the desperate look on the boys' faces. He felt sorry for them. "We're headed to Clackton," he said. "We can take you with us, but we'll be traveling west. Is that going to work for you?"

His question challenged their story further. The boy nodded and offered a meek thank you.

"You can stay in here, out of sight. I'm Jed, and this is my wife Rosa. We'll check on you after we've traveled a few miles."

The boy nodded again, and Jed and Rosa went outside. The caravan was ready to go. Each family's horses were hitched to their respective vardos, waiting for the command to move. Together, the four wagon homes would make a two-day journey to the next town in their summer market circuit. Jed climbed into the driver's seat, followed by Rosa.

"You know those boys are lying to us," he said as he flicked the reins.

Rosa nodded. She grabbed onto his arm and leaned closer as their vardo was pulled into motion.

"I'll tell you something else I know," she said. "The younger one, that's not a boy."

The caravan reached the location where they would camp for the night as the sun was beginning to set. The merchants parked their vardos away from the edge of the road under the cover of some trees. Jed jumped down from his seat, unhitched the horses, and corralled them with the others. He needed to tell the group about the young people hiding in his vardo; he couldn't put it off any longer. Those jittery kids would probably run the first chance they had, but he hoped he could convince them to stay.

Halfway through the day's journey, Rosa checked on them and reported to Jed that they were fast asleep. She was worried they might still be hungry but chose not to wake them. Soon, however, they would have to confront them and get the truth. Jed rolled up his sleeves and motioned the others to gather. He positioned himself so he could see the door of his wagon home.

"Listen," he began, "you know the kids that old man was looking for? They're hiding in my vardo. They're in trouble and I think we can help."

"Jed, you should have told us sooner," Tony said. "What kind of trouble are we talking about? What if they were followed? We can't put ourselves in danger; we have to think about Ira's kids and my ma."

"You're right, I should have told you. But I was trying to work out what to do. We weren't followed, and I really believe they need our help. I think they're running from someone. I want to invite them to stay with us for as long as they need. We can hide them, feed them, and try to figure out who they are and where their family is. Maybe we can get them back to their people."

The merchants slowly nodded their agreement.

"Great," he said. "These kids are scared. I'll see if they're willing to come out for supper."

"Wait," Ira said, halting Jed in his tracks. "What if it's family they're running from?"

Jed sighed and looked at the ground. "I guess we'll figure that out later."

Rosa followed him into the vardo, where they found their guests awake and whispering. The scared young couple stood near the window, watching the group. They quickly hushed their murmurings when Jed and Rosa appeared. The boy held his bag tightly and grabbed onto the girl's hand. Cobra paced happily around their feet.

"My friends and I want to help," Jed explained. "Stay with us for a few days. You can hide in here with Cobra while we're in Clackton if that'll make you more comfortable, but you both look like you could use some food and some rest. You can get cleaned up, and we can look for some clothes that will fit you better. How does that sound?"

"I don't know…" the boy started to say.

"Look," Jed continued, "I can tell it's hard for you to trust people. I don't know why that is, and I am sorry for it. But I do know you've lied about your names and why you're on your own. I also know that this one, here, is not your brother." He pointed at the girl. "And I'm guessing *she* isn't your sister, either. If I can trust you, knowing you haven't been straight with us, then maybe you could try trusting me as well."

The boy clamped his mouth shut, pulling the girl toward himself. He lifted his chin. "No, she's not my sister, and you're right. I don't trust you. Tell me why I should."

Jed shrugged his shoulders. "I can't make you trust me; you'll have to choose that on your own. How about you start by telling me your real names."

The boy shook his head.

"Then tell me if your family is looking for you."

"No," he said, swallowing hard and clenching his jaw.

Tears pooled in the girl's eyes. Rosa cautiously reached for her arm where a dingy bandage peeked out from under her sleeve.

"Oh, honey; are you hurt? We should take a look at that and get it cleaned up."

The girl pulled her arm away and hid it behind her back. "I'm fine."

It was the first time Jed had heard her speak. She sounded older than he had originally thought. Rosa noticed it as well.

"You probably think you've managed well enough on your own," she said to her. "And you might even make it through the summer without too much trouble. But what's going to happen when the weather starts to freeze over? And what will you do if something happens to him?" Rosa indicated the boy with a slight nod. "Winter and sickness and injury, those are rough times. How long do you think you can live as you have been? You need to start trusting someone; it may as well be us. We're safe people."

Worry spread over the girl's face. "We left our blankets back there!" she cried.

The boy's shoulders sagged as he gave into the exhaustion of being on the run. He closed his eyes; Jed and Rosa were about to win him over.

"We'll stay," he finally agreed. "But only for a few days."

Chapter 10

ELI

After agreeing to stay with the merchants, Eli looked more closely at his surroundings. He had never seen a wagon like this before. Jed lit lanterns and hung them throughout the small space, illuminating the ornamental interior.

"You live in this wagon?" Eli asked.

"It's called a vardo," Jed explained, nodding.

The miniature house on wheels was brightly decorated; its cupboards and counters neatly edged with intricate carvings. The velvety curtains hanging by the bed and windows added a layer of texture and warmth. Jed unfolded a tabletop and set it by bench seats built into the wall. He then topped the benches with plush cushions brought from the sleeping area. As he arranged their home for the night, Rosa collected food items from the cupboard and disappeared out the door.

Eli continued to watch Jed, who motioned for them to sit at the table while he worked. He grabbed some wood from a hidden storage area and put it into a tiny stove in the corner. After he lit a fire, warmth spread throughout the space.

"I'm glad you agreed to stay. Are you ready to meet the others?" he asked.

Eli turned to Ada, who was still scanning her surroundings with wide, awestruck eyes. He squeezed her hand to get her attention and gestured toward the door with a slight nod. Cobra bounced to his feet and wagged his tail as Jed led them outside.

A campfire burned under an old blackened grate, upon which a large pot sat. Its contents bubbled, and the steam carried the savory scent of sage and rosemary to Eli's nose, making his stomach grumble. Canvas chairs circled the fire, and a table strewn with onion skins and potato peelings stood nearby. The group sat around the fire pit, engaged in friendly conversation.

"Why don't you join the others," Jed suggested. "Supper should be ready soon. You're welcome to leave your bag inside."

"Thanks," Eli said, holding the bag tighter and leading Ada to the fire.

He picked two chairs closest to the woods, which were set somewhat apart from the others. As he sat, he took his pack off and stepped through one of the straps, securing it to his leg. He wasn't going to let anyone snatch it from him. Cobra stretched out on the ground between him and Jed.

"Okay," Jed said to the group as he pointed to Eli. "This is… well, we don't actually know his name yet, so I guess we're calling him Aaron for now. And this one, here," he said, indicating Ada, "is Adam-ina." Jed winked at her as she blushed. "You two know my wife Rosa," he continued. "And that's Floyd and his wife Hattie. This is Ira and Goldie and their kids, Sammy and Myra. And that's Grandma Mae and her son Tony."

Eli followed Jed's introductions around the fire, nodding acknowledgments to each person. Ada waved her fingers timidly at the new faces. The woman named Hattie returned her greeting with a smile; her plump, soft frame filled the chair as she leaned back and sighed before speaking.

"I still have some clothes from when I was younger that could be altered to fit you—and a warm nightgown you can have. Would you like that?"

Ada nodded, whispering a thank you.

Goldie, who had been standing at the pot stirring, let everyone know supper was ready. Ira took off his hat, and they all bowed their heads. Eli caught Ada's eyes. He bit his lip as guilt cast a shadow across his face. They hadn't remembered to pray for several weeks. Sure, he was pleading hopelessly with God throughout their entire ordeal, but that wasn't the same. Even when he was thankful for a successful snare or finding a source of water, Eli's gratefulness was overshadowed by the pain of what they had lost. He was more focused on his despairing fear than on the trust he should have been asking for.

As he lowered his head, a small flicker of hope regarding these merchants sparked within him, but it was short lived. A larger flame of suspicion, which threatened to consume his heart, snuffed out that hope before it could grow. One prayer and some clothes didn't prove anything.

Eli tugged at the fabric strips on his arm, wondering if these travelers would turn on them as soon as they found it profitable to do so.

"Father God," Ira began. "You are a great provider, and we thank you for keeping us safe on our journey today. Thank you also for this meal we are about to eat. Please Lord, as we arrive in Clackton tomorrow, bless the time we are among those people. Help us show your love to the townsfolk, and please allow our sales to be enough to provide us with what we need for the winter. We would also like to thank you, Lord, for bringing these two young people to us. Even though we don't know them yet, we're grateful that you know them intimately. We ask you to give them courage and give us wisdom in this situation. Lord, continue to protect them and allow them to see your hand in their lives. We pray this in your Son's name. Amen."

Whispers of amen echoed around the fire, but Eli kept his eyes fixed on the ground. He wasn't ready after that prayer to look at anyone, not even Ada.

After a moment, Jed nudged Eli and handed him a bowl of meat and vegetables. He motioned to pass it down to Ada and then handed him another bowl. As Eli ate, he watched the caravan visiting with one another. They were like a family: laughing, joking, and telling stories. He began to relax.

Neither of them could finish their supper; it was more than they had eaten in a long time. Eli picked at his food as he continued to study the people around the fire. His eyes soon landed on Jed and stayed there. He wondered about the pictures peeking out from under the man's shirt. They evoked a faint memory of his grandfather that remained just out of reach.

"You look like you have a question," Jed said, startling Eli out of his thoughts.

"Do those pictures on your skin wash off?" he asked.

"Nope." Jed shook his head.

"But what if you decide you don't want them anymore?"

"These are tattoos; they're permanent," he answered.

"What if you don't like one of them?" Eli persisted.

"Well, a person better make sure he likes a tattoo before he gets it," Jed stated. "I don't regret any of mine."

Eli wasn't satisfied. He could hear the tension building in his voice but was unable to control it. "What if you stop liking one of your tattoos? Isn't there any way to get rid of it?"

Jed looked annoyed by his persistence. "Do you have a tattoo you're trying to get rid of?"

Eli hated how adults dodged questions by asking another; he didn't think it was the right way to end a conversation, but it worked. He shrugged and looked away with a frown. He knew Ada was listening, but he kept his eyes fixed on the dark horizon, hoping to avoid her sympathetic gaze. It wouldn't help his mood.

Finally, Jed sighed and offered an answer. "I suppose the only way to get rid of a tattoo you don't like is to cover it with one you do like. There isn't any other way, so don't get one if you're not sure about it."

Eli nodded but kept looking past the group around the fire, refusing to meet anyone's gaze. They had all hushed to listen to the exchange as it unfolded before them.

Goldie broke the silence. "It's time to put you kiddos to bed," she said to her children. "Goodnight everyone. We'll see you in the morning." She smiled at Ira and whisked Sammy and Myra into their vardo.

"We should all go to bed," Jed suggested. "We have an early start in the morning. Floyd, Hattie, you two have room in your vardo, don't you? How about you take the girl, and Rosa and I will take the boy."

It only took seconds for Eli to understand the full meaning of what was just proposed. "Wait, no! You can't separate us."

He grabbed his pack and stood up, knocking his chair over behind him. Ada was immediately on her feet as well. They resembled cornered animals. Startled by his reaction, the merchants gaped at him. Hearing the commotion, Cobra jumped to his feet and began yowling.

"Yes, we can," Jed stated.

Eli grabbed Ada's hand and backed toward the woods as the man continued.

"You, yourself, admitted that you're not related. And I get it, it's different out there in the cold while you're trying to survive." Jed pointed behind them at the trees. "But it's warm in the vardos, and we have plenty of blankets. If you're not married, you don't get to share a bed here. It's too dark and cold to be running off on your own, so your safest bet is to stick it out with us tonight. I know for her sake you want to do the right thing."

Eli took another step back. He shouldn't have agreed to stay with these people. He set his jaw and clenched his fists, vaguely aware that he was gripping Ada's hand and might be hurting her, but he couldn't relax his hold. He looked first at Ada and then at Jed, trying to figure out what to do. Ada's face furrowed into an expression of either fear or pain—probably both—and Jed stood firm with his eyebrows raised.

Eli knew Jed was right. They wouldn't be safe if they ran into the woods at this hour, especially without blankets. And their last candle had burned away a few evenings ago; it was too dark to find their way among the trees without it. It was also too dark to find the wood they needed to build a bed and a shelter.

They couldn't leave, but if Jed separated them, how could he protect Ada? How could they escape if they needed too? It wasn't fair. These people didn't know what they had been through, but he couldn't tell them; he didn't know if he could trust them. It took every ounce of his will to push down his rage and not fight his way into the woods. Instead, he pulled Ada toward him and put his mouth to her ear.

"I'll come for you, I promise," he whispered. "We'll take some blankets. We can make it if we have them. Trust me. I'll get you out."

He released her and glared at Jed, feeling betrayed by this man who had promised to help. Ada allowed Hattie to guide her away, and Eli followed Jed while Cobra trotted beside him. As he glanced back at Ada, an angry tear slid down his face. He defiantly wiped it away.

It was dark and quiet in the vardo. Eli could hear rhythmic breathing and hoped Jed and Rosa were finally asleep. He wasn't sure how long he had been wrestling with his heavy eyelids, but he knew he couldn't wait any longer. He gathered his blanket around him, stood up, and collected his bag and shoes. Tiptoeing to the door, he gently pressed down on the handle and tried not to make a sound. As he pushed the door open, he stepped to the ground.

He didn't notice he was holding his breath until he turned and saw Cobra standing with his head tilted to one side. Startled by the dog, Eli inhaled quickly. Seeing that Cobra wasn't interested in alerting Jed to his escape, he exhaled and reached out to pet the dog.

As he walked toward Floyd and Hattie's vardo, he grabbed one of the chairs by the extinguished fire. He placed it near the steps leading to their door and sat down to put on his shoes. His heart raced, and his hands trembled as he pulled the Bowie knife out of the pack and set it on his lap. Wrapping the blanket around him, he listened for sounds coming from the vardo. He wanted to wait for the right moment to get Ada; he had to be sure Floyd and Hattie were asleep.

Cobra stretched out on top of Eli's feet. The pressure from the dog's warm body calmed him, and he longed to savor it. He was exhausted; he would need to push himself harder once they returned to the woods. They had to get as far away as possible. Putting as much distance between them and the caravan was his only goal. But for now, he would listen and wait before he made his move. He could afford to close his eyes for just one moment…

Chapter 11

THE CARAVAN

Screams split through the night like a knife cutting fabric. Jed's eyes flew open, and he bolted up from a dead sleep. When Rosa stirred beside him, he let out a sigh, reassured that she was safe. His eyes shot toward the far end of the vardo where their guest should have been sleeping.

～❧

"What's that?" Rosa gasped, clutching at her chest. She turned toward Jed and followed his gaze.

"I don't know, but the boy's gone," he said, leaping out of bed.

As he slipped his feet into boots and grabbed a jacket, Rosa wrapped a blanket around herself and followed him outside.

～❧

Loud shrieks invaded Goldie's peaceful slumber. She sat up and shook Ira awake.

"Mommy, what's that noise?" Sammy asked with a quiver in his voice.

She rushed to the children's stacked beds and picked up Myra, who was rubbing her eyes and whimpering. As she sat on the young girl's mattress, Sammy climbed down from his bed. He sat on the ground and leaned against his mother's leg. Goldie rocked Myra and reached down to put her hand on her son's shoulder.

❧

Ira shook his head, trying to rid himself of his sleepy fog. He threw on some pants and grabbed a hunting rifle from the closet by their door.

"Be careful, husband," Goldie pleaded.

Nodding, he stumbled outside and met Jed and Rosa as they came out of their vardo.

"The boy ran off," Jed informed him and held out his hand for the rifle.

Ira tossed it to him; he didn't mind using it for hunting but preferred leaving the armed protection to someone else. Jed checked the gun and led them toward Floyd and Hattie's vardo, where the commotion was coming from.

❧

As the group passed Tony and Mae's wagon, the door swung open and Tony stumbled outside, dressed in only his thermals and boots. He rubbed his face, running an open hand along the sides of his mustache; with his other hand, he held his rifle. Always the protective son, he ordered his ma to stay put until he knew it was safe. Mae nodded and closed the door behind him.

❧

"Lordy!" Hattie gasped as the screams shocked her into awareness. Her arm shot out toward Floyd, hitting him in the chest.

The strike halted his vertical movement and pushed him back onto the bed. The girl's shrieks continued to pierce the air, and before Hattie could make sense of what was happening, the boy burst into their wagon.

Rushing to the girl's side, he grabbed her shoulders. "Shh. Shh. It's okay. I'm here. Look at me. You're safe."

He held her as she tried to push away. She was unreachable in the clutches of a terrifying nightmare; her eyes were wild, yet vacant. As the boy spoke in a soothing tone, her arms slowly stopped resisting his grip. He placed a hand on either side of her head and pulled her close to him. Her tears streaked over his fingers and she shook uncontrollably.

"We were at the rock quarry again," she cried. "I couldn't find you." Her eyes darted around the vardo. "Where are we? We have to get out of here!"

Hattie glanced at Floyd, her mouth gaping. She wasn't sure what they should do. She grabbed onto his arm for support as they scrambled out of

48

bed. She was about to ask the boy how they could help when the door flung open and Jed rushed inside, followed closely by Ira and Tony.

❧

Jed pushed his way into the vardo; the girl gasped, and the boy spun around to meet his gaze.

"I told you," he said with a glare. "You can't separate us." He turned his attention back to the girl and continued to console her.

"How'd you get here so fast?" Jed demanded as he took in the scene around him. The boy didn't reply.

"Does she do this every night?" Ira asked.

This time he did answer. "Not this bad; not if I'm with her."

The girl let out an anxious moan and sank against him as he put his arm around her and rubbed her back.

"It's all right," he said. "It was just a dream. You're safe."

He pulled his blanket across her shoulders and his voice lowered to a whisper; Jed could no longer make out his words.

Rosa, who had crept in behind the men, placed her hand on Jed's arm. "It's getting crowded in here. Why don't Hattie and I stay with them while the rest of you wait outside?" she suggested. "We can figure out what to do after she calms down."

Jed nodded, and the men filed outside. He stepped down from the vardo and noticed that a chair had been placed close to the door. A knife lay forgotten on the ground. He picked it up and looked at his dog, who sat dutifully by the chair. When Cobra saw his master's countenance, he lowered himself and put his chin on his front paws.

"Some watchdog you are," Jed quipped.

Cobra placed a paw over his nose and whined.

Chapter 12

JED

The men stood together in the cold evening air. As Tony went to his wagon to tell his ma what was going on, Jed peered over at Floyd.

"What happened in there?"

Floyd shook his head and scratched the back of his neck. "I don't know; the girl had a nightmare, I guess. She just started screaming. I think my heart almost gave out. And Hattie wakes up fightin' when she's startled. Between the screams and punches, I'm lucky you aren't digging my grave right now." He rubbed his chest and blew an exaggerated puff of air.

"We might as well start a fire," Ira said with a shiver. "I don't think we'll be leaving in the morning. We need to figure this out; we can't take these kids into Clackton if the girl is going to scream like that every night."

Returning the gun to Ira, Jed tucked the knife into the back of his pants. He gathered kindling and started a fire as Ira put his rifle away. Ira rejoined them just as Tony was helping Mae out of their vardo and into a chair.

"Those poor children," the elderly woman said as she gazed toward Floyd's wagon. "You're right to want to help them, Jed. Nightmares like that don't happen unless there's a reason."

He nodded, waiting for her to continue.

She shook her head and sighed. "I've seen it before, in full-grown men who've experienced a lot of violence. That kind of dream only comes to people when they witness something dreadful."

Jed placed a hand on the knife tucked under his jacket and wondered what dreadful thing could have been done to these kids? For several minutes,

50

the small group sat around the fire, lost in their own thoughts. Goldie, who had been consoling her children, came outside. She walked over to the fire and stood by Ira.

"The children fell back to sleep," she told him. "What happened?"

As Ira filled her in, he put his arms around her, and they warmed each other in the fire's glow. Soon, Hattie came outside and joined them.

"She's doing better. Rosa is sitting with them at the table." She took in a deep breath. "That boy really knows how to calm her down. Maybe he's right, Jed. Perhaps we shouldn't separate them. I don't know—this might be too big for us. Do you think we should get a sheriff involved?"

Jed shook his head, remembering the old man Rake who had been chasing the young couple in the last town. He didn't trust that man, and considering how friendly Rake had been with the town's local law, Jed wondered if any of the sheriffs or deputies in these parts could be trusted.

"Not yet. I'd like to find out what happened first. I wish we could convince those kids that we only want to help."

"Well now," Mae piped in, "we could let them get married."

Everyone stared at the woman; the crackle of the fire filled the silence.

"Why not?" she continued. "He's determined to look after her as if they already are. You all must have seen that as clearly as I did." She pulled her shawl closer around her shoulders. "We don't know how long they've been running—or from what. They're scared, Jed. *Really* scared. They aren't going to trust us unless we give them a reason to. If they get married, we won't have to keep them apart, and that might go a long way toward getting their trust. Then, if she is able to stay quiet through the night, we can go to Clackton without worrying about the attention those nightmares would bring."

Her eyes moved around the circle and finally landed on Jed. "I've been around for a while. Trust me; those two will be married eventually. What does it matter if it's today or next year? At least we can help them do it right."

"You're a pastor, Ira. You could do it," Hattie said.

Jed was not convinced. "They're still young, Mae. I don't know if that's the right answer."

Mae waved a dismissive hand at him. "They wouldn't be the youngest people to get married. In the old country, couples were married even earlier. And they're not much younger than I was when I married my Hanzi. If you're serious about protecting them, you need to find a way to make them want to stay with us. That just might do it."

Jed could feel her watching him as he mulled over her words. He turned to Ira, who was studying the ground, and nudged him.

"Why don't you and I go have a talk with those kids," he suggested.

Ira looked up, nodded, and followed him to the vardo. As the men entered the small home, Rosa and the two young people looked up from where they were sitting at the table by the window. Jed motioned for Rosa to give them her spot. She stood and walked to the other end of the vardo. As the men slid into the seat, Jed set the knife on the table. The boy reached for it, but Jed placed his hand on top of it.

"We're going to have a talk first," he said. "This is a decent knife. I guess it *is* yours." There was a subtle tone of accusation in his voice.

"It's for hunting," the boy replied.

"You had it out. Were you planning on going hunting in the middle of the night?" Jed locked eyes with the boy. "Look, I know you were sitting outside that door before she started screaming. Why was your knife out?"

"It's also for protection."

"Who are you trying to protect yourself from? We have kids; we have families. We're not like the man who was chasing you."

"The knife was in its sheath," the boy said. "I wasn't going to use it on anyone. I only had it out in case you wouldn't let me take—in case you wouldn't let us leave."

"You're making it hard for us to help you," Jed stated.

"Then don't. Just give me back my knife and let us go."

Ira cleared his throat and piped in. "We're not keeping you here against your will."

"But if we leave," the boy said, turning to him, "you're dooming us to starvation if he won't give me back my knife." Silence stretched out before them.

"How long have you been running?" Jed finally asked.

"I don't know; what day is it?"

Jed was about to answer, but the girl cut him off.

"April sixth…" she whispered.

"No," Jed corrected. "It's June eighth—actually, it's the ninth now."

"April sixth is when this all started."

Her voice was low, making it difficult to hear. She glanced at the boy, and he shook his head at her; Jed almost missed it.

"Why won't you tell us what happened?" he asked.

The boy, still holding the canvas bag, shifted in his seat. He avoided the men's eyes. Jed looked at Ira and decided to change the direction of the conversation.

"So, if she's not your sister, who is she?" he asked, nodding toward the girl.

The boy kept his mouth clamped shut and took her hand in his, as if to answer. Jed continued to question them.

"How old are you, fifteen?"

The boy sat up straighter and lifted his chin. "I'm sixteen."

Jed scoffed under his breath. "Fine. And her?"

"Fifteen," the boy answered, lowering his eyes again.

"Did you run away so you could be together?"

They both shook their heads in unison.

"And your parents aren't looking for you?"

"No, they aren't. We didn't run away..." The boy's voice trailed off.

Jed looked at their intertwined hands. Dirty, frayed fabric strips were wrapped around the boy's arm, peeking out from under his sleeve. Jed recalled the girl having something similar. Still holding the girl's hand, the boy moved their arms off the table and out of view.

Jed sighed and rubbed his temples. "Okay, listen. We want to make a deal with you. Stay with us; we'll protect you. But if you think you need to be together to be safe, then you'll have to get married. Otherwise, you're going to have to sleep in different vardos. I promise you can trust us."

"Married?" the boy asked, looking up.

Jed nodded. "Ira is a pastor; he can do it. But before I'll agree to that, you have to tell us your real names. And you have to promise to stay for at least a month—long enough to get some meat on your bones." Jed hoped the extra time would give him a chance to piece together what had happened to them.

"If we get married, you won't separate us?" the boy asked.

"Yeah, kid, but this is for real. Don't do it unless you're absolutely sure. I'm not convinced this is a good idea, but if that's what will make you stay, then that's the deal."

The boy's eyes darted to the window and then down at the knife. "Can we have a minute to talk about it?"

Jed considered the request for a moment and then nodded. He pushed the knife toward the boy. Rosa, who was standing with her arms crossed, shook her head at him. She thought this was just as risky as he did. As the three adults left the vardo, Jed slipped his arm around Rosa's shoulders.

Once outside, Jed pointed to Floyd and motioned for him to go to the other side of the wagon where the window was located. Floyd nodded and went behind the vardo to stand guard. Jed moved closer to the fire.

53

"What do you think?" Ira asked in a low voice.

"I think those kids are going to make a run for it," Jed stated.

As they stood around the fire and waited, the minutes passed. Eventually, Floyd peeked out from the side of the vardo and shook his head. At that moment, the door opened and the boy stepped out. The girl followed close behind. He looked at the merchants as Floyd moved toward the fire and joined the others.

"I'm Eli," he finally said, "and this is Ada. If you promise to do what you said, we'll stay."

Jed let out a slow sigh and glanced at Ira. He figured those kids would run off sooner or later, but for now, they would move forward with the wedding. He prayed they were doing the right thing.

Chapter 13

GRACE

The early summer air was perfect for an afternoon walk. The Duncans strolled hand-in-hand along the road leading to the Gardner home. Grace carried a casserole dish, while Marcus held a basket of kitchen items and table linens. The Gardners didn't own much. Since Grace had a generous heart and more than enough to share, she had assembled this care package, grateful for an excuse to visit the young couple.

Being married to the town's pastor gave her ample opportunity to indulge the giving side of her personality. Marcus often received donations of furniture and household items from his parishioners. The Duncans stored them in their house or attic until they discovered a need in town. Then, they would pass them along. Their sitting room was feeling cluttered, so Grace intended to ask Ada if she would like a small sofa and two parlor chairs. They were in good condition and would match the large area rug rolled up in the rectory attic.

Yesterday during church, the Gardners received their first introduction to the townsfolk of East Haven. The young couple arrived as the singing began. Even though they slipped into a back pew, their entrance did not go unnoticed. A few turned heads grew into many, and curious whispers traveled down each row. After the service, townsfolk lined up to greet the new couple. However, some noticed Eli's tattoos peeking out from under his cuffs, and those introductions became cool and formal. The young couple didn't seem to notice. Grace wondered if they might be overlooking it on purpose.

Well, if the town wouldn't accept them, she was even more determined to make Eli and Ada Gardner feel welcome. Marcus was a good judge of character, and he was impressed with Eli. Grace wanted to get to know them better.

As they passed Evelyn's house, the elderly woman opened her door and waved to them. She was holding a stack of recipe cards tied with ribbon.

"Are you calling on the Gardners?" she asked. "I'll come with you."

Without waiting for an answer, she grabbed her shawl and wrapped it around her shoulders as she descended the steps.

"I wrote down recipes for Ada. Most new brides only know two or three good meals, and they desperately need help coming up with more." She tucked a stray hair back into place. "It is my obligation to pass on an assortment of meal plans to that poor young wife. And I dare say, her husband will appreciate the variety as well." Evelyn giggled to herself, and together they continued down the road.

As the trio approached the house, Eli met them on the porch. Holding a hammer and nails, he worked to secure the loose railing. After shaking hands, Marcus handed the basket to Grace, and Eli motioned for the women to enter the house. They found Ada at her kitchen sink, suds up to her elbows as she washed dishes in a tub of soapy water. She smiled at her guests, grabbed a towel, and turned to welcome them.

"Grace. Mrs. Russell. Good afternoon! Please sit down."

Ada nodded toward the kitchen table, and Grace placed the basket and casserole dish on the counter.

"Forgive me, Ada, but I noticed you didn't have many utensils or tablecloths, so I brought some things for your kitchen. And I also made you some supper."

Ada continued to dry her hands as she peeked into the basket. "Thank you, Grace. That's so sweet," she said with genuine gratitude.

Evelyn seemed anxious to obtain a similar reaction as she held out the recipe cards.

"I thought you might like these. They are modest meals, inexpensive and easy to prepare. But I assure you, Eli will find them quite tasty."

"Thank you, Mrs. Russell. I'm sure he will. He always enjoys what is set before him, and he has never complained about any of the food he's had to try."

Grace noticed a wistful look in the young woman's eyes and wondered what memory might have caused it. Ada put her towel down and reached for the recipe cards, but Evelyn yanked back her hand.

"Oh my goodness, Ada!" she cried out in shock. "What have you done to yourself? Please tell me that isn't real."

Ada looked bewildered by Evelyn's outburst. She raised her left arm and turned it toward the woman.

"Do you mean my tattoo? Yes, Mrs. Russell, it's real."

On the inside of her forearm, there was a silhouette of three flowers—two large and one small. The flowers were surrounded by leaves and delicate vines that twisted around each other. The pattern was feminine, but it reminded Grace of the description Marcus had given of Eli's arms.

"Oh, child," Evelyn said in a disappointed tone. "Why would you do such a thing? Don't you realize heathens and crude sailors mark themselves up like that? Why would you want to be thrown in with that lot? Have you no concern for what others think of you? How could Eli allow it?"

"Evelyn," Grace said. "You're being harsh. Eli has them too. Haven't you noticed?"

"Apparently not," Evelyn huffed. "Well, one can almost excuse a coarse working man for doing such a ridiculous thing—but a young lady? Never!"

The look on Ada's face was filled with dismay, as though she were trying to calculate how to respond. Evelyn, however, persisted with her scolding.

"What a thoughtless and selfish choice, Ada. Your body should be a temple, one that the Lord would want to dwell in. Well, you have simply ruined yourself. That will never come off, and you will regret it."

Evelyn put her hand to her chest; she wasn't done. "Oh, the disappointment your parents must feel! I suppose you didn't even think of them. You are so young and naïve, Ada. You can't possibly know what a mother feels for her children or what she suffers because of them. Your mother would have been better off to never—well, to have never known of this, certainly. And what kind of a parent do you expect to be, parading that thing around so proudly? You'll teach your children to have no respect for themselves."

Evelyn truly looked as though she might cry, despite her angry tone. "I will pray for you, Ada. I will pray for a change in your heart and for repentance."

"Evelyn, that's enough," Grace said.

Ada's brows knit together as she lowered her head and peered at the ground. She slowly shook her head as she clenched her fists.

"You think *I'm* naïve?" She was barely able to control her voice. "You, in fact, are the ignorant one, Mrs. Russell. You've decided I'm selfish, but you don't know my heart or my motives."

Her voice grew louder as she looked squarely into Evelyn's face. "Nor can you possibly know anything about my parents. You think this tattoo ruins me? You have no concept of what truly ruins someone—or how completely destroyed one person can become by the whims of another. You judge and convict me without even trying to know me or my past. Only God knows my life and my character better than I know them myself—and He is the only Judge I have to face."

She took a step forward. Evelyn stood her ground as Ada continued.

"I can see that you think I'm beneath your acquaintance, Mrs. Russell. Well, please don't feel as though you need to prolong your visit. I will not hold you to your neighborly obligations. You may leave."

Evelyn's mouth was drawn tight. She blinked a few times and sniffed as she raised her chin.

"I believe I *will* leave. You certainly need time to calm down before you can listen to reason and graciously accept the wisdom others share with you."

She turned and marched out the door, taking her recipe cards with her. Grace rushed after her, hoping to convince her to come back and apologize. As Evelyn stepped onto the porch, she turned to Eli and glanced at his wrists with a scowl.

"I see you're just as impulsive as your wife. I wonder, Mr. Gardner, if you have an unbridled tongue as well."

Having spoken her mind, the self-righteous woman stormed off. Eli followed her departure with a stunned gaze and then turned toward Grace.

"What was that all about?"

"I'm sorry, Eli. Evelyn saw Ada's arm and scolded her terribly. I might have kicked someone out of my home, too, if I had been spoken to like that."

"Ada kicked her out? What did Mrs. Russell say?"

Grace glanced at Marcus, not wanting to repeat the woman's cruel words.

"It's all right, Grace," Eli assured her.

A quick recap of the incident didn't make it any easier; with each word, the knot in her stomach tightened. She watched Eli's face move from puzzled to troubled and finally to stern grief. She wanted her husband to step in with his usual ability to smooth over conflict, but Marcus only stood by and watched Eli's reaction. The young man peered at the ground and sighed.

"Well," he said in a quiet voice, "Mrs. Russell couldn't have chosen worse words to say to Ada." He frowned as though he were remembering something painful. "We both lost our parents several years ago. And last year—"

He swallowed hard, unable to continue, and kept his eyes on the ground. Taking in a deep breath, he finally looked up with an aching expression.

"Ada knows well enough what a mother feels for her child," he said and went into the house.

Grace glanced at Marcus with a furrowed brow before they followed him in.

Ada sat at the table and leaned on her elbows. Her eyes remained closed, and her cheeks were damp with tears. Her forehead rested in her hands as she formed silent words uttered for God alone to hear. Eli called to her and she stood to meet him. She placed a hand on his arm as he reached out to support her.

"Ada." He looked deep into her eyes, communicating more than just her name. "Did I bring you here too soon?" he asked after a quiet pause.

"No. It doesn't matter where we live; you're my home, Eli. If I'm with you, I'm where God wants me to be."

As Grace watched this exchange, she realized the Gardners were not new to marriage or difficult times. She vowed to defend this couple to the entire town. She prayed she wouldn't have to.

Chapter 14

ROSA

"Who cut your hair?" Rosa asked, rubbing more soap onto the girl's scalp.

Ada sat in a steaming tub of water, hugging her knees to her chest.

"Eli," she said.

Rosa wasn't surprised. Her hair had been chopped off in large, uneven clumps. Something would need to be done with it.

After the stressful events of the night before, the caravan members were finally able to get a few hours of sleep, but by early morning, the wedding preparations were in full swing. Hattie, who was in charge of the meal, hummed a melodic tune as she chopped and diced. Goldie was altering the dress she had found for Ada, and her children helped Grandma Mae make simple but quaint decorations. Ira wrote the ceremony and drafted a certificate for the young couple to sign. Floyd and Tony set up a makeshift tent using the oilcloth canopies from the markets. It would act as a temporary home for the newlyweds.

Rosa and Jed were left with the difficult task of helping the bride and groom look as though they hadn't been living in the woods for the last two months. Rosa convinced the young couple that baths would be a good start. While Jed heated water drawn from a nearby stream, a large tub was brought out and blankets were hung for privacy.

Ada took her bath first, and though Rosa had already washed her hair twice, the clumps of unruly tufts flipped this way and that, defying any hope of control. Rosa poured water over the girl's hair to rinse out the last bit of soap. As clean as Ada now was, she still refused to take those dirty bandages off her arm. While she washed the girl's hair, Rosa tried to think of a way to coax her into removing them.

"Why don't you climb out and dry off?" she said. "Here's a towel and an extra blanket. If you'd like, I can cut your hair to even it out. Would that be all right? I have scissors in my vardo."

Ada nodded her consent, and Rosa stepped out of the bathing area while she dried herself. As Rosa rushed the bundled up girl into the warmth of the vardo, Jed began preparing a new bath for Eli. The next batch of water was already heated, and soon the tub was refilled for the groom.

Once inside the wagon, Ada slipped into one of Rosa's nightgowns while they waited for the wedding dress to be altered. Rosa suggested she cut Ada's hair outside. If they set a chair behind the tiny home, her clippings wouldn't get all over the vardo floor, and Eli wouldn't see his bride before the ceremony.

With shoulders draped in a towel, Ada sat in the mid-morning sun. Rosa brought her comb and scissors out from the pocket of her apron and began snipping bits of the roughly cut locks. As she blended chunks of hair, the stubborn flips eased into soft, tame curls.

"Ada, your hair is beautiful," Rosa said. She peered down at the girl and noticed her silent tears. "Oh honey, if you're not sure about getting married, just say something. You don't have to do this, you know."

"No," Ada said through her sniffs, "that's not it. I want to marry Eli, but—Oh, Rosa! I wish my mother could be here." Her soft cries grew louder.

Rosa knelt in front of the girl, setting aside the scissors. She reached for Ada's hands.

"Getting married is a big decision. You and Eli *should* wait until your parents can be with you. We can help you get home safely; I'm sure they want to know you're okay."

As Ada's weeping escalated, there was a growing element to her sobs that made Rosa uneasy. She had calmed frantic women down before, but this was different. This was a terror filled panic that she wasn't used to, and it quickly surpassed last night's episode. Ada's breathing was quick and erratic; her tense shoulders heaved with each sob. Her eyes, puffy and swollen, darted around, unable to focus on anything. She tried to speak but struggled to form sentences between gasps and only sputtered out a few words.

"They're—*dead! Oh*, why? Rosa, I…"

As the words tumbled out of her, Rosa noticed that the wet fabric strips on her arm had stretched and shifted. They didn't cover an injury; they were hiding something. She grabbed Ada's wrist and pushed at the strips with her thumbs, revealing the skin underneath.

"What is this, Ada? What does it mean?"

She raised Ada's arm slightly and squeezed her wrist, trying to draw her attention. The exposed part of her forearm was covered in symbols and numbers, injected under her skin with an ugly, rough hand.

Ada continued to gulp back tears and grasp at words.

"Killed! Rosa… they *killed* them. Right in front of us!"

She covered her face with her free arm, and her whole body shuddered as she moaned.

"Your parents? Who killed them, Ada? The people who did this? Tell me who did this to you."

She was still holding Ada's wrist, attempting to keep the girl focused on her questions, but it was Eli who answered. He and Jed must have heard Ada crying and came to investigate.

"They did it to both of us," he said with a strained voice. "Strange men—I don't know who they were. They rushed into my house and shot our parents. I don't know why they did it; they just killed them. They put bags over our heads, threw us into the back of a wagon, and took us away. They had guns. We couldn't fight them off."

He stepped toward them, his hair still wet from his bath. Jed followed behind as Eli knelt beside Rosa and took Ada's marked arm from her grasp. Ada grabbed onto him, and as she looked into his eyes, her trembling began to subside. He picked up the scissors and cut strips of the fabric from each of their arms. The strips relaxed and began to fall away from their skin as they unwound.

Eli continued in a low voice. "They took us to an abandoned rock quarry and locked us in cages. Then they marked us up like this."

He pulled the remaining strips away, revealing all the black markings. He rubbed at Ada's arm as if trying to wipe it clean and pointed to some unfamiliar symbols.

"I don't know what this means, but I think it's supposed to tell people who we belong to—like cattle brands."

Jed stood over them and peered down at their arms. "Those are symbols identifying a gang of criminals. I've seen tattoos like these before, but not forced on a person."

Ada continued to cry. Eli focused on her as if nothing else existed.

"These numbers here," he said, rubbing his thumb over the list on her forearm. "They get bigger. They're bids. Every night, men would come and stare at Ada in her small cage. They never said a word; but they would reach in, grab her arm, and look at the last number before going away. After they left, the men who locked us up would come and add a new number onto her arm—the largest bid of the evening. They did this for five nights, but I was able to get out of my cage and free her. We ran away before the highest bidder could claim his prize."

As Eli spit these words out, tears welled up in his eyes, but they didn't spill over.

"What's that number for?" Rosa asked quietly.

The same number was etched into both of their arms, but on Ada it was placed above the other numbers. It was larger than the first two bids and was preceded by the letter *R*.

Eli hesitated before responding; he kept his eyes on Ada.

"The *R* stands for reward," he said after a long pause. He turned toward Jed. "That's how much those men will pay if you return us."

Rosa finally understood why the boy had been unwilling to tell them anything, and why it was so hard for him to trust people. That reward was big. Jed furrowed his brows at Eli's next words.

"Now you have to tell the truth. Are you going to turn us in for the money?"

Jed knelt beside the boy and looked him in the eyes.

"No, Eli. I won't do that," he promised. "But I will help you conceal this. Permanently." He placed his large hand over the boy's forearm, completely covering the numbers and symbols. "No one will ever be able to see it again. Then maybe you can stop running. But I won't lie to you; it's going to hurt."

"It already hurts," Eli said. "It can't feel any worse." He lowered his face, unable to continue.

Jed patted him on the shoulder. "Come on, you have a wedding to get ready for."

He helped Eli up and led him in the direction of Ira's vardo. As Jed walked by Rosa, he squeezed her arm. If anyone could help these kids, their little group could, perhaps Jed most of all.

Rosa turned her attention back to Ada. She smiled as she wiped the girl's tears away.

"Well, at least he didn't see you in your dress. Come on, let's wash your face so it won't be red for the ceremony."

Chapter 15

ELI & ADA

A lantern hung from the center beam of the tent, casting a dim light over the young couple's temporary home. They were married. It was another adjustment Ada was forced to navigate. In the last two months, she and Eli had changed who they were so often, and there was no time to process it.

They had started out as ordinary kids, about to finish school and plan the next stage of their lives. But in the blink of an eye, they became orphans and captives. After escaping, they were homeless and on the run. Now they were married and living, at least for the moment, with a caravan of traveling merchants.

The only thing Ada was sure of through all of this was that God had allowed Eli to remain her constant protector. She wouldn't have survived without him. She would have been dead by now—or worse.

Eli sat on a thin mattress, the same one Ada had slept on last night. It had belonged to Floyd and Hattie's son, but he was grown up now and making his own way in the world. Hattie assured them that he wouldn't be back anytime soon.

As Eli looked around the tent, he noticed that someone had placed his canvas bag in one of the corners. How did he forget about it? He couldn't let his guard down. He wanted to keep the bag packed in case they needed to leave in a hurry.

He grabbed it and dug down deep, relieved to find everything still there. He closed his eyes as he thought back over the last two days. Everything had happened so quickly; it made his head spin.

Ada joined Eli on the other side of the bed; both were silent. Even though she knew he was still on edge, she was beginning to trust the caravan more with each hour. The marriage ceremony took place late that afternoon. Floyd asked Ada if he could give her away. She gratefully accepted, not wanting to walk alone with all those eyes on her.

Sammy guided little Myra down a short aisle that led from Jed's vardo to a tree with white ribbon flowers hanging from its branches. He had to remind the young toddler to throw petals out of her basket as they walked.

Floyd smiled at Ada and held out his arm for her. She took it, and they moved toward the tree. Ira and Jed stood with Eli; he looked nervous.

When Eli saw Ada walk toward him, his heart jumped. She wore a pale green dress. Someone had made her a crown of flowering vines, which rested lightly in her curls. She looked like an angel. Floyd walked her right up to him and placed her hand in his.

Ira opened the ceremony with a prayer and spoke on the importance of putting God first in their marriage. He explained what it meant to love and respect each other. He asked them to repeat promises, and even though they didn't have a ring, he talked about the significance of it anyway. Hattie stood and interrupted the ceremony with an excited shout. She had made a ring by braiding thin strips of leather into a continuous band. She handed it to Eli, and he slid it onto Ada's finger; it fit perfectly.

As Ira pronounced them husband and wife, he told Eli to kiss his bride. Eli had forgotten all about that part of the ceremony. He felt his face growing hot and Ada blushed openly. He leaned in and kissed the corner of her mouth, then awkwardly apologized for it. He thought about trying again but knew he would be just as clumsy the second time. Instead, he grabbed her hand and grinned at her. She gave him an encouraging smile in return. The group clapped as they gathered around the couple to congratulate them.

Ira pulled them aside to sign their marriage certificate. They would need witnesses to sign as well, so they chose Jed and Rosa. Eli picked up the pen, and dipping it in the ink, he wrote down his first name. He was about to write his last name but stopped, his hand hovering over the paper.

He wasn't sure if he should write Noble on the certificate; they were still on the run, after all. Those men knew their names, so he needed to pick a new one. Not wanting to give up his family's name, he wrote the letter *N* as a middle initial and then looked up at Jed.

"What's your last name?" he asked.

"Gardner," Jed replied. "Why?"

Eli turned his attention back to the certificate and wrote Gardner—Eli N. Gardner.

Ada understood what Eli was doing. When he handed her the pen, she followed his example. She dipped it into the ink, and wrote Ada Y. Gardner.

"Eli and Ada Gardner." She spoke the names out loud for the first time. "I like it."

She glanced toward Jed and Rosa, who nodded their approval. As soon as Jed, Rosa, and Ira had signed the certificate, Hattie announced it was time to eat.

During the celebration, the couple received gifts for their new life together: pillows and blankets, the mattress, and a cedar chest that could double as a table or bench. It was full of clothes that fit them better and included some skirts and blouses for Ada. They were given a couple of lanterns and some flint and steel to light them. Tony gave them a beautiful wooden document box, taken from the merchandise he sold at the markets. Ada couldn't wait to put their marriage certificate in it.

After the festivities, Jed and Eli set up their new furnishings in the tent. The sun had just begun to set, but Ada was exhausted. After thanking the group and bidding them all goodnight, she and Eli went to bed early. They now found themselves sitting on their new bed, in their new home, contemplating their newest situation.

Eli reached up and snuffed out the lantern. In the dark, they slipped under their blankets.

"Ada." He paused, not sure how to say what he was feeling. "Those men took a lot of things from us. They took away our parents, our home… even the future we thought we would have."

He reached over and took her hand in his. Ada was quiet, which gave him courage to continue.

"I'm glad we got married, and I want to protect you, but I can't do it alone. We're not completely grown up yet; I don't think we need to be in a hurry. We've already lost so much."

When she remained quiet, he felt the weight of their loss pressing down on him. Why was it so hard to say what he was feeling? He swallowed, and after a few moments he tried again.

"Jed said if we're still with them in the fall, we should consider staying at their winter camp. We could finish our schooling. He said Ira would be willing to help us. He's smart; he went to a university. I don't want to decide yet, but… Well, maybe we should think about it. Maybe we—"

His voice cut out. He knew this was an important decision, and he should be strong enough to make it, but his mind was stretched so thin. Every thought and every action was to keep Ada safe. One wrong choice, one ounce of misplaced trust, would mean his failure. He could not fail.

❦

Ada heard him sniff, and even though it was dark, she knew his face must look as strained as his voice sounded.

"I'm just… I'm really tired, Ada. I'm tired of running."

He put his arm over his eyes, and for the first time in nine weeks, Ada heard him cry.

These were not angry tears, like when he told Jed and Rosa of their kidnappers; or the shocked and scared cry they both shared as they watched their parents die. This was a complete surrender to the sorrow, the stress, and all the demands the last two months must have forced upon him. Ada had never heard him cry like this before. It wasn't loud or sloppy. It was quiet and persistent, making it seem all the more unsettling. She wasn't sure how to calm him—or if she should.

Maybe it was better for him to let out his pent-up heartache. He had been so brave and had taken care of her all this time, while she had cried at every turn. Now, in the safety of this dark tent, he was free to let go and not hide his feelings for her sake. Now it was time for her to be the strong one and let him finally grieve.

"Okay," she whispered and put an arm around him. She didn't try to quiet him; she just held him.

67

After several minutes his breathing slowed. They continued to hold onto each other, and in the hushed darkness, they fell asleep. It was the most uninterrupted and deepest sleep they had experienced in a very long time.

PART 2

And we know that all things work together for good to those who love God, to those who are the called according to His purpose.

Romans 8:28

Chapter 16

ELI

*E*li knelt in the dirt. Another wilted plant lay on the ground in front of him. He pushed a small stake into the earth beside the plant and grabbed a piece of string out of his pocket. His body was stiff. His knees and back hurt. His hands were dirty and blistered, but he couldn't stop working. The field was big and there were so many plants to care for. As he tied the young plant to the stake, he could still hear the request ringing in his ears: "Eli, will you tend my crops?"

He scooped dark, fertile soil out of the bag next to him and spread it over the exposed roots. The bag was made of heavy canvas, similar to the one he had carried with him for weeks. This one, however, was filled with an endless supply of dirt. He drizzled water around the base of the plant. The work was slow and delicate. He glanced behind him at the ones he had already staked and sighed as he thought about how many still needed to be done.

Ada sat at the edge of the field next to a potted plant with flowering vines spilling over the sides. She held one of the vines in her arms and carefully wrapped it around her shoulders, admiring the soft petals. She wore a playful, childlike smile that conveyed peaceful happiness and a sense of security.

"Eli, don't forget about my plants; tend to them."

He looked toward the voice. A man several rows ahead had already turned back to his work after speaking.

"Dad?" Eli took in a deep breath.

Was that his father? He stood and was about to run to him but stopped. It couldn't be; William Noble was dead. Eli continued to stare at the man's back as he lifted the bag of dirt and moved farther down the row.

Kneeling again, Eli tied up the next plant. How could he have mistaken that man for his father? He placed his hands in the warm dirt and noticed how full of life it felt. He spread it around the plant in front of him and looked toward the man again. He was facing away but seemed to sense the boy's curious gaze.

"Eli, my crops. Will you tend them with me?"

As the man started to turn, Eli felt a tickle on his hand. He looked down and saw the plant growing around his wrists and creeping up his arms.

"I'm sorry. I got distracted," he said as he glanced back up.

The man was gone. Eli scanned the empty field. He heard a whisper behind him but close to his ear.

"Eli..."

His eyes fought against the dawn. Eli felt the steady rise and fall of Ada's breathing and realized he had been dreaming. He rubbed his eyes and waited for his mind to move from dream to reality.

"Eli," Jed called again as he flicked the wall of the tent. "You and Ada need to get up. Worship is about to start."

Eli reached over and gently shook his new bride. "Okay, we're getting up," he said as he sat up and stretched.

The couple quickly got ready for the day and stepped out of their tent. Ada shivered in the cold morning air.

"You may want to grab a blanket," Hattie called out to them. "It's brisk this morning."

Almost before the woman had finished speaking, Ada twirled around and leapt back into the tent. When she reemerged, she was wrapped in one of their blankets. Cobra trotted up to her and danced around her feet as she skipped to the fire and sat in a chair next to Rosa. Eli detected a bounce in her step that had been missing for a long time. He sat in the empty chair to her left, and she reached for his hand.

"No nightmares last night," he observed with a smile.

"None," she said, grinning.

The fire was warm, and everyone sat around it as they waited in peaceful anticipation. Breakfast was heating on the edge of the fire. It smelled both sweet and savory. Myra sat on her mother's lap, sucking her fingers and staring at Ada, who waved playfully at the girl. The toddler grinned around her fingers and giggled.

Tony and Jed had musical instruments next to them. Eli didn't know what they were; he had never seen anything like them before. The instruments were both shaped similar to a violin but were bigger and had more strings. Unlike a violin, there was a round hole in the center of each. Eli wondered what they sounded like.

Jed picked his up and held it against himself. With the fingers of one hand, he pressed the strings along the instrument's neck. With his other hand, he reached around it and began plucking at the strings over the hole. It had a deep, full-bodied sound; its warm tone had a solid ring. Eli enjoyed the whimsical rhythm it produced. Tony soon joined in, and the melody and harmony mingled together.

The song sounded familiar, but it wasn't until the group began to sing that Eli recognized the hymn. He had heard it played on a piano many times before, but this morning the song was livelier, and he couldn't help tapping his foot to its quick pace. He glanced at Ada, who smiled back at him as she started to clap in time with the rest of the group. Together they sang the well-known lyrics of praise. Eli had previously thought of this hymn as being solemn and serious, but singing it with this faster tempo gave it a joyous and hopeful mood.

A majority of the songs that were sung that morning had an energy and a sense of celebration to them, even when they were slower. With each one, Eli sat taller, and his mind grew more alert. He wanted the singing to continue all morning, but soon Jed announced the last song. As he began to play, Tony didn't join him right away, and everyone else was quiet. Rosa swayed with closed eyes as Jed's rich, deep voice sang a hymn Eli had never heard before. The words caught his attention. They spoke of walking in a garden with Jesus and talking with Him. It described the Savior's voice as being so sweet that all of creation couldn't help but listen. The hymn was full of joy and beauty.

Eli's thoughts drifted to his dream. He longed to go back to the field and work harder. He wanted those wilted plants to spring up as healthy as the flowers in the song Jed was singing. Perhaps it was only a dream, but Eli was filled with a sense of importance in the job he had been given. Why didn't he understand this before waking?

"Yes, Lord. I *will* care for your crops," he whispered. "Show me what I need to do."

Tony joined the song, slowly strumming the strings on his instrument, and everyone sang together as the chorus repeated two more times. Soon the music ended, and the worship time moved seamlessly into a prayer led by Ira. After praying, he opened his Bible and read aloud. His sermon focused on a verse about being adopted into God's family. Ira didn't stand and preach dryly to the group; he sat with them and leaned forward as he spoke. He used examples from their own lives to emphasize his topic. He didn't mind when someone chimed in with a comment, an example, or even a joke. They laughed and nodded and shared with each other. The morning flew by. Eli never felt impatient for breakfast. He never wondered about the time or thought about rushing out to play ball with his friends as he had done during so many church meetings in his past. He listened and understood everything Ira said.

Before he knew it, the service was over and breakfast was being passed around. The conversation, however, still lingered on Ira's sermon. More examples were shared, and there was genuine and natural praise woven into the entire morning. As breakfast came to an end, Jed brought the discussion back to business.

"Even though it's Sunday, we should get back on the road. We need to get to Clackton soon."

Everyone agreed, and they talked over the details. The caravan worked efficiently together; they were soon cleaned, loaded, and hitched up. Eli and Ada rode with Jed and Rosa as the four vardos journeyed along the road. Cobra sat with his head on Eli's lap.

"Jed," he said as he rubbed the dog's ears, "what was that instrument you played this morning?"

"That's a guitar."

"Could you teach me how to play it?" Eli asked.

"Sure," he said, winking at Rosa. "It'll take longer than a month, though. You're gonna have to stick around for a while."

Eli peered at Ada, who was nodding. "Okay," he whispered, returning her nod.

He leaned against the wall of the vardo and closed his eyes. Sunshine fell on his face as the horses pulled them along. The day was going to be warm after all.

Chapter 17

ADA

Ada sipped her tea and leaned back in one of the parlor chairs Grace had given them. Wrapped in a blanket, she gazed at the fire in the hearth, knowing it would be the last one until fall. As she watched the fire crackle, Ada thought about that morning's church service. After experiencing three Sundays in East Haven, it was easy to notice the differences between the church meetings in town and the worship times with the caravan.

East Haven's services were quiet and contemplative. They were formal compared to the caravan's energetic worship. Marcus Duncan spoke with just as much love, enthusiasm, and knowledge as Ira. But it seemed like most of the congregation wasn't able to catch his excitement, and that surprised her.

Ada appreciated many things about both styles of worship. This church reminded her of the one she had attended as a child, before her parents had died. It gave her a warm, nostalgic feeling that kept her connected to her past, whereas the caravan's worship time filled her with joy and gave her hope that, despite every trial, the future still had potential. She longed to experience both styles together.

"Ada, you seem far away," Eli said as he sat on the sofa, watching her.

She smiled and moved to sit with him.

"That's better," he said, putting an arm around her. "But it isn't what I meant. You may be here, but I think you're also sitting around a fire with Jed and Rosa and the rest of them."

"I was," she admitted as she rested her head on his shoulder. "It'll take a while to adjust to this new life. I'm sorry."

"Don't be. I understand. But I know we're supposed to be here. I can't explain it; I just need you to trust me."

"I do, Eli. I always have. I'm not sorry we're here, though I will need time to get used to it." Ada sat up and turned toward Eli. "Or maybe it's the town who needs to get used to us. You shocked a few people this morning when you spoke up in the middle of the sermon."

He chuckled and shook his head. "Marcus asked a question. I simply answered it."

"I think everyone assumed it was rhetorical."

"Maybe, but he paused," Eli pointed out. "I assumed he was waiting for an answer."

Ada sat up straight and employed her best imitation of Mrs. Russell's offended voice. "That pause was for effect, young man. No one in East Haven *ever* speaks out in church. The very idea!"

Eli started to laugh. "You do that well. Maybe you don't need as much time as you think to fit in. Anyway, Marcus seemed to welcome my answer. He didn't even notice all the gasps; he just rolled it right into his sermon as if he had planned for someone to speak up."

This time Ada laughed. "There really were a lot of gasps, weren't there? I wonder what the town would think of our music. I miss that most of all."

"Well *that* I can help you with, Mrs. Gardner."

He winked at her and went to the corner of the room where his guitar rested against the wall. He put the strap over his shoulder and started to play as he walked back to the sofa. He didn't sit down again but stood in the firelight, strumming a lively version of a hymn from earlier that morning.

As he moved with the tempo, a grin grew on Ada's face. She stood and clapped along with the song. An impish smile spread over Eli's face as he watched her dance. He increased the tempo; she knew he was just playing around. He wanted to see if she could keep up with him. Well, two could play at that game.

Her cheeks felt warm as she danced faster. She laughed and hooked her arm around his waist. As she spun him, he maintained his ability to form chords regardless of how animated their dance grew. She was impressed anew with how good a player he had become.

Just as Ada couldn't dance or spin or sing any faster, there was a knock at the door. She ran to their front entry. Eli followed, removing the guitar strap from his shoulder. Ada's face was still flushed when she opened their door.

Edith Taylor and her daughter Laura stood on the porch, each with a different expression. Laura, who was seventeen, smiled with wide, inquiring eyes. She peeked past the door, searching for the source of excitement within. Edith, on the other hand, looked displeased; her mouth was drawn into a frown.

"Mrs. Taylor. Laura. How are you?" Ada said between breaths, surprised by their unexpected arrival.

"Hello, Ada," Laura replied. "The music, was that you?"

"Laura!" her mother snapped. "Mrs. Gardner is a married woman, and you are not. Address her properly."

Ada flashed a sympathetic smile at Laura. "Eli was playing his guitar. I suppose we got a little carried away with our dancing. Won't you please come in?"

Laura stepped forward, but her mother grabbed her arm.

"Thank you, I think not. We are only here to invite you to the women's Wednesday evening prayer meeting."

As she spoke, Edith peered sideways at Eli and her frown deepened. Even Laura seemed to grow cautious, though curious, as he stepped up to the door. The girl's gasp was barely audible, but her widening eyes were hard to miss.

Most people in town had only seen a small bit of the tattoos around Eli's wrists. But this afternoon, in the comfort of his home, he was dressed in a casual, short-sleeved undershirt. The vines continued up his arms and even over his shoulders and down his back, though few people would ever see that.

"Thank you for the invitation, Mrs. Taylor. What time does it start?" Ada asked, drawing Edith's attention away from Eli.

"Six o'clock. We meet at the Johnsons' home. But if you can't make it—"

"I can be there. Will you be there too, Laura?"

"Oh no, not exactly." She glanced timidly at her mother. "I watch the children. The men hold a meeting at the rectory that night as well."

"Laura is still a child herself," Edith said. "Our meeting is for married women."

"I see," Ada replied. "Thank you; I'm sure it will be interesting."

Edith raised her eyebrows. "Yes… Well, please do come. If you're a true prayer warrior, you'll find it invigorating and not merely interesting. Now, we really must be moving along. We have other visits to make."

"We do?" Laura looked as though this was the first she had heard of it. Her mother made a quick, sharp sound to hush the girl.

"Good day, Ada." Edith said, glancing at Eli once more before turning away. "Come, Laura," she ordered, much like Jed had often done with Cobra.

Laura obeyed, following her mother down the steps but looking back to wave at the couple standing in the doorway. Ada closed the door and looked at Eli. He had a smirk on his face.

"That was a reluctant invitation," he said with a laugh.

"Perhaps she thought I wouldn't accept," Ada said, baffled by the encounter. "Well, at least it will give me a chance to get to know the other women. Are you hungry? I can start supper, if you'd like."

Eli rubbed his stomach as he placed his guitar against the wall. "I think I'll help," he said with a grin and chased her into the kitchen.

Chapter 18

ELI

Having arrived in Clackton late Sunday evening, the caravan set up camp and prepared a quick supper. After eating, the merchants soon drifted off to bed in anticipation of Monday's early start. The oilcloth canopies were needed for the market, so the young couple couldn't use them to make a tent as they had done the night before. Instead, they slept in the vardo with Jed and Rosa. They folded the table away and set their mattress on the floor by the woodstove.

In the morning, the tables, canopies, and merchandise were all transported to the town's main street. The merchants were rarely able to locate the market on the same street as their camp, making the first and last days the most difficult to set up and tear down. If they had arrived in Clackton on Saturday as planned, they would have set up the tables and canopies right away and then rested and worshiped on Sunday. By Monday morning, setting out their merchandise would have been the only task remaining.

To make up for lost time, they had to start their day earlier than normal. No one seemed to mind, though, which helped put the newlyweds at ease when they realized it was their arrival and wedding that had caused the disruption in the caravan's routine.

The merchants chose someone to remain at camp with the young couple each day while the others shared the responsibility of selling for the one who had stayed behind. Rosa sat with them on Monday. She gave them clean fabric to wrap their arms until Jed could cover their markings with other tattoos. Even with their arms covered, Eli and Ada felt safer staying in the vardo and only came out for supper.

When the merchants returned to camp on the first evening, Jed and Ira carried a large roll of oiled canvas between them. Floyd followed, hauling several lengths of wood in one of the caravan's carts. He informed the young couple that he would stay with them for the rest of the week.

On Tuesday, rather than sitting in the vardo with them, Floyd began to measure and cut the oilcloth. Occasionally, Eli would peek out the window to see what he was doing. Floyd constructed a tent frame with the wood, much larger than the one he and Tony had rigged up with the canopies on Saturday. Then, he began stitching the lengths of oilcloth together. It was a tedious process, and he was only able to sew two of the tent sides together before the light began to dim and the others returned.

On Wednesday, he continued working. Eli ventured out of the vardo in the late morning, tugging at his sleeve and asking if he could help. Floyd gave him a leather hand guard to protect his palm and showed him how to stitch the heavy fabric. It was hard to push the needle through all the layers, but when Floyd confirmed that the tent was for him and Ada, Eli was glad to help.

By Thursday, Ada was brave enough to sit with Cobra on the steps of the vardo. She listened to their conversation as they worked and soon joined in with a few witty comments of her own. The tent was finished late that afternoon, and when the rest of the group returned to camp, the men helped secure the canvas to its frame. Earlier, Floyd had cut a large piece of oilcloth to cover the ground and guard against the damp, dewy earth. He helped Eli spread it out as Ada peeked through the door to admire the finishing touches.

While eating supper, everyone complimented Floyd on how well-made the tent was. Eli realized that the caravan members must have pooled their money together to buy the supplies. He glanced at the people around the fire, touched by their willingness to give freely to somebody they hardly knew. Why would they do that? His heart felt torn between doubt and gratitude—between fear and relief. He closed his eyes and wondered if he would ever feel truly safe again. When he opened his eyes, his gaze locked with Jed's. He wondered how long the man had been watching him.

"Thank you," Eli said suddenly, looking at each of them. "You've all done so much for us. I can't... I don't know how we can ever repay you."

Ada nodded as she grabbed onto his hand.

"It's our pleasure," Jed said. "Some of us know what it feels like to teeter on the edge of despair."

When they retired for the night, Eli and Ada were able to sleep in their new, more permanent dwelling. Maybe it was just a tent, but it was their tent. Eli had helped make it, and after two long months, it finally felt as though they had a home again.

❧

Jed stayed with the young couple on their second Monday in Clackton. Eli was glad; he wanted to get to know the man better. They sat in his vardo with a deck of cards. He showed them a few simple games to pass the time, but he said his main goal was to design tattoos that would cover the marks on their arms.

"Start thinking of something you will want to have forever. I know you think these tattoos will help you forget what happened, but they won't do that; you're always going to remember. But you can choose a tattoo with a stronger message. Pick an image that carries a positive meaning behind it."

"What about you?" Eli said. "What do your tattoos mean?"

Jed glanced at his arms and rubbed the pictures. A distant look passed over his face.

"Every one of my tattoos reminds me of either a blessing God has given me or a lesson He has taught me. Even my first, the one I got before I knew Christ."

"Which one is that?" Eli asked.

Jed turned slightly to show the image of a lion on his upper arm. He pointed to it, tapping his finger lightly. "I got this one when I was twenty-six. I thought it would make me look tough. I was the Lion; that's what they called me. The king of the jungle—ruler of my own life."

He shook his head at the memory. "My brother and I had just moved to the roughest part of the city, and the people we hung around with were not good. They picked people's pockets and swindled them out of their hard-earned money. They constantly fought amongst themselves, hoping to gain respect. The only way they could get others to follow them was through intimidation." He tapped the deck of cards on the table. "I never did those things, except maybe the fighting—I was a boxer. But I didn't care what they did. Who was I to tell them it was wrong? My brother and I were on a dangerous path."

Jed shuffled the cards in his hand. "And then one day, my path crossed with that of a young theology student. I don't know what he saw in me, but he went out of his way every week to buy me a coffee. He was determined to be my friend. I was only interested in the free drink, but he was persistent. He talked to me about God and the Bible. He didn't force it on me; he just spoke in a way that got me thinking. Ira—" Jed chuckled. "He's smart. He knows God's word, and he makes it interesting. But back then, I was stubborn; I didn't think I needed to change. It wasn't until I met this beautiful nurse that I started to rethink my life. She was way too good for me and I knew it."

"Rosa?" Ada asked with a smile.

Jed laughed and nodded. "Still too good for me, right? Yeah, I don't think I'll ever be as good a man as she deserves, but she loves me anyway. She's something special. You know, she used to help the poor women in the city. She was their midwife when it was time for them to have their babies, the ones who couldn't afford to see a doctor."

He dealt the cards as he continued his story. "Well, I knew I would have to make some real changes if I was ever going to have a chance with her, and Ira was up for the challenge. We started meeting *every* day. I asked him so many questions. He was patient and answered them all, and then one day I got it. I finally understood that I am not enough. When left to my own efforts, I'm lost. I desperately need Christ, and He truly wants me. I asked Him to be the Ruler of my life, and from that day on, this tattoo meant something new to me."

Jed paused for a moment. When the man looked at his hands and sniffed, Eli realized he was trying to compose himself.

"I tried to tell my brother about Jesus, but the criminal life was too tempting for him. It didn't take long for that life to kill him."

As Jed continued, Eli picked up his cards and began to arrange them into suits. He thought about his parents and felt the same pain he heard in Jed's voice.

"It was hard on me when my brother died, and Ira knew I needed to get away from the city. He had recently met Tony and his father Hanzi. They wanted him to join their caravan, and Ira asked me to come along. Rosa and I got married and we both went. Rosa had seen so many babies and mothers die; she was ready for a change."

He looked at them and sighed; his voice changed as the mood of his story lifted.

"That was over a decade ago, and even though I'll always miss my brother, the caravan is my family now. We've lost a few along the way, but we've gained a few as well. When we joined the caravan, Hanzi was alive and Floyd and Hattie's son was still with us. Goldie lived with her parents in their vardo, but it didn't take long for everyone to see how perfect she and Ira were for each other. They got married two years later, and now we have Sammy and Myra. Every single one of these people has been a blessing in my life, and each of them has been an inspiration for another tattoo."

Jed leaned back in his seat, looking as though several more memories were running through his mind.

"Where are Goldie's parents now?" Eli asked.

"Goldie's folks stay at the winter camp year-round," he explained. "They have a garden and take care of things for us. Thanks to them, we have enough food for winter. You'll meet them in September when we return."

Jed peered closely at him. He knew Jed was looking for some kind of reaction, but Eli remained quiet and shifted his eyes to his cards.

Ada broke the silence. "I want my tattoo to represent people and blessings too." She rubbed her arm. "The flowers that were in my hair during the wedding, I'd like two of those; one for me and one for Eli. And the leaves—I want those to represent the caravan, surrounding the flowers in a protective cluster. Can you do that, Jed?"

The man set his cards aside and grabbed a stick of charcoal and some paper. He began sketching ideas while she looked across the table at his design.

The image of Ada from his dream flashed into Eli's mind. The flowering vines she had been playing with were the same flowers that had been in her hair, the ones she now asked Jed to put on her arm. A deep longing stirred in his heart; he couldn't put it into words, but he knew it was connected to his dream.

Jed and Ada wanted their tattoos to remind them of what God had already done for them and of people God had placed in their lives. They wanted something commemorative. Eli wanted his tattoo to remind him of something more continual, something ongoing. He wanted it to motivate him. The question from his dream repeated in his mind: "*Will you tend my crops?*"

"I know what I want my tattoo to be."

Jed and Ada glanced up at him. Jed slid the paper and charcoal across the table. Eli set his cards down and started drawing.

Chapter 19

JOHN

John Miller slapped the reins impatiently as he guided his wagon down the road. He needed to repair a few of his cattle pens, so he was heading into town to pick up a load of lumber. John was the largest landowner in East Haven. He owned approximately one thousand acres, and running a farm that size kept him busy.

Ray Larson owned a good-sized farm as well, which happened to border John's westward fields, but his was only six hundred acres. Ray used his land to grow a few crops—mostly hay—and he was successful enough. John, however, grew more high-profit crops than his neighbor and owned twenty-six dairy cows as well. Those cows provided most of the town with milk, butter, and cheese. Both he and Ray needed to hire workers in order to keep their farms running smoothly. So, it could easily be said that they were important men who helped ensure the town's prosperity. Since John employed far more men than Ray, he was well aware of his greater responsibility to East Haven.

Picking up lumber was not his only reason for going to town. Isaac Weber had asked him to meet with Eli Gardner and possibly offer him some work. To be honest, John was irritated by Isaac's request. If this new neighbor of his really wanted a job, he should have come to John himself. He was not impressed. And it didn't help that there were some pretty shocking stories flying around town about this new couple. The things his wife Agnes had repeated to him were not stacking up favorably for the town's newcomers.

She had heard from Edith Taylor that the Gardners were lewd performers who used to travel with a band of gypsies. They corrupted the youth of every town they visited. Edith herself had witnessed the wild dancing and loud, detestable music—all on a Sunday afternoon too! If that wasn't bad enough, people were saying that both of them— even the wife—were covered in tattoos under all their clothing.

Evelyn Russell had told Agnes that the "snippy girl in the house next door" was rude, disrespectful, and had a nasty temper. And the husband seemed to have his own faults. The Gardners had been in town for almost a month now, and Eli still hadn't sought out any work. Well, that spoke for itself. John got the impression that this gypsy boy was lazy, and in his experience, lazy people tended to drink. He wondered if the wife was so bitter and angry because of her husband's idle ways—or if the husband was so apathetic because his wife was a pestering nag.

The more he thought about the things he had heard, the more he regretted agreeing to meet with Eli. Isaac probably saw them as a charity case, but John had a farm to run. Handing out charity jobs was not good for business. Let the church take care of the poor. That's what John's tithe was for, wasn't it?

It wasn't as though he had no compassion for the needy. There were plenty of poor, large families in town, and he was willing to offer those men some modest wages once they proved to be hard workers. John had no tolerance for men who were only poor because they weren't willing to work. His dad was a lazy drunk, and John had to work harder than most just to make sure he and his mother and sisters had enough to eat. He resented his father for it, but he was also aware of this simple fact: having to work harder back then contributed to his success now. He could either take after his pa or rise up and be better. John refused to take the first route.

He pulled his wagon up to the lumber mill, and as a millworker began to load his order, John strolled over to the general store. Isaac was standing outside Johnson's Mercantile, but there was no sign of Eli.

"Your boy didn't show up, huh?" John sneered as he walked up to him.

"Eli is at the bank talking with Mr. Holden," Isaac explained. "He'll be here soon."

It was early in the month, and due to Eli's lack of work, John figured he must be having trouble coming up with his mortgage payment. He was probably trying to work out some sort of deal with the banker. John shook his head as his patience grew thinner.

Just then, Eli and David walked out of the bank, deep in conversation. David was relaying some anecdote as Eli laughed and nodded. The men shook hands before Eli jogged across the road toward the general store.

"Eli," Isaac called out, "have you met John Miller?"

"Briefly, a couple Sundays ago," he said, holding out his hand.

John shook it, turning Eli's arm to give his tattoo an obvious examination.

"Looks tough," he said. "I hear you're looking for work. What else can you do with your arms besides mark them up?"

There was a short pause before Eli answered. "My trade is fine wood-working, but if you've got something you need help with, I can do just about anything."

"Fine woodworking… like carving?" John wasn't really interested. "I don't have any use for that. But I'll tell you what, I do need someone to muck out my barn every morning. I was going to give the job to Henry Carlson, but you can do it instead."

Mucking out a barn was a dirty, unpleasant job, but it revealed who the most humble and hardest workers were. John wanted to test his theory on what kind of man Eli was.

"I didn't know Henry Carlson was looking for extra work," Isaac piped in.

"Yeah, he's got his tenth kid on the way. What do you say, boy? You want the job?"

Eli was slower to answer than he liked.

"Thank you for the offer, Mr. Miller, but I think I had better keep looking."

"Not quite what you were hoping for, huh?" he said with a snort.

"I just don't think I should take work away from a man with ten kids. I only have Ada and myself to take care of."

Well, that sounded noble enough, but John guessed there was another reason for Eli's refusal. He suspected it was either pride or laziness—probably both.

"You sure about that? I won't offer again. Once the other employers in town hear that you've refused a perfectly good job offer, they'll be less willing to hire you."

"Go ahead and give the job to Henry," Eli insisted.

As Isaac listened to their conversation, he raised his hand and beckoned to Ray Larson, who was walking toward them.

"Don't worry, Mr. Miller. I asked Ray Larson to meet with Eli as well. I'm sure he'll have some work." Isaac greeted the old farmer. "Mr. Larson, you've met Eli, haven't you? Mr. Miller wasn't able to hire him, so if you have any work, I'm sure he'd be grateful for it."

As Ray shook Eli's hand, John spoke up in a sardonic tone.

"Yeah, if you've got any *whittling* you need done, this is your boy, Ray." He slapped Eli roughly on his back.

"Whittling? No, I don't think so…" Ray began. "I assume you've got other skills, though?"

Eli glanced sideways at John before answering. "Yes, Mr. Larson. I can work the land. I also know a little bit about building, and I'm good at odd jobs if they're needed."

"Oh, we have a lot of those around my place," Ray said, chuckling. "Come by the barn tomorrow morning, and I'll get you started on some of those odd jobs. I can't pay you as much as John pays his workers, but I'm sure we can figure something out."

"Whatever you pay will be fine. I just appreciate the chance to work," Eli replied. "And I don't know what his skills are, but I understand Henry Carlson is looking for some extra income. If you have a lot of work, you may want to call on him also."

"I wasn't aware. Thanks for the tip, Eli. I'll definitely do that."

John grimaced. He could not believe Eli had just given up half his work to someone else. Well, that was one way to ensure a person didn't have to do a full day's work. He was starting to understand why Eli's wife might be so bitter. Having a husband who dodged his responsibilities would shrink any woman's heart. Maybe he should feel sorry for her.

"Well, I need to get going," John grumbled. "Farm work is never done. Isaac, I hope you've had a productive day off; see you in the morning. Eli, looks like you found a job you're willing to do. Good for you. And Ray…" He shook his head. "Good luck with that."

As he walked back to his wagon, he wondered how long it would take his neighbor to get fed up with Eli's casual work ethic. Knowing Ray, he'd probably never figure it out—the guy was a pushover. But then, Ray only had six hundred acres, whereas John had almost twice that. He was too big and too important to let himself be pushed around.

Chapter 20
ELI

When it was time to start working on their tattoos, both Jed and Rosa stayed in the camp with the young couple. Rosa put on her apron, grabbed a cooking pot, and stepped outside. Eli watched her through the window as she walked up to one of the caravan's small barrels that was filled at the public well. After dipping her pot into the water, she brought it back inside and placed it on the woodstove. While the water was heating, she collected supplies from the cupboards and closets. Jed opened a drawer and brought out a pen and a bottle of dark red ink.

"I'm going to draw the designs right onto your arms with this," he explained. "Once you've decided it looks right, I'll use black ink to make it permanent."

He grabbed a rolled-up leather pouch that contained a set of wood carving tools. "These belonged to my grandpa," he said with a proud grin. He removed one of the tools from the pouch. It was only a wooden handle; the chisel's blade had broken free a long time ago. He placed the handle on the table and set the pouch aside.

Rosa handed Jed a bottle of clear liquid, along with a spool of thread and an ink cake wrapped in waxed paper. She opened a small tin container that was filled with sewing needles and put five of them into the pot of boiling water.

While Rosa spread clean cheesecloth over the top of a large mixing bowl, Jed used his knife to cut a small piece off of the dry ink cake. He scraped it into a shallow cup and mixed the black ink with a small amount of water.

After a few minutes, Rosa poured the pot of water into the mixing bowl. The cheesecloth caught the needles as the hot water filtered through it. She brought them to the table, along with the bowl. Jed washed his hands in the water and held the needles together. He inserted them into a groove on the edge of the handle and tied them securely by wrapping them several times with the thread. He poured liquid from the bottle over the tool he had assembled.

"What's that?" Eli asked.

"It's grain alcohol," Jed explained. "It's better for cleaning than for drinking. So, who wants to go first?"

Eli looked at Ada. "Are you nervous? I want your marks to get covered as soon as possible. If you aren't too scared, I think you should go first."

"I'm a little scared," she said. But after a pause, she agreed.

Ada sat across from Jed and held out her arm. He studied the marks in silence before beginning. Picking up the pen, he dipped it in the red ink and drew a simple sketch of their earlier design directly onto her arm. She smiled and said it looked good. When the ink dried, Jed used his right hand to stretch her skin taut. With his left hand, he dipped the needles into the black ink and began pricking her skin along the red lines. Ada's eyes widened, and she reached out with her free arm.

"Eli…" she said through a quick, wavering breath as she grabbed onto his wrist.

"Does it hurt more than last time?" he asked.

"No. It feels the same, but it brought back memories. For a second, it felt like I was back in that cage."

Her eyes were moist, and her grip tightened; Eli had to stifle a wince. She turned her head and stared at the pattern painted along the edge of the shuttered window.

"Do you need me to stop, Ada?" Jed asked.

She shook her head. "The marks need to be covered. You can't stop."

He continued to work on her tattoo. Eli was impressed with how long she withstood the pain before needing a break. Jed gave her several short rests throughout the day. It was a slow process, but eventually the outline of the flowers and leaves was finished.

As Jed began to fill in the first flower, Eli was relieved to see her marks covered by the fresh, dark ink. When he started the second, Ada finally asked if they could stop for the day. He suggested she take a few days to heal before they worked on it again.

Rosa mixed a small amount of grain alcohol in some water and washed Ada's arm with the solution. She spread ointment over her skin and wrapped it in clean, gauzy fabric.

"We'll start on yours tomorrow," Jed said to Eli as he and Rosa cleaned up.

While they ate supper with the others, Eli felt empty—drained of all his energy. Ada was the one who had suffered the most that day, but having to watch her relive their time in the rock quarry opened a hole in his center, and everything poured out of him. He wondered how tired Ada must be. He wasn't surprised when she went to bed early. It didn't take long for him to follow.

Chapter 21

ADA

The Johnsons, who owned the mercantile in town, lived in a beautiful two-story house. Ada tapped their bronze knocker lightly. It was time for the women's prayer meeting, and she wasn't sure what to expect. The caravan didn't set aside a formal time for praying; they didn't have to because they were always together. If someone needed prayer, they would stop what they were doing and pray as a group. After Ada's second knock, Nora Johnson opened the door and ushered her to an elegant table spread out with tea cakes, preserves, and a crystal pitcher of rose water.

"Please help yourself to some refreshments and join the women in the sitting room," Mrs. Johnson said.

Ada poured water for herself and chose a chair in the corner. Glancing around the room, she was disappointed to find that Grace and Hannah were not among the others.

"When will Grace Duncan be here?" she asked.

"Oh," Mrs. Johnson said, shaking her head. "Mrs. Duncan rarely attends. Pastor Duncan holds a meeting for the men as well; he insists that she stay to serve them. Hasn't Eli received an invitation to the men's meeting?"

"Yes, Marcus invited him when we first moved here," Ada said. "But he hasn't mentioned seeing Grace there."

Mrs. Johnson pursed her lips. "Well, *Pastor Duncan* would have her stay in the kitchen until the men are ready for their pie."

Ada noted her condescending emphasis on the propriety of using titles. That sarcastic tone remained when the woman spoke again.

"Perhaps he was too focused on his dessert to notice who had served it."

As more women arrived, the small talk continued. Mrs. Turner turned to Ada just as she lifted her water glass to her mouth.

"I understand Eli is doing odd jobs for Ray Larson."

Ada nodded, and Mrs. Turner pressed her mouth into a flat smile.

"Hmm… Well, I'm sure he must be grateful for the work."

Nora Johnson clapped her hands quickly to get their attention. "Ladies, let's get started, shall we? Why don't we start with our newest guest tonight? Ada, do you have anything you would like us to pray for? Please don't be shy."

Ada looked up, unprepared. "Oh, let me see… I've been praying that Eli and I will make some meaningful friendships here."

The group nodded and continued to stare at her, as if expecting her to continue. What else was she supposed to say? She let out a nervous laugh.

"That's all, really. Thank you for praying with me about this."

"Isn't there anything else you'd like us to pray for, dear?" Mrs. Turner asked. "Your husband spends more time at the bank than he does at the Larson farm. Perhaps you need financial prayer."

Ada's mouth dropped at the woman's assumption. "I'm sure we're fine. Eli has lunch with David once a week. They get along well and are becoming good friends." Her eyes darted amongst their skeptical gazes.

"Well," Edith Taylor said, "husbands don't always tell their wives about their money problems." She looked at Ada with raised eyebrows.

Mrs. Turner inhaled loudly through her nose. "Oh, Edith, that is so true! Now then, Ada. You must tell us when you find yourself in need. We will want to know—so we can pray for you, of course."

Ada's stomach tightened along with her jaw. She nodded and forced a polite smile. When she remained silent, they moved on to the next woman.

Each of them spoke in great lengths of their prayer requests, most of which included complicated backstories of all the people involved. Ada wondered when they were going to finally pray and if she would remember what to pray about when they did. The women listened to each other and shook their heads, asking leading questions. The stories and inquiries went on until Ada realized that many of these women were using their prayer requests as an excuse to gossip.

Their attention soon turned to Helen Blake, whose husband owned the post office. She sighed heavily, preparing to share some troublesome news.

"We need to keep Evelyn Russell in our prayers," she told the curious listeners.

Ada scanned the group of women; Evelyn was missing from the circle. Mrs. Blake continued, unable to hide her enjoyment.

"The poor woman has just received a telegram. Her son has been sent to prison! She is greatly afflicted and has confined herself to her bed tonight."

The others gasped, lamenting over Evelyn's trial. Ada didn't even know her neighbor had a son.

"Oh, dear. What has he done?" Mrs. Martin asked.

Mrs. Blake sat up straight, assuming a well-informed attitude. "Apparently, he started a fight—in a tavern, no less! He beat a man within an inch of his life and was sent straight to the Middletown Penitentiary. He will be there for two years."

The women all patted their chests and shook their heads. Edith Taylor sanctimoniously commented on how embarrassing this was for the *entire* town.

"Evelyn must be so sad," Mrs. Martin observed. "Two years is such a long time."

"Well, it isn't that long," Nora Johnson chimed in, "considering he's been away for longer. I don't know what I would do if my little Eddie was sent to prison. Just between us ladies, I'm not sure how comfortable I will feel if Evelyn's son ever does come back. I am so glad Edgar keeps his gun behind the counter at the mercantile."

Ada was disgusted by Nora's callous comment. She wondered how Evelyn would feel about what was being said. Her neighbor might be outspoken and narrow-minded, but no one deserved to have their hardships talked of in this heartless manner. Not interested in hearing any more of their gossip, she leaned forward to stand. But then Edith Taylor said something that shocked her even more and caused her to sit back down.

"Goodness! He will probably come out of there all covered in…" She stopped short, catching herself. "Um…" She glanced at Ada.

"Tattoos," Ada finished for her.

There was an uncomfortable hush as the women peered around the room. Some looked nervous, while others looked curiously entertained.

"I was going to say scars," Edith said after a long pause. "A penitentiary is a vicious place, full of violent men."

The silence stretched on until Agnes Miller finally broke it.

"Has Eli ever been in prison?"

Ada blinked at the brashness of the question. Her stomach flipped, and a tired frown dusted the corners of her mouth as a painful memory of the rock quarry cages flashed in her mind.

93

"No, Mrs. Miller," she whispered, "he has never been in prison."

The judgmental looks of the women drilled holes into her heart. She longed to be anywhere but here. Ada stood and excused herself, promising to take their requests home with her. She would pray about them later. Unfortunately, she was developing a headache and felt as though she ought to leave. Nora Johnson, Edith Taylor, and Agnes Miller raised their eyebrows as they glanced at each other.

"Well, Ada, we hope you feel better soon," Edith said over her shoulder as Nora walked her to the door. "We'll be sure to keep you on our prayer list."

"Thank you," Ada managed to say as she walked out the door.

Chapter 22

ELI

The summer was passing quickly. It was already early August, and the evening air was warm and heavy. After leaving Clackton at the end of June, the caravan had traveled first to Westmill and then to Orston before moving on to Linland and beyond. Jed had explained that they would stay at each town for approximately two weeks. The caravan had just arrived at Briggmoore, the second to the last town in their summer market circuit.

After that, they would travel to Woodhurst and then home to Oak Springs and the West Woods, where their winter camp was. The West Woods was part of a large property owned by a well-to-do widow. In exchange for living on a corner of her land, the men of the caravan helped the widow's hired workers with her harvest and other small projects.

As Eli sat by their small cooking fire, he tried not to scratch the newest section of his tattoo. Ada's had only taken a couple of days to finish, with a week in between for healing. But his was taking longer. He didn't mind; he liked what Jed was doing. He had used the idea of the plant from Eli's dream, the one that had started to grow around his wrists, and made it look better than the sketch Eli had drawn to explain it.

Jed designed a thick, twisting vine that started on the top of Eli's hand, close to his wrist, and branched in several places as it spread up the front of his arm and wrapped around the underside. He was going to make the branches coil together randomly to cover the marks on the inside of Eli's arm. But then, Eli confided in Jed that it was hard to believe Jesus was around when their parents were killed or when they had been locked away in those cages. Jed suggested having two of the branches twist together into a cross that covered Eli's marks. He said it might help Eli remember that Christ had never left them alone in their troubles.

Eli agreed, and while Jed pricked the cross into his arm, memories of their time on the run flooded back into his mind. They weren't the bad memories, though. It was as if God were using his memories to say, "*See, I was right there.*"

Eli remembered how easy it was to break the bar free from his cage and how well he fit through the space it made. The fact that all the men except one had left the rock quarry on the night of their escape was a detail he couldn't ignore. He recalled feeling the urgent push to keep moving—and the circumstances around finding the coin raced through his mind. Finally, he remembered the perfect timing of meeting up with the caravan just as they were about to leave Ashbrook.

As Jed worked on his tattoo, he told Eli that Jesus had often used images of vines and branches, as well as crops and harvests, to teach about God. When Jed had finished the cross, Eli asked if he could work on his other arm too. Over time, he hoped Jed would continue to add to it, and if he didn't mind, they could talk more about the things Jesus said. It was his way of letting Jed know they planned to stay with the caravan.

Eli started to scratch his arm again, but Ada grabbed his hand. She shook her head at him and smiled.

"Don't scratch."

Eli could tell she was happy, and that encouraged him. She rarely had nightmares anymore, and when she did, she would only sit up and gasp in the dark. The screaming had not returned since the night before their wedding.

He sighed as he looked at the group of people with him. Just like Jed, this was their family now—and they were good people. In this peaceful moment, Eli could feel Christ sitting right there among them, and he didn't need to look at his tattoo to know it was true. He felt himself relax for the first time in months. Maybe he and Ada were finally safe.

Chapter 23

DAVID

D avid Holden locked the bank doors at three o'clock every weekday. After three, he would take off his banker's hat and put on his accountant's hat. He and his son Daniel managed the books for most of the farms in East Haven, including the Larson and Miller farms. It took many hours to balance ledgers, fill out purchase orders, track wages paid, and record accounts received—each with three hand written copies. Father and son rarely left the office before six o'clock, but neither of them minded working the late hours. David's wife had passed away several years ago, so there was no need to hurry home.

Despite the long hours, there was always a rush to finish the paperwork at the end of the week. So, on Fridays David hid in his office all day and only took a break during the lunch hour, which he usually spent with Eli Gardner. Daniel worked with the customers while his father was in his office, and he knew not to disturb him until Eli's arrival.

David looked forward to their weekly lunch. He had liked the young man from the moment they met. Both Eli and his wife had displayed an enjoyable blend of excitement and politeness when David had shown them the Colebrook house. He didn't care about their eccentric style; he liked the couple. After deciding to buy the house, they went back to David's office to talk about payment options and fill out some forms. He could easily see Eli's tattoos but didn't even bat an eye. Tattoos were nothing new to him.

David had grown up in a small town similar to East Haven, but he moved to a busy port city when he attended the university. After finishing his education, his first banking job had been in that same port city. Many of his customers were sailors, and they almost always had several tattoos.

He could tell, though, that Eli was not a sailor. He also knew that the young couple was not easily defined by normal standards. In some ways it seemed as though they had a small-town feel to them, but maybe that was from their earlier past—surely not recently. He did know, however, that they were not from a large city either. During their first meeting, he couldn't quite put a finger on what made the Gardners so unique. But there was definitely something different about them, and David delighted in it.

When Eli returned on the following Thursday to pick up his house key, he brought the information David needed to transfer his account from Bradford's bank to East Haven's bank. While the men conducted their business, Ada walked across the street to the mercantile to buy a few items for their pantry. After she had left, Eli hesitated, not wanting to hand over the account ledger that Harold Ross had provided.

"David," he said with a slight furrow on his brow. "When I decided to buy my wife a house, I asked Mr. Ross to recommend some towns with good banks owned by decent men. You were at the top of his list. He told me you run your bank honestly and efficiently. He also said you know how to be discreet."

He continued to hold onto his paperwork. "I would like to know if he was right. I already come into this town with a disadvantage. I know what people will think of me, and I know what I'm asking my wife to endure by moving here. I don't want to give the town any more reason to judge me."

David assured him that he was bound to privacy, not only legally but morally as well. It wouldn't have made a difference to him what kind of mess was on that ledger; he was impressed by Eli's straightforward and honest manner. No matter what challenges the young man faced, he had a good character. From that day forward, David considered him a friend, and when they started to have lunch together on Fridays, their friendship grew.

Eli told him about their time with the merchant caravan. It sounded like an interesting life and was probably what made the young couple seem so unusual. Living in such a close and dependent community gave the Gardners an ease with others that David found refreshing. Perhaps this relaxed and informal manner had contributed to why they were so misunderstood. Personally, he felt comfortable around Eli's casual nature; it was the reason they had become friends so quickly.

It was now eleven o'clock, and there was a light tap on David's door. After opening it, he greeted Eli with a handshake. From the doorway, he could see the counter where his son was working. John Miller was there, making his weekly withdrawal—four hours earlier than usual.

David nodded at the farmer. "Good morning, Mr. Miller. You're here early."

"Yeah, well, I have to pick up some supplies in White Falls. And as you know, it's payday. I want to make sure my men get their wages before I head out." He paused as he peered at David's guest. "Eli... Didn't expect to see you here. I thought you were working for Ray Larson these days. Guess he ran out of work for you."

"No, I'm still working with Ray. I was there earlier." Eli replied.

"Oh? I didn't realize the workday was already over. But then, Ray has always been more laid back with his hired help than I am with mine. A little too laid back, if you ask me. I sure could show him a few things about efficiency that would put some profit back in his pocket. It's too bad he's so set in his ways."

"Ray's a good employer," Eli said. "His men appreciate working for him, and they keep his farm running well. I'm heading back this afternoon."

"Well, you're pretty lucky to have such a long lunch break, aren't you? Especially if he's paying you daily wages." He made a subtle scoffing noise as he dismissed Eli and turned his attention back to Daniel.

Eli looked as though he might say something but chose to remain silent. He watched John for a moment longer before shaking his head and turning away.

"Have a good afternoon, David," John called over his shoulder to the banker only.

"You too, Mr. Miller."

David motioned Eli into his office. After closing the door, he glanced at his friend.

"John doesn't like you."

Eli laughed. "No, he sure doesn't, but I don't really care. And besides..." He changed the subject with a grin. "Ada packed us some cookies."

"Ah, your wife is very thoughtful," David replied as they walked to his desk. "Now, let's see those cookies."

Chapter 24

ELI

Eli's lantern barely lit the dark tent as he rummaged through the chest full of clothes given to them as a wedding gift. It was early morning; he didn't want to wake Ada, but somewhere in the chest was a wool sweater he needed. Jed was taking him fishing, and now that it was late September, the mornings were getting colder.

The caravan had arrived at their winter camp on the first day of the month. Eli had liked the West Woods and the camp immediately. The caravan's winter home felt permanent, and that was why it appealed to him. The merchants continued to live in their vardos, but this place had a few amenities that couldn't travel with them in the summer.

Stretched out over the fire pit was an oversized canopy to protect the merchants from the damp weather. An ancient looking brick oven had been built near the large fire pit, and a simple wooden storage shed stood by a path that led to Badger Creek. A short distance away from where they parked their vardos, the merchants had constructed a small smokehouse out of stone. In it, they cured the meat and fish that was sold in the markets.

The winter camp had a fenced in area for horses. It was attached to a stable that could house a dozen animals when the weather was cold. A hitch wagon with a bench seat was parked under a sturdy cover built against the stable. The merchants drove the wagon into town when they needed to buy supplies.

A short walk toward Badger Creek revealed a clearing of land where Goldie's parents, Levi and Bea, planted a modest garden every spring.

Surrounding the garden were small, well-pruned fruit trees: apples, pears, and plums. The merchants always gave some of their best produce to Mrs. Perry, the widow who owned the land.

The West Woods reminded Eli of the forest near his childhood home. He had explored those back woods with Ada or his father often, and he was itching to roam these as well. Soon after arriving at the winter camp, Rosa brought up the subject of school. Jed had talked to them about it earlier, but now she was insisting they make a decision. Even though Eli would have preferred to explore the woods all winter long, he understood that lessons were important. They agreed to start their schooling the following week, and Rosa and Ira began planning straightaway. Ira would teach arithmetic, grammar, and rhetoric, whereas Rosa would tackle their history and geography lessons.

School started early each weekday and lasted until noon. After lunch, Ira and Eli would join the other men, who were either working the land for Mrs. Perry or stocking up on their wares for the markets. They worked for the widow on the first three days of the week and then worked for themselves on the other three days, as needed. Sundays, of course, were set aside for worship and rest.

Tony showed Eli how to work with wood. Jed let him try out his grandpa's carving tools, and he caught on well. The men also took him fishing and hunting. They showed him how to prepare meat for the smoke house, and they taught him how to tan the animal hides using a different method than his father. Floyd and Levi used most of the leather to make pouches, belts, and toys for the markets. Hattie used the remainder to make her unique jewelry.

Eli was not the only one learning new skills. Rosa was teaching Ada how to crochet and weave bobbin lace, while Goldie and Bea picked up her sewing lessons where her mother had left off. All of the women—and especially Grandma Mae—taught her how to cook, bake, and can food.

Best of all was when Jed offered to help Eli build their very own vardo. Eli was too excited to concentrate on his lessons for three whole days. Jed pointed out that it would take several months to build, so it would be best for Eli to focus on his schoolwork. Later in the month they could take the hitch wagon to town and purchase some lumber.

At last, the day had come! Jed promised to take him to Bradford, which was a big town located a few miles past Oak Springs. They would leave as soon as they returned from fishing. Jed knew a wheelwright who lived in Bradford. He had worked with the tradesman before and hoped he would have some seasoned timber to sell, along with four well-made wagon wheels and their axles. Eli could hardly wait.

As he sifted through the chest, he could hear Jed collecting the fishing poles from the shed. Cobra panted loudly and tromped around in anticipation of their fishing trip. Eli pushed aside clothes, still looking for the wool sweater. As his hand grazed canvas, his stomach clenched tight; it was the bag from the rock quarry. The morning after their wedding, the caravan had hastily packed in order to get back on the road to Clackton. In the hustle and bustle, Eli threw the bag into the chest, still fully packed—and there it stayed. He hadn't thought about it in months.

Now, he pulled it out of the chest and set it on the ground in front of him. As he wiped his trembling hands on his knees, he contemplated what was in the bag. He started to reach for the cinched cord but stopped. Under the bowl and cup, under the plates and utensils, under all those clothes, something else was in the bag.

As he stared at it, a murky thought crept into the corner of his mind. Maybe he should burn what had been hidden in it for all these months. Could he do that? He wasn't sure. He sat in the low light of his lantern, imagining different ways he could sneak it out to the fire without anyone noticing. Suddenly, a loud, stern voice rang in his ears.

"*Eli!*"

He jumped, feeling a hint of guilt. It must have been Jed, though it didn't sound like him. Eli glanced at Ada, surprised that the voice hadn't disturbed her sleep.

"What?" he asked. The only answer was Ada moaning quietly as she rolled over.

He picked up the bag and threw it back in the chest, finally seeing the sweater. He grabbed the wooly garment, quickly put it on, and closed the lid. Snatching up his lantern, he climbed outside, irritated that Jed hadn't answered him. He didn't understand what had warranted the man's angry tone. He walked over to him.

"What?" he repeated.

Jed turned around and shook his head. "Hmm?"

"You called my name. What did you want?" Eli asked again, feeling impatient.

"I didn't say anything. You ready to go?"

Jed handed him a fishing pole. Eli narrowed his eyes and pressed his lips together. He did hear something, didn't he? Jed raised his eyebrows at the long silence.

"Are you ready?" he asked again.

Eli nodded. "Yeah…"

He followed Jed down the path toward the creek. As they walked past the corn stalks still waiting to be harvested, Eli was reminded of the plants from his dream.

Chapter 25

ADA

Ada knocked for a third time on Mrs. Russell's door. The woman was home; Ada wasn't going to give up. She soon heard shuffling footsteps, and Evelyn peeked out her half-opened door.

"Oh… I wasn't expecting you." The woman's voice sounded tired. Her hair was put together, and she was ready for the day, but her eyes were red and swollen.

"Mrs. Russell, I haven't seen you in church recently. I want to make sure you're feeling well."

Evelyn looked mildly surprised. "I'm all right, but I haven't been sleeping well." She spied the dish in Ada's hands and sighed. "You brought me a meal. You didn't have to do that. Pastor and Mrs. Duncan checked on me earlier this week. I assured them I'm fine and don't need any help."

"May I please come in anyway?" Ada asked.

"Yes, of course." Evelyn peered behind herself with another sigh. She opened the door the rest of the way and led Ada into her home. "I suppose I could make you some tea."

"Why don't you sit and rest," Ada suggested. "I'll make us both some tea—if you don't mind me in your kitchen."

Giving in to the idea, Evelyn showed her where the teapot and cups were. While Ada checked the fire in the woodstove, Evelyn fetched the tea caddy and some cheesecloth from the pantry. After handing them to Ada, she sank into a chair by the table that was tucked into her kitchen nook.

Ada filled the kettle and placed it on the stovetop. As the water was heating, she wrapped some leaves in the cheesecloth and put the bundle into the teapot. She placed two cups and saucers on the table, one set in front of Evelyn, the other across from her. Once the water had boiled, she poured it into the teapot, placed a cozy over it, and set it on the table to steep. She sat down and peered at the elderly woman. Evelyn glanced away first.

"You seem quite efficient in the kitchen." There was less judgement in her voice than Ada had anticipated. "I didn't expect to see that in someone so young."

Ah, there it was...

"I'm glad you're feeling well, Mrs. Russell," Ada replied, sidestepping the woman's comment. "I was hoping to discuss something with you."

"I suppose you'd like to ask about my son; that's what everyone wants to talk about these days. Well, I don't know much. Don't worry, I'm sure he won't be coming back here... after..." Evelyn's voice cut out and her lip quivered.

"I did hear about your son, but that isn't why I came over." Ada filled their cups with tea. "I feel bad about what took place between us last month. I apologize for not talking to you about it sooner."

Evelyn shifted in her seat as she listened.

"Oh," she said quietly. "Well, I suppose I came across a bit strong, especially since you can't do anything about your tattoo. It's no secret that I don't like them. I never have. And I guess it's no secret that I'm outspoken about my opinions as well. That's just who I am; I can't change it."

Even as Evelyn defended herself, Ada noticed that the vitality behind the older woman's argument was lacking, giving her courage to continue.

"The things you said hurt me, Mrs. Russell; I won't pretend they didn't. But I should have controlled my anger. When you spoke of my parents, it brought back the grief I still feel over their deaths."

"I didn't know they died," Evelyn said. "I'm truly sorry about that."

"Thank you." Ada appreciated the woman's sincerity. "I don't expect you to start liking my tattoo, but please respect the fact that I do, and I'll never regret it. I didn't get it on a whim. It has a purpose, and there was a lot of thought that went into it. It means something important to me."

While Ada spoke, Evelyn's eyes lowered. She looked at her hands as she rubbed them together.

"My son has a tattoo," she whispered. "He got it soon after he moved away. When he wrote to me about it, he also said it had a special meaning. I thought he only wanted to look tough. I thought he was just being defiant." She looked up at Ada. "Is it common that someone's tattoo has meaning attached to it?"

"I think so," Ada said, nodding. "But I can only speak for myself. Did your son tell you what it meant?"

"He said it reminded him of me—of how I helped him cope with his father's passing. I thought he only said that so I wouldn't be angry." She hesitated. "I told him I never wanted to see it. I guess he thought I never wanted to see *him*; he hasn't been home since."

Tears formed in Evelyn's eyes. "Oh, Ada, he's not a bad man. I know people think the worst of him now that he's been sent to prison. Even I thought little of him for so long. I thought he was being disrespectful when he wasn't interested in what I thought he should do with his life."

She picked up a letter from a small stack on the table and unfolded it.

"I just received this from his lawyer. My son is not violent. He didn't get into a pointless fight; he was defending a young girl. But she won't come forward. She's afraid for her reputation, and now he will spend two years in prison for it."

Evelyn pulled out a handkerchief that was tucked into her sleeve and wiped her eyes.

"He refuses to write me and asks that I don't come to see him. I didn't realize he was so… Oh, Ada. I don't think he will ever forgive me for rejecting him." She covered her eyes and began to weep.

"I'm so sorry about your son." Ada placed her hand on Evelyn's. "I wish there was something I could say to make you feel better, but I'm willing to sit with you. Being with someone when you cry is better than crying alone. I know this personally."

Evelyn nodded as she continued to weep. "Thank you, Ada." After a pause, she sniffed and began to compose herself.

"Well, now." She chuckled through her sniffles. "Enough of that. Thank you for the meal; it looks delicious. And to be honest, I could use a break from cooking tonight."

Evelyn sipped her tea properly. Ada could tell it was hard for her to let down her guard.

"Eli wanted me to ask you something," she said to lighten the mood.

Evelyn nodded, jumping at the opportunity to change the subject.

"He noticed the fence along the back of your property and said it could use some repair. He would be happy to do that for you. We have lumber in our shed. It's the same kind as your fence. There's more than enough to repair it as well as build one along the back of our yard. Would you allow him to do that?"

A broad smile spread over the older woman's face, adding some vigor to her tired eyes.

"Oh, that would be such a blessing! I've worried about what to do with that fence for over a year. I never found the time to arrange for it to be fixed. What would he like as payment?" she asked.

"Oh, no, Mrs. Russell. He wouldn't want you to pay him. You're our neighbor, and he'll already be working on our fence anyway."

"That is very thoughtful. Please thank him for me, Ada." The woman patted her on the hand. "You know," she added with a grin, "I think I have some cookies in my pantry. We really should have some with our tea, don't you think?"

"Definitely," Ada agreed with a laugh. Her eyes followed her neighbor as Evelyn walked into her pantry to retrieve the treats.

Chapter 26

JED

Jed and Eli sat in silence as they waited for the fish to bite. Fishing was Jed's favorite activity, even on a cold fall morning. If they caught enough, they would not only have supper for this evening but could also begin stocking the smokehouse. Before the fish could be smoked, though, it needed to sit in brine for a few hours. Since the caravan was running low on supplies, he intended to pick up some salt and brown sugar when they went to Bradford later in the day. But the main reason for the trip into town was to buy lumber for the young couple's vardo.

He glanced at Eli, who was wrapped in his wool sweater. The boy was quieter than usual. Jed looked forward to helping him build the small home and knew Eli was excited as well, but this morning the boy gazed at the river with a slight frown in the corners of his mouth.

"I was thinking about something," Jed said, breaking the silence.

The boy turned to him, still looking distracted.

"I have a feeling your vardo won't be finished by the time we need to leave for our next market season in May."

Eli looked thoughtful for a moment. "So, we'll need to bring the tent with us."

"Maybe not. Rosa and I could stay here with you and Ada this summer, while Levi and Bea go with the others. We could finish the vardo, and you could start living in it by next fall—maybe sooner."

"Would Goldie's parents be okay with that?"

"They used to go to the markets with us all the time," Jed explained, "and Bea was just saying how much she missed it. I could talk with them about it this evening. You're getting pretty good at carving, but I doubt you'll have enough merchandise to sell at your own table by then. You can always send a few things with Tony, or you can save it for next summer. What do you think? Do you want to stay here?" Jed was hoping Eli would perk up at this idea.

"Yeah... Sure. That sounds good," he said, looking back toward the river.

"Are you okay?" Jed asked. "It seems like you have something on your mind."

"I was thinking about what Ira said on Sunday," Eli admitted. "Do you think all those bad things happened to us because God wanted them to, so He could use them somehow? God can do anything, right? Then why does He need the bad stuff?"

Jed sighed—that was a tough question. Where was Ira?

"I think you're looking at it wrong," he said. "Those bad things didn't happen to you because God wanted *or* needed them to. Those things happened because some sinful men chose to hurt you. But God can take those bad things and use them to accomplish good things in and through you. Can you see the difference?"

"I guess. It's just hard to believe anything good can come from what happened to us."

"I know," Jed agreed. "But faith is a hope in things you can't see. The trials God allows in our lives can cause us to grow and mature. Trials reveal the genuineness of our faith. You have a choice in front of you, Eli. You can be angry and bitter about what happened, or you can choose to believe God will use it for good. You may not get to see how He uses it, and He may not use it the way you think He should. But God is bigger than our trials, and He sees things we can't imagine."

Jed shifted on his feet. "Our faith needs to be strong and patient. That's what makes us complete, like it says in the Bible. That's what James meant when he said to count it all joy. He didn't mean our trials are good, but what they produce in us *will* be when we trust God with the things we don't understand."

Eli was quiet as Jed continued. "I'm probably not saying this as well as Ira could, and I don't have a Bible in front of me to get the words just right, but in the book of Romans it says all things work together for good to those who love God and are called according to His purpose. And in James we're told that every good and perfect gift is from above, coming down from the

Father who doesn't ever change. That means we can always trust in God's plan for our life, even when bad things happen."

Eli nodded slowly. "So, God can use the bad things to do good things through me? But... What if I can't let go of my anger?"

"Eli, if you trust God and let go of your bitterness, then that's a good thing. But even in our anger, He can still work in our lives. Look at that logjam; it doesn't stop the water, it only slows it. That's what unforgiveness does in our lives. Forgiving others removes the logjam, and then God's goodness can't help but shine through us and touch others. Don't you think *that* is a good and perfect gift?"

Eli remained silent as he peered over the water. After a while, he looked at Jed with an uneasy expression.

"Jed, I need to tell you something," he said. "I need your help. I have something I don't think I should have." The boy sounded worried and a little bit scared.

"You can tell me anything; we can figure it out together," Jed assured him. He waited as the boy gathered his courage.

Finally, Eli took in a deep breath and began to speak.

Chapter 27

GRACE

Plump, feathery snowflakes drifted to the ground outside the Gardners' dining room window. The pastor's wife smiled as she gazed at the view. Grace loved wintertime. She loved snow, mittens, hats, and scarves. She loved crackling fires and hot drinks that fought off the cold December air. For Grace, winter made friendly gatherings even cozier. Tonight was no exception.

Twice a month the Duncans, the Gardners, and their next-door neighbors, the Webers, shared supper together. They alternated hosting the meals between the three houses. This evening, they were gathered at the Gardners' home. Their small abode was warm and comfortable. Grace was impressed by the inviting atmosphere, considering how little they owned and how simply they lived.

When it was the Gardners' turn to host, they moved their kitchen table to the dining room. They only had the one table, and it only had four chairs, so they also moved the two parlor chairs to the dining room. It was a snug fit and elbows occasionally bumped, but the young couple never appeared insecure by their shortage. Perhaps it was their contented attitude that contributed to the pleasing atmosphere.

When the three families started having meals together, Grace insisted they all bring food to share. She wanted those evenings to be focused on their time together, and she didn't want the Gardners to feel the burden of having extra mouths to feed. But Grace was the first to admit that she greatly anticipated whatever dish Ada prepared. The young woman was an amazing cook. The food she made wasn't showy; it was as simple as her home, and just like her home, Ada's contribution seemed that much better because of it.

Little Noah Weber was always a fun addition to the group. The young boy was well behaved, even though he was a ball of energy. Whenever supper was at the Gardners' home, Eli set a wooden chest by the table and stacked it high with pillows, allowing Noah to sit with the adults. He was going to be four in a couple of months, but despite his age, the youngster politely sat with them and didn't mind being the only child.

After supper, Eli always managed to find a toy or two, and Noah entertained himself with them while the adults moved into the front room to visit around the fireplace. It was endearing that Eli had kept some of his childhood toys. They were well made and still in good condition.

That evening, as the snow continued to fall, the three couples enjoyed a pleasant conversation around the supper table.

"Oh, I just heard," Grace informed the group. "Jacob Martin and Laura Taylor are now engaged."

"Really," Ada exclaimed. "I'm so happy for them. I adore Laura; she's such a sweet girl. I enjoy visiting with her on Sundays. She seems quite devoted to Jacob. Are their parents excited?"

"They are—for the most part," Grace said. "However, I think Edith Taylor wanted them to wait, but Laura is eighteen now."

"Why did Edith want them to wait?" Eli asked.

"Well, long engagements can be difficult," Grace explained. "And they can't get married until Jacob saves a bit more money. He's been working for his uncle at the mercantile, but I believe he just began working at the Miller farm on weekends as well."

"I didn't know Mr. Johnson was Jacob's uncle," Ada said.

"Jacob's mother is Edgar Johnson's sister," Isaac replied.

"Hasn't Jacob been working there for a few years?" Eli asked. "Why does he still need to save up? I'm sure David has a few properties he could afford now. This house wasn't much at all; he keeps his prices reasonable."

"I think Laura's mother has greater hopes for her daughter," Hannah said cautiously.

Eli shook his head and scoffed.

"Well, I hope she doesn't make them wait too long," Ada said, glancing at her husband.

Soon the friends relocated their conversation to the front room, and as the conversation moved, so did the chairs. Once by the fire, Grace noticed a small display hutch that was new to the room. It sat against the wall adjacent to the fireplace and was only two feet wide and three shelves high. The doors didn't have glass yet, but they were embellished along their top edges with an intricately carved design.

Inside the hutch was a doll with a wooden head and hands. She wore a red dress edged with white lace. The doll was stunning. Grace would have loved to own a doll like that when she was younger. Hannah also noticed it and went immediately to the hutch.

"Ada, is this your doll?" she asked. "Oh, she is so beautiful! Can I pick her up?"

Ada's eyes darted toward Eli, and she smiled. She handed the doll to her neighbor, who couldn't help but give its soft body a gentle hug.

"You've taken such good care of her. My dolls were so dirty and scratched."

"She looks like you, Ada," Grace observed.

"She should," Eli said. "I used Ada as a model when I carved it."

"You made this doll?" Grace asked.

"I carved the head—and the hands and feet," he said with a slight shrug and a quiet chuckle. "Ada made the body and the dress. It's only a few years old, so it hasn't been played with much."

The group looked at him with amazement.

"We used to make toys and sell them at summer markets before we moved here."

"So, the other toys," Hannah said, "the train and horse Noah is playing with—you made those also?"

Eli nodded and glanced at the smirks on Marcus and Isaac's faces. "I suppose you two are going to tease me now."

Isaac donned an innocent expression and shook his head. "No, but I can think of a few men who might, so your secret is safe with us. We won't tell anyone about your dolls. Right, Marcus?"

The men chuckled as the same faces seemed to come into all of their minds at once.

"Well," Isaac continued, "Your kids will have the best toys in town, that's for sure."

Grace watched the smile on Ada's face melt away. Eli's eyes darted to his wife.

"Yeah... maybe so." Without pausing, he added, "Ada has some hot chocolate warming on the stove. I don't know about the rest of you, but that sounds really good to me right about now."

113

Noah, who had been playing quietly up to this point, clapped his hands in agreement. Eli grinned and scooped the boy into his arms.

"I think you and I should have the first two cups. What do you say, little man?"

He flew the boy through the air and into the kitchen, laughing playfully as the others followed close behind.

Chapter 28

ELI

The voice from his dream repeated in his mind. *"Tend my crops..."*

As Eli stretched out on his bed, he used his interlaced hands as a pillow behind his neck. He was tired; the day had been full. It began with an early morning. As soon as he woke up, he spent several hours in the garden. After that, he and Jed took a mid-day trip into Bradford. When they returned, they spent the latter part of the day working on the interior of the young couple's vardo. Now, as the evening came to an end, Eli and Ada shared a quiet moment of solitude in their new wagon home.

Eli enjoyed starting each day in the garden and never neglected it. Goldie's father Levi had asked him to look after it while he and Bea were away. Before leaving with the rest of the merchants in May, the quiet-spoken man had instructed him on the best way to care for the plants. Eli didn't want to let him down, so after weeding, he would gather water from Badger Creek and irrigate the entire garden before the sun reached its zenith. It took three hours every morning to weed and water, but the garden was important. The vegetables would be canned in the fall and used all winter to help feed the caravan.

Whenever he watered, he always gave each fruit tree an additional bucket or two. Bea said if they were given extra water, the fruit would be larger and juicier. He didn't know if that was true or not, but he wasn't going to chance messing up the crop's yield. After giving the nicest fruit to Mrs. Perry in the fall, the women would make the rest into preserves, which would then be canned—half for the markets and half for the caravan's personal stock.

It was early August, and Eli had already grown four inches since last summer. The exercise from working in the garden and carrying heavy buckets of water had built up the muscles in his shoulders and back. He and Ada had been underweight when they first joined the caravan, but after a year of eating regular meals, playing hard, and working hard, they had both filled out and gained a healthy glow. Now at seventeen, Eli looked more like a man and less like a boy. Ada, however, had only grown half an inch, and he couldn't help teasing her a bit.

He was glad they had stayed in the West Woods over the summer, but even Jed and Rosa commented on how lonely it was without the others. He didn't know how Levi and Bea could stand to be by themselves during those months. As close as Eli had grown to Jed and Rosa, he still missed the rest of the caravan and looked forward to their return.

He was excited to show everyone the progress on his vardo. Their wagon home was almost finished, and the young couple had moved into it the week before. All that was left were some final touches, such as cupboard doors, cushions, and a woodstove before winter. The tent Floyd had made was dismantled and placed in the storage shed. The oilcloth had held up well in the winter cold and summer heat; it still had some life left in it and was worth keeping.

At the end of March, two months before the others had left for the markets, Jed and Tony gave Eli a set of carving tools for his birthday. He had never owned his own tools before and treasured them greatly. Normally, Jed took Eli into Bradford each week. They had a standing appointment in town, but they also used the time to buy supplies for the rest of the caravan. One day, however, Jed insisted on taking Tony with him instead. That was the day they had purchased the set. The gift was from everyone, of course, but Eli couldn't help thinking of the tools as being mostly from the two men who had picked them out.

Eli looked forward to showing Tony the merchandise he had been making. He had carved some toys, doll heads, and wooden spoons with decorative handles. He had also started shaping some strips of wooden trim that he would use as embellishment in the vardo. Tony would be pleased to see how much he was enjoying the craft. Eli was improving every day and hoped to carve some pen handles and maybe some beads for Hattie, but those items were small and might require more skill than he had.

Over the summer, Eli practiced playing Jed's guitar when he wasn't carving or taking care of the garden or working on his vardo. He wanted to play for the group on Sunday mornings, but first he would need to buy his own instrument. Mrs. Perry took a liking to Eli and offered to pay him for a few extra jobs throughout the year. He used a majority of that money to pay Jed back for the vardo lumber, but he also put some aside for a guitar.

The past year had been a full time for both Eli and Ada—full of deepening relationships, acquired knowledge, security, and healing. But most importantly, the year had been full of God in the midst of it all. Eli viewed the lessons gained as the groundwork for a future God had long been planning, and he looked forward to finding out what that future held. The hardest trials—the darkest days—were now behind them. At least, he hoped they were.

Eli leaned back in bed and looked around at their homey vardo. Ada was working on a length of lace; her fingers skillfully flipped the bobbins over and under each other in the dim lantern light. Eli turned his attention to her and watched her work. Earlier that day, he had thought of a question while he and Jed were in Bradford, and he needed to know her answer.

"Ada," he said after a few minutes.

Her fingers paused as she looked up from her project.

"Would you go with me anywhere, even if it meant leaving the caravan?"

"Are you thinking of leaving?" she asked, mildly surprised.

"No, not right now. Maybe someday, though. I think God is calling me to do something. I don't know what it is yet, but I think it might take us away from here."

"Of course, I'll go with you. Why wouldn't I?"

"Because you're happy here."

"I *am* happy here," she agreed. "But I'm happy here with you, not without you." She tied off the lace and set it aside. "When you decide to go, I'll go with you. If you're supposed to do something, then so am I."

He smiled as she snuffed out the lantern. He had been feeling restless, but her answer calmed him. He put his arm around her in the dark.

"Don't worry," he reassured her. "Jed and I just finished this vardo. I won't take you away anytime soon."

Chapter 29

ADA

This October was colder than last year's. Even though the church had a large woodstove, Ada leaned closer to Eli for warmth as Marcus gave his sermon. It was hard to believe they had been living in East Haven for over a year now. While several townsfolk still displayed a subtle disapproval of them, the young couple had been able to form a few close friendships. It gave Ada hope that this town might feel like home someday. Naturally, her heart was with the caravan; they would always be her family. But as time went on, she was growing fonder of her East Haven friends.

The Gardners continued to have supper with the Duncans and the Webers at least once a month. In addition to spending time with those friends, Eli never missed a Friday lunch with David. He still worked for Ray Larson, who respected Eli as much as Eli respected him. As for Ada, she often sat with Evelyn and listened to her neighbor read the latest letter from her son. He had finally written to her, and their correspondence was regular. Mother and son were getting to know each other better than they ever had when he lived at home.

Ada also felt a strong affection for Laura Taylor. She wanted to take the young girl under her wing, especially considering the trials Laura and her fiancé Jacob were now facing. The past three months had been filled with misfortune, and Ada's heart wept for what they would still have to endure. But this morning Laura looked happier than she had in a while, and Ada prayed for a chance to talk with her away from Edith Taylor's ever-listening ears.

Last April, four months after their engagement in December, Jacob and Laura had finally set a date for their wedding. The joyous event would take place in just over a year, on the first of May. It was a long time to wait, but after calculating how much Jacob could save in that year, all those involved in the decision agreed. By May, he would have enough money to provide Laura with a respectable lifestyle. The main decision maker, of course, was Edith. When Laura cried at her mother's final word on the subject, Edith pointed out that a year was a much shorter time than *she* had anticipated.

Ada liked the day they chose for two reasons. Spring was a beautiful time for a wedding, with flowers beginning to bloom, and the first of May happened to be her birthday. On the following May Day, if all went as planned, Laura and Jacob would be getting married and Ada would be turning twenty-three.

But all didn't go as planned, and three months ago, Jacob fell from the hayloft of John Miller's barn, breaking his leg in several places. The men tried to set Jacob's leg, and John drove him to White Falls where a doctor could tend to his injury. It was a sticky summer day, and the two-hour journey in a jostling wagon must have been agonizing.

Once in White Falls, the doctor reset his leg and stabilized it in a splint. Because of the severity of the fractures, he recommended Jacob stay in town for at least three weeks while he observed how his bones were healing. After only one week, Jacob's foot turned a dreadful color, and the doctor had to remove it just above the ankle. Four weeks later, Jacob was finally sent home to finish healing and learn how to live with only one foot.

The wedding was postponed for an undetermined amount of time, and Jacob fell into a depression. He tried to convince Laura not to marry him, but she refused to leave him. Together, they began to rethink their former plans in a way that better fit his altered state. Under the best circumstances, they might be able to get married in two years, but much would depend on the type of work Jacob could do after he healed. The entire situation was hard on them, and they both lost some of their youthful spunk. Today, however, Laura looked better, and Ada couldn't wait to talk to her.

After the service, Laura stood near her mother, who was visiting with Agnes Miller. When she saw Ada walking toward her, she stepped a few paces away from the women so they could talk privately. She grasped Ada's hand and smiled.

"You'll never guess," she said in a barely controlled whisper. "Jacob has been given some money. It will pay for our wedding and should be enough to cover a few living expenses until he can return to work at the mercantile. We can still get married in May!"

"Laura, that's wonderful," Ada said, scarcely able to contain her joy for the girl. "I thought you looked happy this morning."

"It's such a generous blessing," Laura continued with a beam. "Jacob is convinced that John Miller gave it to him. He thinks Mr. Miller feels bad because the accident happened on his land, but I think Mr. Miller is too heartless to make such a grand gesture. I believe it was Mr. Johnson; he *is* family, after all. And he said Jacob could always have his job at the mercantile. He promised to pay Jacob the same, even if he has to work at a slower pace."

"Well, that is a kind offer," Ada agreed. "Mr. Johnson must recognize what a hard worker Jacob has always been."

As Laura nodded, her mother grabbed her elbow, demanding the girl's attention. Edith kept her voice low but stern.

"This is not an appropriate topic to discuss in public. Mrs. Martin is looking for you; don't keep your future mother-in-law waiting."

Laura turned back to Ada and rolled her eyes.

"Congratulations, Laura," Ada said. "I can't wait for your wedding."

"Thank you." She gave Ada a quick hug before leaving to find Mrs. Martin.

Laura's mother peered down her nose at Ada. "I was hoping to have a word with you."

Edith Taylor rarely sought Ada out for anything. The woman's eyes were cold as she continued to speak.

"My daughter is now attached to a man who will never be able to completely provide for her. You, of all people, can appreciate the situation she finds herself in. From this point on, all their decisions will be based on what the cost will be. I hope you realize not everyone will receive an invitation to the wedding."

"Oh." Ada was too surprised to say more.

"It would be dreadfully embarrassing if a person who did not receive an invitation tried to come to the wedding anyway. That would be an extremely unpleasant scene."

"I agree, Mrs. Taylor," Ada said with forced politeness, having found her voice again. "It would be unfair to Laura if *anyone* were to make a scene that day. I would hope—"

"Furthermore," Edith said, ignoring Ada's insinuation. "Despite Laura's circumstances, I do not wish for her to associate with inferior society. She does not need to be influenced by people who make willing choices to lower themselves." The woman glanced at Ada's arm as she spoke. "So, please don't be surprised when you are not extended an invitation to my daughter's wedding."

"I'm sure you *think* you're doing the right thing—"

"Good," Edith said, cutting her off again. "I'm glad we understand each other."

She turned and walked away, leaving Ada alone in her dismay.

Chapter 30

ELI

There was nothing between Eli and the cold, hard ground except his blanket and an oiled canvas tarp. He sat with Sammy, dealing a deck of cards, while the rest of the caravan waited quietly around the fire. Even though the two boys were wrapped in blankets, the icy February chill seeped through their layers, giving Sammy a noticeable shiver.

"We should sit by the fire," Eli suggested to the seven-year-old. "Ada looks warm over there, doesn't she? I bet she'll let you sit on her lap."

The boy nodded and jogged over to Ada. Eli was relieved; playing the same three games grew tedious after a while, but he had been trying to distract Sammy as much as possible.

The young boy climbed into Ada's lap and leaned against her. He looked worried. He would have been too young to remember what it was like when Myra was born, but this time he was more aware of what was happening with his mother. Myra, on the other hand, stood next to her father, giggling. As she leaned against him, Ira focused her attention on little hand games and sing-song rhymes. It was easier to distract the little girl; she was only four.

Goldie had told the group about the baby back in July while working their summer market circuit. That summer had been the third since Eli and Ada joined the caravan. After staying at the winter camp to finish their vardo during their second summer, the young couple had at last been able to return to the markets. Eli enjoyed taking their vardo on the road. It pulled smoothly behind the horses, and he couldn't help but feel proud of their little home.

While visiting the eight towns in the circuit, Eli and Ada were finally able to experience the markets as merchants themselves. They set up their own table, and their toys and dolls sold well. The caravan had visited the same towns as when they had first joined them—with the exception of Ashbrook. They decided it would be safer to go to Newcrest instead, just in case the old man Rake was still there.

After having a summer off, Levi and Bea happily returned to their responsibilities of looking after the winter camp. They had enjoyed revisiting the nomadic market life, but as they got older, they preferred staying in one place all year. That meant, however, that they did not learn of their future grandchild until Goldie climbed down from her vardo with a slightly rounder belly than when she had left in May. Naturally, they were excited and doted on their expecting daughter until the winter due date arrived.

It had been several hours now since Goldie had announced it was time for the baby to come. Eli thought it should have been born already. Since no one else seemed concerned by how long it was taking, he figured this must be normal. Rosa and Hattie were with Goldie in her vardo, while everyone else lingered anxiously by the fire. It was warmer inside, but the group wanted to be together, and none of the vardos were big enough to hold that many people.

Mae quietly hummed while knitting. Tony and Floyd worked on wood and leather, taking occasional breaks to breathe warm air onto their stiff fingers. Jed tapped his foot absently as he stared into the fire. Levi walked in irregular circles, and Bea played one solitary card game after another on the tray in her lap. Even Cobra was quiet, except for a concerned whimper now and then.

Ira pulled his daughter onto his lap and bounced her on his knee. He sang a little homespun song while she grinned.

Ira and Myra, dancing in the sun.
Father and daughter, having so much fun!
Myra and Ira, two peas in a pod.
We raise our hands high and, for our blessings, thank God.

As they bounced, Ira moved her hands through motions made to go along with the song.

Eli scooted his chair closer to the fire and held his hands over the flames. Hearing Goldie struggle through her birthing pains added to his nervousness; he was ready for this to be over. He chewed on his thumbnail and glanced at Ada as she calmly told a story close to Sammy's ear. Eli could only make out a few of her words, but the story captivated the young boy, whose tense shoulders visibly relaxed. While she spoke the tale to Sammy, her eyes drifted to Eli's and stayed there. He didn't need to hear the story to be affected by her calming charm. Just watching her was enough.

Suddenly, Goldie's groans were joined by the baby's cry, and everyone expelled a collective sigh accompanied by grateful smiles. Praises were offered up. Ira's relief was mingled with a visible awe. Hattie stepped out of the vardo and beckoned him over. She gave him a quick hug before he disappeared into it. After a few minutes, Rosa came outside, drying her hands on a towel. She walked over to Jed, who stood and engulfed her in a supportive hug.

"It went well?" he whispered close to her ear.

"It went well," she affirmed with a sigh.

Rosa sat down and relayed important details to the grandparents while the others listened. Goldie had a healthy baby girl, possessing the right amount of body parts. Both were doing well with no complications. Tense bodies relaxed as the earlier anxious quiet was replaced with animated laughter and happy tears. Soon everyone dispersed to their own vardos, knowing the baby would be presented after the family had rested and bonded. Sammy and Myra stayed with their grandparents that night, but not before a quick introduction to Lily, their new baby sister.

There was an unspoken understanding that each family would fend for themselves for supper. Once in their vardo, Ada made a simple meal of bread and cheese. After eating, Eli felt less tired as the concerns of the day melted away. He stoked the woodstove and slipped into their warm bed.

"I want to hear the story you were telling Sammy," he said with a grin.

Ada smiled and snuggled in next to him. Gently laughing, she began to tell him the tale of brave Samuel, the bear tamer, while the night stretched out before them.

Chapter 31

JOHN

There wasn't a cloud to be seen, and a clear sky in May is exactly what a farmer liked to see. As soon as John Miller was certain there would be no rain for the next few days, he rushed his men through their morning chores. Even so, it was half past ten before he was able to order a majority of them onto his wagon. He knew the minimum number of men needed to keep his farm from falling behind on the milking schedule, so he left a small crew in charge of the livestock. The rest he took to Ray Larson's land to work the first hay harvest of the season.

Ray grew several acres of hay, whereas John used his land for more profitable crops such as oats, wheat, and corn. He kept aside a small portion of land for his cattle to graze on, but he still needed to store up enough hay to sustain his dairy cows throughout the cold weather. He got that winter feed from Ray.

Just as John suspected, his neighbor's crew was already busy cutting and stacking the young hay. Spring produced the sweetest and most tender feed for his livestock. Since John was Ray's biggest purchaser, he had worked out a deal with the man. If his workers helped with the harvest, Ray would cut John's price by sixty percent. The next few days would be long and grueling, but for that price, it would be worth it.

As his men piled out of the wagon, John waved at Ray, who was standing to the side talking intently with Eli. What a pathetic sight. Everyone else knew what to do; they didn't need detailed instructions. While watching the two men engaged in such a focused conversation, he wondered what Eli couldn't understand about the work at hand. Ray did not need Eli's distractions. That boy just needed to get onto the hay field and figure it out for himself.

Soon Ray was nodding. They shook hands and Eli walked off the field and down the road—away from the work. You've got to be joking, John thought to himself. There were plenty of workers, even without Eli, but who would walk away from the wages a week like this could offer? He doubted anyone would see Eli again for the rest of the week. John walked over to Frank Stevens, one of Ray's lead men.

"Does Eli leave like that often?"

"Oh, yeah. He keeps his own schedule. Sometimes he works a full day, sometimes only a half day. Other days he don't come in at all. He and Mr. Larson figure it out, though, so I don't much worry about it."

John shook his head as he watched Eli walk down the road. He didn't know why he was so surprised. Of course, Eli would choose one of the busiest weeks to skip out. Why would Ray keep such a lazy, undisciplined person around his other workers? That kind of attitude spreads if left unchecked. He started to wish he had hired Eli, just so he could have had the satisfaction of firing him.

"I sure hope Ray doesn't pay him for a full day when he leaves early," John said with a scoff.

"I don't really know, Mr. Miller. Maybe he pays Eli per job," Frank suggested.

As John continued to watch Eli walk away, he pictured that idler sitting slothfully in a group of other lazy gypsies, picking greedily at a greasy chicken bone. Why would someone want to live that kind of lifestyle? That boy didn't appear to have any desire to change. So, why would he move his wife to hardworking East Haven?

John might have understood Eli's choice if he were trying to provide a better life for Ada, but he stuck her in that small, pokey house and seemed content to keep her there. As John's loathing increased, he turned away and walked farther onto the field. He shook his head, hoping a hard day of work would purge that annoying gypsy from his thoughts—at least for the time being.

Chapter 32

LOUISE

L ouise Evans sat in one of her two faded rocking chairs, enjoying the clear view from her porch. On a warm May morning like this, the farmers would be busy bringing in the hay. If her husband George were still alive, he would be out on those fields working alongside the young men, trying to prove he was just as spry as they were. She placed her hand lovingly on the empty chair next to hers.

East Haven had three widows. Louise was the oldest, yet she was the most recently widowed. George had passed away two short years ago, only a few months before that young couple had moved into town. She was more fortunate than many to have had him with her for so long. They had married when she was twenty-two, and they had a full forty-eight years together before his passing.

Though George wouldn't admit it, he had been slowing down for a good decade before he died. The evidence of his slower pace could be found in the condition of their home. Floorboards squeaked, windows were stuck, walls were chipped, and porch steps sagged. Louise wasn't always able to get herself to church anymore, but whenever a thoughtful couple came to pick her up, she never failed to offer a small bit of wages to the husband if he would help with some of her home repairs.

Unfortunately, these young men were always too busy to come by that week and promised to come the next. But they must have forgotten, because no one ever took her up on her offer. She couldn't pay much and had often suspected that this fact may have contributed to their lack of interest.

Not wanting to be a burden on the church, she kept the extent of her need hidden. But earlier that year, she had developed a strong suspicion that she shouldn't lean too heavily on the railings leading down her porch steps. Louise would need to ask Pastor Duncan for help soon, but she wasn't looking forward to it. She kept putting it off just one more day, and the weeks slipped by.

As she sat in the warm spring air, she noticed someone walking along the road. The figure drew closer, and she soon recognized him; it was that Gardner boy. He touched the brim of his hat.

"Good morning, Mrs. Evans."

"Hello, young man," she said, not sure if she was remembering his name correctly. She stood and moved to a spot on her porch that allowed her to converse easily, but she was careful not to lean on the railings.

"I'm Eli Gardner. I think you may be more familiar with my wife Ada."

Louise nodded. "Ah, yes. I spoke with her after church last month. I was disappointed when she wasn't at the Martins' wedding; I was hoping to visit with her again. You have a sweet wife, Mr. Gardner."

Her visitor smiled at the compliment. "Thank you. Please call me Eli."

The young man seemed polite enough. Why did some people think poorly of him? Perhaps the dark lines on his arms made others nervous. Well, it wasn't as though they spelled out bad words or twisted into inappropriate pictures. As he stood by her gate with a workbag slung over his shoulder, she wondered what brought him by her place.

"Well, Eli, I'd say you were arriving at work a bit late if I hadn't just seen you walking away from the fields."

"I already met with Mr. Larson earlier this morning," he explained. "I walked by your home as the sun was coming up. You have a beautiful view here."

Louise smiled proudly. "Yes," she agreed. "When my George was alive, we would wake early and sit out here to watch the sunrise." She glanced at the two old rocking chairs placed close together. She could almost see George sitting there now.

"Mrs. Evans, I was wondering if I could check your porch railings," Eli asked. "I know a loose handrail when I see one."

"Oh, my. Why, yes. Yes! Please come in."

Louise moved forward to better greet her thoughtful guest. Eli passed through the gate and walked up to her steps. Grabbing hold of the handrail, he gave it a test shake.

"This isn't safe, but I can fix it for you," he said.

Louise thanked him with an eager smile and offered to pay him some of the money she had tucked away in a jar on the top shelf of her pantry.

"No thank you, Mrs. Evans. This is a small job; it won't take long."

While Eli worked, Louise went into her kitchen to see what sort of lunch she could scrape up. She brought him a plate as he was finishing up, which he graciously accepted. After he ate, he asked Louise if there was anything else he could take care of while he was there. She invited him in and pointed out all the disrepair her home was suffering. Eli fixed a few other things, and as the afternoon grew later, he promised to return the next day.

Louise poured him a glass of water and insisted he drink it all before leaving. They talked in length about her property, and he commented on some areas along the outside of the structure and around her yard that also needed attention. After finishing his water, he thanked her and placed his workbag back across his shoulder.

"Please," she said, "you must let me pay you."

He shook his head and refused, but an idea came to her.

"I know the perfect solution. Come, follow me to the shed."

She led Eli to a crooked outbuilding, which he offered to repair as well. Inside the shed was an array of tools that had belonged to her husband.

"You should have these, Eli. If you won't let me pay you, then please take these instead."

"No, that's too generous. I couldn't take them," he argued.

"You must. What is an old woman like me going to do with all these tools? It would make me so happy to know they were being used again instead of collecting dust."

He contemplated the tools. "Thank you, Mrs. Evans," he said, finally conceding. "But would you allow me to leave them here? That way, when I come to work on your house, I won't have to carry this heavy bag with me."

"Oh, yes." A grateful smile spread across her face. She took his hand in hers and gave it an affectionate pat before he left.

As Eli walked down the road, she waved at him until he was too far away to see. Her heart felt lighter as the oppressive weight of worry lifted. She was so thankful that God had sent her this willing helper. Her home would soon be safe again.

Chapter 33

ELI

Eli carefully shaped the doll head in his hand and thought about the child who would one day own it. The dolls sold well, and he enjoyed seeing the excitement of the little girls who were fortunate enough to have one placed in their arms. Two summers ago—the first year he and Ada were able to have a table at the markets—almost all of their dolls had sold by the end of the season. Last summer, their stock was depleted early, and the last town had to miss out on the popular toy altogether.

Peering closely at Ada, Eli scraped away the wood around the doll's chin, duplicating what he considered to be the perfect face. The sun had moved lower in the September sky, giving her a soft glow. His hand hovered over his project as he watched his wife plant soft little kisses on Lily's chubby cheeks. Maybe it wasn't the sun. Perhaps Ada's glow came from cooing and cuddling the baby in her arms.

Lily had grown so much over the summer. She had only been three months old when the caravan left for the markets in May. As hard as it was to stay behind, Ira kept his family at the winter camp that season. The other merchants missed having his family along, but Ada especially missed the baby. When they returned last week, she practically leapt out of the vardo while it was still moving just to get to Lily sooner. The baby loved to be held and snuggled, which suited Ada perfectly. She was always first to offer to hold Lily whenever Goldie needed a break.

Over the summer, Eli had finally purchased a thin gold wedding band for Ada. He admired how it looked on her finger as she caressed the baby's cheeks and tickled her nose. Ada looked good with a baby in her arms; it would be nice to have their own someday. Now that he was nineteen, the thought of having children didn't seem as daunting as it used to.

"If you spent as much time carving those doll heads as you do staring at their model, you might make enough to last until the end of summer," Hattie teased with a chuckle.

Ada glanced up and caught Eli's blush. He grinned at her and winked.

"You can't rush perfection, Hattie," he teased back.

"Ooh... Rosa!" Hattie called out. "I think we need to make some humble pie for supper."

Jed laughed at the woman's remark and suggested giving Eli a double helping. The rest of the merchants joined in the light bantering as the women pulled out supplies to make their evening meal. Ada smiled as she handed the baby back to Goldie and helped with supper preparations.

Eli returned to his task while he still had sunlight. Throughout the evening, however, he managed to steal small glimpses of his wife without anyone else noticing.

Chapter 34

ADA

The low candlelight cast long shadows in the dark room. As Ada brushed her hair for the night, Eli watched. He was lying on their bed with his chin in his hands, most likely remembering the time he had cut off her braid. That was over eight years ago, and she still wasn't sure if it had happened in April or May. She did know, however, that tonight was an extremely dry September evening—the kind of dry that made her skin feel tight. It had been more so than normal all summer long. Even the spring brought less rain than usual.

The arid weather was difficult on the farmers, who had to work harder to irrigate their fields; but it was good for Laura and Jacob, who had been blessed with a clear May sky on the day of their wedding. True to her word, Edith Taylor made sure the Gardners never received an invitation, even if Laura had written one. Ada shed a few tears on her birthday, partly in joy for the young couple, but mostly for having to miss their wedding.

She set her brush down and rubbed some lotion into her hands and face.

"Ready for bed?" Eli asked as he spun around and bounced under the covers.

Ada went to her side of the bed and climbed in. As soon as Eli blew out the candle and leaned in to kiss her, Ada noticed something wasn't right about the darkness. An odd glow flickered outside the window, filling her with hollow dread. She halted his advance and nodded toward the window.

"Eli…"

"Yeah, I see it." He hopped out of bed, walked to the glass, and peeked out. "It's the Webers' barn. It's on fire!"

As he sprinted to the back door, Ada followed, throwing a shawl over her shoulders. Eli stepped into his shoes and grabbed a bucket from the back steps. As they ran toward the Webers' barn, Hannah rushed out of her house, holding a bucket of her own.

"Isaac's in there!" she cried.

Eli ran faster, and as he got to the wide door, Isaac limped out on an injured foot. He grasped onto his friend for support.

"Darn loft ladder. I should have fixed that loose rung." Isaac rubbed his head. "I think I blacked out for a minute and knocked over the lantern."

When Ada reached them, she grabbed the bucket out of Eli's hand. Hannah was already at the water pump filling hers. The horses whinnied hysterically as Eli ran into the smoke to free them. Isaac hobbled after him, despite his wife's protests.

The fire was spreading quickly. As Ada threw one bucket after another onto the flames, she doubted the building could be saved. She didn't like how long it was taking to free the animals. Eventually, first the horses and then the men stumbled out of the barn. Isaac carried two more buckets. As they rushed to the pump, Ada's gaze drifted upwards. Her eyes followed the red glowing embers that lifted with the wind.

"Ada, the bell pole—go ring the bell!" Eli shouted as he took one of the buckets from Isaac.

She nodded, dropped her bucket, and ran toward the direction of town. As she passed Evelyn's house, the concerned elderly woman popped her head out the door. Ada quickly informed her of the fire. Minutes later, she reached the bell pole at the end of town and pulled on the rope. She was breathless, and her heart was pounding.

The bell had been placed there for just this type of emergency. It echoed throughout the street, and soon people were rushing out of their homes, startled but alert. As Ada continued pulling the cord, she pointed up the road.

"The Webers' barn," she gasped between breaths. "It's on fire!"

The townsfolk grabbed buckets and ran in the direction she was pointing. She saw the Duncans, the Martins, David, and Daniel. Even the Johnsons and the Taylors and the Blakes, along with many others, hurried down the street—all pulling together to help one of their neighbors. Ada continued to ring the bell for several more minutes, and eventually she ran back as well.

As she approached their property, she couldn't believe what she was seeing. The chaos seemed to unfold in slow motion. The fire had spread to the Webers' house and was burning out of control. There was a frantic commotion as men and women alike threw buckets of water onto a lost cause. Isaac held back his panic-stricken wife as she shrieked negatives and pushed against him. Ada's heart raced as her eyes skimmed over the scene in front of her. She felt a light touch on her elbow and spun around to look into the troubled faces of Evelyn and Grace.

"Where's Eli?" she asked in a low voice, her stomach twisting into a knot.

"Ada, honey," Evelyn shouted over the roar of the flames. "He ran into the fire to look for Noah."

Chapter 35

ELI

The air was thick with blinding smoke. The floor was the only thing Eli could see. He crouched low to the ground and felt along the wall as he made his way into Noah's room, calling out for the boy. There was no reply. His skin felt as if it were burning under a scorching desert sun, and he imagined his sweat boiling away as soon as it hit the hot air. Before he ran into the house, he had taken off his shirt and plunged it into a bucket of water. Eli held it up to his face.

"Noah! Where are you, little man?" he called out. The fire's roar blotted out his words.

His eyes stung and there was a bitter taste in his mouth. As he reached into the sweltering darkness, his hand bumped the edge of Noah's bed. Eli threw the wet shirt over his shoulder and cried out again as he rushed forward and felt along the top of the mattress. Nothing.

"Noah!" he yelled louder.

The faintest whimper reached him. Eli swept his arms under the bed and felt the boy's trembling fingers reaching back. He grabbed the tiny hands and pulled Noah into his lap as he leaned against the bed. The boy was crying and coughing.

"Here, put this on your head," he said as he spread his dampened shirt over the boy. "Breathe through this and hang on to me. We're going to be okay, Noah."

Eli tried to recall the layout of the room. The darkness was disorienting, but he was sure there must be a window on the wall he was facing. He reached behind him and grabbed a pillow from the boy's bed. Putting an arm around Noah, he pushed himself up. As he groped the air ahead of him, his hand hit the wall. He felt along its surface, relieved to find the window frame. Pushing the curtain aside, he tried to open it, but it stuck.

Noah clung to him as he placed the pillow against the window and punched through it. He swept the frame with the pillow, knocking the shards loose. Eli pushed the boy out the window and into someone's receiving arms. As Noah was whisked away to safety, Eli climbed out, desperate to breathe fresh air.

He coughed and wiped at his watering eyes as he stumbled forward. His arms were streaked with soot. And blood. He must have cut himself when he broke the window. Eli scanned his hand and arm but couldn't find the wound under all the dirt and ashes.

As he walked away from the searing heat, the commotion in front of him was a blur. The only thing he could see was Ada running toward him. She jumped into his arms, knocking him to one knee. He was exhausted and shaky, but he held onto her tightly. He pulled her hair to one side and looked over her shoulder as she pressed her face into his sooty cheek.

Isaac and Hannah were doting over their son. Hannah smiled through tears and wiped at Noah's face with her shawl. Isaac turned his eyes to Eli, and with arms grasping onto his family, he nodded his gratitude. Eli nodded back.

Chapter 36

MARCUS

Two nights ago, the Webers' house and barn burned to the ground. Isaac was nursing an injured ankle and a mild concussion, while Noah and Eli, who suffered from smoke inhalation, were already beginning to feel better. Thankfully, these were minor injuries, but the property loss was devastating. Between smoke and fire damage, there was little that could be salvaged.

Marcus would soon be meeting with a group of men at the church to discuss how to help the Webers in their time of need. But first, he walked to the bank, hoping to catch David at his office and consult him on how much money Isaac would need to rebuild. The banker's assessment would give the men a goal to reach for. When he arrived, David was stepping out of the building.

"Hey there, Marcus," he said. "I was just about to head over to the church, but I'm glad you came by. I need to talk with you."

"Perfect," Marcus replied. "I was hoping you could give me a rough estimate on what the Webers will need to get back on their feet. I want to start a collection as soon as possible."

David nodded as Marcus explained the reason for his visit. Looking up and down the street, he opened the bank door and ushered Marcus in.

"Let's talk in my office," he said.

The conversation with David took longer than Marcus had expected, and now the two men were walking toward the church at a fast pace. He didn't want the men to have to wait for long. This meeting was disrupting their workday, and it was a busy time of year.

A dry heat lingered in the air. The church doors were propped open, and as he and David scaled the front stairs, Marcus heard a heated argument unfolding within. The voices belonged to John Miller and Eli Gardner. Eli should have been at home recovering; Marcus was surprised to find him there.

"Listen," John said with contempt in his voice. "The only way we're going to help the Webers is if everyone in this room contributes monetarily. That means money, Eli. So stop complaining and start digging into your pockets."

"I'm just saying we need to wait for Marcus before discussing this," Eli insisted. "You want to give that much, fine. But you can't demand the same amount from the rest of the men here. Each man should decide on his own how he can best help Isaac."

"Okay," John said as Marcus stepped through the door. "If every man here gave only a third of what I'm prepared to give, it would still help Isaac more than playing your *ghee-tar* while you saunter down the lane. If you worked half as hard as the rest of these men, you could give your neighbor some real help. Come on, Eli. You must have something hoarded away. I bet you have a tin can filled with a few coins buried in your yard somewhere. We live in a community. You're the one who decided to move here and join the civilized world. It's time to jump off the gypsy wagon and act like a man."

Eli took a step toward John, his fists clenched and jaw set. Marcus didn't like where this confrontation was headed. John was sneering, and Eli looked ready to strike.

"Hey," Marcus said, stepping between them. "I called this meeting; I'll be leading it. You both need to calm down."

The two continued to glare at each other over his shoulder. The other men stood by and watched as the silence clamored with a tension that wouldn't be ignored.

David grabbed onto Eli's arm. "Come on. Let's stand over there."

Eli relented and allowed the banker to lead him to the far side of the sanctuary where they leaned against the wall. John snorted through his smirk and sat down.

"All right, listen," Marcus said, turning his attention to the entire group. "I appreciate that everyone wants to help, but money isn't the issue. David just informed me that an anonymous donation has been given to Isaac. It's more than enough to replace everything they've lost."

As Marcus explained this, the men turned their astonished faces to the banker and started murmuring. David confirmed the news with a slow nod. Eli peered at the ground, barely shaking his head. He crossed his arms and poked at the ground with the tip of his boot before finally turning his eyes to David as well.

"What? Who—" John began.

"He said anonymous," David pointed out before the farmer could finish.

"Okay," Marcus continued, "the Webers are staying with the Gardners, correct?"

Eli nodded as his eyes drifted back to the ground, his jaw still clamped shut.

"That sounds cozy," John said under his breath.

"So, lodging is taken care of," Marcus said, choosing to ignore him. "What the Webers will need, however, is help with the clean up and with transporting lumber. They have to finish building their home and barn before the weather turns. If you have any skills in that area, we're going to need you. And of course, they'll need help picking up some new furniture later on. I know it's almost time for harvest, and you're all going to be busy, but we only have a few months to get this done. We'll have to rotate our manpower. I brought some paper. I want everyone to write down the days and times you're available to help. Just list it in the columns I've made, and we'll contact you when we're more organized."

"Yeah, I can help," Eli said, looking up.

"You're quite the hero, Eli," John mocked. "It's pretty easy to volunteer when you know the money's been collected. But everyone heard you balk at having to give, and that's what we're all going to remember. You know, Pastor. How about you put me down for one of those nice relaxing lumber runs. Maybe I can get out of some work too."

"John, you need to stop…" Marcus began.

But before he could finish, Eli walked to the front of the room, scribbled something on the paper, and left the building.

"Eli, wait," he called out.

Eli shook his head and wouldn't look back. Marcus glanced at the paper. Eli had scrawled his name at the top of the list. Under the days column he wrote *all*; under times he wrote *any*.

Chapter 37
ADA

It was difficult to watch her neighbors suffer, but Ada was happy to offer her home to Isaac and his family. She had once lost everything also, and she remembered how desperate it made her feel. She wanted to give them the same unconditional love and acceptance that the caravan had given her.

The Webers kept to themselves in the back room. Ada didn't mind; she understood their mood and encouraged them to spend as much time alone as needed. It was important to let Noah rest, and their time together would help them heal. She appreciated the solitude as well, needing her own time to process what had happened. The fire was a frightening experience for everyone who had witnessed it.

Several hours after the fire had begun, the flames died down to a red glow. It was decided that the displaced family would stay with the Gardners. Ada took them to her home and helped the dazed parents clean up their little boy. Evelyn offered to lend a bed since the Gardners didn't have an extra one. As a handful of men kept the smoldering ruins contained, Marcus and Eli followed the widow to her home and retrieved it. While there, she asked Marcus if it would be better for the Webers to stay with her.

He thanked her for the kind offer but suggested Isaac might prefer being closer to his own property once they started the clean-up process. Evelyn nodded and tearfully asked how else she could help. Eli suggested she make one of her delicious meals for the Webers. The woman wasted no time in preparing supper for the next day.

Now, as Ada sat at her table, fighting the emotions that were threatening to overtake her, she delayed preparing that evening's meal. With eyes closed, she listened to the silence around her until the back door opened, startling her back into the present. She glanced up and noticed Eli's expression.

"How was the meeting?" she asked. "You look upset."

He shook his head, dismissing her concern. "There were some differences of opinion, but everything's fine now." He sat across from her and picked at his bandaged arm. "I told Marcus I could help with the rebuild. I promised to help every day—until it's done."

"Oh. And how does Ray feel about that?"

"I don't know; he arrived later. I saw him come in as I was leaving. I didn't have a chance to talk with him. Marcus had us write down the days we could help. I was at the top, and I'm sure Ray has seen the list by now. The work I do for him doesn't have a deadline, so he can manage without me for a while."

His eyes drifted to the far end of the kitchen as he grew quiet and chewed on his thumbnail. Ada wanted to talk, but this didn't seem like a good time. She reached over and unwrapped the bandage on his arm. He had cut himself on Noah's window, and she wanted to make sure he was healing well. When Eli spoke again, he sounded far away.

"Do you remember when I told you about my dream? God was asking me to do something for Him. I'm still not sure what it is, but I'm getting closer. I can feel it."

Ada lowered her eyes and looked at her tattoo, caressing the smallest of the three flowers as he continued.

"The fire made me think of it again. I want to help people. I think I'm supposed to..." He stopped. "Ada, what's wrong?"

She tried not to cry, but that one tear wouldn't stay in her eye. It trickled down her cheek and gave her away.

"When Mrs. Russell told me you had run into the fire, I was scared. I've been afraid in the past, but never like that. You were always with me before, but this time was different. It felt... lonely."

"I'm sorry." He reached for her hand. "I wasn't thinking. I shouldn't have—"

"No, you did the right thing, Eli. It doesn't matter how it made me feel. If you hadn't run into that fire, Noah would have died. God used you to save that little boy. How could I possibly let my fear stand in the way of that? And when Noah's life was saved, Isaac and Hannah were saved from a grief that would have been..."

She closed her eyes, losing the fight. "God spared them from a pain they would have felt forever."

She couldn't stop the tears now. She glanced at him, unable to finish what she was trying to say. She leaned forward and covered her face.

"I'm sorry... I think I need to go home. Eli, I miss her," she whispered under her breath, giving in to her quiet sobs. "I didn't even get to have her for very long—Oh Lord! I miss our Ruth Ann so much."

Eli put his arm around her as she wept.

"Can we please go home for a little while?" she asked, sinking against him.

"We can leave tomorrow," he promised, blinking away his own tears.

Chapter 38

ELI

It was a cold morning, but December was still a good time of year to catch a few lethargic bass. With the right kind of bait, the fish would be eager to bite. Located a mile downstream from the winter camp, there was a small lake with a few warmer pockets where the fish tended to congregate. After two hours spent shivering on the edge of the water, Eli and Jed walked home with a full basket. When they arrived at camp, Lily ran up to Eli with her chubby arms held out.

"Fishies!" she squealed as Eli scooped up the toddler.

"You like that, Lily?" he asked. "We can have fish tonight."

He lifted the lid of the basket and showed her its contents. She wiggled out of his arms, giggling. As she ran to Goldie, she babbled about fish in an indecipherable baby language. Eli scanned the camp, noting Ada's absence.

"She's not up yet?" he asked as he handed Rosa the basket.

Rosa shook her head. "I haven't seen her all morning. She didn't come out for breakfast, but we left some for her."

"She wasn't feeling well yesterday," Eli said. "Maybe some extra sleep will help."

He and Jed put their poles away. After washing his hands, he sat by the fire and worked on his doll heads. Last summer had been another good season for sales, making it necessary for Eli and Ada to increase their inventory again.

All the merchants had been able to travel to the markets that year, including Ira's family. Goldie stayed at the vardo with her two younger children, but Sammy, who was almost nine, ran their table with his father. Ira and Goldie's children were growing up quickly. It was hard to believe it had already been four and a half years since Eli and Ada first met the caravan. Yet at the same time, it seemed as though they had always been with them.

After several minutes of carving, Eli decided to check on Ada. He set his project aside and walked over to their vardo. Once inside, he pulled back the curtain that divided the bed from the rest of their home and gently rubbed her shoulder.

"Hey, are you going to get up today?" he asked.

Ada stretched and asked what time it was.

"It's after ten," he said. "Rosa left some breakfast out for you."

Ada covered her nose with her blanket. "Ugh, you smell like fish. I don't think I'm hungry."

Eli laughed. "Wow, Miss Grumpy. I just got back from fishing with Jed. I guess you do need more sleep." He started to walk to the door, but Ada threw back the covers.

"No, I'll get up." She got out of bed and wrapped herself in a shawl. Eli held the door open for her.

"Well, there she is!" Hattie called out.

Ada took a few steps toward the fire and then hesitated. She turned and reached for Eli as her eyes rolled back, and she began to fall. He caught her and called out to Rosa. As he lowered her to the ground, Rosa and Hattie ran to the couple. Concern for the girl swept through the group, and the other merchants jumped up as well. The women knelt beside Ada as her eyes fluttered back into consciousness.

"Are you okay?" Eli asked. "Rosa, what's wrong with her? Is she sick?"

"Let's get her back to bed," the woman suggested.

Helping Ada up, the three of them walked her back into the vardo. Rosa sat her on the edge of the bed and felt her forehead while the other two looked on.

"I don't think she ate supper last night," Hattie said.

She opened the cupboards, found some bread, and tore off a large piece. Ada shook her head and put the back of her hand up to her mouth, squeezing her eyes shut. As Eli rubbed her back, her face turned a slight shade of grey. She stiffened and tried to push him away. Her eyes popped open, and there was a quick glance between the older women. Hattie grabbed a bowl from the counter and shoved it into the girl's hands. Ada leaned forward, but the feeling seemed to pass.

"Eat some bread," Rosa ordered. "I think it will help."

144

As Ada nibbled at the bread, her color slowly returned.

"Is she sick?" Eli asked again.

Rosa shook her head. "No, she doesn't have a fever. Ada, is it possible you're expecting?"

"Expecting what?" Eli said.

Hattie snickered, but he didn't see what was so funny about any of this.

Ada's eyes widened. "Oh, Rosa…" She turned pale this time instead of grey.

"Wait, a baby?" Eli felt the color drain from his own cheeks.

"Now he gets it," Hattie said, laughing louder.

"Ada, are we going to have a baby?" A grin spread over his face as he sat down.

Ada looked at Rosa, who smiled and asked some questions related to her symptoms. Rosa then said she was sure of it; they could expect their baby to arrive sometime toward the end of July or early August. Eli laughed as he hugged Ada, and her energy seemed to return. They began discussing what ought to be done regarding the next market season.

Rosa insisted they stay in the winter camp with her. "Someone else can sell the dolls, Eli. Ada is having your baby here."

He nodded, and they continued to talk of the future as they held each other.

Rosa rubbed Ada's arm. "Keep eating that bread. It will settle your stomach. I'm sure everyone is worried. Should I tell them about the baby, or would you like to?"

They asked her to tell the others and chose to stay in their vardo. They wanted to let the news sink in for a bit. Rosa and Hattie each gave them a hug before leaving the couple to their planning. When they were alone, Ada glanced at Eli.

"You don't mind missing the markets?"

Eli smiled and shook his head. "We're having a baby, Ada. I couldn't be happier."

Chapter 39

ADA

It was March twenty-sixth, Eli's twenty-first birthday. Ada had been full of energy earlier, but by this time of night, her swelling body was usually tired. When Eli first noticed how drained she felt in the evenings, he insisted they start going to bed early. Of course, they always stayed awake and talked for an hour or two longer, but being alone in the vardo was relaxing.

"Thank you for the raspberry tart." Eli propped himself on his elbow as he lay next to her.

She leaned closer to him. "They weren't fresh raspberries, though," she said with a hint of regret. "Preserves were the best I could do."

He put his hand on her growing belly. "Well, at least they weren't under ripe," he said, winking.

She thought about the time he had given her berries while they were hiding in the woods. She recalled their sweetly sour taste, and her heart warmed at the memory.

"No, it was perfect," he reassured her. The baby pushed against his touch. He smiled and rubbed her stomach.

"He's wishing his daddy a happy birthday," she said with a grin.

"He? Do you think it's a boy?"

Ada shrugged. "I don't really know. Hattie said I'm carrying low, and Bea said that proves I'm having a boy. But Rosa told her not to fill my head with silly wives' tales. I guess the only way to know for certain is to wait until the baby is born."

"Then we better have two names picked out," he said. "I thought a pretty girl's name could be Ruth Ann."

Ada smiled. "After our mothers. I love it. And if we have a boy, we could name him after our fathers."

"I thought of that, also," Eli admitted.

"William Arthur," she said. As they smiled, the baby kicked again. "Oh, ho! He likes the name." Ada laughed. "Maybe it *is* a boy."

Eli continued to rub her stomach and coo through her nightgown at the baby tumbling inside her.

"I think you love my big, fat stomach more than me," she teased.

"I love this baby," he said. "And I love you, too. You'll be a good mother, Ada."

Her face grew pensive and she glanced down. "Sometimes I'm scared, though. I know I shouldn't be, but I want to protect our baby from all the awful things out there. It feels overwhelming when I think about what might have happened to us. Even our parents couldn't protect us."

"And we couldn't protect them." Eli sat up. "We can't think about those things, Ada. It'll just shut us down and keep us from living. I know it's hard, but we have to trust God."

"I do trust Him, but that doesn't always make the fear go away. I have a head and I have a heart, but they don't always agree. Sometimes my feelings don't match my thinking."

"Well, that's one of the things we need to pray about. Can I pray for you now?"

She nodded. They closed their eyes and put their foreheads together. Eli placed a warm hand on her stomach.

"Lord," he began quietly. "You are a good Father, and we know You love us. Thank you for this baby. Please give us the wisdom to be the best parents we can be. Help us keep our child safe and show us how to trust You with the things we can't control. Please bring peace between our hearts and our minds so our focus can always stay on You. In Jesus' name, we lay our hearts, our minds, and our baby at Your feet. Amen."

Eli smiled at Ada as she leaned in and kissed him.

"Thank you," she said.

They turned down the lantern and snuggled into bed. Ada slept comfortably in Eli's safe arms and in God's peaceful embrace.

❧

Ada carried a basket of clothes down the path leading to the river. Normally, the women washed their clothes together, but she didn't want to wait. Even though the others would be doing their laundry in a few days, she was restless and decided to do hers today, hoping to get her mind off the uncomfortable clenching in her middle. It wasn't exactly painful, but it was distracting enough to stop her whenever it happened. It was only the end of April; she wasn't looking forward to another three months of this.

She mentioned the sensation to Rosa, who said it was probably just her body practicing for the delivery. It was fine, as long as it didn't hurt. After asking her a few more questions, though, she suggested Ada take it easy and rest, as a precaution. Perhaps Ada was imagining it, but something in Rosa's eyes looked concerned—more than her calm voice portrayed. It was difficult to ignore the nagging suspicion that Rosa was worried.

Washing a small basket of clothes might help her refocus her thoughts. The delicate items needed cold water, and she could easily wash them in the river. It shouldn't use up too much of her energy. At least this was something she could still do. Eli already did more of her work than she wanted; she would feel bad if he had to start doing their laundry as well.

When Ada reached the river, she placed the basket on the ground and knelt on a large rock hanging over the creek. She grabbed an item out of the basket and scrubbed soap into the garment. After rubbing the fabric together to loosen the dirt, she rinsed it thoroughly in the water. As she placed it on the rock, her insides tightened up again. She sat back on her heels to wait it out. When her muscles had relaxed, she noticed an area farther down the river that was more convenient for washing clothes.

She put the wet item back in the basket and stood up, but her foot slipped and splashed into the river. She landed hard on her heel and it sent a shock through her whole body. Her heart skipped a beat. That was close! The thought of falling and landing on her stomach made her shiver. Maybe she shouldn't be out here by herself. Before she could step out of the river, a surge of intense pain grew in her abdomen and spread out, engulfing her completely. She doubled over and grabbed her belly. Her eyes dimmed at the height of the pain, and a low moan escaped her as she rode the slowly subsiding wave to its end.

A seed of dread began to grow in her mind as she picked up the basket and walked toward camp, giving up her plans to launder anything. Farther along the path, another rush of pain swept over her, forcing her to stop. She held onto a tree for support and fought the panic that threatened to grip her.

This did not feel right. Once again, the pain receded, and she continued to work her way back to camp.

She walked faster, but it only triggered another flood of pain, this time so intense that she dropped the basket and feared she might fall over. Tears came to her eyes, blurring her vision.

"Please, God, make it stop..." was all she could manage to pray. She needed to get back to camp; she needed to find Rosa. As the pain faded, Ada stumbled forward again, leaving the overturned basket behind.

Chapter 40

ELI

Eli held up the wood and studied the design he was carving. He was making a cradle, and this would be the headboard. He could have left it plain; he knew he should be working on merchandise for the markets, but he didn't want to. He was excited to be a father and it influenced what he chose to work on.

In less than a month, the caravan would travel the summer markets. He and Ada would stay at the winter camp with Jed and Rosa, like they had done when Eli built their vardo, but this time they would be having their baby.

Tony agreed to help the couple sell their merchandise at his table. Two weeks ago, they had packed up most of it and were storing it in his and Grandma Mae's vardo. Eli wasn't concerned about adding to the merchandise; whatever sold was fine with him. He had other things on his mind, and he didn't care about the money. He was already going to be making less than he did last summer since he was planning to give half of it to Tony for helping them. His focus was on the baby's arrival.

Many of his other projects had fallen to the wayside that spring, including the one that took him into town every week. But they were safe where they were; he could pick them up again in the fall. The cradle, however, was a project that couldn't wait.

As he sat by the fire with his back toward the river, he continued to carve on the wood held between his knees. Rosa and Jed sat across from him, whispering together. Suddenly, there was a shift in their mood, causing them to stand.

"Oh, no," Rosa gasped, looking past Eli.

He turned to see Ada holding herself up against the shed as she cradled her stomach. The color had drained from her face, which twisted in a grimace of pain. Eli's gut plummeted as he jumped up. He dropped the headboard and ran to her. When he got to her side, she seemed to recover but was shaky and weak. She leaned into him as Rosa reached them.

"When did your contractions start, Ada?" she asked, holding onto her other arm. She motioned Eli toward their vardo.

"While I was at the river. I slipped on a rock just before they started. Is this my fault?" Speaking the question aloud caused an onset of new tears.

"No, honey. Of course not," Rosa reassured her. "Did you fall?"

Ada shook her head.

"She can't have the baby yet," Eli said. "It's too soon. Can you stop it, Rosa?" He couldn't control the waver in his voice.

"We're going to try."

Jed held the door open, and they helped Ada to the bed. Rosa grabbed Eli's arm and led him a few steps away.

"You need to be calm," she said in a low voice. "Try to help her relax. I need some things from my vardo, I'll be right back."

He nodded and went back to comfort her.

"Eli…"

Ada held her breath while another wave of pain gripped her. He felt helpless as she squeezed his hand. The pain faded and she let out her breath in short gasps.

"I'm sorry," she said between her panting.

Eli rubbed her hand. "Look at me. You're going to be okay." He didn't think he sounded convincing, but she hung onto every word. "Breathe with me." He inhaled and exhaled slowly as she followed his lead.

Jed started a fire in the woodstove and lit the lanterns. Rosa and Hattie reentered the vardo, each with an armful of supplies.

"Oh good. You started a fire," Rosa said as Hattie set a pot of water on the stove. They placed the supplies on the table, and Rosa handed a small, brown bottle to Eli. "Rub this onto her stomach; it's lavender oil. It might help stop the contractions." She turned to Jed. "Time for you to leave, my love."

She held onto his arm and steered him toward the door. As Jed stepped out of the vardo, Eli heard Rosa whisper: "The best help now is for all of us to pray."

While Rosa washed her hands, Eli turned his attention back to Ada. She uncovered her round belly for him. Her skin was hot to the touch, and as he rubbed oil onto her stomach, he felt it clench tighter than an angry fist. She moaned through another contraction. He wanted to make it all end. He wanted to take away her pain, but he knew he couldn't.

Rosa, Hattie, and Eli continued to soothe her as the minutes stretched into hours. Rosa told Ada to kneel in different positions in an attempt to relieve the pressure that might be causing her early labor. Nothing seemed to help. Hattie brought a warm mug to her and placed it in her hands, encouraging her to drink.

"Sip on this, Sweetie. Nettle leaf tea has been known to slow down labor," she explained. Ada nodded and brought the mug to her lips.

"Try not to tense up," Rosa said in a soothing voice. "We need to stop your contractions."

Ada closed her eyes and let out a slow breath as Eli rubbed her shoulders. She tried to sip her tea, but her face scrunched up again; another contraction took over. Eli shook his head in frustration and took the mug away before it spilled. He caught the concerned look that passed between Rosa and Hattie. As he set the mug down, his hand trembled.

"All right, Ada. It's time to let me check you," Rosa said. "Eli, maybe you should wait with the others."

"No, I'm not leaving," he insisted.

She considered him for a moment and then nodded. "Fine. But you've cut yourself with one of your tools. Go wash your hands."

He looked down; the side of his knuckle on his left hand was gouged and covered in dried blood. The tool he was using earlier must have slipped when he saw Ada stumble into camp. He had been too distracted to notice. He poured some warm water from the stove into a basin and washed his hands. The soap caused his knuckle to sting, but it was nothing compared to what Ada was feeling. He closed his eyes, trying to push away his emotions. Ada wouldn't be able to calm down if she knew he was upset.

Hattie put a hand on his shoulder. "Let me dress it for you, Eli."

He nodded and kept his eyes closed as she wrapped his finger in gauze. Ada moaned again, louder this time. How long had this been going on? Her reaction to the pain was getting worse. He turned and saw Rosa urging him over.

"Sit with your wife," she ordered. "Ada, I am so sorry, but your baby is coming now."

"No! Ooh, no…" she cried as Eli slipped his arm around her.

His heart was racing; he hated this feeling. Ada squeezed her eyes shut. She went rigid and held her breath.

"Ada, don't," he pleaded with her. She opened her eyes and looked at him with an expression that tore at his heart.

"Our baby cannot come now. It's too early," she cried. "Eli, please. Help me."

"I can't," he whispered. "I'm sorry, Ada. I don't know what to do…"

⁓

"It's a girl," Rosa said as she handed the tiny bundle to Ada.

Eli sat behind Ada, supporting her against his chest. He looked down at the baby in her arms. She could have fit in one of his hands.

"She's so small," Ada said as tears rolled down her cheeks. The infant's arm moved slightly as she struggled to breathe.

Eli looked at Rosa. "Will she be okay?" he asked, pleading for some good news.

Rosa turned to him and shook her head. "No, honey. She's just too little."

"Is she in any pain?" Ada asked with a shaky voice.

"I don't think so," Rosa answered.

Ada closed her eyes and continued to cry in silence.

"How long…" Eli tried to ask, but his voice broke.

"A couple of hours, perhaps. I am so sorry." Rosa's face was wet with her own tears. She placed a hand on each of their arms. "I want you both to listen carefully and try to hear what I'm saying. I know this is hard, but please try to put your grief aside for later. There will be a time for that. Hold onto your baby and give her as much love and attention as you can. This, right now, is the time you've been given. This is what you will remember when you think back on her short life. Try to take in every detail and cherish every second you have with her." She reached up and wiped Ada's eyes. "Make this time something you will remember fondly. It won't be void of sadness, but don't let it be without a little bit of joy as well."

Rosa leaned in, kissed both of them, and then stepped aside. Hattie took their hands in hers and gave them each a hug before she left the vardo.

Eli held onto Ada and gazed at their baby girl. "Ruth Ann…" he whispered. He didn't know if they sat like that for one hour or for three. It didn't matter. It was forever, and it was a blink of an eye. It was both. They held her in silence for the entire time. Together, they held her until she slipped peacefully out of their arms and into the Savior's forever.

153

Chapter 41

JED

The caravan was silent as everyone grieved the loss of Ruth Ann. Jed sat in front of the fire and watched the flames flicker into the air. Rosa was next to him, gripping his hand. It had been a long time since she had lost a child she helped deliver. It was always tragic when a mother or child died, but for her, this would be felt more deeply. Ada was like a daughter to them; her baby was also theirs, a grandchild they never thought they would have. Ada's body would recover, but this loss was going to be devastating for the young couple who had already lost so much.

Yesterday while the caravan prayed for Ada's labor to stop, there was no way for them to know that Ruth Ann had already been born. She never cried; her lungs were too weak. When Rosa came outside and told them the news, their prayers changed. From that moment on, they asked for comfort and healing instead.

A few hours later, Eli stumbled out of the vardo in a daze, holding his baby. He handed the lifeless bundle to Hattie. Tony walked up to her, whispered a few words, and carefully took the baby from her.

"One of my boxes," he said, looking at Jed. "Do you think that will do?" Jed nodded, and Tony disappeared into his vardo. Knowing Tony, he would choose the nicest one he had.

Everyone took turns hugging the bereaved young man. Eli moved from one embrace to another, asleep in his grief, and then disappeared back into his home. Rosa checked on Ada throughout the evening to make sure she wasn't experiencing any complications.

Jed hardly slept that night. He lay in his bed, slipping in and out of a half-sleep until he heard quiet rustling by the fire pit. He got up and opened the door to see who it was. Eli was walking down the path that led to Badger Creek, holding something in his hand. Cobra slid past Jed's leg and hurried after him. When the dog caught up to him, Eli reached down and rubbed his ears as they disappeared into the night.

By late afternoon the following day, Ada was still resting in the vardo, and Eli had not yet returned. Jed was beginning to wonder if he should look for him. As he considered leaving, however, the young couple's door opened, and Ada stepped out. He jumped up and ran to her, offering his arm for support. He hugged her for a long minute.

"Come sit with me by the fire," he said. "It's good to be around other people, and no one will make you talk about it if you don't want to."

Ada scanned the group and then bit her lower lip. She dipped her head slightly and let him guide her to a chair.

"Do you know where Eli is?" she asked.

"I think he's down by the river. He probably just needs to be alone for a while."

She sat with the others but kept her eyes downcast. By joining the group, she had made a small step toward working through her sorrow. Everyone understood that and didn't expect any more. Occasionally, someone would pat her on the shoulder or rub her hand as they walked by, but they respected her need for quiet. Jed sat in the chair next to hers, waiting for Eli's return.

After two more hours had passed, the women began to prepare supper. Jed stood and moved closer to Rosa.

"I think I'll go for a walk," he told her, but she knew where he was going.

"Tell him supper will be ready soon."

Jed walked down a path that led to their favorite fishing spot, and as he stepped into the small clearing, he found Eli sitting against a fallen tree. Cobra was lying next to him. Undetected, Jed watched his slumped back for a moment.

Eli rested his forearms on his knees. As he looked out over the water, he held his Bowie knife in front of him. He turned his eyes to a piece of wood next to him and threw the knife into it. After a pause, he grabbed the handle, rocked it back and forth to loosen the blade, and repeated the action. Jed step forward and took a closer look; it was the headboard for the cradle.

As Cobra jumped up and jogged toward him, Eli lowered his head and left the knife where it had landed. Jed sat down next to him; his mind raced back to another time when he tried to comfort that grief-stricken and confused boy. What did he say then? Did it help? What could he possibly say now, at a time like this? He prayed for the right words.

"Why…" Eli started to ask with a strain in his voice. "Jed, I don't understand." He grabbed onto his forehead, unable to say more.

"I don't know either," Jed said, shaking his head. "I wish I had a good answer for you, but I don't."

Eli moved his hand over his eyes and leaned forward. As his shoulders shook under silent sobs, Jed placed his hand on the back of Eli's neck. After a few minutes, his weeping slowed; he sniffed and squinted at Jed.

"Tell me this happened for a reason," he begged. "Please… I need to know God has a purpose for this. I have to believe it happened for a reason… Even *this*. Otherwise, it's just…" He squeezed his eyes shut and shook his head as if he were trying to clear his thoughts. "Otherwise, it's just cruel," he finally said, covering his face again.

Jed sighed a deep, long breath. "Eli, that's your sorrow talking. You know God isn't cruel. We live in a fallen world, and with that comes pain and death. He had every right to leave us here in our mess, but He didn't. What you're suffering right now—the death of your child—God understands that. You can be certain that He knows what you're feeling. He allowed His one and only Son to be sacrificed for our sins. He did that for you, and He did that for me; He did it for all of us. God is powerful and just, but He is also merciful. God is many things, but cruel is not one of them."

Eli looked back toward the water and dug his fingers into his arms, fighting against his tears.

After a pause, Jed continued. "This loss you're going through, it's now a part of you forever, just like your tattoo. Right now, it's an open wound. You don't even have to bump it to feel the pain; just having the air touch it is enough to make it hurt. But like any wound, you need to take care of it. You're at a crossroads again, like you were five years ago. You can rub the salt and dirt of despair into this wound, and it will heal into a gnarled and disfigured scar that no one wants to look at. Or you can cover it in the comforting ointment of God's promises, and it will eventually heal into compassion and wisdom. It'll still leave a scar, but it won't be an ugly one. And when you or anyone else looks at it, it will point back to God."

Eli shook his head again. "I don't know how I'm going to get through this one, Jed. This is too much. I can't do it," he moaned. "I don't want to be around anyone; I don't want to *feel* anything."

"Secluding yourself isn't going to make your pain go away," Jed pointed out. "You can't do this on your own, Eli. I know you're heartbroken, but

Ada is hurting too. You need each other now more than ever. Lean on one another for support, and then when you both reach for God together, you'll be lifting up four hands instead of only two."

Eli glanced at his hands and relaxed their grip on his arms. His eyes drifted to the sky as he took in several deep breaths, blowing each one out slowly.

"You and Ada are not alone in this," Jed added after another pause. "If you let us, we will all come alongside you and help hold up your arms when they get tired. And trust me; you will get tired. There are no magic words that will make your pain go away. The only things that will truly help ease it are faith, support, and time. This sadness will never completely leave you, but one day, your perspective on it will change. I promise."

He put his hand on Eli's shoulder and they sat in silence for several minutes. Eventually, Eli cleared his throat and rubbed his eyes.

"Thanks," he said.

Jed patted his back and stood up. "Supper must be ready by now. I'm guessing you haven't eaten today." He started to walk away, but stopped and turned. "I thought you might want to know that Ada's awake. She's been up for a while."

"Would you tell her I'll be back soon? I need a little more time."

Jed nodded and walked back to camp. When he reached the shed, Ada glanced up. He walked over to her and placed a hand on her arm as he sat down.

"He'll be back in a bit."

Supper was served and eaten, but still there was no sign of Eli. Ada barely ate; she watched the fire as she picked at her food. The sky began to dim while Jed helped Rosa wash the supper dishes.

"Is he coming back tonight?" she asked.

They looked at Ada, who had closed her eyes. As she wiped the tears flowing down her cheeks, Eli finally appeared on the path near the shed, followed by Cobra. He held the top part of the headboard in his hand, broken off at the spot where he had thrown the knife into it. He hesitated for a moment, looked at Jed, and then walked toward Ada. Everyone around the fire knew they needed a private moment and turned their attention toward each other.

When Eli touched her shoulder, she opened her eyes and looked up at him. She pressed her lips together as tears continued to flow. He squatted in front of her, and she leaned into him. They put their foreheads together and sat with their eyes closed. Jed could see Eli's mouth moving as he spoke, and he could see Ada nodding as she bit her lower lip.

Eli stood, squeezed her shoulder, and placed the wood on her lap. He walked to the table where supper had been left for him, and as he filled a bowl, Ada turned the wood over and looked at it. She smiled and dabbed her eyes as he carried his meal over and sat in the chair beside her.

From where he stood, Jed could see the piece of wood. Along its top was the design Eli had been carving before Ada's labor, but in the center was a new carving. In beautiful scrolling letters, Eli had carved the name of their baby: Ruth Ann.

Chapter 42

ELI

Eli caught sight of a large willow tree as he guided his wagon down a lane that cut through the back of Mrs. Perry's property. He knew that tree well. It sat alone on a low grassy hill between the widow's grain fields and the edge of the West Woods. He turned his eyes toward Ada; she was also watching the tree as it glided past them. She glanced at him and smiled wistfully before peering down at her lap. Eli put his hand on her shoulder.

"We're almost there," he said.

Her eyes were moist when she looked up, but there was also anticipation on her face. He felt it too. He was looking forward to seeing everyone again. Even so, there was a small pang of guilt mixed with his excitement; they should have visited sooner.

As the narrowing lane turned, the trees crept closer to the wagon. The woods thickened and the road became less maintained, causing the wagon to jostle along. It was late September; the merchants would have rejoined Levi and Bea at the winter camp three weeks ago. By this time of day, they would be preparing supper and settling in to enjoy a peaceful evening.

A smile cut deeper into Eli's face as they rounded the last bend and saw familiar figures sitting around the fire pit. One animated cry after another rang out as the wagon's approach was discovered. Eli pulled to a stop and they jumped down to meet their family as the merchants ran to them. He could scarcely hear what was being said as joyful voices overlapped each other. Rosa put her hands on the sides of Eli's face.

"You're the best thing I've seen all day," she said as she hugged him. Jed grabbed onto his arm and drew him into a strong, fatherly embrace. "Welcome home, son. How long are you staying?"

"About a week." Eli knew the answer would be a disappointment.

Jed nodded as though he were expecting it. He squeezed Eli's arm again before giving Ada an affectionate bear hug. Eli turned away, and Hattie threw her soft arms around him.

"Two years," she whispered into his ear. She held him at arm's length and let a frown hint at the edge of her mouth. "Don't do that to them again. You hear me?" She glanced at Jed and Rosa as they took turns embracing Ada.

"I'm sorry, Hattie. I lost track of time."

"Well, don't. You're not that far away."

"I won't. I promise."

She nodded and let go of him. Floyd stepped up and slapped him on the shoulder as they hugged. Ira, Goldie, and her parents each took a turn welcoming him. And then he saw the children.

"Sammy! Wow, you've gotten tall. And you, Myra! You're even more beautiful than the last time I saw you."

They laughed and hugged him. He felt a tug on his shirtsleeve and turned to see Lily staring up at him. He knelt down and looked into her eyes, afraid she wouldn't remember him.

"Eli!" She was still tugging his sleeve. "See? I lost it yesterday." She grinned and pushed her lower teeth at him. There, in the center, was a gap.

"Wow, Lily. That's incredible. Can I have a hug?"

She wrapped her little arms around his neck and squeezed him quickly before running to Ada. When Eli stood, Tony and Mae met him; they had taken longer than the others to reach them. Eli was shocked at how frail Mae looked, but he was careful to hide his surprise. After hugging her gently, he took her arm and helped her walk back to the fire, followed by the rest of the group.

They shared a lively supper, full of welcomed conversation. Later, Jed and Ira helped the young couple settle into their old vardo. When Eli and Ada had moved away, the merchants started using the space for extra storage. Soon, heat was crackling from the small woodstove, and Ada was fluffing pillows and spreading blankets onto the bed.

After they were finished unpacking, they joined the group by the fire and continued to chat as the night grew long. Bedtime had come and gone, yet another log managed to find its way onto the flames; the visit was long overdue. Before Eli was ready for the night to be over, the fire died down and the conversation ebbed.

"So, are you up for some fishing in the morning?" Jed asked him.

"I was counting on it," he replied.

The group rose and shared another round of hugs as they drifted to their beds.

Chapter 43
ADA

Ada knelt among the roots of the large willow tree and brushed dried leaves off the piece of wood nailed to its trunk. Though weather-beaten and faded, she could still see Ruth Ann's name carved into it. It was the headboard Eli had made, marking their baby's grave. She and Eli would visit the tree together before they went back to East Haven, but this morning she wanted to be alone. When Eli left to go fishing with Jed, she walked to the willow tree in the orange glow of the sunrise.

The caravan had been so supportive during that difficult time; it would have been hard to get through it without them. Jed and Ira met with Mrs. Perry right after Ruth Ann had died and told the widow what had happened. She insisted they take time to mourn the loss. She told the men not to work her fields for at least a week and attend to the young couple instead. Her other workers could manage the planting season without them. She then offered the old willow tree as a place to lay the baby to rest.

Tony gave one of his most intricately designed boxes to put her tiny remains in. Rosa lined it and covered Ruth Ann with some of her mother's embroidered handkerchiefs. She looked so peaceful, as though she were only sleeping.

By the third morning, Ada felt strong enough to walk with the caravan to the tree. Eli and Jed stood on either side of her to offer a hand if needed. But whether she needed the support or not, Eli never let go of her arm. Rosa followed behind, carrying the box for the young couple.

When they reached the tree, the widow's hired men were working in the fields. One of them walked Mrs. Perry up the hill to meet the grieving parents. He carried a shovel and began to dig a hole at the base of the tree. The widow took Ada's hand in hers and told her how sorry she was for their loss. She then turned to Eli and hugged him. He thanked her quietly.

Ada smiled through her tears as she remembered Ira leading them in a prayer. The workers came to the edge of the field and stood with their hats in their hands. They lowered their heads for the duration of the burial. Ada was moved by their show of respect. It was a good funeral—simple but full of love and support.

Rosa had once said that these memories would never be void of sadness, and that was so true. But she also said there would be joy in them. At the time, Ada didn't believe her. Rosa had urged them to find some small happiness while holding Ruth Ann. Though she tried, Ada still couldn't find any joy in that memory; it felt more like a constant ache in her heart that varied only by waves of intensity.

Now, three years later, she understood what Rosa was trying to say. She could finally feel the bitter sweetness of those days, but not in the way Rosa had suggested. The peace in her soul came from the Savior, and her joyful memories centered on the people He had put into her life. They had walked that journey with her, and despite everything she had ever lost, she felt more than blessed because of them.

Chapter 44

ELI

E li could feel the gentle tug of the river on his line. He and Jed stood on the bank of Badger Creek in the dim early morning, not caring if they caught anything. They were simply enjoying each other's company.

Jed turned toward him. "How have you two been doing? Are you settling into that town all right?"

"We're doing okay." Eli watched the moving waters. "We've made a few friends, but some people still don't... Well, you know how it is. A town like that will always be uncomfortable with someone like me."

"Yeah, I get it," Jed replied. "Speaking of that, you might lose some ink when the cut on your arm heals. I can touch it up for you the next time you visit."

Eli turned his arm to look at the injury. A piece of glass had sliced through one of the vines on his tattoo.

"I got this during the fire I told you about. It really shook Ada up. Our neighbors' boy was trapped in the house. He would have died if..." Eli sighed, shaking his head. "Anyway, it brought back memories of losing Ruth Ann. It'll be good for her to be here."

"And what about you?"

Eli looked at him with a question in his eyes.

"I'm just wondering if you've found what you're looking for in that town," Jed clarified. "I want to know if you're ever coming back home. I get the feeling this visit was for Ada, not you."

The pang of guilt resurfaced and clutched at Eli's gut. He looked at the ground but kept silent.

"Eli, you've been searching for as long as I've known you. Most of the others think you took Ada away so the two of you could heal, and I'm sure that's part of it. But it isn't the only reason why you left. You told me about your dream a long time ago—the one about the crops. I know you're trying to figure out what it means. I'm asking if you've found what you're seeking. Have you discovered what you think you're supposed to be doing?"

Eli sat on the ground and Jed joined him. "You and I both know what I'm supposed to be doing," Eli said as he wedged his pole between two rocks and scratched at a pebble in the dirt. "What I don't know is how God wants me to do it."

"Well, there's definitely some truth in that," Jed agreed. "What you're supposed to do—what we're *all* supposed to do—is glorify God. That's our purpose. How we do it is something we all have to figure out for ourselves. But I can tell you one thing. The best way to glorify God is to put Him before everything else in your life, Him and nothing else. Anything you choose to do in life—anything you choose to do with what God has given you—do it all for Him. If you do that on a daily basis, even while you're still searching, then you will be fulfilling your purpose."

Eli nodded. "But you know what I mean, Jed. You know what else I'm trying to figure out. I want God to show me what I'm supposed to do with it all. I don't understand why He's so quiet now."

"Maybe He doesn't want to show you yet, or you're not ready to know." Jed jabbed him with his elbow. "Maybe you aren't listening the way you should."

"I *am* listening." Eli flung a small rock at a sapling near the edge of the water.

"Listening and searching are not the same," Jed pointed out. "God wants to see that you're listening, not just hear you say you are. Sure, we both know what gifts He's given you, but you're still holding onto something, Eli. You need to let go of it and sit back and be still. Sometimes God's answer comes in pieces. He gives you the part you're ready for and holds the rest back. Don't expect it too soon. You'll be the one who gets frustrated, not God. He's more patient than you. He can still work through you if He wants to, even if you fight against Him the whole time. Don't forget—you're the one who needs Him, not the other way around."

Eli nodded again and dropped his shoulders. "Okay. I know I'm stubborn. I'm just anxious to start doing something. Waiting is hard."

"I know it is, but it sounds to me like God has already brought you something to do. Focus on helping your neighbors through their ordeal. Maybe it will calm your spirit."

He put a hand on Eli's shoulder. A fish tugged at Jed's line, and he grabbed his pole tighter.

"Ha! I got the first one. See if you can catch up to me, now."

Chapter 45

MARCUS

It was Saturday afternoon and tomorrow's sermon was ready, but Marcus felt restless. Something still needed to be done, but since he couldn't think of what it might be, he decided to go for a walk. If a brisk stroll could help him write his sermons, then perhaps it could help him figure out what he was forgetting. He bundled up against the late November air, kissed Grace, and headed out the door.

As he turned toward the backcountry roads, he sifted through a mental list of his parishioners. A few of them were going through some big life changes, and he made sure he was always there for them. But maybe he had missed something. He intended to walk until he figured it out.

Could it be Jacob and Laura Martin? They seemed to be doing well, despite Jacob's recent mishap. His leg had healed, and he was able to get around using his cane and a wooden peg strapped to his ankle, but it slowed him down. He told Marcus that he was hoping to get a prosthetic foot. He needed to save up for it, though, and wasn't ready to tell Laura about his plan yet. Saving the money would take a while, especially now that she was expecting a baby in May. Marcus congratulated him and promised not to say anything to Laura until Jacob did. No, the Martins were not the source of his restlessness.

What about Evelyn Russell? Her son had been released from prison a month ago. He wrote to her about the possibility of moving back home, and though some people in town would oppose this plan, none of them knew yet. His return to East Haven wasn't a certainty anyway; that couldn't be it either.

Perhaps his unrest had to do with Louise Evans. Two Sundays ago, she asked Marcus if he and Grace could take her home. After a short visit in her parlor, Mrs. Evans asked him for some advice. She had been contacted by a Mr. Dixon from the White Falls bank. He claimed that her husband had taken out a loan shortly before he had passed away. Well, she had no idea this loan existed, nor had any idea why he would do such a thing. No payments had been made toward the loan for three years, and now Mr. Dixon insisted she pay it in full by the beginning of the year, or she would lose her house and land.

She had resigned herself to losing her home, but she was worried that this would alter the town's opinion of George. He wasn't alive to defend himself, and the thought of anyone speaking poorly of him broke her heart. She was hoping Marcus could help her move into a different situation without ruining the reputation of her late husband. It would need to be affordable, though, since she had very little to live on.

"I'll do my best to think of something," he told her. "Perhaps I could talk to Mr. Dixon and see if he will give you more time."

"Thank you, Pastor Duncan," she said with a sigh.

"In the meantime, is there anything you could sell to help with your expenses? What about George's tools? I know it'll be hard to see them go, but he has some nice ones. You could sell them for a decent price if you're willing."

"Oh, I can't do that," she said. "I gave those tools to Eli Gardner."

Marcus was surprised. "Eli has George's tools?" Why would Eli allow her to do that? Surely, he knew their value.

"Well… not exactly," she explained. "He asked if he could keep them here and use them while he works on the repairs around my house."

"I see," Marcus said, nodding. "I'll explain the situation. I'm sure he won't mind if you sell them."

"No, no. Please don't do that. He has worked so hard for me. And if you tell him, he'll know about the loan. I can't do that to George. Please, Pastor. We must think of something else."

"Okay. I'll give it some thought. Don't worry, Mrs. Evans. I'll come up with a plan."

The widow thanked him. She seemed relieved now, knowing he would help her. That week, Marcus rode out to White Falls and confirmed that there was indeed a loan, but Mr. Dixon wouldn't give her more than an extra month to come up with the money; by February, it must be paid. So, yes, Louise Evans would need his help soon, but that wasn't what was eluding him.

Isaac and Hannah Weber had recently moved into their new home. Now that they were settled, Marcus no longer needed to worry about them. The rebuild had been a fast project, and it wasn't without its moments of stress. Eli, who had signed up to help every day, came to see Marcus a few hours after the meeting. He had decided to leave town for a while. He wanted to take Ada home to see their family and planned to be away for about ten days. He would not be able to help with the cleanup after all.

Eli thought it might be good for the Webers to continue living in his house while he and Ada were gone. That way, they wouldn't feel as though they were being a burden. By the time the Gardners returned, the Webers would feel comfortable enough to stay for as long as they needed. Marcus agreed and assured him that the men could handle the cleanup without him.

Of course, John Miller did not miss the fact that Eli was absent; he wasn't at all surprised to hear how "that boy" had gone back on his word. He failed to notice, however, that Eli worked on the house every day after his return. It didn't matter how much Marcus tried to defend Eli. John saw what John wanted to see, and he didn't see anything wrong with trying to goad the young man into a fight.

It seemed as though John would throw around snide comments intended to push Eli to the point of swinging his fist, and thus show everyone some flaw in his character. But Eli held his ground and kept his frustrations to himself. There were times when Marcus feared John might succeed, so he was relieved when the house was finished and those two were finally separated, except on Sundays when everyone was better behaved.

"You know, Pastor," John said to him once, "that gypsy boy has bewitched you. I want to be there when you finally figure out he is not the man you think he is. I hope you're not too disillusioned when you see what kind of person he really is."

"John," Marcus said, "maybe you'll be the one who sees Eli differently someday."

As Marcus thought about all these events, his walk took him down the road that passed in front of the Gardners' home. He stopped at their gate. There was something different about Eli these days. It was a subtle change, but Marcus noticed it. The young man was not as talkative as he used to be. Even though Eli was a confident man, Marcus had sensed something slightly guarded in his manner from the first day they met. But since returning to town, there was a shift in Eli's attitude. He was still guarded, but his lack of humor seemed to reflect an internal struggle with whatever he was hiding.

Grace had noticed it too, but she was convinced it was something else. She thought Eli spent too much time helping the Webers, and perhaps it was hurting the young couple. He hadn't worked for Ray Larson in two months, and that couldn't be good for them.

Marcus pushed the gate open and walked toward the house. He finally realized what had escaped his notice. There was a question he needed to ask Eli.

Chapter 46

JED

As Jed watched the wagon depart, he wondered when he would see the young couple again. This day was inevitable; it had been a hard year, and every moment of it pointed to right now. After Ruth Ann had died, the devastated parents didn't want to go to the markets with the rest of the caravan. Jed and Rosa chose to stay with them at the winter camp. It was important to be with Eli and Ada as they grieved, and Jed couldn't imagine leaving them, even for a few days. That summer they shed several tears, offered up many prayers, and talked through hard emotions.

In July, Ada asked Jed to add a small flower to her tattoo. She wanted a memorial to Ruth Ann. While Jed pricked the flower onto her arm, her eyes drifted off, and she commented to Eli that she could barely feel it. As August hinted at the end of summer, the couple's energy and mood began to rise. Eli played his guitar more often, and they shared frequent smiles with each other. By the end of the month, the couple had recovered a small bit of their playful spirit. However, losing a child had forced them to grow up even more than when they had lost their parents.

Though they regained their happiness, they stopped making merchandise for the markets. When the others returned in the fall, the young couple still helped with group projects. Eli went hunting and fishing with the men and helped them smoke the meat and prepare the leather. Ada helped with the canning, but neither worked on their toys anymore. Instead, Eli worked for Mrs. Perry every chance he could, and she gladly found extra jobs for him to do. Jed sensed a growing restlessness in him.

When April came around again, there was a dip in their moods as they remembered all the losses this month had brought them over the years. Shortly after that, Eli started going into Bradford more often. Jed knew he was meeting with Harold Ross, the town's bank owner, during those visits, but Eli wouldn't talk about it. Jed wasn't surprised when Eli finally told him and Rosa of his plan to buy a house.

By the time the caravan was ready to leave for the markets again, Eli and Ada began to visit towns in the opposite direction. Jed and Rosa stayed behind once again, promising to catch up with the others when they knew the young couple was finally settled. It only took three trips into three towns for the young couple to return with success. They had found the perfect house and would be moving right away.

Jed and Rosa helped them pack the wagon. They closed up the young couple's vacant vardo and rode into Bradford together. Once in town, Eli bought a used hitch wagon and a couple of horses. They also purchased a few pieces of furniture and some dishes.

After loading the new wagon, there was a flurry of goodbyes, and soon Eli and Ada were riding away from their days with the caravan and moving toward their next chapter. It was a difficult year, but it was the fastest one Jed had ever experienced. He sat in the wagon seat with Rosa and sighed as he watched them go.

"I told you those kids would run off some day," he said, clearing his throat.

Rosa held his hand and leaned her head on his shoulder. "They'll be back, Jed, at least for visits," she promised, attempting to comfort him.

"Yeah, but I'm not ready for them to go," he said, struggling to get his words out.

"We may never be ready for that," Rosa agreed.

Jed's eyes lingered on the road until he couldn't see the wagon anymore.

Chapter 47

ELI

There was a knock at the door. Eli opened it to find the pastor standing on his porch, shivering.

"Hey, Marcus. Come on in. You look like you could use a few minutes in front of the fire."

He led the pastor to the parlor chairs. Ada stood and gave up her seat. She offered to make them some coffee and went into the kitchen. As Marcus sat down, Eli put another log on the fire. He enjoyed visiting with Marcus, but the man's lack of smile told him this was not a casual call.

He sat in the other chair, and they talked about nothing important while Ada made their drinks. After she placed a tray on the table between them, Eli winked at her and nodded his head toward the other room; the men needed to talk privately.

"If you'll excuse me, Marcus, I need to get a few things done in the kitchen," she said.

"Of course." He stood and thanked her for the coffee.

Eli leaned back in his chair and waited until Ada was gone. "So, what brings you to my door, Marcus?"

The pastor sighed as he sat back down. Eli could see that he wasn't looking forward to the conversation.

"I want to make sure you and Ada are doing all right," he said after a short pause.

"Yeah," Eli answered with a half-nod. "We're fine."

"You can talk to me about anything," Marcus assured him. He sipped his coffee, obviously waiting for a response, and then continued speaking when Eli only nodded. "I know you haven't been working for Ray lately; you've spent two months helping the Webers instead. I need to know you're okay."

"We're fine, Marcus," he repeated, but the pastor pressed on.

"I hope you know you can trust me, Eli. People tell me things they aren't ready for others to know. It's part of my job to listen."

Eli studied the man sitting across from him and slowly leaned forward in his chair. "I promise I'll come to you if I ever need help."

"Fine," Marcus said. He shook his head and frowned. "It's just that I... Look, Eli. I need you to understand that a lot of people come to me when they're in trouble."

"What are you getting at?" Eli asked.

Marcus shifted in his seat. "Was it you?"

Eli shook his head, puzzled by his inquiry.

Marcus sighed. "The money. I need to know if it was you who gave it to the Webers."

Eli leaned back in his chair, crossed his arms, and stared at his friend for a long moment.

"Why would you ask me that, Marcus?"

"Because you didn't react the way the rest of the men did at the meeting. When I told everyone about the money, they were all surprised except for David, who had just told me about it. And you."

When Eli remained silent, the pastor's resolve seemed to falter. Eli exhaled slowly.

"That isn't what I meant. Why do you need to know who gave the money to Isaac?"

Marcus dropped his shoulders in defeat. "I'm sorry. I shouldn't have sprung my question on you like that. I need to know because one of the widows is in trouble. She's having a problem with a loan her husband took out before he died, and she might lose her house. I have to find a way to help her." Marcus glanced at the ground. "I just thought if I could figure out who gave the money to the Webers—and to Jacob Martin, for that matter—maybe there would be something left to help her." He looked up again. "I was just trying to avoid taking up another collection. She doesn't want anyone to know about it, but I don't see any other way. Maybe I can go to a few people privately and ask if they can help."

"I don't think you should," Eli said. "Louise Evans is the only widow whose husband has died recently enough for a defaulted loan to be a problem. If I can figure that out, so can others."

"I don't know what else to do," Marcus said, shaking his head. The men sat in silence.

"I do," Eli said after a pause. "I can help her. I did give the money to the Webers and to Jacob. I'll help Mrs. Evans pay her husband's loan." Eli leaned forward and peered closely at the pastor. "But you better be as discreet as you claim to be, Marcus. I don't want *anyone* to know it's me."

PART 3

But let him ask in faith, with no doubting, for he who doubts is like a wave of the sea driven and tossed by the wind.

James 1:6

Chapter 48

ELI

Eli stood in David Holden's office, holding his account information. This conversation needed to happen, but now that it was here, he hesitated. David handed him the house key.

"Here you go, Mr. Gardner," he said. "I should let you know; I've already unlocked your house. A few of the townsfolk are giving it a good wipe down. It should be ready for your arrival."

"Thank you; I appreciate it. But I thought we agreed to use our first names."

David gave him a relieved smile. "We did. I'm glad you remembered, Eli. I prefer being informal, but I don't often get the chance. When it comes to money, most people expect me to use their proper titles. I suppose it makes them feel as though their accounts are more secure." He laughed. "Speaking of accounts, I assume that's your ledger from Harold Ross."

Eli glanced down at the leather document folder in his hand and brought it closer to his chest.

"David," he said with a slight furrow on his brow. "When I decided to buy my wife a house, I asked Mr. Ross to recommend some towns with good banks owned by decent men. You were at the top of his list. He told me that you run your bank honestly and efficiently. He also said you know how to be discreet."

He continued to hold onto his paperwork. "I would like to know if he was right. I already come into this town with a disadvantage. I know what

179

people will think of me, and I know what I'm asking my wife to endure by moving here. I don't want to give the town any more reason to judge me."

"I understand your concern," David said with a nod. "I assure you, Eli, I take the privacy of your finances very seriously. I am bound by law; I cannot discuss your account with anyone unless I have your written permission. Even so, it's an ethical issue for me as well. You can trust me. And I'd be more than happy to give any financial advice you need. I've helped many people settle their debts and work their way out of poverty in the thirty years I've been doing this. Sometimes it takes a while, but if you're willing to follow my guidance, you'll be amazed at what can be done with a little discipline."

Eli held onto his account information for a moment longer before stepping closer to David's desk and handing it to him. David sat and motioned Eli to take the chair across from him. He opened the folder and scanned the information written on the ledgers. Eli watched his eyes move from one paper to another, and then back again. After a pause, he looked up and shook his head.

"I have to admit, this is not what I was expecting."

"I figured as much," Eli responded.

David seemed to carefully consider his next words. "Please don't take this the wrong way; I'm simply trying to make sense of what I'm looking at. I got the impression you were just a tradesman."

"I do have a trade," Eli said. "Woodworking. Ada and I spent the last six years living with a traveling merchant caravan. I sold carved goods." Eli chuckled. "And toys."

"Well, I think I need to change my profession then," David said with a shake of his head. "But I'm guessing that isn't where a majority of your money comes from."

"No," Eli admitted. "I've done a bit of investing during those years as well."

"A bit…" the banker repeated. "I'd like to know your secret."

"I don't really have one," Eli insisted. He tried to think of the easiest way to explain his experience. "Some investments just feel right, and others don't." He shook his head. "Please don't repeat that to Mr. Ross. He spent almost six years teaching me everything he knows. I doubt he'd want to hear it all summed up like that."

"You're probably right," David agreed with a chuckle. "I won't say a word. So, I see you have two accounts. I can combine these if you'd like."

"No. I don't want those accounts to mix."

"Are you sure? Having one account is easier."

"I have my reasons. I'll pull our living expenses from the smaller one and…"

Eli stopped speaking when David began to chortle. He cast a questioning look at the banker.

"Sorry," David said, "but I hope you realize your use of the word 'smaller' is only relative to your other account."

Eli remained silent. When it came to his banking business, his usual relaxed humor was replaced with a more serious demeanor. David apparently got the message.

"And the bigger account?" he prompted more professionally.

"That one isn't mine." Eli leaned back in his chair and looked past the banker, deep in thought. "That account belongs to God."

"Okay," David said, nodding. "And what's the plan for God's money?"

Eli shrugged. "I don't know; I'm still not sure how I'm supposed to use it. He hasn't shown me yet." He looked at David. "But whatever it is, I think it's going to be big. See there?" He pointed at the additional papers in the stack. "I have a lot of active investments and they're all growing."

David picked through the papers as he dug into the pile. "So…" he said as a captivated expression spread over his face. "What are you doing for lunch tomorrow?"

Chapter 49

MARCUS

The late November wind blew crunchy leaves down the street. Marcus stepped into the inviting warmth of the bank and glanced around. Daniel stood at the counter, copying figures into a book. He shifted his attention to Marcus.

"Good morning, Pastor Duncan. Are you looking for my father?"

Marcus nodded. "Yes, thank you. Is he in?"

Daniel gestured toward a door behind him. "He's in his office. You can go right in; he's expecting you."

Marcus thanked the young man again and walked toward the door. As he entered the office, he found David sitting at his desk and talking with Eli. David stood and gestured to the empty chair.

"Have a seat, Marcus."

After they shook hands, Marcus took off his coat and hung it on a coat rack before sitting down. David went to the small woodstove in the corner of the room, put a thick piece of wood into it, and rejoined the other two.

"So, Eli was just telling me about the situation Mrs. Evans finds herself in. Were you able to get any more details?"

Marcus nodded and handed him some paperwork from the White Falls bank. David shook his head as he skimmed over the papers.

"What were you thinking, George?" he said under his breath. "You know, he came to me earlier that year and asked about a loan. I told him it wasn't a good idea. I guess he didn't like my answer." He glanced up.

"Do we know where the money from this loan ended up? It's not in their account."

"No, we don't," Marcus said. "Louise didn't know about the loan until she was contacted a few weeks ago. If George took out the loan from a different bank, I wouldn't be surprised if he had an account somewhere else as well, but it isn't with Mr. Dixon in White Falls."

"This is all very odd," David said. "It doesn't seem like George. He must have been getting confused in his old age. We have to assume that the money is lost." He glanced at the papers again. "Three years of interest… If this had been caught earlier, her house might not be in danger. I've never been impressed with the way Mr. Dixon runs his bank over there."

He handed the papers to Eli, who began reading the information. Marcus was still trying to get used to the idea that this young man could help. He had no idea how much money Eli had, and that worried him. What if he was asking too much? Eli was generous enough to give away everything, and since he and Ada lived so simply, it wouldn't be surprising if he gave until it hurt.

"Are you sure you can do this?" Marcus asked, trying to offer his friend a way out.

Eli nodded dismissively as he continued to look over the paperwork. Then he looked up at David.

"Can you make sure this is paid without my name attached to it?"

"Of course," David said. "The easiest way would be to move the money into the church account and pay it from there. How do you feel about that, Marcus?"

Marcus shrugged and gave his consent.

"Okay, then," David continued. "I can get this all wrapped up in a few days and Louise can forget there was ever a debt." He turned to Eli. "Shall we handle it the same way as before?"

"Yeah, let's use the smaller one," Eli said, nodding.

Marcus wondered what that meant. He was about to ask, but Eli continued to speak.

"David, this loan might be taken care of, but will Mrs. Evans still be struggling? I suspect she doesn't always have as much money as she needs."

David looked at Eli with a straight face. "I'm sorry, friend. You know I can't give you that information. You get to know details about the loan because you're settling it, but I don't have permission to tell you anything beyond that. And I can't ask for it without revealing your involvement."

Marcus could see the wheels turning behind Eli's eyes as he considered the banker's words. He wasn't going to accept David's answer.

"Marcus," he asked, still peering steadily at David. "East Haven has three widows, correct?"

"That's right."

"Would you say they all have enough money to live on?"

"I would say—generally speaking—most widows don't," Marcus answered carefully.

Eli directed his next question back to David. "And do you know what a yearly income for a widow should be?"

David barely had time to nod before Eli added, "So, if you were to compare that amount to what each of the widows actually has, you could add up those deficits."

David continued to nod. "Yes, but—"

"Then I suggest you have that amount in mind when you advise me on how much I should deposit into the East Haven Widows' Fund."

"The East Haven Widows' Fund?" David asked.

"Yes," Eli said with a decisive nod. "And I'm sure it's part of the pastor's job to inform his parishioners when they're the beneficiary of a fund like that. Especially if the fund is set up with the church as the trustee. Am I right, Marcus?"

"Uh... yes. That's correct," Marcus answered as he grinned at David.

The banker shook his head and started to chuckle. "Okay," he said, "let's set this up." He opened one of his desk drawers and pulled out some forms.

As David began to write up the funding terms, Marcus marveled at how well Eli had orchestrated the scene as it played out. He had never seen this side of his friend before; he was impressed with Eli's grasp on financial matters and his fast thinking.

"Promise me you won't get yourself into trouble by giving away too much," he pleaded, still wrestling with his earlier concern.

A grin spread over Eli's face, and he laughed as though he had heard a good joke.

"I promise," he said as he clasped Marcus on the shoulder.

The men turned their attention back to the paperwork in front of David. The fire crackled in the woodstove, drowning out the sound of the crisp autumn wind.

Chapter 50

ELI

Eli stood a few paces away from Jed on the rocky bank of Badger Creek. It was a cold morning in late September, but the wool sweater from the wooden chest kept him warm. He cast his line out to the center of the stream, but his thoughts were not on fishing. Jed was talking about staying at the winter camp through the summer. He suggested it would give them more time to finish construction on the vardo. As excited as Eli was to build their home, even this conversation couldn't pull his mind away from what lay hidden in the bottom of his canvas bag. And what was in the bag reminded him of the horrible things that had happened less than six months earlier.

"Are you okay?" Jed asked. "It seems like you have something on your mind."

"I was thinking about something Ira said on Sunday," Eli admitted. "Do you think all those bad things happened to us because God wanted them to, so He could use them somehow? God can do anything, right? Then why does He need the bad stuff?"

Jed sighed. He paused for a moment, and then proceeded to explain the difference between man's sinful choices and God's ability to use evil for good, but the whole subject made Eli's gut twist into a knot. Whatever good thing God was going to do, didn't feel good right now.

"…can you see the difference, Eli?"

"I guess," he said.

Eli felt the knot tighten as he remembered what those men had done to their parents. As the scene replayed in his mind, he blinked back angry tears, trying not to imagine what kind of life he and Ada might have had if they hadn't escaped.

"It's just hard to believe anything good can come from what happened to us."

"I know," Jed agreed, "but faith is a hope in things you can't see. The trials God allows in our lives cause us to grow and mature…"

Jed went on to explain that Eli also had a choice. He could remain bitter and angry, or he could trust that God was going to do a good work in him. Jed's words stirred up a memory from his dream: *"Eli, tend my crops."*

He knew God wanted him to do something; he felt a conviction deep in his heart. He even had Jed cover his marks with a tattoo that would always remind him of that calling. Maybe God planned to use Eli because of those bad things; maybe that was the good that could come out of everything that happened. Eli locked onto that thought and held fast to the idea. The only problem was that he didn't know what he was being called to do. What if he couldn't do it well? What if he wasn't good enough?

Jed continued to speak. "…every good and perfect gift is from above, coming down from the Father who doesn't ever change. That means we can always trust in God's plan for our life, even when bad things happen."

Eli nodded as he took in everything Jed was saying. "So, God can use the bad things to do good things through me? But… What if I can't let go of my anger?"

Eli didn't know if he would ever be able to do that; he felt so angry. How could he just let it go? And along with his anger came a hatred for what was hiding in his bag. He was sure there was nothing good about that.

Jed pointed at a logjam near the far end of the stream and compared it to anger and unforgiveness. Eli remained silent as he continued to gaze out over the water. Jed was right; his anger made him feel all jammed up inside. He wanted God's goodness to be in him; he longed for His purpose. Eli wanted to do whatever was asked of him, but he knew he wouldn't be able to do it well unless he could let go of his resentment.

In order to do that, he would need to get rid of what he had been carrying in his bag for all these months. He realized he couldn't do whatever he wanted with it; he would need to handle it in the right way. Up until now, Eli had only trusted Jed to a certain point, but this morning, he decided to trust him with everything.

"Jed, I need to tell you something," he said. "I need your help. I have something I don't think I should have."

As the man looked at him with compassion in his eyes, Eli knew he was doing the right thing. Even so, he was still scared.

"You can tell me anything, Eli; we can figure it out together," Jed promised.

Eli tried to gather his courage but shook his head. "No, I need to show you." He began to pull in his line. They wouldn't be catching any fish today.

Chapter 51
JED

Jed knelt next to the wooden chest in the young couple's tent and watched Eli dig through its contents. What could cause so much fear and hesitation in the boy? Eli pulled a canvas bag out of the chest and set it on his lap. It was the same bag he had been carrying when he ran into Jed's vardo as the caravan was preparing to leave Ashbrook back in June. Jed never noticed it again after they had reached Clackton, and he had forgotten all about it. Seeing it now reminded him of the stubborn way Eli had held onto it, refusing to let it out of his sight.

After the wedding ceremony, Jed had found the bag sitting against a tree. The boy must have set it there when he took his bath. In all the excitement, it had been forgotten, and whoever emptied the tub had failed to see it. The bag was left where it was. It might still be there to this day if Jed hadn't stumbled upon it in the twilight. He put it in the newlyweds' makeshift tent, and now—nearly four months later—he was looking at it once more as Eli held it reluctantly between his knees.

"When Ada and I were locked in those cages," he began, "there were usually four or five men who never left the rock quarry, but only one of them held the key. I know this because he always let in the man who marked up Ada's arm each night. I think it was his job to be our guard. Even though there were others, the man with the key was the only one who stayed close to us the whole time. The rest of them sat at a distance and played cards."

Eli paused briefly. His hands seemed to have a mind of their own as his grip on the bag repeatedly squeezed and relaxed.

"He would stand outside Ada's cage and stare at her. He said awful things that made her cry. That's how I found out those numbers on her arm were bids. He told her she brought in higher bids than he had ever seen before. He said the men who bid on her were willing to pay a high price for an 'untouched' souvenir from their travels to our country. Whoever won the bid would be able to show off his wealth by parading her around, and he could loan her out—over and over—to barter for more power and loyalty."

Jed could hear disgust in the boy's voice; he felt it too. What had happened to these kids was unimaginable. Eli proceeded to relay more of their story.

"I hated listening to that man's voice and seeing how his words upset Ada, but every time he focused on her and ignored me, I was able to work loose one of the bars. Then one morning, all the men except for him left the quarry. He seemed anxious, and after a while, he left too."

Eli fidgeted with the straps as he spoke. "He was only gone for a moment. He walked away to where I couldn't see him, but he was banging things around and making a lot of noise, so I knew he was still somewhere in the cavern. While he wasn't guarding us, I broke the bar completely free. I had to hold it in place when he came back. I thought he would notice, but he was distracted and kept looking around like he was nervous."

Eli indicated the bag in front of him. "He had this when he returned and began stuffing clothes and food into it. He seemed to be in a hurry, but then he stopped in front of Ada's cage and said things that made her cry even more. I didn't hear what he said because I wasn't really listening. I knew I had to make my move while he was looking away."

The boy kept his eyes locked on the bag. "I pulled the bar out, slipped through the space, and came up behind him. I hit him hard over the head and knocked him out. I found the key to Ada's cage, and we took the bag and ran until we reached the edge of the woods. That's how we got away."

Jed listened closely to the details of their escape. Eli finally looked up at him.

"We never stayed in one place for more than a few days. It didn't take long to eat all the food in the bag, and the clothes turned out to be more important anyway. We layered them to keep warm; I think it kept us from freezing those first nights. I took that man's knife also, and I used it to hunt for food."

When Eli paused, Jed nodded, encouraging him to go on.

"After several days, we found an old shack. I thought we would be safe there; I even thought we could hide in it for a long time. While there, I dumped out the bag to make sure there wasn't any more food, but I found something that made me realize we weren't safe at all. We had to keep moving."

Eli opened the bag and dug down to the bottom. He pulled out a leather satchel and handed it over. Jed untied the cord on its front and opened it. Inside the satchel, he found a stack of banknotes. He had never seen that much money before and wondered about the amount. As though Eli could read his thoughts, he continued to speak.

"I counted it. It's the same as the last bid on Ada's arm. Jed, I think these were going to pay for her." The boy looked down again and wiped at his eyes and nose. "I don't know what I should do. Do you think they can find us if I still have these? I thought about burning them. Our parents died for this, and I almost lost Ada because of them. I don't want to keep them with me anymore, but I don't want to leave them for just anyone to find. I don't want these notes to get back to those men. Please. Help me find a way to get rid of them."

When Eli looked at him, there was a desperate plea in his eyes. Jed flipped through the banknotes, trying to think of what to do.

"What if…" he began slowly, "what if we could use these to find the people who killed your parents?"

Eli shook his head, his eyes widening. "No! I don't want to find them. I don't want those men to know where we are."

"That isn't what I meant. I just thought if we take these into Bradford, we can have the bank owner look at one of them and tell us if it can be traced back to the person who had them drawn up."

"But that wouldn't be our kidnappers; it would only be the person who was going to pay for Ada."

"But that man might know who he was paying, and that would be the men who took you." Jed could see doubt on the boy's face. "It might not work. We may not be able to find the person who this money belonged to, especially if he's not from around here. But it's worth a try, isn't it? I doubt you and Ada are the only kids these criminals have hurt. Wouldn't you like to help them as well? I know the bank owner. Mr. Ross is a good man; we can trust him. We don't need to tell him everything, only that you found the banknotes and want to see if he can find out who they belong to. Then we can decide what to do."

Eli hesitated. "Please don't let them find us."

"I won't let anyone hurt you," Jed promised. "Let's head out as soon as we're done with breakfast."

Eli finally agreed with a nod. As they climbed out of the tent, Jed tucked the leather satchel under his jacket.

Chapter 52

ELI

"Mr. Gardner, it's good to see you," Harold Ross said as he shook Jed's hand. "How was your summer? How did the markets treat you this year?" He looked at Eli and offered him a hand as well. "I don't think we've met."

Eli shook his hand timidly. In return, Mr. Ross gave his hand a firm shake, followed by a nod.

"This is Eli," Jed stated.

"I didn't realize you had a son. It's nice to meet you, Eli. What can I do for you today?"

Eli and Jed exchanged a quick glance. "Could we discuss something in your office?" Jed asked without correcting the banker.

"Of course. Follow me."

Mr. Ross ushered them into his office. After closing the door, he offered them each a chair. Jed pulled one of the banknotes out of his breast pocket and handed it to the banker as he sat down. Mr. Ross raised his eyebrows and took a seat behind his desk.

"This is a nice little treasure. Do you want to open an account?"

"My boy found it. We want to know if the owner can be located."

Eli remained silent. He felt as though he were in a daze as he listened to the men talk casually about the banknote.

"Let's see." Mr. Ross studied it closely. He looked up and shook his head, pointing at the paper. "See this here? It says, 'payable to bearer on demand.' This note isn't issued to a specific person. It can't be traced back to anyone. I believe you're stuck with it."

The bank owner tried to hand it to Eli, but he leaned back. "It's not mine. I don't want it." He looked at Jed again.

"Mr. Ross, there's the name of a bank printed right here." Jed tapped it with his finger. "Wouldn't that be the bank that issued the note? Is there any way to check with them and see if anyone has reported it missing?"

"Of course, I can check with the bank," Mr. Ross said. "But I doubt I'll find anything. Even with a good-sized note like this, I can almost promise that my inquiries will turn up empty."

"What if there were more of them?" Jed asked.

"How many more?"

As Eli's eyes moved back and forth between the two men, the room grew dim.

Jed leaned forward a bit. "Enough to make me think someone would want to report them missing."

He brought out the satchel from under his jacket and handed it to the banker. Mr. Ross looked at the banknotes and then at Eli.

"Where exactly did you find these?"

Eli took in a deep breath before answering in the calmest voice he could muster. "I found them in the woods." He hoped Mr. Ross wouldn't ask for more details. The banker was quiet. He finally glanced at Jed after thinking for a moment.

"Mr. Gardner, I'll tell you what I believe. I would wager that these notes belonged to someone with nefarious intentions. Criminals have been known to exchange money at drop points in out-of-the-way places like the woods. I think your son stumbled upon one of these drops before the person it was intended for could get to it. If that's the case, then I am one hundred percent sure that these banknotes will not have been reported missing. But if it makes you feel better, Eli, whatever crime these notes were meant for probably didn't happen because you found the money first."

Eli wondered what Mr. Ross would think if he knew how close his guess was to the truth. Jed then asked the banker the same question forming in the recesses of Eli's own mind.

"If these notes can't be traced back to their original owner, then the criminals can't trace them forward to my son either, correct?"

"Not unless they saw him take it." He turned to Eli. "They can't come after you, if that's what you're worried about."

"Could you check with the bank anyway?" Eli asked.

"But… be careful about it," Jed suggested. "Just in case."

"Sure. I'll send a telegram first thing Monday morning. If I find out anything, I'll let you know. But I'll be very surprised if I do."

"And if you don't find anyone, Mr. Ross," Eli said as his relief seemed to brighten the room, "then could you destroy them for us? They aren't worth anything without a name, right?"

Mr. Ross and Jed looked at him with surprise on their faces. Eli looked back at them innocently.

"I mean, if it isn't issued to anyone, then it's just paper, isn't it?"

"Eli, this is legal tender backed by a very stable bank. These notes are worth exactly what is written on them. If I can't find who they belonged to, then you own them. You might want to get used to the idea that you could soon be very wealthy."

Eli shook his head as that familiar weight slammed down on him once again. "I don't want criminal money."

"It's not 'criminal money' if it isn't owned by criminals," Mr. Ross pointed out. "Listen, I'll keep the notes in a security box in my vault while I look into it. But if I don't find the owner, I'm going to open an account for you. Agreed?" He didn't wait for an answer. He peered over at Jed. "Do you want the box assigned to you?"

"Nope. Eli found the money. If you can't trace it, then it's all his."

Eli fell back into a daze as Mr. Ross filled out the papers for the security box. This was not how he imagined the day going. But at least the notes were now in the bank and not with him. Maybe he could simply forget about them. If he didn't see them, he didn't have to think about them.

"Check back with me in two weeks, Mr. Gardner. I should know something by then."

Harold Ross shook hands with them as they left the building.

"Well, let's get the lumber for your vardo," Jed suggested.

Eli had almost forgotten the other reason they were in town. He nodded and forced a weak smile. Building the vardo was something he could allow himself to think about. As the buzzing numbness in his head began to fade, he climbed into the wagon and willfully pushed all thoughts of banknotes and criminals out of his mind.

Chapter 53

ADA & LAURA

Ada wanted to get to Jacob and Laura's house as fast as possible. She held onto Eli's hand and tried not to pull him, but she was having trouble holding herself back. He stopped walking, which forced her to stop as well. She glanced at him impatiently but checked herself when she noticed his face; his eyebrows were raised, and he wasn't smiling.

"Ada, you need to calm down before we get there," he said. "If you don't, you'll only add to their anxiety. They may not even want visitors so soon after having the baby. I know you're worried, but you may not get to talk to Laura today."

He was right. Why did he always have to be right about these things? She sighed and closed her eyes.

"Mrs. Russell spoke with Laura's mother last night." She tried to sound as calm as she could, but there was a tremble in her voice. "Edith told her something was wrong with Laura's baby."

"I know," he said softly. "But we both know what Edith Taylor is like, so we can't rush in there with any assumptions."

Ada opened her eyes again and looked at him. "Okay, Eli. But can we please try to see them?" She blinked back a tear.

He nodded, pulling her into a warm hug. When he let go of her, they continued walking to the Martins' home at a more relaxed pace.

Jacob must have seen them coming. When they arrived at the door, he hobbled out of the house before they could knock. He leaned heavily on his cane, but the grin stretching across his face conveyed his relief that they were there. He grabbed onto Eli's hand and shook it wholeheartedly.

As a tiny piercing cry came from somewhere in the house, Jacob pulled them inside. Ada's eyes met a forlorn looking Laura with a red face. She sat on the sofa, holding her baby against her shoulder.

"It's a boy," she managed to say.

"Does he have a name?" Hope filled Ada's heart. Edith must have been exaggerating; the baby's cry sounded angry, but there was a healthy energy behind it.

❧

Laura shook her head. "We were going to name him Walter after Jacob's father. Now, I don't think we should; he might not want us to."

Pressing her mouth into a frown, Laura fought against her tears. She was so tired. She hadn't slept since her baby was born. Being a mother was supposed to feel better than this. She never realized how much her heart could ache from the unconditional love she felt for her child.

"Laura, you need to rest." Ada stepped closer to the sofa. "Can I hold your baby?"

"Do you really want to? Even my mother couldn't hold him for very long."

"Please. I want to hold him for you. Let me take him so you can sleep. You'll feel better after you rest."

Supporting his small head, Laura brought her baby forward and handed him to her friend.

❧

Ada reached for the newborn. He stopped crying when he moved from one set of arms to another. She cradled him lovingly and gazed into his face. His upper lip had a large gap where his skin hadn't grown together. The gap stretched up to his left nostril, and his mouth resembled a large, pink triangle.

Despite this disfigurement, his eyes were wide and full of wonder as he stared at the light coming from the door behind Ada. She closed her eyes and sighed with relief, lifting praises that this baby was healthy. He was strong and alert.

She pulled him close to her and brought his face to her neck, longing to feel his warm, soft skin against hers. She breathed in his smell as tears

196

wet her cheeks. She wasn't able to hold her baby like this. Because Ruth Ann was so small, Ada was afraid to. She hugged Laura's baby against her, savoring the weight of him.

"Oh, Laura," she whispered. "He's an angel."

❧

Laura began to sob. "He is! Ada, you're the first person who hasn't handed him right back to me. Why can't they see it too? And why do I wish he didn't look like he does?"

She covered her eyes with her hands, and her sobbing increased. "I feel so guilty. Do you think he can see it in my face? I just want him to feel loved. I know everyone will stare at him, and he'll have to grow up with that. But he can't ever believe that I might see him as others do. That would break my heart."

"Don't feel guilty for wanting the best for him," Ada said.

Laura felt a gentle squeeze on her arm. She uncovered her eyes to find her friend kneeling next to her, smiling through her own tears.

"You aren't wishing he were a different child. What you hope for is that he won't be looked at by others as though he were, but you can't control what they think or say. All you can do is make sure your son knows who he is and how much he is loved by Jesus and both of his parents. I think you should pick a name for him soon."

Laura nodded and looked at her husband. "He *is* an angel, Jacob. I want to name him Angel."

He smiled at her. "Then it's Angel."

Laura closed her eyes and laid back on the sofa. After two days, she was finally willing to sleep. She sighed, knowing there were others who loved Angel as unconditionally as she did—three other people and a great and glorious God!

Chapter 54

ELI

After Jacob lowered himself onto the porch steps facing his back yard, Eli joined him. He rested his elbows on his knees and glanced at the new father, studying his face.

"Thanks for coming over," Jacob said to him. "I'm glad Ada is taking care of the baby—I mean Angel. I don't think Laura has slept through the night for a few weeks, even before all this." He sighed and lowered his head. "I just don't know what to do."

"You might want to get some sleep too," Eli suggested.

"Maybe later. I couldn't sleep now anyway. There's got to be something I can do, right? You ever feel helpless? I hate that feeling. I just need to be doing something, you know?"

"Yeah, I know exactly what you mean. I don't think it's in a man's nature to sit still when his family is in a crisis." The men looked out at the horizon. After a long silence, Eli spoke again. "You should take Angel to White Falls in a couple of weeks. The doctor there can take a look at him and tell you if anything could be done."

Jacob let out a short, cynical laugh. "You mean in a couple of months. I have some money saved but not enough. I was going to get myself a foot." Jacob shook his head and lowered his eyes. "You know, one of those wood and metal ones shaped like the real thing so a shoe can fit on it. I heard they even have some with hinged ankles. But my priorities have shifted. The foot can wait—it doesn't seem as important anymore." He leaned forward and balanced the center of his cane on one finger.

Eli watched him for a moment, calculating his next words. "What if someone could help you? Someone who could pay for the trip to White Falls and the doctor's visit?"

"No. No charity, not again." Jacob shook his head. "I know Laura told Ada about the money that was given to us so we could get married. Did she mention it to you?"

He nodded and glanced down as Jacob continued. "It was supposed to be a secret—you know, anonymous. But I know who gave it to us."

Eli looked up in surprise and searched Jacob's face.

"Laura figured it out; she was pretty sure it was my Uncle Edgar. When she asked him, he finally admitted it."

"Mr. Johnson…" Eli said slowly. "He said he gave it to you?"

"Yeah. I mean, I appreciated it at the time. We couldn't have gotten married without it, so it really did help. But I want to be the one who takes care of my family. Everyone assumes I can't provide for Laura now that I've lost my foot, but I can. I can still work."

"Not everyone, Jacob," Eli corrected him. "Maybe some people in Laura's family think that, but not the rest of us. We see how hard you work; no one else doubts you. Right now, you're overcoming things other people don't have to deal with, and those things are coming at you, one right after another. I don't think there's any shame in accepting help when you need it. And your uncle didn't…"

He paused to rethink his words. "When you were given that money, it wasn't meant to make you feel as though you weren't providing. I'm sure it was given with compassion, not judgment. You were going through a lot back then. And now you're going through tough times again, but this involves your child."

"Well, I'm still going to take care of it myself," Jacob said with firm resolve. "Angel isn't sick. He can eat without too much trouble, so there isn't a hurry to get him to White Falls. I can still put money aside while I am paying back my uncle, just like I've been doing for the last six months. Then, when I have enough—"

"Wait… You've been paying back your uncle?" Eli asked, cutting him off.

"Sure, I insisted. I calculated how long it would take. If I work without pay for one day every week—"

"And he agreed to that?"

"It's the same thing," Jacob said. "Instead of paying me so I can turn around and give it right back to him, he just keeps it."

Eli shook his head, trying to process what Jacob was saying. It was hard enough to hear that Edgar Johnson took credit for giving the money; even so, Eli might have been willing to let it go. But allowing Jacob to pay him back? That was too much. Edgar had crossed an inexcusable line into thievery.

"That was a gift, Jacob. You shouldn't have to give it back. I wouldn't have let you." He swallowed down his anger as he chewed his lower lip.

"Gift or not, I'm paying him back anyway. I can always get a second job if I need to; I've done it before. I could put some of that income aside each week, and in a few months, I'll take Angel to see the doctor in White Falls. I'm going to be the one who takes care of my family."

Eli remained quiet. He looked out across the yard, wrestling with his thoughts. He wasn't sure what to do. Jacob deserved to know that the gift wasn't from his uncle, but Eli wasn't willing to tell him who it was really from. He didn't want anyone to know he had money. He chose not to tell Jacob or Isaac or Mrs. Evans because he didn't want them to feel obligated to repay him. It wasn't really from him anyway. The only reason he had money to give was because God had provided it. They sat on the steps for several minutes before Jacob finally spoke again.

"You know, I think I am starting to feel tired. You're right; I should lay down while I have a chance."

"Yeah, good idea," Eli said under his breath as Jacob walked into the house.

Eli stayed outside for another hour, wondering what to do with this new information about Edgar Johnson. Eventually, Ada joined him, carrying Angel in a bundle of blankets. She sat next to him and leaned against his shoulder.

"You've been out here for a while," she whispered. "I think all three of the Martins are finally asleep."

"Ada, don't go to the mercantile tomorrow."

"Oh, okay. Why not?"

"I need to go to White Falls. If you go with me, we can do our shopping there. We could make a day of it." Eli put his arm around her. "Come on. It'll be fun."

Chapter 55

HAROLD

Harold Ross stood at the counter assisting one of his customers when Jed Gardner walked into the bank. He had been hoping Jed would come in soon; he needed to speak with him.

Harold had thought about Jed's boy often during the last two weeks. He had made several inquiries about the banknotes, and just as he suspected, nothing had been reported missing. Two days ago, he filled out an account ledger in Eli's name and started the transfer process with the other bank. Now, Harold looked forward to telling Jed about an idea he had.

As he finished logging his customer's deposit into the book, Harold waved Jed over. He was fascinated by Eli's situation; it reminded him of a book he had read recently, written by an author from across the ocean. It was about a boy of little means who ended up with a large amount of money unexpectedly. But that was fiction, whereas in Eli's case—well, this was a real life rags-to-riches story playing out right in front of his eyes. Even better, Harold might get to have a hand in this story if God permitted it. Jed stepped up to the counter and nodded.

"Good morning, Mr. Gardner. I was hoping I'd see you," Harold said. "I've got some good news for you."

"Did you find the owner of the money?"

"No... I didn't."

Jed bobbed his head and sighed. "Well, at least we tried. Thank you, Mr. Ross. I appreciate the time you put into it."

"Mr. Gardner, that money is being transferred into an account for Eli. You do understand that your son is considerably well-off now, don't you?"

"I'm aware of it," Jed replied with a straight face.

"Good, because he's still young. He's going to need your help managing his money. Here's a pocket ledger for him. I took the liberty of filling in the first line. Eli can keep track of his deposits and withdrawals on this." He handed the ledger to Jed.

"Thanks."

Jed glanced at it briefly before shoving it into his pocket. Harold thought the man would have been more excited for his boy than he appeared.

"Your son isn't overly fond of this money, is he?"

Jed shook his head. "I can think of other attitudes that would be worse."

"I agree," Harold said. "But if the right attitude is fostered in him, I believe Eli could do great things. I'd like to assist you with that. You live in Oak Springs, don't you? Is your son going to school there?"

"No, he's schooled at home."

"Well, that works out perfectly then. I have a proposal for you; I'd like to set up a weekly class with Eli. I could teach him how to handle his money wisely and show him some investment strategies. I can help him use those techniques in a practical way that will cause his money to grow. More importantly, I want to teach him how to have an attitude of stewardship. You'd be welcome to sit in on the classes—in fact, I would encourage it. What do you say?"

"It sounds like a good idea, but I'd say you have your work cut out for you. Eli can be stubborn."

"Well, I like a good challenge," Harold said. "I'll pray God gives me the right words to get through to him. Let's start next week, shall we? Which day works best for you?"

"I'll need to convince Eli, but Thursday is probably a good choice."

Harold nodded. "The bank closes at three. Have Eli here every Thursday at three o'clock sharp."

"Okay, we'll be here."

The men shook hands again and Jed headed out the door. Harold smiled as he watched him leave. It looked as though he might have a small part in Eli's story after all. He was going to enjoy this.

Chapter 56
ADA

Ada was about to climb into bed, but at the last minute, she threw her shawl over her shoulders and walked to Evelyn's house. At first, she had considered going to the Webers', but their home was dark. It looked as though they had already gone to sleep. Evelyn's window, on the other hand, had a faint light shining from it. Ada tapped on Evelyn's door. Even though the early summer days were growing longer, she felt bad for disturbing the woman so late in the evening.

As she heard footsteps approaching, relief trickled into her heart. The door opened a slight crack and Evelyn's face appeared. With a furrowed brow, she pulled her door open the rest of the way.

"Ada, is everything all right?" She glanced toward the other houses.

"I'm sorry to bother you, Mrs. Russell. I saw a light in your window and hoped you might still be awake."

"I was, my dear. It seems as though I need less sleep as I get older. I was reading, but you haven't disturbed me. It's too dark anyway; the lantern isn't giving off enough light. I'm sure it isn't good for my eyes. Are you okay, child?"

"I'm all right," she said, but her face didn't convince the woman; concern remained in Evelyn's eyes. "If it isn't too much trouble, may I come in?"

"Of course. Come sit in my parlor and tell me what's troubling you." Evelyn ushered Ada inside, and they sat in the room together as the lantern cast a dim light between them.

"Eli left town this morning; he'll be gone for a week. Perhaps I'm being silly, but I haven't spent an evening without him since we were married. I'm feeling uneasy."

"Oh, I see." Evelyn's sympathy replaced her worry. "I remember the first time my husband went away. It only happened once or twice a year. It was especially hard in the first few years, but it does get easier. I'll tell you a secret, though. By the time we had been married for five years, I came to look forward to our times apart. Don't misunderstand me. I loved my husband and preferred to have him home, but a short time away from each other can be a nice break." Evelyn giggled. "And the homecoming makes the time apart worth it."

Ada realized that her neighbor still thought of them as newlyweds, but in truth, she and Eli had been married for nine years. She chose not to correct Mrs. Russell. She didn't want to explain the circumstances that led to their early marriage. Bringing up those memories while Eli was away didn't seem like a good idea.

"I think it's harder to be away from him now because tomorrow is our anniversary," she explained instead.

"I see." Evelyn nodded her head with compassion. "What was so important that it couldn't wait?"

"We received a telegram this afternoon. A good friend of ours passed away, and Eli has gone to be with her son. We decided I should stay and continue to help Laura. It's hard not to go, but she does need the help, and we'll be visiting our family in September anyway."

Ada blinked as a tear slipped down her cheek. Evelyn reached over and patted her hand.

"I'm sorry for your loss. It's hard to lose someone close to you, especially when you couldn't be with them at the end."

"Mae was like a grandmother to us," Ada said. "She was seventy-nine and lived a good life. But it won't be the same without her when we go home." She cried quietly while Evelyn continued to hold her hand.

"Ada, you told me once that it's better to cry with someone else than to cry alone. You can sit here and cry for as long as you need to."

Ada smiled and they sat together for several minutes. It felt good to be with a friend. Her tears slowed after a while, and she dabbed her eyes with a corner of her shawl.

"How's your son doing?" she finally asked. "Has he decided when he will come home and stay with you?"

"Oh, no... he won't be able to after all. At least not any time soon. He feels bad about it, but he's working on a project that could take longer than a year to get established. He promises to come home for a short visit afterwards." The woman sighed and looked down at her lap.

"I'm sorry you won't get to see him. That must be hard."

"It is," Evelyn admitted. "But he writes often, so at least I have that to look forward to. In fact, he writes to me more than my daughters do." She shook her head and huffed. "Well, don't worry about me, Ada. I have many friends, and I'll never be lonely as long as I have a thoughtful neighbor like you." She smiled and patted Ada's knee. "I think it's too warm for tea tonight, but I could get us a treat to nibble on."

After going to the pantry, Evelyn brought back a tray of goodies and the two kept each other company late into the evening. Outside, the crickets joined the conversation as they chirped at the stars in the sky.

Chapter 57

ELI

"I'm glad you're home," Ada said as she and Eli walked down the road toward the Martins' house. "I missed you."

Eli was carrying a basket full of food. If his hands had been free, he would have grabbed onto hers. Instead, he smiled and winked.

"I missed you too, but I'm glad I went. Tony appreciated the company."

"How's he doing?"

"He's having a rough time; he misses his ma. He's the only one left in his immediate family now that Mae is gone. But he has the caravan, so he'll be okay."

Ada glanced at the ground and nodded. He knew she had wanted to go with him, but it wasn't practical this time.

"It was just Tony, Levi, and Bea; the others were all at the markets. I didn't get to see anyone else. I think this is the first summer he hasn't gone with the rest of them. Levi and Bea have been a big support for him. They spent the entire time I was there sharing stories about Mae. They had known her the longest."

"Oh, I miss them all so much," she said. "I can't wait to see everyone this fall. But you were right; Laura was glad I stayed. Between Grace, Hannah, Mrs. Russell, and myself, someone was with her every day. I know she's grateful, especially when it's time to make supper. It takes her so long to feed Angel."

The cheer in Ada's voice increased as she continued. "Mrs. Russell suggested she hold him in an upright position while nursing, and it has made such a difference. He doesn't swallow nearly as much air, which means his little tummy isn't upset as often. You'll see; he doesn't cry much. I wish Jacob would accept help, though, and take him to the doctor soon. I don't think waiting is a good idea."

"Jacob is stubborn," Eli said. "But so am I, so I can't fault him for it."

A shadow darkened his eyes as he thought about Edgar Johnson. He knew he ought to tell Jacob about his uncle, but he still struggled with how.

Ada placed her hand on his elbow. "You mean like insisting we not go to Johnson's Mercantile anymore? You still haven't told me why."

"I'm sorry. I know it's hard to go to White Falls every time we need something, but I can't go into that store until I figure things out."

He was worried that talking with Jacob might expose more than just Edgar's secrets. He had a few of his own. At least his secrets didn't hurt anyone; however, his inaction did. The longer he waited, the more it hurt Jacob.

Ada moved her hand from his elbow and rubbed his lower back. "I don't mind going to White Falls, but I'll be praying for whatever you're struggling with. I hope you'll figure it out soon. I can tell it's upsetting you."

Eli smiled. He finally understood what Jed had meant all those years ago when he said he could never be as good a man as Rosa deserved. Eli felt the same about Ada. She kept her hand on his back as they walked down the street.

As soon as they arrived at the Martins', Ada would help Laura with the baby, and he would help Jacob with anything his friend needed. They would prepare a delicious meal with the food they brought, and the four of them would spend an enjoyable evening together. And through all of this, Eli would try to convince himself that he was still a good friend—despite not telling Jacob the truth.

Chapter 58

JOHN

John stepped through the mercantile door. The morning light glowed through the windows as he sauntered to the counter. He had planted a large crop of corn that spring—larger than normal—and it would be ready to harvest in a month. He would need to hire extra men this season; therefore, he needed more tools. The mercantile only had a few scythes and sickles, but he knew he ought to buy what Edgar had before heading over to White Falls. John was going to be bringing in more profit this fall than ever before, so it was only right to support the local store whenever possible.

"How's business, Edgar?" he asked as he tapped the counter.

"Hey, John, I'm surprised to see you. Isaac Weber usually delivers your morning milk supply." The store owner called to his nephew. "Jacob! The milk is here. You need to get it into the icehouse."

As Jacob hobbled in from the back of the store, he smiled at the two men.

"Sure, Uncle. How are you today, Mr. Miller?"

"Doing good, as usual, Jacob. How's fatherhood treating you?"

"Well, I'm definitely not getting much sleep, but I'm sure that will improve in a few months."

"It will," John promised. "Listen. Out in my wagon, along with all the milk, there's a smaller container; it has about two gallons in it. It's from the last half of my best cow's milking this morning, so it's nice and thick. I left all the cream in it. I want you to give that to your wife; she'll benefit from the extra milk right now."

"Thank you, Mr. Miller. That's kind of you."

Jacob limped toward the door. John shook his head as he watched him go, knowing the job would take Edgar's nephew twice as long as anyone else. Having to use a cane meant that Jacob could only carry one container at a time.

"So, how's that working out for you, Edgar?" John nodded toward the young man as he left the building.

"Well, he's slower now that he lost his foot, but he is family. He makes a good effort, considering his peg-leg. He seems to be exhausted all the time. That baby takes more work than most. He and Laura are getting a lot of help, though. Even your buddy Eli and his wife go over there a lot."

John snorted at the remark. "Yeah, he's my 'buddy' all right," he said with a sneer. As the men laughed, the door opened and a bell rang, announcing another customer.

"You know, neither of the Gardners have been in here for months," Edgar remarked.

"Why not, can't afford to? I've given up trying to figure out how that boy justifies not working. I doubt he's at Ray's more than a couple times a week. So, if he's not coming in here to buy anything, how's he keeping his poor wife fed? It's a good thing those gypsies don't have any kids; I suppose God knew what He was doing there." John let out a scoffing chuckle.

At that moment, Mrs. Taylor came up behind him. "I'll tell you how," she said with an irritated scowl. "They go to my Laura's house twice a week. They say they're helping with that baby, but more often than not, they stay past supper and eat half her food! I told Laura she can manage on her own, but she won't listen. They have her convinced that she needs their help. I've tried talking to Pastor Duncan, but he won't listen either. Those Gardners have him just as deceived as my daughter. When they aren't eating up all her food, they're eating at the Duncans or the Webers."

"Wait a minute…" John was stunned by the woman's claims. "Is that true?"

Mrs. Taylor nodded with raised eyebrows.

He shook his head. "You know, Isaac Weber has always had a soft spot for anyone he thinks is a charity case. If he wants to give the Gardners a handout now and then, well, that's his business. But you're telling me Eli is scrounging meals not only off of the pastor but also the cripple with the disfigured baby?"

A shocked gasp escaped Edith as she brought her hand to her forehead and fluttered her eyes.

"No offense, Mrs. Taylor," he added quickly.

She dismissed him with a wave. "Oh, my poor little girl! Why is this happening to me?" She grabbed onto the store owner's hand. "Thank you for letting Jacob work here. I don't know how they could manage without you."

Edgar smiled smugly at his nephew's mother-in-law, but John frowned, still stewing over what he had learned about Eli. He slammed his fist on the counter, startling the other two.

"I didn't think it was possible to dislike him even more," John muttered under his breath.

Why didn't more people see it? How could they let themselves be fooled by that gypsy boy?

"You need to put your foot down, Mrs. Taylor. I wouldn't let Eli around that baby if I were you. I know he has a violent streak in him. I've seen it in his eyes. When we were working on the Webers' house, I barely had to say a word to him. His rage was bubbling just under the surface."

"Oh, dear!" she said.

John didn't care if he had frightened the woman. The spell that boy had on this town needed to be broken. Mrs. Taylor let out a worried groan. Abandoning her errand, she said her goodbyes and ran out of the store, no doubt rushing to her daughter's house to warn the girl about what she had just learned.

John purchased the harvesting tools. When Jacob returned and told him the milk was unloaded, he left for White Falls. He continued to brood over Eli as he guided his wagon down the road. Ever since finishing the Webers' house, John had been able to avoid him. As long as no more homes burned down, he only had to see Eli on Sundays. Even then, he was usually able to dodge talking to him, which was aided by the fact that John slipped into church late and rushed out as soon as the service was over.

Having a dairy farm made it difficult to get to church on time. If God wanted man to rest on the seventh day, He should have told the cows to rest also. Every Sunday morning, after the cows were milked, John quickly changed into church clothes and headed to town. His wife and children had already left in their smaller carriage. They always saved him a seat in the second row, and he would stride in to join them right after the singing had ended. That suited him just fine; he didn't like to sing all those songs anyway. And when he came in late, he didn't have to talk to anyone until after the service, especially not Eli.

Once the congregation was excused, John only had time to talk to a few people before heading back to the farm. That made it easier to escape interacting with Eli. However, he wasn't able to escape noticing how many people sought out the gypsy boy. Pastor Duncan always spoke a few words to Eli immediately after the service, usually followed by a robust laugh. Jacob Martin, Isaac Weber, and Ray Larson were all chummy with him as well. Even David Holden seemed to like the guy. John didn't understand it; these were smart men with good work ethics. What did they find so interesting about that lazy idler?

Well, it didn't matter. One of these days, Eli was going to let his guard down, and then those men would finally realize they had all been played the fool. Even if John were too busy with his corn harvest to see it all go down, he would hear about it. He imagined that glorious day as he drove his horses down the road. A grin crept onto his face and he began to chuckle.

Chapter 59

ADA

As Eli visited with everyone around the fire, Ada helped Hattie wash the morning dishes. Spending time with the caravan was peaceful. She missed them terribly and loved how natural it was to pick up her life with them whenever they visited. It felt as if they had never left.

When she and Eli had arrived two evenings ago, there was a sadness mixed with the joy of coming home. Mae was not there to greet them, and Tony was quieter than usual. At the end of the day, however, being together had lifted his spirits, and the men agreed to rise early the next morning to go fishing before breakfast. By the next afternoon, Tony was joining in on the bantering Eli often provoked.

"Oh, Hattie," Ada said with a sigh. "I'm so glad to be here. I've made some close friends in the last three years, but you are all so dear to me. I wish both the caravan and the town could be with me every day."

Hattie laughed and put an arm around her. "This group certainly isn't the same without the two of you," she agreed. "We wish we could see you more often as well."

"The kids are growing up fast," Ada observed. "Sammy is almost as old as I was when we first joined the caravan."

"You best not call him Sammy," Hattie warned. "It's Sam now. Ever since he moved into Tony's vardo, he has become quite the young man, you know."

Hattie's voice grew more serious. "I think it's been good for both of them, though. When Mae died, Tony was lost for a while. We weren't sure if he was going to stick around. Then Ira suggested Sam move in with him since their family's vardo was starting to feel a bit crowded. I think it gave Tony a new purpose to look after the boy and mentor him."

As Ada watched the children, Hattie returned to her jovial self.

"Well, those three kids are something else, that's for sure. The little man, the princess, and the spit-fire—that sums them up! And what about you, Ada? I expected you to roll in here with a bundle of your own." Hattie nudged Ada with her elbow and said in a softer voice, "I know losing Ruth Ann was hard on you, but I hope it hasn't scared you away from motherhood altogether."

Ada looked down at the tub of dishes in front of her. "No, I *do* want children. But that's up to God, not me."

"Now don't you give up, honey. Hoping and even praying that God will give you a child someday doesn't mean you haven't accepted what His plan might be. There's room in every heart for hope and acceptance. They don't cancel each other out."

"Thank you, Hattie," she said, smiling. "I needed to hear that."

Ada watched Eli as Lily sat on his knee. They were playing a fast-paced hand clapping game. The little six-year old, who was obviously winning, was doing so despite giggling at his blundered attempts to follow her clapping patterns. He noticed Ada watching him and winked at her right before messing up again. Eli rolled his eyes and made a silly face at Lily as they broke into laughter and began another round of their game.

213

Chapter 60

ELI

There was something calming about moving water. Eli sat on the edge of Badger Creek, watching the water flow downstream. Earlier that morning, he and Ada were sharing memories in their vardo as they packed for their return trip. After a pleasant weeklong visit, Eli's goal was to be home by Saturday evening. It took two days to travel from the West Woods to East Haven, and if they left by ten o'clock, they could easily make it by then.

However, just as they finished packing, he decided to walk to the creek one last time and spend a few minutes by himself. He kissed Ada, promising to be back in thirty minutes. Those few minutes turned into several hours, and now the sun was low in the sky. It was late afternoon, too late to leave, but he couldn't pull himself away from the creek. The bushes rustled behind him, and he knew who would step out from the trees.

"So, you decided not to leave," Jed observed.

"I didn't really want to travel on Sunday, but I guess I messed that up." Eli continued to watch the water. "Is Ada worried?"

"No, not too much. I think she's just surprised by the change of plans. You can always leave on Monday, you know."

"No, I want to be home before then. If we leave early tomorrow, we should be able to make it to Clearwater before it gets too late. We can stay there for the night and go to church in the morning before heading out again."

"Suit yourself," Jed said as he sat down next to Eli. "But you seem reluctant to leave. I think you're trying to avoid something. People don't usually disappear for six hours unless they have something heavy weighing on their mind."

"Six hours?"

Eli glanced at Jed. He didn't realize how long he had been gone. He shook his head and threw a rock into the water, watching the ripples spread. As he picked up another stone, he spoke again.

"After our talk last year, I really tried to listen to God more closely—you know, about the money. I found a few people who were in need, and I was able to help. It made a big difference for them, but it barely made a dent in my account. I know the money was meant to help them; it felt right to give it—just like my investments." He chuckled. "Mr. Ross never understood how I could make decisions about money based on feelings rather than figures, but it works for me. I can't ignore those feelings."

Eli appreciated how patiently Jed listened as he stumbled through his thoughts. "Staying here for one more day *feels* important, so I'm going to follow my gut on this decision as well."

He was silent for a moment before continuing with a heavy sigh. "I don't know, maybe I *am* just trying to avoid a problem. I discovered something about a person in town. I'm going to have to deal with it, but I don't know how to do that yet."

"What did you find out?" Jed asked. "Maybe there's an easier solution than you think."

Eli told him about giving money to Jacob. He told him about the frustration he felt when Edgar took credit for it and allowed Jacob to pay him back.

"Hmm… that is a tough one," Jed agreed. "But I think you know what you need to do; you just don't want to do it."

"Well, yeah. Jacob needs to know what his uncle is doing. But if I tell him, I'm going to be the cause of a broken relationship—possibly even two. If I tell him about Edgar, he'll know I gave him the money. Sure, he's going to be angry with his uncle, but he's also going to be unhappy with me. He's stubborn and prideful; he won't like hearing it was from me."

"Pride is difficult to get over," Jed said with a sigh. "We all struggle with it. But pride doesn't always look like we think it should. It's easy for someone to get caught up in it without realizing they are." He peered at Eli for a moment before continuing. "I don't think you should tell your friend yet; you should talk to his uncle first. Go to Edgar privately and tell him what you know. Give him a chance to make it right. God gives us second chances all the time. We need to follow His example and do the same for others."

215

"That's a good idea," Eli said quietly. "It's still going to be hard, though."

"Well, you need to pray about it. Ask God to show you the right time and way to approach him." Jed slapped Eli on the back. "Now, if you're going to stay one more night, you may as well spend the time with us instead of this creek. We aren't going to see you for another year."

Eli laughed as they stood up. Talking with Jed always gave him perspective. As they walked back to camp, he looked forward to another evening with good company.

Chapter 61

ADA

The church in Clearwater had a warm wood décor throughout the sanctuary. Ada sat in the last pew next to Eli. They had slipped into the back row just as the first hymn had ended. Now, they listened to the pastor as he promised a short sermon followed by a guest speaker. Ada scanned the congregation, wondering who would be speaking. She suspected the man sitting in the front. A subtle difference in his style gave her the impression that he came from a big city, but she had never been to one, so she couldn't be sure. The biggest town Ada had ever experienced was Orston, one of the towns in the caravan's summer circuit, and even Orston was small compared to the cities by the water.

The pastor finished his sermon with a prayer and introduced the guest speaker.

"We have the privilege of hearing from a gifted surgeon from Lambury. Doctor Nathan Keeler has an amazing ministry that he would like to share with us this morning, so let's welcome him warmly."

As the congregation clapped, the pastor gestured toward the man in the front pew and stepped aside. Dr. Keeler came forward to address the church. He spoke in a clear, crisp voice; he had obviously presented to the public before. He told the church about his work with children who were in desperate need of surgeries that would improve their lives.

He explained how he traveled to the hometowns of these children and appealed to the members of their churches in an effort to help raise money for the much needed procedures. But even with fundraising, there was often a need beyond what the town could raise; that was where the church at Clearwater could help. As he continued his speech, Dr. Keeler leaned large pictures along the back wall of the pulpit.

Ada could feel Eli sit up taller as his interest piqued. The pictures were drawings of children before and after surgery. They looked like Angel Martin! These children suffered the same affliction that Angel had. Some were similar in age, while others were a few years older—but all of them had an after picture.

As Dr. Keeler continued to speak, Eli tapped his leg rapidly and leaned forward. Ada reached for his hand to steady his restlessness. When she touched him, he glanced at her and their eyes locked. She knew what he was thinking. They would not be leaving the building without talking to this man first.

At the conclusion of his presentation, the doctor announced that he had some professional card portraits to share with the congregation, depicting children before and after their procedures. He explained two ways to donate to his ministry. A collection would be taken after the service, and he would be handing out information on where a contribution could be wired. He would also be happy to answer any questions they had.

After a well-worded prayer from the doctor, a small group of people crowded around him. Men with baskets walked around the sanctuary as others dropped coins into them. Ada watched Eli empty his pockets into a basket while keeping his eyes fixed on Dr. Keeler. They stood a pace or two away from the mingling group and waited for the crowd to thin. Soon there were only a few persistent enthusiasts, and the pastor began to usher the doctor toward the door. Eli grabbed Ada's arm and stepped toward the men.

"Excuse me, Dr. Keeler," he called out. The doctor stopped and turned. Eli held out his hand. "My name is Eli Gardner."

Dr. Keeler clasped it and nodded, waiting for him to continue.

"My wife Ada and I are traveling home today. We had planned to leave earlier but were delayed. Had we left on time, we would have missed hearing your presentation. Do you have any time to spare? I need to know more about what you do."

"I believe I have some time right now. We were just heading to the rectory for a quick meal." Dr. Keeler turned to the pastor. "Would your wife mind if we were a bit late?"

"Oh, she'll mind if we're late, but I know she won't mind extra guests." He glanced at them with a kind smile. "Why don't you and your wife join us, Mr. Gardner?"

Eli nodded. "Thank you."

"No, thank *you* for speaking up," Dr. Keeler countered. "If such an accidental circumstance caused our paths to cross, I believe it was more likely orchestrated. There must be a reason God allowed us to meet."

Chapter 62

DR. KEELER

Dr. Nathan Keeler sat at Pastor Greene's table, ready to answer questions from the energetic young man who sat across from him. This was a familiar scene to the doctor. He was usually offered lodging in the home of the local preacher whenever he visited a town. And more often than not, Sunday's meal included an unexpected guest following his presentation.

There were two reasons why Nathan presented his ministry. The first and most frequent was to raise funds for a specific child whose family belonged to the church where he was speaking. If there was no child in need associated with the church, the other reason was to raise general awareness of—and possible funding for—the many surgeries he provided. He was visiting Clearwater with the latter purpose in mind.

Regardless of whether a specific child was being represented or not, many of his presentations resulted in the acquaintance of someone who knew of a child like the ones in his pictures. These meetings accounted for nearly a third of the children with whom he worked. He could almost predict where today's conversation was headed. This young man was probably related in some way to a child who needed the surgery. He had the same look in his eyes that Nathan had seen in others.

"Mr. Gardner, let's get right to it. I'm willing to bet you know a child with a facial disfigurement."

"Please call me Eli—and yes, I do. Our friends had a little boy four months ago. Do you think something can be done for him, or is he too young?"

"It's actually easier on the child if the initial surgery is performed within the first year," Nathan explained. "It becomes increasingly more difficult as the child gets older. However, I've worked with children as old as ten, and most need second and third surgeries to help support their adult teeth as they come in. As far as what can be done in your friends' case, I would need to assess their child myself to know what to tell you. A lot of advances have been made recently in regard to this type of surgery, but the procedure is still fairly new. Has the child been seen by a doctor yet?"

"No," Eli said. "Dr. Keeler, you work with families who can't afford this surgery, correct?"

Nathan nodded. "I started my ministry about five years ago. I mentioned in my presentation that I used to work for the hospital in Lambury, but I began to notice a shift in the attitude of the medical profession. The hospital was being run more like a business, where profit mattered more than the patient." He shook his head. "I watched more and more families walk away from cost prohibitive surgeries that would greatly improve their children's lives. I became a doctor to help people, not to fill my pockets. I felt as though God were calling me to these families, so I decided to work with them directly. I looked for ways to lower the cost of the surgery without jeopardizing its quality."

As Eli ate his soup, Nathan continued. "Even so, the cost can be as high as a year's worth of income for many families. It takes quite a long time to save that much. Therefore, I began a fundraising program that appeals to the communities for whom the children belong, and I seek out other contributors to cover the funds that can't be raised by the communities alone. As I said before, oftentimes the children need more than one surgery, so fundraising is an important part of my ministry."

"And how many surgeries do you perform in a year?" Eli asked.

"Not as many as I would like. I help about twenty children per year." Nathan smiled and shook his head again. "I know it doesn't sound like much, but twenty children equates to more than twenty surgeries. And if you add in all the travel time for the fundraising… well, my year fills up quickly.

"My wife assists me during the surgeries, but we are the only two involved in the medical side of our ministry. There are a few women who volunteer to clean our facility and cook for the families who stay there while their children recover. I would love to have another surgeon on board, but that dream will have to wait. We have a bigger priority to purchase some new equipment, and the money we raise barely covers the cost of the surgeries." Nathan paused to take a bite.

"Wow! Do you have any regular donors?" Eli asked.

Nathan nodded. "Oh, sure. We have several that give yearly donations. I couldn't do this without their contributions, and I'm grateful for them. Even with their help, though, I have a fair amount of legwork to do myself, but it's all extremely rewarding. I've witnessed how tight a community bonds together when it has a common goal to work toward. I enjoy having a part in that."

Eli asked many more questions regarding the cost of the surgeries, the type of equipment needed, what their facility was like, and about the procedure itself. He then asked about Nathan's goals, what he was looking for in another surgeon, and how many more children they could help if they had assistance. He also wanted to know how many additional surgeries could be done if less time was spent on fundraising.

His questions seemed to cover a wide range of interests. Some were related to helping his friends' child, but most were not the typical questions asked for that reason. Nathan began to suspect that Eli had a hunger for knowledge; the young man might have made a good doctor. He finally had to stop the questioning.

"Eli, I assume you would like me to examine this couple's baby and help them raise the funds."

He nodded, but his shoulders sank a bit. "That may be a problem. Jacob, the father, won't ask for help. I'm not sure he would want you to talk to our church."

"Then I suggest we take this one step at a time." Nathan pulled a pamphlet out of his coat pocket. "Give this to your friend. It explains the benefits of the surgery as well as the lifelong complications his son will have to deal with if he doesn't have it. Find out if he would be willing to let me examine..." Nathan raised his eyebrows and held out his hand.

"Angel," Eli offered.

"Thank you. Find out if he'll let me examine Angel. I'm good at what I do. Even if he chooses to pay for it himself, he won't find a less expensive way to go. Here's my card. Where are you from?"

"East Haven. Do you know the town?"

"That's close to here, isn't it? Less than a day away, I believe."

Eli confirmed Nathan's assumption with a nod.

"Well then, after you've talked to your friend, write to me and let me know what he says. If he agrees, I'll come to East Haven the first weekend I have available."

222

The men shook hands, and as Eli pocketed the pamphlet and card, Nathan said a quick prayer that Angel's parents would allow him to help their son. He hoped to hear back soon, but from what he could gather about this spirited man, Nathan suspected there was a good chance he would be traveling to East Haven before the end of October.

Chapter 63

JACOB

The sun sat low in the sky as Jacob held the pamphlet in his hand and listened to Eli talk about the doctor he had met while he was away. He hadn't seen his friend this animated for months. Eli only wanted to help, but Jacob didn't need to read the pamphlet to know his answer. It was, and always would be, no. He was not going to accept a handout.

"I appreciate what you're trying to do, but I'm not going to look at this," Jacob said. "I told you before, I can take care of it myself." He tried to hand the pamphlet back, but Eli refused.

"You have to at least read it. Angel needs the surgery sooner rather than later. It's going to affect his whole life, and there are complications that could show up later. I know you want to do it yourself, but look at how much you'll have to save to do that. Jacob, your son can't afford to wait until you have enough."

"You think I'm a bad father."

"No, I think you're a great father," Eli said. "But we all need help sometimes. When I was sixteen, my parents died, and I lost everything. I had no home, no family, no money of my own; I could barely feed myself. I don't know what would have become of me if Jed and Rosa hadn't taken me in when they did. There's no way to put a price on that, and it's not about the money anyway. Some help can only be accepted and then given to someone else—not paid back. I actually tried for a while. Whenever I had extra money, I gave it to Jed."

Eli shook his head and rubbed the back of his hair. "He just put it into another account for me. You see, here's what I didn't understand at the time: he wasn't helping because he was expecting me to pay him back. He did it because Ada and I needed help and he could give it. He cares about us." Eli put his hand on Jacob's shoulder. "Let the town care for you; let them help. And then someday when someone else is in need, you can pay the town's kindness back by helping that person. It doesn't matter if you do so with money, time, or service. That's how God's economy works. It's only in man's economy that things get paid back dollar for dollar. Jacob, you are too stuck in man's ways."

Jacob glanced at the pamphlet. Maybe Eli was right. He didn't want his own stubbornness to hurt his son. He should read what this Dr. Keeler had to say before making his decision, and he should discuss it with Laura. He hadn't even considered how hard this might be for her.

"Okay, I'll look at the information. I'll give it some thought."

"And pray about it," Eli encouraged. "This town isn't perfect, but I've seen it work together to help others before. It's good for us; it makes us stronger."

Jacob nodded as Eli patted him on the back, and together they walked into the house for supper.

Chapter 64

HAROLD & ELI

Harold now realized how accurate Jed had been; Eli *was* stubborn. He placed a folder of information in front of the boy, who barely looked at it. Eli flipped through the papers and pushed it back across the desk.

Harold had spent every Thursday since October teaching Eli about finances and investing. He even showed him how it worked by getting the boy's permission to invest a small amount of his money into a low-risk venture. Harold was able to demonstrate that it could grow over time. Sure, there were ups and downs, but the trend over the last nine months was an unquestionable increase. Eli wasn't fazed; he still held onto a feeling of disdain toward his money. How could Harold get through to him?

"Look more closely at that information," he urged. "I spent a lot of time putting it together. Think about everything you've learned and tell me which of these investments you'd like to try. I want to see if you can put into practice the things you've learned so far."

Harold tried to ignore Jed's look that said: *I told you so.* The boy remained silent and shrugged.

He decided to try a different approach. "All right, look at me for a second."

The boy raised his eyes.

"What is it about this money that makes you feel uncomfortable? Let's talk about it."

Eli glanced at Jed and chose his words carefully. "It's bad money, Mr. Ross. You said it was going to be used for a crime. What if it already has, like...?" He stopped and licked his lips, unable to continue.

"And that makes you feel guilty," Mr. Ross said, "as though you're somehow associated with those bad things because the money is now yours."

Eli dropped his eyes again; the man's words hit their mark square in his heart. Mr. Ross sighed.

"Whatever this money was intended for, it has either already happened, or it hasn't. You didn't do it, Eli; someone else did. No matter what the crime was, you can't undo it by locking the money up and ignoring it. You can't let yourself feel responsible for the actions of others."

Eli frowned. He understood what Mr. Ross was saying, but it didn't make him feel better.

Harold could see that Eli was struggling. He reached across the desk and patted the boy on the arm.

"As far as the money is concerned, you need to remember that God doesn't want us to fear the things of this world. When we do, we're placing what we fear above Him."

The boy swallowed hard; his face seemed to beg Harold to take away some misery locked inside him.

"Your money is just a thing, Eli. It isn't good, and it isn't bad. It's nothing more than a tool, like a hammer. In the wrong hands, a hammer can be used to destroy something. In the right hands, it can help build something beautiful. I don't pretend to know what God is thinking, but I *do* know I would rather you have the money than the criminals. Maybe finding it was God's plan all along. You can be the 'right hands' building something good—and more importantly, you can glorify God through whatever you build."

Eli blinked; something Harold said had finally struck a chord with the boy.

"I could use the money to do something for God?"

Eli turned toward Jed, who had remained quiet throughout their lesson. Jed, and everyone else in the caravan, had taken him and Ada in when they had nothing. Maybe Eli should help others who had also lost everything. At least he'd finally be rid of it.

"I could just give it to orphans right now," he said.

"You could," Mr. Ross agreed. "You could find an orphanage, give it all to them, and that would be a good thing. Then the money would be gone. However, if you spend a few years learning how to make it grow and keep it growing, you can fund ten orphanages for several generations. There are a lot of good things you can do with this money. We live in a big world full of many worthy causes. Stewardship is more than just using the money for good. It's also being wise with what God has given you and making responsible choices. Think of an investment as fertile soil…"

Eli's mouth dropped open at Mr. Ross' words.

"…An investment is like warm, life-giving dirt that can feed your money and make it grow."

"What did you say?" Eli asked, thinking of his dream.

"Okay, maybe that's a bad analogy," Mr. Ross said, chuckling, "but do you understand what I'm trying to say? If you can increase your money responsibly and with the right attitude, you can also increase the impact you make with it. So, how do you feel about looking at these investment choices again?" He spread the papers across the top of the desk.

Eli picked them up and looked at them with renewed interest. He began to think of the money differently. Mr. Ross called the investments life-giving dirt, but what if the *money* was the soil? In his dream, the dirt was in a canvas bag, and that was where he found the banknotes. And maybe the *bag* represented the investments. The dirt in the bag didn't decrease as fast as he used it, and that's what Mr. Ross was suggesting he could do with the money if he invested it wisely.

Whichever the case, Eli still needed to figure out what the crop was supposed to be. Mr. Ross said there were all kinds of things he could do and many places he could go. What if it took him away from the caravan some day? Would Ada be willing to go with him? As he sifted through the information in front of him, he decided he would ask her before the day was over.

Chapter 65

DR. KEELER

"Liz, could you pass the bread, please?"

Nathan Keeler sat with his wife Elizabeth at their dining room table. It was a rare evening in which they could sit quietly and eat their supper without rushing. There had been no surgeries, traveling, or fundraising that day. Elizabeth handed him the basket of warm bread. The glow from the gas lamps filled their small apartment with a faint light, while the noise of the city buzzed outside their window.

"I went to the post office today," Elizabeth said as Nathan took a hardy bite.

She walked over to a desk tucked into the corner of the room and picked up a stack of letters. She read the sender's name on the top letter aloud before handing it to him. As Nathan opened the letter and glanced over it, she read the next name. She continued to read names until she reached the middle of the pile.

"Here's one from an Eli Gardner in East Haven," she said.

"Oh, that's the young man I was telling you about—the one I met in Clearwater a couple of weeks ago."

"The inquisitive one?" she asked.

He answered with a nod. "Could you read his letter to me while I look over this invoice?" Nathan indicated the paperwork he had just received in the previous correspondence.

Elizabeth flashed her warm smile as she broke the seal and unfolded the paper. Inside was another sealed note, which she set aside.

"Dear Dr. Keeler," she read. "I enjoyed meeting you on the last Sunday of September. I appreciated the time you spent with me. Thank you for answering my questions. I gave your pamphlet to my friends, Jacob and Laura Martin, and they have asked me to inquire if you would still be willing to examine their son. You mentioned that you could come to East Haven as soon as you have a free weekend. I would like to extend an invitation to you and your wife to stay at my home while you are in town; Ada would love to meet Mrs. Keeler…"

Elizabeth looked up from the letter in her hands. "Oh, that sounds wonderful! I would love to go," she interjected before continuing.

"…I have included two train tickets to White Falls. Once there, someone will pick you up and bring you the rest of the way. I have also sent a letter from my accountant detailing my contributions to your ministry…"

Again, Elizabeth glanced up and commented on the young man's thoughtfulness.

"…Please put the larger amount toward the new equipment you require. The smaller amount is the first installment of an ongoing quarterly donation. I hope this will help you reach some of your goals sooner. Sincerely, Eli Gardner."

Elizabeth set the first letter aside and started to open the second. "Well," she observed, "he is very considerate."

Nathan carried the invoice to the desk and quickly filed it away. "That was my impression as well when I met him," he commented as he closed the file drawer. "He was also better spoken than his rugged appearance had suggested. Of course, he *was* traveling…"

Nathan's voice trailed off when he turned toward the table and saw Elizabeth's stunned expression. She skimmed the contents of the second letter. Bringing her hand to her mouth, she let the paper fall from her grasp.

"Liz, what's wrong?"

"Oh, Nathan," she whispered, "we can buy our equipment now."

He picked up the letter and read the information as he sat down. Making a quick calculation of the installments, Nathan glanced at Liz, donning a similar expression.

"You say considerate, but a more accurate word might be generous. Either way, that young man has just doubled our funding! I think I had better find another surgeon to join our team."

Chapter 66

MARCUS

Far in the distance, the smoke from the train billowed into the air. Marcus was waiting at the White Falls Depot for Dr. Keeler and his wife Elizabeth. Eli would have come with him, but an hour before the pastor had left East Haven, Ada tapped on his office door and informed him that her husband would be unable to make it. Eli and Isaac were currently fixing Evelyn's roof. Last night had brought with it a heavy October rain, revealing a leak directly over her woodstove. The repair could not wait, especially when considering the ominous color of the overcast sky. Marcus thanked her for letting him know and traveled to the station alone.

As the train pulled up to the depot, the small crowd on the platform took a synchronized step forward in anticipation of seeing their loved ones. The train whistled, and the cheerful "halloos" of the people had to be shouted above the noise. Railway workers in tidy uniforms were busy unloading the luggage car. Marcus studied the passengers as they stepped off the train. Not knowing what the doctor and his wife looked like, he searched for a couple that was not greeted by others, hoping they would be his charge. But he soon realized his concern was unwarranted; the doctor seemed to instinctively know who had come to meet them. He waved at Marcus as he helped his wife step onto the platform.

"Dr. Keeler," Marcus said, holding out his hand. "It's nice to meet you. I'm Pastor Duncan."

"Good afternoon," the doctor replied, shaking his hand. "This is my wife Elizabeth."

231

Marcus tipped his head at her and touched the rim of his hat.

"Shall we collect your luggage? If we hurry, we should stay ahead of the rain. Eli sends his apologies. He would have been here to meet you, but something came up."

Once on the road, Marcus asked what the standard itinerary was for this type of visit. It was Friday afternoon, and the Keelers would be leaving Monday morning. He wanted to ensure that their quick visit ran as smoothly as possible.

"Tomorrow," Dr. Keeler began, "I'll visit the Martins and examine Angel to determine what his surgical needs and follow-up care will be. That should give me an idea of how much the church should raise to help offset their medical expenses. On Sunday, I'll talk to your congregation about my ministry, and Angel's situation in particular. I should only need about forty minutes. To be honest, though, Eli's donation negates any need for the Martin family to raise funds."

"Ah, yes…" Marcus said. "Eli asked me to discuss that with you before we get to East Haven. He was impressed by something you mentioned in Clearwater. You noted how much a community benefits when it works together to help a child in need. He didn't want to take away that opportunity. He offered to cover the remaining cost of Angel's surgery after we've had a chance to come together and help. However, he insists that this information not be made known to anyone."

"I see," the doctor said. "Does he think the town won't contribute as much if they know the cost will be covered, regardless of what they give?"

"No, that isn't the issue," Marcus said. "Dr. Keeler, you need to understand something. Eli is a very private person, especially when it comes to his finances. There are only two men in East Haven who know how well-off he is, and he wants to make sure it stays that way. In other words, he has asked that you not make his involvement known beyond the fact that he introduced you to the Martins."

"Okay, I can do that," the doctor replied. "To be honest, it will be refreshing to work with someone who doesn't boast about their donation. Most of my larger contributors tend to be prideful about their wealth."

Marcus glanced at Dr. Keeler and shook his head. "Oh, I'm not saying Eli doesn't struggle with pride. I know he does. His struggle just looks different from most men in his situation. Eli's pride lies somewhere in his humility, and I think there will come a day when he will have to wrestle with it and take control before he can reach his full potential."

Dr. Keeler nodded at his words, and the three of them sat in thoughtful silence. Soon they would arrive in town. They would pick up Grace and head to the Gardners' home to enjoy a casual supper. As the carriage rolled forward, the sun moved lower in the sky. Thankfully, the weather remained dry.

Chapter 67

ELI

During his examination, Angel sat in the reassuring comfort of his mother's arms. While the Martins answered Dr. Keeler's questions, Eli leaned against the wall on the other side of their living room. He watched Nathan peer inside Angel's mouth and thought about their conversation during supper the previous evening.

When the Duncans and the Keelers had arrived on Friday, Eli and Isaac were finishing up the repair on Mrs. Russell's roof. Marcus waved to Eli as they rode by. He returned the greeting and quickly gathered his tools. Asking Mrs. Russell to forgive him for not staying longer, he darted to his house to meet his guests. He entered the back door, came through the kitchen and dining room, and joined Ada at the front door. She was already ushering the two couples in.

"Dr. Keeler, welcome." He grasped the doctor's hand and gave it an eager shake. "I'm sorry I couldn't meet you at the station. How was your journey?" Eli noticed his dirty hands and wiped them on his work coat. "Sorry."

Dr. Keeler waved away his apology. "The journey was comfortable, but please no titles, Eli. Tonight, I'm your guest."

"All right, Nathan," he replied. "Let me show you to your room before I wash up for supper."

He led the couple to the same back room that the Webers had stayed in a year ago. Since that time, they had returned Evelyn's bed and furnished their guest room with a quaint bedroom set.

Once cleaned up, Eli joined his guests in the dining room. The women were in the kitchen finishing supper preparations while the men visited. Eli was relieved to see that Nathan had also dressed casually—rolled up sleeves and no jacket. After a few minutes Ada, Grace, and Elizabeth brought the meal in from the kitchen. Eli jumped up, took the hot dish from his wife, and placed it on the table. He continued to relieve the women of their dishes until the meal was completely set down. After Marcus led them in prayer, they sat and began to eat.

"You have a nice home, Ada," Elizabeth said. "It's so charming. How long have you lived here?"

"Thank you. We've lived in this house for about three and a half years."

"You must have moved in shortly after you were married. Are you from East Haven? Do your parents live in town as well?"

"Um, no…"

Ada glanced at Eli. He wondered what she was saying no to: Elizabeth's assumption about how long they had been married or her question about their parents. It would have worked for either. He winked and was about to rescue her, but Nathan spoke instead.

"It is a nice home, but I was expecting something bigger. I don't mean to sound critical, though. I admire you for choosing to live in a smaller home. I have a few associates who live in houses much bigger than they need, just to make sure everyone is aware that they can."

Eli's eyes darted toward Marcus before he responded with a quiet laugh.

"I think it's all about perspective, Nathan. For Ada and I, this is a big house—at least structurally. We lived in a very small home for several years before moving to East Haven, but in many ways, it felt bigger than this one. Every fall when we visit our family, we stay in it. That home will always be dear to us; I built it myself and it's filled with memories, some good and some sad."

"You know, Eli," Marcus said, "I've known you for a while now, but I still don't know much about your past. Nathan, did you know Eli and Ada used to be traveling merchants?"

"Really?" Nathan tilted his head toward Eli.

"It's true," Marcus said. "They used to make and sell toys at town markets. What do you think of that?"

Eli wondered if Nathan would take the bait Marcus was throwing.

"I didn't realize selling toys at markets was so lucrative," Nathan replied.

There was a long pause as Eli leaned back in his seat and looked at the men.

"My investments were lucrative," he remarked. "The markets were… marginal. Selling toys was something we sort of stumbled into."

When the men looked as though they wanted a better explanation, he continued before they could ask anything specific.

"Almost ten years ago, Ada and I lost our parents…"

As he relayed parts of their story to his guests, he rubbed his tattoo and his eyes drifted to Ada. She peered at her hands, head down and silent. The low candlelight felt heavy as he told his spellbound guests of their struggles to survive on their own after their parents had died. He mentioned how they had quite literally stumbled onto the caravan, but his words trailed off before he could explain why they were running toward them.

After a pause, he opened his mouth again, and for a brief second, he believed he might tell them everything—the gruesome details of their parents' deaths, their abduction, even the banknotes—but Ada glanced at him, and his throat closed. He let out an uncertain chuckle and his eyes dropped.

"Well, anyway… the caravan took us in and adopted us. We married young and learned a trade from our new family. We sold our toys at the markets as we traveled through different towns during the summer months. It was a good life with good people. They taught us about acceptance and friendship." He turned to Nathan. "They showed me what it looks like to help others. I might have grown up bitter and angry if it weren't for them."

"Well then, I guess I have your caravan family to thank as well as you," Nathan observed. "But I think there's more to your story than you've just told us."

"There is," Eli admitted. His eyes shifted between the men. "But not all of it is conversation that should accompany a meal."

There was a drawn-out silence, and finally, Nathan nodded and pointed to Eli's arms.

"In that case, I'd like to hear where that art came from. That's one of the best tattoos I've ever seen. Whoever did it has some real talent. But I bet it must have hurt."

Eli smiled at his comment. "It was a little uncomfortable." He turned his arms so Nathan could get a better look. "Jed worked on this for several months. He's one of the men from the caravan. He's the closest thing I have to a father now. My tattoos remind me that God has a plan for my life. Helping you is part of that plan, Nathan. But I don't think you're the whole picture; you're only one of the branches on this vine."

~&

As Eli remembered this conversation from the night before, he was brought back to the present when Nathan sighed. He continued to examine Angel and then sat back, smiling at the parents.

"I have some good news for you. Angel has a unilateral cleft that does not extend into his gums or palate."

The parents looked at him vacantly, unsure of what he meant.

"It's the best scenario with the simplest fix," he clarified.

They both let out a relieved sigh.

"I'd like to schedule his procedure for the spring, so you won't have to travel with him during the winter months." He opened his scheduling book as he spoke. "You should plan to stay in Lambury for about ten days; I want to observe Angel during the week after his surgery. Our facility has accommodations, so you don't have to worry about where you'll stay. I think he will only need one operation, but I won't know for sure until after his follow-up exam."

He flipped through the pages of his book until he found an empty week.

"Here we go. Let's schedule it for March twenty-first. You can take the train on Saturday the nineteenth and return home on Monday the twenty-eighth. Today is October twenty-third; that puts his procedure out five months. Angel will be almost ten months old by then. That will work out well."

Nathan wrote the information in his calendar. The visit continued with the Martins asking more questions. Eli watched the young family as they planned for this life-changing event and wondered what branches God would bring him next.

Chapter 68

JOHN

John listened as the doctor talked about a surgery that would fix the Martin baby. It all sounded impressive, but there was no way Jacob could afford it without help. He wasn't surprised when the doctor's speech turned into a proposal that the church members raise money for Angel's surgery. Dr. Keeler told them how much was needed and suggested they collect as much as possible over the next four weeks. Even though the procedure was scheduled for March, he insisted on having a deadline for the collection. John glanced at Jacob and rolled his eyes when he saw Eli sitting next to him; apparently, *he* had found the doctor.

As usual, that idler had been out of town avoiding the harvest when he happened upon the surgeon. He met him in some town between East Haven and wherever he disappeared to every fall. He invited the doctor to their humble little town and convinced Jacob to let his kid get the surgery. Obviously, John was happy for the Martins, but why did it have to be the town gypsy who came to the rescue? Eli must be tickled with himself over this discovery. Bringing a doctor to town would make him look like a hero. But John could see right through his hypocrisy.

He had not forgotten their argument last year when the Webers' house had burned down. Eli had made such a big deal about John's suggestion that everyone give Isaac a certain amount of money. How was this any different? Did he think this was okay because it was his idea? John was going to have to knock him down a peg or two.

After the service, everyone crowded around the doctor and the Martins, asking questions and offering words of support. Eli hovered close to the group with what John assumed was a self-important attitude. John walked up behind him, gripped his arm, and pulled him away from the others. He felt Eli tense up as a defensive look cast a shadow across the gypsy's face.

"You must feel pretty good about yourself, right about now," John snorted in a low voice.

Eli frowned at him but remained silent.

"You know, finding this guy and bringing him here is not enough, boy. You're going to need to step up and do more this time. You don't get to bring this doctor to town, and then expect the rest of us to do all the work; you have to give something too. Got it?"

"You're joking, right?" Eli said, shaking his head. "You think you have some great insight that qualifies you to tell others what they should be doing? You need to manage your own affairs, John, and let me manage mine."

"I don't think so. I know what 'managing your own affairs' means to you. You *are* going to donate money to the Martins; you don't get to claim poverty this time. And this is how you'll do it: instead of skipping out on work, you're going to get yourself over to Ray's every single day—assuming he'll have you—and you're going to give Jacob all the extra money you earn. Heck, you might even discover how good self-respect feels. Wouldn't that be something?"

Eli jerked his arm out of John's grasp. "Are you done? Because this conversation is over."

He walked away, scowling. John watched him go to his wife, say a quick word in her ear, and storm away with fists clenched.

Chapter 69

ELI

Two weeks after Dr. Keeler had talked to the church, Angel's fundraising event—which had reached its halfway point—was going well. Eli sat in the pastor's office with Marcus and David as they looked over the donation ledger. The funds were trickling in on a daily basis. Marcus wrote down each amount after the name of the person who gave it and added up the total. The town had already raised over a third of the cost; Eli was impressed.

"Well at this rate, I think we're going to get really close," David said.

"*If* it keeps up," Marcus agreed. "But I expect the giving will taper off during these last two weeks. Even so, we should raise just over half of what is needed, and that's still exceptional. Dr. Keeler said half would be a great success for a town our size."

David ran his finger down the column of names. "We might get a surge of giving at the end. There are a few people who aren't on this list yet. Some told me personally that they're planning on giving."

"Regardless of what anyone has said, we need to keep our focus on the total column, not the names," Marcus insisted. "By the way, here's the collection from today. Can you deposit it?" He handed a box to David.

"Sure, and you'll probably want to add this to your list." David pulled a piece of paper out of his pocket. "Edgar Johnson had me transfer money directly from his account to Jacob's. It made more sense to do it that way, since it's a fairly good-sized donation."

He handed the paper to Marcus, who smiled as he looked at the numbers written on it. The pastor added the information to the ledger.

Eli watched him scribble down the amount; a flicker of anger ignited in his gut. He hadn't thought about Edgar for weeks. He wondered if that donation came anywhere close to what the man had stolen from his nephew. He didn't deserve any credit for it; that money should be considered Jacob's own personal contribution.

Eli had allowed himself to be distracted after meeting Nathan, but now that the conflict with Edgar flooded back into his mind, he recalled Jed's advice. He was right. Eli couldn't put it off any longer; he had to face the man.

"Well, that helped tremendously," Marcus said after adding up the new total. "We are very close to the halfway mark. I'm so pleased." He looked up at the other two with a grin. "This encourages me. The people of this town are quite generous, wouldn't you both agree?"

Eli looked at the pastor with a straight face and forced himself to nod.

Chapter 70

EDGAR

It was four o'clock and no one had passed through the mercantile door for over an hour. That was typical for November; shorter days tended to close the shops of East Haven early. Edgar had sent his nephew home forty minutes ago. Keeping Jacob at the store was pointless when there were no customers to help.

He brought the cash box out from under the counter and opened his registry book. As he counted his sales and jotted down his income for the day, the entrance bell on the front door rang. Edgar glanced up, surprised to have a customer at this hour. When he saw Eli walk into the building, he scooped up the coins in front of him. He threw them in the cash box, shut the lid, and swiftly stowed it out of sight. Eli hadn't been in the mercantile for months, what could he possibly want? Edgar reached under the counter and moved his searching fingers along the top shelf.

"I've already started closing up for the night," he stated.

"I can see that." Eli walked up to Edgar and placed his hands on the edge of the countertop. He wasn't smiling.

"Why are you here?" Edgar asked as his fingers finally found the revolver. His hand rested lightly on the grip.

"I was hoping to catch you alone," Eli said, keeping his voice quiet. "Have you sent Jacob home?"

"He left almost an hour ago. We don't have any business to discuss, Eli. You best be leaving."

"Not yet." Eli shook his head. His tense posture reminded Edgar of what John Miller had speculated about his violent streak.

"Boy," he said, clearing his throat. His eyes darted briefly toward the shelf under the counter. "Whatever you came in here for, you may want to reconsider."

A scoffing noise escaped Eli's throat. "You think I came in here to rob you?" He removed his hands from the counter and took a step back.

"What am I supposed to think? You haven't been in my store for months, and suddenly you waltz in here, hoping to find me alone. Everyone knows you don't like to work, and I sure as heck know you haven't bought anything for a while. I don't think you have any money, Eli. And that makes me wonder how desperate you are."

"I came here to talk."

"Then talk."

"How about you show me your hands first," Eli demanded.

Edgar brought his hands up and rested them on the countertop. His right hand still held onto the gun. Eli sighed and looked him in the eye.

"Jacob told me you gave him some money."

"Are you seriously asking me for a hand-out? Ray has plenty of work; figure out your own means. I'm not giving you anything."

"You didn't give your nephew anything either," Eli stated.

"Oh, really? How would you know?"

Edgar flinched and leaned back when Eli took a sudden step toward the counter, ignoring the gun. He raised his hand and pointed at Edgar.

"Because I know who did give him that money. It wasn't you."

"You don't know anything, boy."

"Okay then, let's go talk to David. Is he going to back up your lies?"

Edgar was silent, he could feel his cheek twitching. He replaced the gun under the counter but raised his chin and squared his shoulders. Eli curled his lip and let out a short scoffing noise.

"How could you let Jacob pay you back for something you never even gave him? Tell me, Edgar, which one of us is the thief here." Eli's grip tightened on the edge of the counter. "You need to tell him it wasn't from you, or I will."

"I'm not a thief," Edgar muttered under his breath. "I'm giving that money to Angel."

Eli's hand shot out. He grabbed Edgar by the shirt and pulled him toward his face.

"You mean your donation toward his surgery? You don't get to take credit for that, either."

A sniveling gasp squeaked out of Edgar as he turned his head and cowered against Eli's hold. Eli scowled at him for a moment and then pushed him away. As he turned to leave, he said over his shoulder, "Tell him the truth."

Edgar smoothed out his shirt, snorting disgust over his mistreatment to hide his embarrassment.

"That is my donation; I swear it is. I've been putting Jacob's money into a savings account. Go ahead and ask David about that. It's in Angel's name."

Eli turned and glared at him. "You think that'll make up for what you're doing? Jacob could have been using that money to take care of his family. You don't get to make financial decisions for him. You need to come clean, Edgar."

The two men stared at each other for a drawn out moment before Eli finally turned again and walked toward the exit, shaking his head.

"All right," Edgar said, spitting out the words.

Eli paused briefly at the door and then left the mercantile without looking back.

Chapter 71

JOHN

Today was the last chance to give money toward the Martin baby's surgery. John was holding out for this day. Jacob needed to wire his payment to Dr. Keeler in the morning, and Pastor Duncan had reminded the congregation of the deadline several times during the church meeting. John was waiting until the very end to give his contribution; he wanted to make sure everyone else got their money in before he did. He lingered after the service until there were only a few people left. The pastor and his wife were visiting with Jacob and Laura, while Louise Evans waited for them to be done. The Martins would take her home as soon as they finished their conversation.

John caught the pastor's eye and indicated that he would wait by the office. As he walked down the hall, he glanced back to make sure the small group was distracted, and then he slipped through the office door and walked up to Pastor Duncan's cluttered desk.

After moving a stack of papers and several books, he found the Martins' fundraising ledger. John grinned. He ran his eyes quickly down the list of names, noting each donation amount. He wanted specific information, but before he found it, a few other things caught his attention. All three widows, for one thing, had donated more than John would have thought possible. None of them had given a large amount, but their gifts were bigger than a strict budget should have allowed.

The next thing he noted was Edgar Johnson's contribution. It was sizable compared to the majority, but he was family. Nevertheless, John tucked that number away in the back of his mind and continued to scan the list.

He finally found who he was looking for—Ray Larson, the second largest farm owner in East Haven. If anyone had given a large contribution, it would have been Ray. John took a mental note of his neighbor's donation. Then on a whim, he added together Ray and Edgar's gifts. He considered that total for a moment but decided to knock off a few dollars before settling on what *he* would give to the Martins.

He peeked toward the door. He could barely hear the conversation, but it still stretched on. John had time to check one more thing. He finished scanning over the list of names, and then just to be sure, he ran his eyes over them a second time. John sniffed back his contempt; there was a name missing. He wasn't surprised. Even so, he had held onto a small bit of hope that he might be wrong. Every family in the church was represented on that ledger, every single family except one—the Gardners.

Chapter 72

ELI

The March air was chilly, but the evening was clear. The Gardners had invited the Martins over for supper. Tomorrow morning Eli would take them to the train station in White Falls, and the little family would travel to Lambury. Ada had suggested having them over, hoping to relieve their workload as they packed for the trip. Eli realized the wisdom in her proposal after detecting a subtle anxiety lying under the surface of their conversation throughout the evening.

Ada warmed some cider, and the men sat on the front porch after supper, while the women visited inside. Eli could tell Jacob was pretending to be calmer than he was; he nervously picked at the arm of his chair while he sipped his drink.

"Dr. Keeler has done this procedure a hundred times," Eli said, hoping to reassure him. "And Angel's surgery is one of the least complicated. Try not to worry; in a couple of months, this will seem like ancient history."

"I know," Jacob said. "But before then, it's going to be rough. Angel will be in a lot of pain and he's not going to understand why. I keep thinking about how it will feel to watch my child suffer, knowing there's nothing I can do to help. How does a parent deal with that?"

Eli thought about Ruth Ann. "You deal with it because you have to. You do it by relying on God's strength, not your own."

Jacob sighed and rubbed his forehead. "I've been praying! And I'll be praying non-stop for as long as I'm Angel's father. I think it goes along with the job."

"It has to," Eli agreed. "Being a father is one of the toughest jobs a man will ever have, but it's also the most rewarding."

"That's a good point," Jacob said through a tired laugh. "You and Ada will make great parents. You two should hurry up and have some kids. Being a father is like nothing else you'll ever experience."

"I know." Eli glanced down before looking at Jacob again. "I'll never forget what it felt like to hold our daughter, even though it was only for a few hours. And whether or not we have any more children isn't up to us."

"Oh… I didn't know," Jacob said quietly. "I'm sorry."

Eli shook his head. "It was a long time ago. She would have been five next month." He peered out at his yard and imagined Ruth Ann playing on the lawn. After a pause, he turned his attention back to Jacob and smiled. "We don't know yet what God has planned, do we?" Eli patted him on the shoulder. "So, how is your uncle going to manage without you next week?"

Jacob's brows creased over his eyes. "I'm sure Edgar will manage just fine."

Eli noted the cool edge in his voice.

"What happened?" he asked, already suspecting the answer.

"A few months ago, he came by the house," Jacob explained. "He said he didn't give me any money after all. I don't get it. Why would he say he did and allow me to pay him back? Who does that?" Jacob sighed and crossed his arms. "At least he didn't keep it. He put it into a savings account for us. But still. It was a lousy thing to do."

"It was lousy," Eli agreed. "But we're all vulnerable to temptation. Your uncle must be struggling with something. Somewhere deep inside, he must have felt bad about his actions or he wouldn't have told you about it, and he wouldn't have given back the money. Let's pray the Holy Spirit is working in him."

"Yeah well, I don't know if I'll ever be able to trust him again," Jacob admitted. "I'm still angry; I'm not sure I can forgive him."

"God requires us to forgive, Jacob; if you don't, then why should He forgive you? You'll have to figure out how to let this one go—but forgiving him doesn't mean you have to trust him. Edgar will have to earn that back himself."

"I'm trying; I really am, but it's hard. Maybe Edgar regrets keeping me on at the same pay. I know I'm slower. I'm sure it's difficult to pay me as much as he does when I only get half the work done. I probably shouldn't be working at the mercantile, but I don't know what else to do. Who's going to hire me?"

"Have you considered a desk job?" Eli asked. "Maybe you should talk to David. Even if he doesn't have any work for you, he might have some ideas."

Jacob nodded at the suggestion and sighed. "I'll talk to him when I get back."

"Speaking of that, you and Laura should head home; we have an early start tomorrow," Eli reminded him.

"Yeah. Listen, Eli. Thanks for taking us to the train station—and for supper tonight. That helped Laura out a lot. You two are good friends. We appreciate everything you've done for us."

Eli smiled as they stood up. "You'd have done the same, Jacob."

The men moved their conversation inside, knowing it would take several more minutes for the women to wrap up their visit.

Chapter 73

HAROLD

Harold scratched his chin as he glanced at the information in front of him. He was in awe every time he looked at a report on Eli's capital gains. The young man, now almost twenty-one, had invested in several different companies, properties, and inventions over the last four years, all of which had done well. And this report... well, this was yet another surprise. He himself would not have bet on it.

Eli had two accounts with Harold. The first one, his largest, had been opened with the banknotes found in the woods. His second was the one Jed had opened for him. Mr. Gardner came into the bank one day with a pocket full of coins and crumpled bills. Eli had been trying to pay him back for something he didn't want to be paid back for, and the man decided to put the money into an account.

Eli was frustrated when he first found out, and it took him several weeks to accept that Jed wouldn't take his money. But after a while, he gave up his protests and thanked him. He added to it after every market season or whenever Mrs. Perry paid him for a job he had done. As the account increased, he asked Harold to invest a portion of it into several ventures. Some were low risk, and some were medium risk, but all were extremely successful, and the account grew quickly.

Eli seemed to have a natural gift when it came to money. He knew exactly where to invest it, but more impressively, he knew exactly when to pull it back out. Eli was so successful that Harold had been tempted to follow his investment trail with his own money. He was smart enough to pray over the idea, though, and ask God if it was something he should do. God's answer, which Harold felt deep in his heart, was a resounding *no*. So, Harold decided to make his own investment choices before showing the options to Eli. He wrote them down to eliminate any temptation to change them, especially when they differed from Eli's choices. God blessed Harold's diligence by allowing most of his investments to have an overall upward trend, but none of them matched the boy's success.

Harold was impressed with the rate of growth in Eli's smaller account over the years and laughed at himself for continuing to call it *small*. But the growth in the larger account was not only impressive, it was extraordinary! Eli had invested some of the money from the banknotes into the same ventures as his lesser account, and those parallel investments created a steady growth for each account. What made the larger one so remarkable, however, were the investments which the boy isolated to that account. He chose high-risk ventures and moved the money from the banknotes between so many different investments that, if it weren't for his uncanny success rate, Harold would have thought he was being reckless.

He remembered the first time the boy had done this. Harold had selected a stack of investment choices for Eli to look at. He had mixed a variety of risk into the pile just to see what he would do with it all. After studying the information for a few minutes, Eli pointed to one of them, insisting Harold invest a substantial amount from his bigger account.

"That's a high-risk investment, Eli. Even with the potential of a high return, I didn't think you would choose that one. I only put it in there to see if you'd recognize it for what it is."

"I do; it has a high return," the boy said.

"It has a high risk," Harold pointed out. "That's what you need to consider. High-risk means the high return may not happen. You could lose a lot of money."

"I could make even more," Eli countered. "I thought that's what you were trying to teach me."

"I'm trying to teach you how to grow your money responsibly. Are you being a good steward of your money by taking such a high risk?"

"Mr. Ross, it isn't my money. If God wants it to grow, it will. I can't explain it, but this investment is the right choice. It feels like a good investment."

"You can't make your choices based on feelings, Eli."

"Why not? It works for me. And not just with the money. Please, let me try it."

Harold decided to let him. If he lost the money it would be a hard but important lesson. However, Eli didn't lose it that time… or the next time… or the next time after that. And even with all those successes, Harold still sat at his desk, rubbing his chin in wonder. Eli's wealth had grown at an unprecedented rate in a short amount of time. Harold had never seen anything like it. He *had* to give God the credit; there was no other explanation.

He gathered the paperwork in front of him. In a few hours, that blessed young man would be sitting in Harold's office discussing the latest state of his accounts. Eli would soon be a father, and the baby's arrival was an understandable distraction. But hopefully, Harold could draw the soon-to-be father's mind out of his future excitement in order to conduct a small amount of business today.

Chapter 74
ELI

The mid-September glow in the early evening sky cast a golden hue on the hills as Eli walked home from the Larson farm. Over the past several weeks, he was able to get a considerable amount of repairs and preparations done for his friend. Ray had commented that this fall's harvest was stacking up to be one of the smoothest yet. He couldn't imagine running into any bumps or hitches for the rest of the season, thanks to Eli's help.

That morning, Eli talked to Ray about having some time off. He wanted to take Ada to Oak Springs for their yearly visit with the caravan later in the month. Ray assured him that the timing would not be a problem and, once again, gave him the okay to leave. While walking home, Eli's mind drifted to their travel plans.

As he rounded the bend, he saw Isaac walking along the road leading away from the Miller farm. Isaac waved as he approached. Eli waited for him, and they walked the rest of the way together.

"Hey, Eli. Are you heading over to the church tonight?"

"What for?"

"For John's meeting, of course," Isaac said.

"John Miller? I don't know anything about it."

"Well you should come anyway. I'm sure he won't mind."

"What's the meeting about?" Eli asked.

"I don't know exactly, some sort of investment. John seems to think I'll be interested. But if it's that good, we should both take a look. What do you say?"

Eli hesitated. "Is David going to be there?"

"I don't know that either," Isaac said, laughing. "Come on, it might be worth it. I'm going home to change and then I'm heading over there. Let Ada know you might be late for supper and come with me."

"Okay," Eli said. "This should be interesting."

The men went into their homes, changed out of their work clothes, and walked into town. When they got to the church, Eli made a quick note of who was and who wasn't there. Most notably absent were David, Marcus, and Ray. He also noticed the disdain on John's face when he saw Eli walk into the building.

"What are you doing here?" John blurted out.

"Isaac invited me."

"Of course he did," John said, narrowing his eyes.

The men settled into their seats and John began to talk. Eli listened as the farmer explained a too-good-to-be-true product to the group. Throughout his speech, John avoided looking at Eli, even though he sat in the front pew. After listening for a few minutes, Eli didn't need to hear any more. He tried to wait for a pause in the presentation, but the more John spoke, the more Eli was unable to hold his tongue.

"Miracle Corn? Come on, you can't be serious."

John finally looked at him. "It's just a catchy name to help market it." He sounded as though he were explaining a difficult concept to a child. "This company is above board, Eli. Their corn has a forty percent higher yield than other corn; it's all science. Look, I know this is probably hard for you to wrap your brain around, but these men can invest in the company as well as in the seed itself. They'll get returns as the company grows *and* from their higher crop yields. That means more profit in their pockets all around. You see? This meeting really wasn't intended for you."

Eli stood up. "What about Ray, why isn't he here? Did you forget to invite him, or was he just too smart to come?"

"Ray! Are you kidding? He's too stuck in his ways. He's not going to have the guts to put himself out there."

"This is a bad investment, John. It's a mistake."

"What would *you* know about investing? You can't come in here with your simple understanding of things and try to tell me I don't know what I'm talking about. The testimonies for this corn are staggering; we'd all be idiots not to invest." He picked up some fliers and turned to the rest of the men. "If we don't move on this quickly, we're going to miss out."

Eli snatched a paper out of John's hand and glanced over it. "Who are these testimonies from? Look at this. These are all from men directly involved with the company. They're going to tell you what they want you to believe. They all have something to lose if more people don't invest. Show me something from a non-investing farmer—or an impartial scientist. These testimonies are worthless."

"And that's your quick assessment, is it?" John said. "You're suggesting we all steer clear just because *you* don't want to trust what's being said about it. Don't you think the men cultivating this corn seed would know more about it than you? You keep complaining that I tell people what to do with their money, and then you come in here and tell these men not to invest. What do you think you're doing? Maybe you should take your own advice and let these intelligent men make up their own minds."

Eli turned to his neighbor. "Isaac, you're not considering this, are you?"

"Well... I don't know... I'm no expert. What if John's right?"

"He's not. You have to believe me. Don't invest in this."

"You know, Eli," John said, his voice rising to a near shout. "Just because you like wallowing in poverty doesn't mean the rest of us do. How dare you come into this meeting and tell these men not to do something that could change their lives. This is why I didn't invite you. You know nothing about money. You're poor. You're pathetic. You're lazy. You have no work ethic. What makes you think anyone here would even listen to you? You obviously don't care about the people of this town or their success. And you pretend to be all great and heroic bringing that doctor here. You've got this poor, humble do-gooder act going on, but I know the truth, boy! You didn't contribute a cent to that Martin baby's surgery."

John wiped at his mouth as he glanced around the room. "You hear that, men? How much of your hard-earned money did you all give for that baby? Eli, here—he didn't give anything."

Eli's anger boiled over. "You have no idea what I gave toward Angel's surgery..." he began to say, but John cut him off.

"Oh, yes I do. I saw the ledger; I saw what everyone gave. You weren't even on that list."

As Eli's mouth dropped open, Marcus and David stepped into the church, looking concerned.

"What is everyone doing here?" the pastor asked. "We could hear you shouting all the way down the street. I didn't approve this gathering. What's going on?"

Eli barely heard him. "That ledger was none of your business." He took a step closer to John. "Why don't you tell Marcus how you've been snooping around his office? Go ahead, there he is." He pointed at the two men who had just entered the building. "Hey David, listen to this. John has some foolish investment idea he thinks everyone in town should jump on. How about that? No, wait. I mean everyone except the people who might actually know how bad it is."

As Eli spoke, John clenched his teeth and breathed through flaring nostrils. Eli pressed his finger into John's shoulder and pushed him toward the front of the room.

"You know, John, I really thought you were smarter than this. But I guess you've thrown away any intelligence you might have had, and you've focused whatever brain is left into all your angry, prejudiced ideas. I am done with your insults. You're the one who doesn't know anything. If you invest in this, *you're* the idiot."

With that last word, John's fist shot out. Eli's instinct was triggered by his anger, and he countered the attack. He sidestepped John's strike, grabbed his wrist, and twisted his arm behind his back. Eli pushed the farmer's shoulder toward the front wall of the church and pinned his chest against it with the weight of his body. He brought his face close to John's ear.

"You really want to fight me?" he growled, "Is that how you want this to go?" He brought his fist up and let it hover in the air, level with John's face. Blinded by his anger, Eli was oblivious to the other men in the room.

The pastor's voice cut through all the murmuring. "Stop!"

Eli glared at John's grimacing face, unable to lower his arm. Before he knew what he was doing, his fist shot forward and sunk into the wall a mere inch from the farmer's nose. He pushed himself away and spun around to face the others. Some of the men looked ready to jump on him. David held his arms out in an effort to block them. Marcus stepped forward with his hands held up, palm side out.

"You need to calm down," he said in a composed tone. "It's over, okay."

Eli raised a hand and pointed at the pastor as he turned and backed toward the door. "You're right, it *is* over," he said, spitting out the words. "I'm *done*, Marcus." He looked around the room and his eyes landed on the banker. "Tell them whatever you want, David. This is a bad investment. Maybe they'll listen to you."

He spun around and stormed out of the church, ignoring Marcus as he called after him. He blindly walked toward his home, cradling his swelling hand as he went.

Chapter 75
MARCUS

Marcus knocked on the Gardners' door. He waited as the seconds stretched out in front of him. Just as he was about to knock again, the door opened halfway. Ada blocked the entrance with her body, neglecting to adorn her face with her usual welcoming smile. She stood in silence, peering at him as he waited in the low twilight.

"Is he here?" Marcus finally asked. "I need to talk to him. Can I please come in?"

She pressed her mouth together, considering his request. "Not until you tell me something first. What does the other guy look like?" Her voice wavered slightly.

"The 'other guy' is a dent in the church wall," Marcus replied. "But John Miller probably thinks that dent landed a little too close to his face for comfort."

Ada bit her lip and looked down. After a pause, she opened the door the rest of the way. "He's in the kitchen," she said, gesturing him in.

Marcus found Eli sitting at the table. He leaned back in his chair and held a cold, wet rag against his knuckles. Reddish-pink smears of blood stained the cloth.

"That's going to hurt," Marcus said.

Eli kept his face straight. "What do you want?"

"Isaac filled me in on what transpired between you and John before I got there. Look, Eli, this is going to have to be dealt with."

"Dealt with!" he said, cutting Marcus off before he could say more. "What is that supposed to mean? John has been after me ever since I moved here. I haven't done anything to deserve it. There wasn't a single man in that room who came to my defense tonight. What am I even doing here?"

"Eli…" Marcus started to say.

"No, you saw it yourself. John swung at me, but who did you choose to call off? Not one man, Marcus. Not even you."

"Okay, you're right; he swung first. But from what I could see, you had the upper hand. You may not have hit him, but your fist flew also. We need to resolve whatever is going on between you two. Take the night to cool off and come to my office tomorrow afternoon. I'll have John meet us there as well. We can lay everything out on the table and figure out what's causing this."

"I won't be there." Eli peeked under the rag at his knuckles. "Ada and I are leaving in the morning."

"What do you mean?" Marcus asked.

"We're going home."

"For how long?"

Eli scowled. "I don't know." He wouldn't look up.

Marcus glanced at Ada, who remained quiet as she peered back at him.

"Listen," he said, sitting in the chair across from Eli. "Why don't Grace and I join you? I'd like to meet your family and see where you grew up. I can't leave until after the service on Sunday, but we'll come as soon as we can. What do you say? Just tell me how to find you."

Eli turned his head away from Marcus and remained silent as he clenched his jaw tighter. Marcus looked at Ada again for an answer. She dropped her shoulders.

"It will only take you two days to get to Oak Springs if you go through Clearwater. If you leave as soon as the service is over, you should arrive around five o'clock on Monday evening. There's a coffee house at the Inn; it stays open late. You can meet us there and follow us the rest of the way. But Marcus, come prepared. We spend a lot of time outside."

He nodded and thanked her as he watched Eli closely. "You will meet us there, right?" he asked. "Promise you'll be there."

Eli stood, still avoiding his eyes. "Ada, show Marcus out. We need to start packing," he said and walked out of the room.

Chapter 76

ROSA

"Jed..." Rosa nudged him as the wagon approached. "They're here."
She wasn't expecting them to arrive for another week, and certainly not on a Friday. She figured they would have waited for a weekend to travel. As everyone set their supper aside and moved to greet the couple, Rosa noticed a subtle difference in Eli's posture. He wore a thin smile as he greeted them, and there was no energy behind it. Maybe he was just tired. But when she hugged Ada, she knew something was wrong.

"Is everything all right?" she whispered.

Ada glanced at Eli. "We'll see..."

Jed and Rosa helped them clear out their vardo and unpack the wagon. Eli's responses to their questions were short. Jed must have picked up on the tension as well, but he didn't press the subject. As they carried their things into the vardo, Eli kept his work gloves on and favored his right hand.

Soon, they joined the group around the fire, and Hattie offered the couple some supper. Eli sat with his hands stuffed in his coat pockets, claiming he wasn't hungry. He watched the flames flickering into the dim night, barely responding to the inquiries about their journey. Even Lily's playful prodding was unable to elicit more than a faint smile from the young man. His words remained few as she tried to show him her new toy. He brought his left hand out of his pocket when she begged him to hold it.

Rosa stood and carried her chair toward them. She placed it in the space between him and Jed and sent the little girl back to her mother. She raised her eyebrows at Jed before sitting down and turning to Eli.

"Let me see it." She held out her hand.

"It's all right, Rosa," he insisted, not budging.

"I'll decide that. Show me."

The rest of the group was quiet. He pulled his right hand out of his pocket and placed it in hers. It was bruised and swollen; the knuckles had barely started to scab over.

"Oh, Eli…"

She sighed and gently pressed around the top of his hand. He winced as she checked his bones.

"Well, I don't think you broke it, but I'm going to wrap it anyway."

She stood and went to her vardo to collect a few things. When she returned, she rubbed ointment onto his knuckles and began wrapping his hand in strips of bandages.

"Who'd you hit?" Jed asked, breaking the silence.

Eli's eyes shifted from his hand to the question. He shook his head and glanced at the ground, letting a quiet scoff escape his throat. Jed tried again.

"Was someone messing with Ada?"

"No, Jed, I was just angry. I hit a wall."

"Eli, every man has a responsibility to protect his family, and I've never told you to back away from that kind of fight. But if you only needed to let off some steam, then it doesn't matter if you hit a face or a wall. When your anger moves to your fist, you need to walk it off."

"I've been walking it off for four years!"

Rosa scarcely finished wrapping his injury; he pulled his hand away and nodded a quick thank you to her. Standing, he glanced at Ada.

"I'm going to bed," he said and left the group.

Rosa flashed a look toward Jed, who sighed and turned to Ada.

"What's going on? Who's he fighting with?"

She shifted her worried eyes between them. "I think… I think he's fighting himself."

Chapter *77*

ADA

Ada peeked at the late Monday sun as Hattie told her about last summer's markets. The cheerful woman laughed while relaying a humorous event involving a clumsy man and one of their tables, but Ada found it hard to concentrate on the anecdote; she was worried about Eli. Even though he had disappeared every morning since their arrival and stayed away for hours, she had prayed that—at least today—he would be back by now.

On Saturday, he spent the entire day fishing at the lake. He left camp before any of the other men could wake up and join him. Long before the sun had risen, Ada heard him dig the fishing gear out of the shed and call quietly to Cobra.

In the late afternoon, Jed went to look for him but returned unsuccessful. Eli must have hiked out farther than usual. He had a lot on his mind, so she didn't start worrying until the sun went down and he still hadn't returned. Several hours after Ada had gone to bed, the door opened, and he stepped into the vardo.

Ada sat up. "Eli, where have you been? I couldn't sleep."

"Sorry. I went to the other side of the lake." He changed and climbed under the covers.

"You're cold. Did you eat?"

"I cooked some of the fish I caught. I didn't mean to worry you." That was the only explanation she got that night.

During worship the next morning, Eli sat in silence as he stared into the fire. He didn't move the entire time. He didn't sing any of the songs or share in the comments as he normally did. Ada couldn't tell if he had heard a single word of Ira's sermon. After breakfast, he grabbed a pole and started down the path to the creek. Jed called after him and asked if he wanted company, but Eli shook his head and continued to walk away without turning around.

Again, he didn't return until after dark. Ada didn't scold him when he slipped into bed. She wrapped her arms around him, warming him up as they fell asleep in silence. When he climbed out of bed the next morning, she rolled over and watched him get ready for the day.

"Eli," she said, causing him to pause at the door. "Marcus and Grace will be arriving at the coffee house tonight."

"I know," he replied and walked out.

The sun had now made a significant arc in the sky. Hattie continued to relay her story as a knot grew in Ada's stomach. Eli wasn't going to be back in time. She turned to the woman, who was attempting to distract her.

"I'm sorry, Hattie. Do you know what time it is?"

Hattie stopped speaking and glanced at Floyd. He pulled a watch out of his pocket. "It's ten past four," he informed her.

"Will you please excuse me?" She stood up.

Jed and Rosa had been talking in their vardo for the past hour. She walked to their door, and after she tapped lightly, Jed pulled it open and peered down at her.

"Could you take me into town?" she asked. "Our friends will be here soon."

He looked past her and scanned the camp. Sighing, he grabbed his coat and said, "Yeah, let's go." As they walked to the wagon, he stopped and placed his hand on her shoulder. "I'm sorry, Ada. I don't think he'll let me help this time."

"No," she agreed. "He's going to have to figure this one out for himself."

Chapter 78

ELI

*E*li tied a small, weak plant to the stake. One of its leaves was torn and dangling. He wondered if this one would survive. Nevertheless, it still deserved a chance. He spread dirt around the roots. The dark soil had rubbed into his skin, lessening the contrast between the pigment of his flesh and the ink in his tattoos. As he drizzled water around the base of the plant, he heard a voice.

"Eli, I want to show you something."

He stood and stretched his aching muscles. As he stepped forward, he was no longer in the field but on the edge of a steep hill. The man from the field stood next to him. Eli could vaguely see him in the fringe of his vision.

"There." The man pointed at a town below.

Eli followed the direction of his gesture. Faceless, nondescript people walked along the street of the town, nodding greetings to each other as they went about their business.

"Why there?" He didn't see what was so special about that place.

The man put a hand on his shoulder. "Does it matter? That's the place because I said it is. How badly do you need to know all the 'whys' and 'whats' before I'm ready to tell you?"

Eli's eyes drifted across the figures in the street. As he turned toward the man, he discovered he was alone again, but he could still hear his voice.

"Eli, wake up. It's almost time..."

263

Eli's eyes sprung open as a shadowy, echoing voice faded from his mind. He became aware of Ada's body pressing against his back. Turning over, he put an arm around her. As he felt her sigh, he thought about the night he had asked her to go with him when it was time to leave. Would she still agree all these years later? They had just lost Ruth Ann, and she barely had time to grieve. He closed his eyes and whispered into the night.

"Lord, I promise I'll go, but please let me give her a little more time."

Chapter 79

MARCUS

Marcus sat at the table with Grace and pulled his watch out of his pocket again. It was a quarter past five.

"I'm sure he'll be here," he said, hoping to bolster his own confidence by reassuring Grace.

He put his watch away and took another sip of his lukewarm coffee. They had made good time, arriving at the coffee house twenty-five minutes after four. Now, fifty minutes later, the shop door opened and Ada finally entered. She was accompanied by a tall, broad-shouldered man with a beard. Eli, however, was not with her. She smiled and waved at them. They stood to give the young woman a hug as she asked about their journey.

"This is Jed." She indicated the man standing by her. "Jed, this is Pastor and Mrs. Duncan."

"Marcus," he insisted when Jed took his hand. "And this is Grace." As they followed Jed out of the shop, Marcus turned to Ada. "Eli didn't come."

"He couldn't make it." There was an apologetic tone in her voice.

Ada sat in the carriage with the Duncans while Jed led them to the camp in his hitch wagon. When they arrived, a pleasant group of people met them, but Eli was still nowhere to be seen. Jed ran through the introductions, and a woman named Rosa took Grace by the hand. She smiled at Marcus and reached over to Ada as well. Though she directed her words to the young woman, she spoke to all three of them.

"Eli set up the tent after you left. He moved your things out there so your guests could stay in your vardo."

"Is he here?" Ada asked.

Rosa shook her head. "He brought some fish home for supper. He knows it will be ready soon; I'm sure he'll be back."

Eli didn't return for the meal, though. Marcus was worried about him, but despite his absence—and Ada's quieter than normal temperament—he enjoyed getting to know the couple's adopted family. Soon it was time for bed. As they retired to the quaint wagon home, Marcus marveled at the workmanship Eli had put into it and wondered if he would see his friend in the morning.

A meal cooked over a campfire always made the food seem more nourishing. Marcus sat by the open flames, enjoying a full stomach after an amazing breakfast. As the caravan entertained them with tales about their lives, his admiration for them continued to grow. He was gaining a deep respect for Jed, who had a strong yet gentle way that was reinforced by his confident presence. Now that he had met Eli's mentor, Marcus could see Jed's influence in the better side of the young man's personality.

Earlier that morning, Marcus emerged from the vardo to find Eli sitting in a chair next to Ada. The young man stared despondently into the fire, unable to find his way back to his good-natured self. Even though Eli barely acknowledged anyone all through breakfast, Marcus was relieved to see him.

"You know, Jed," he said as the conversation lulled, "I've enjoyed coming here and meeting all of you. It's been a good eye-opener to see the life Eli and Ada had before moving to our town. I'm glad to know the people who have been instrumental in their growth. I can see Eli's best qualities in you folks. I'm sure he appreciates what a blessing you are."

He looked at Eli and took on a more serious tone. "But I hope he also realizes that he has been a blessing to his friends in East Haven. Our town is better with him there."

Eli glanced up from the fire.

"I have to admit, though," Marcus said as he continued to look at Eli, "I'm worried we're going to lose him. He may decide not to come back, and that would be a great loss to me."

Eli peered at him in silence, and Marcus sighed when his unreadable expression didn't change.

After a drawn-out pause, Jed nodded. "You're right, Marcus. You just might lose him. Once he makes up his mind about something, it's hard to convince him otherwise."

Still looking at Marcus, Eli stood and shook his head slowly. "Don't…" he began. "I haven't decided anything yet." He turned and walked down a path leading away from camp.

"Do you know where he's going?" Marcus asked Jed as he watched him leave.

"Yeah. If you follow that path, you'll find a tree with a broken limb. To the left of the tree is a small trail that will take you to a clearing by the edge of the creek. He's probably going there."

Marcus nodded and went after him. He found Eli sitting on the bank, throwing rocks into the creek. He joined him on the ground, and they watched the water flow by. The creek gurgled as a twig snapped somewhere in the woods.

"I am truly sorry that I made you feel as though I agreed with John," Marcus said. "I don't know why he dislikes you so much, and I don't know where his opinions come from, but they're not mine. And they're not the opinion of anyone who has taken the time to get to know you." As he spoke, the young man's head lowered. "I've always known you to be confident, Eli. I know you don't care what John thinks of you. His ignorance provokes you, but he's not the one you're wrestling with. Why did you come to East Haven anyway? There must have been a reason for you to leave all of this."

Eli looked up. "I really thought God was calling me there," he said, finally opening up. "I thought I would find some answers, but men like John make me think I must have heard wrong."

He sighed, sounding defeated. "I had a dream when I was younger. God was calling me to do something for Him, but I still don't know what it is. That dream put a desire in my heart to serve the Lord, and I have been trying to fill it ever since."

Eli shifted his body and rubbed his bandaged hand. "There are only three things in life that I desire. I want to take care of Ada, I want to be a father someday, and I want to live for God. I *have* to do whatever He's asking of me, but He won't tell me what it is."

After a pause, Eli squinted his eyes and frowned. "You're right, Marcus. I don't really care what John or anyone else thinks of me. What I don't understand is why God would put this desire in my heart, ask me to move Ada away from our family, and then leave us there with no answers. I feel like I've wasted years, and I'm no closer to discovering it now than I was before I started." He lowered his eyes again and stared at the ground.

"I don't think you're looking at the whole picture," Marcus said. "You're struggling with a couple of things. First of all, you're mad at God, and that means you can't see clearly."

Eli shook his head. "I'm not mad at God. What would be the point of that? I get it; His plan is best. I'm just mad that I can't figure it out. It's obviously not in East Haven."

Marcus pointed at his friend. "That, right there. That's what I'm talking about. You're angry with God because He's taking you down a path that doesn't look like you thought it should, and He isn't backing it up with any answers. You won't admit you're mad at Him, and because you won't, you can't deal with it. You've let your anger build up so much that you doubt your own calling. You're willing to give up just because God won't give you the answers you're demanding. Why should He? You're not ready yet."

Eli squeezed his eyes closed. "You sound like Jed," he muttered.

"Good," Marcus said with a short laugh. "He's a smart man. Look, Eli. It's okay to admit that you're frustrated with God's timing. It's even okay to admit that you're mad at Him; He can handle it. But don't stay there. Confess it and try to start trusting Him again. I know it's hard, but you won't get past this until you do. Ask Him to give you the patience to wait on Him. Waiting on God means you're resting on a fine line between the hopeful expectations of His promises and the contentment of where He has you. It's easy to fall off of that line when you're not holding on to God for balance."

Eli nodded at his words. "Okay," he whispered. "I admit it; I *am* angry at God. I hate how it feels, Marcus, but I don't know how to get rid of it."

"You can start by thinking about all the times God *has* given you answers, and then list everything He's done for you. That might help you remember how to trust Him. Make a choice to let go of your anger, and then keep letting go of it—every hour if you have to. One day, you won't want to pick it up again." He gripped Eli's shoulder. "Come on, let's pray about it right now."

They lowered their heads and Marcus asked Jesus to fill Eli with trust. He asked Him to help Eli with his anger and, as they prayed, he felt the young man's tension melt away.

After a long pause, Eli asked, "So... what's the other thing? You said I'm struggling with a couple of things."

"Hmm." Marcus sighed. "How can I explain this? Try to hear me out, Eli. Why should John or anyone else in our town accept who you are if you won't even accept it? You say you want to live for God; that's great. But you won't embrace His gifts. He has given you the gift of giving and the means to do it, but you hide those gifts away as if you're ashamed of them."

"No, Marcus, now that's where I think you're wrong. I was willing to learn how to make that money grow. I *do* use the tools God has given me, and I try to use them in a way that honors Him. I want to help people; I want to give. That's what I need Him to show me. I want to know how to use that money for His glory. I'm not ashamed of it."

"Then why are David and I the only ones who know you have it?" he asked.

Eli's expression faltered. "I don't know... I guess I don't want people to treat me differently because of it. I want to know who my true friends are, regardless of the money. I don't want anyone to put me on a pedestal."

"Okay, I get that," Marcus said. "You don't have to put your money out there for everyone to see. But you also don't have to hide it as if it's some big secret. You're like a person who's been given the gift of song, but instead of using that talent to draw people into worship, you never share it with anyone for fear of the vanity it might give you. How is that glorifying God? How is that being a good steward of the gifts He's given you? You're trying to be humble, but it's selfish. You're a good man, Eli. Don't trip yourself up with misplaced humility. God doesn't make mistakes, and it's prideful to think that He does."

"Ouch. You just keep knocking me down. I'm not sure I can take much more of your insight."

"Well, I'll stop then. I think we've reached the end of my wisdom anyway," Marcus said with a grin.

Eli picked up a rock and rolled it around in his uninjured hand. He chuckled at himself. "I've been pretty awful these last few days, haven't I? I think I need to apologize to everyone. I'm sorry for how I treated you through all of this. I'm not sure why you still like me."

"Who said I did?" Marcus replied, laughing. "I'm only here for the fish. Jed said you all have some good-sized salmon in this creek. You know, I don't know why it's called a creek; this here is a river."

The two men laughed together.

"You want to go fishing?" Eli said. "We'll go first thing tomorrow. You haven't experienced early until you've gone early-morning fishing with Jed." He threw the rock into the river.

"Hey!" Marcus yelled. "Don't scare away my fish."

A mischievous smile grew on Eli's face as he picked up another rock.

Chapter 80
ELI

Eli had converted one of their two extra rooms into an office. A comfortable chair sat next to a small desk made from dark-stained hardwood. The document box Tony had given them rested on top of the desk. Their marriage certificate could be found at the bottom of the box, and above that was a stack of letters from Nathan Keeler.

The letters contained stories of some of the children who had undergone surgeries over the past year. Dr. Keeler sent a letter faithfully every month. He didn't write about every child he worked with, only those benefiting directly from Eli's quarterly contributions, which averaged about two per month. Eli only skimmed over the stories before throwing them into the box. It made him uncomfortable to read the letters. But after listening to Marcus point out his weaknesses ten days ago, he thought it might be good for him to pay closer attention to the letter he currently held in his hand.

After returning from the West Woods, Eli had gone to the post office to collect his mail. In the stack, he found this current letter detailing the children who had received surgeries back in August. It took the doctor a month to get his letters out, which was why Eli would be reading about these at the end of September. Ironically, now that he intended to read through his discomfort, this letter felt thicker than the previous ones.

As he leaned back in his chair, he read about the first child, a little boy named Paul. The tiny eight-month-old had undergone the first of several surgeries to close a gap in both sides of his upper lip as well as his pallet.

His disfigurement had made it difficult to eat, and his parents were worried about his growth. In addition to his eating challenges, he had chronic ear pain with a suspected loss of hearing. Eli wanted to read more about this boy's progress in the future, and for the first time, he appreciated Nathan's efforts to keep him informed.

The next page told of a six-year-old girl named Sarah who had a small gap in her lip. She had a single surgery that had fixed the problem immediately, just like Angel. The sad part of this little girl's story was that she had been abandoned as an infant. Her parents were unwilling to keep a child they thought was damaged. They left her on the steps of an orphanage, forcing her to deal with her disfigurement on her own. Her life must have been difficult as other children teased her. It was a shame to suffer that kind of isolation when there was such a simple fix. He paused briefly and prayed for the young girl.

As he finished reading about Sarah, he turned to the final page. It wasn't another child's story; it was an invitation. The doctor and his wife were holding an appreciation banquet for their donors on the tenth of December. Nathan asked the Gardners to come to Lambury to participate in the event.

Eli's first thought was no thank you! But then he remembered Marcus' poignant criticism and decided to give it more consideration. Would it really be so horrible to let the Keelers thank him along with all their other donors? Even though the thought of attending Nathan's banquet filled him with apprehension, under that hesitation was a feeling that he ought to go.

"Okay, fine," he thought, "I'll go." In that moment, Eli chose to step out of his comfort zone. He would take his wife to the banquet in Lambury no matter how anxious it made him feel.

Chapter 81

JAMES

James O'Conner stood in the banquet hall, scanning the crowd of people dressed in tails and lacy gowns. He did not want to be here, but his good friend Nathan Keeler had insisted. Nathan said he wanted to introduce James to someone who would be at the dinner, but he and Elizabeth were both busy hosting. James would have to fend for himself. He knew he should mingle with some of the well-to-do men with money to spare, but he felt awkward pushing himself on them. Nathan said that was part of his problem and why he didn't have more success. He looked around the hall, trying to decide which group to chat with first. Catching sight of a young man standing by himself, James gathered his courage, walked up to him, and nodded.

"You look about as uncomfortable as I feel," James said.

"Is it that obvious?" the man asked.

"At first, I thought you might be a reporter for the paper. But you aren't talking to anyone, so that wouldn't make for a very good story, would it?" James chuckled.

"Reporters?" The man looked around the banquet hall. "They won't be here, will they?"

"I was joking," James said with an apologetic laugh. "Nathan keeps his banquets closed. Though, I'm sure a few of these men wish he wouldn't. You know, 'the press is good for business,' and all. Are you here with an organization?"

"No, I'm here with my wife. She was just pulled away to meet some of the other women. What about you, are you one of Dr. Keeler's donors?"

"No, a friend and sometimes-volunteer. Oh, I'm sorry. My name is James." He held out his hand.

"I'm Eli," the young man replied, taking his hand. "So, how do you know Dr. Keeler?"

"Nathan and I met at the hospital," James explained. "We both used to work there years ago. Actually, my wife Sophia and I still do, but Nathan moved on so he could focus on his ministry." He laughed. "You know, I have a ministry of my own. It's nothing like Nathan's, but my wife and I work hard at it. Nathan and Elizabeth inspire us. He insisted I come here tonight and talk to some of these gentlemen about what I do. He thought I might find a few people who would be interested in donating to my cause. Lack of funding is my biggest challenge."

"And I'm guessing you haven't done that yet," Eli said.

James chuckled and shook his head. "Nope, you're the first person I've talked to. Maybe you'll laugh, but I find all these rich men hard to engage. They look at you as though they might fall asleep if you don't hurry up and get to the point. You know what I mean? You and I, we're just a couple of regular fellows; but not them. People with money tote around a self-important attitude that I find unapproachable."

"Well, I'm sure not all of them are like that," Eli said.

"Oh yeah, I'm generalizing. But when you put me in a situation like this, knowing I need to put myself out there and talk to them… well, that's where my insecurities take me," James confessed.

"So, why don't you practice on me then," Eli suggested. "I'll listen to you talk about your ministry, and you can be comfortable knowing that I'm just a regular guy, like you."

"Okay, you've got a deal," James said, smiling. "I make legs. I'm the leg man."

"The leg man?" Eli looked intrigued.

"Yeah. I make prosthetic legs for children. You see, these legs can be expensive. Now, when an adult needs one, he saves up and eventually buys one. One, mind you! He might be able to go the rest of his life with that one leg, if he takes good care of it." James paused for effect.

Eli nodded. "I think I see where you're going with this."

"Exactly! When a child receives a limb, he's going to grow out of it quicker than his parents can save up for a new one. Walking on a prosthetic leg that's too short or doesn't fit correctly can have negative effects on their posture. My belief is that it doesn't matter if the parents can afford another leg or not; that child will still need a new one. So, twice a year I have a leg run." James laughed at his pun. "It's an event where families can come and have their child's limb repaired or exchanged for another when needed. The limbs can be reused by other children over and over again as long as they're still in good condition. These previously used legs aren't as expensive, and often times, I can repair them quickly or make adjustments on them right there in my studio.

"The families pay what they can," James continued. "But no child is turned away without a new or adjusted limb, no matter how creative we have to get. You should see how my wife and I rig some of these legs up when supplies start to get low. They're always safe, but they aren't always pretty." James grinned proudly, exposing most of his teeth.

"So, you said funding is your biggest challenge. I assume whatever the families can pay isn't enough."

"Not even close!" James said. "Sophia and I pay for a lot of it ourselves. We both work at the hospital, like I mentioned earlier. But we moved out of our apartment, and now we live in my studio. It saves on money and time."

"Wow, that's dedication," Eli said. "It sounds like a great ministry, and you've explained it well. I don't see why you're worried about talking with these men."

"Well, it was easy talking to you about it," James replied. "Thanks for listening."

At that moment, Dr. Keeler announced it was time to sit down. He wanted to say a few words while the food was being served. James glanced at Eli.

"It looks like *this* event has just started. Maybe I'll have enough courage to talk to a few gentlemen afterwards. Enjoy the evening, Eli." He held out a hand to him again.

"Do you have a card?" Eli asked, taking his hand. "I'd like to contact you later."

James nodded as he reached into his pocket and pulled out a card for this friendly, regular guy.

Chapter 82

ELI

Eli found Ada, and they sat at their assigned seats. He felt out of place as he glanced in either direction to spy out the proper etiquette for the evening. From their table, he had a clear view of the stage at the front of the banquet hall. Near the back of the stage sat an odd piece of decoration that he couldn't help wondering about. It wasn't very attractive. It was nothing more than a twisted network of metal branches attached to a wooden base. It reminded Eli of a dormant, leafless tree one might find in the winter woods—an odd choice for a decoration, considering the opulence of the banquet hall.

As the guests politely ate the fancy meal placed in front of them, Nathan stood on the stage and spoke of his various donors. He called them up, one by one, to receive a plaque inscribed with a grateful sentiment from the doctor and his wife. Eli was getting nervous.

He had hoped Nathan would make a quick and general speech about his appreciation, and then let them all enjoy a nice meal in peace. But now he realized that Nathan would talk specifically about him, and he would eventually have to cross the stage to receive an obligatory plaque. Eli's food lost its flavor as he simultaneously lost his appetite. Soon, however, Nathan seemed to be concluding his presentation and there were no more plaques on the table next to him. Perhaps he realized an event like this would make Eli uncomfortable and mercifully chose to spare him the distress.

"All of the men presented with plaques this evening have been important to my ministry over the years, and I greatly appreciate the interest they have shown in my work," Nathan said, gesturing out to the audience. "Gentlemen, again, I thank you."

He gave a respectful bow to them as light applause rose from the tables. The doctor continued.

"There is one more gentleman I would like to recognize this evening."

Eli's heart began to race; this was it.

"I had the privilege of meeting Mr. Gardner a year ago this September. It was a meeting in which our paths barely crossed, but I believe it was God ordained. This young man is a humble and private giver. To be honest, I'm worried he won't be pleased that I'm bringing attention to him tonight.

"However, I choose to recognize him in this way because I truly believe he doesn't understand how far-reaching his contribution to my ministry actually is. Not only has he made it possible for our facility to purchase all new equipment, but he has also been instrumental in our ability to reach more children this year than ever before. Because of Mr. Gardner's dona-tion, we have almost doubled our surgeries for the year, which has led to our partnering with Dr. Albert Jackson." Again, a polite applause moved through the hall.

Eli glanced around the room one last time and took a sip of water to relieve his dry mouth. He leaned over and whispered in Ada's ear.

"I don't think I can do this…"

She smiled at him and took his hand. "Yes, you can."

"I would now like to ask Mr. Eli Gardner to join me on stage please."

The applause continued as Eli walked to the stage and stood next to Nathan. He smiled at the crowd and tried to leave quickly, but Nathan held his arm and pulled him back.

"I've invited several families here tonight whose children have been the recipients of surgeries funded by Mr. Gardner." He indicated the ugly branch sculpture on the stage. "I have asked them to tie fabric leaves to this tree for every person affected by his donation."

At this point, Nathan made a beckoning gesture with his hand. Families carrying babies and toddlers with small pink scars on their upper lips began to cross the stage. They stopped at the tree and tied their leaves onto it while others lined up behind them. Eli couldn't see the end of the line as it continued out the door on the side of the stage. The tree began to fill up with light and dark green leaves while Nathan continued his speech.

"This includes not only the children, but all of the family members as well. The light green leaves represent those who have had the surgery, and the dark green leaves represent their family members. For the families that could not travel to Lambury tonight, I have asked other guests to tie their leaves onto the tree."

People continued to cross the stage as the scene began to blur. Eli rubbed his eyes, trying to clear them. Nathan turned to him, indicating the tree.

"This, Eli, is how far-reaching your contribution has been. This is how God has been using you. This, as you said last year, is 'only one of the branches' on your vine."

Even though he had skimmed the letters Nathan had sent him, Eli only thought of his gift in terms of helping the doctor, Angel, and a few other children. He never allowed his understanding to extend beyond that. With this visual, he couldn't help but see God's impact through his giving.

He continued to watch the leaves multiply and finally saw the last family cross the stage. Laura held Angel as Jacob tied their leaves onto a branch. They walked toward Eli, and when they reached him, Jacob grabbed onto his arm.

"Why didn't you tell me it was from you?" he asked quietly.

"It wasn't," Eli said. "God gave you that gift."

Jacob reached up and patted him on the back as they hugged.

"Thank you, my friend," he said.

Chapter 83

ADA

Ada climbed into bed. She was about to put out the lantern and cloak their vardo in darkness, but Eli stopped her. She turned to give him her full attention. She had noticed earlier in the day how quiet he had been, but he was often quiet when something important was on his mind. She wasn't surprised that he wanted to talk now.

"Do you remember when I asked if you would be willing to leave with me?"

"Yes."

"Would you still go with me? Is your answer still the same?"

"Of course it is. Why do you keep asking that?"

"What if I said it was time to go now? We're both still grieving. If we leave now, I'll be taking you away from Jed and Rosa. I'd be asking you to leave your family."

"Eli, you're my husband." She put her hand on his arm. "You *are* my family. I'll go with you whenever you tell me it's time."

"I think God wants us to go soon. I'm going to talk to Mr. Ross about finding a town to buy a house in. It might take a few months, but I wanted to see how you felt about it."

"Where do you think we'll go? What town?"

"I don't know," he admitted. "But I'll know it when I see it. I think it will just feel right. Do you trust me, Ada?"

"I do trust you; you know I always have. God gave you to me. When I trust you, I'm also trusting Him."

Eli sighed as she extinguished the light.

Chapter 84
ELI

Eli was relieved when Nathan finally closed the door and asked the driver to take them back to their hotel. The noise of the carriage was quiet compared to the banquet, but the buzzing clamor of meeting so many people still rang in his ears.

While Ada looked out the window at the city, Eli sank into his seat. He leaned his head back and sighed. The other donors had swarmed him after dinner, introducing themselves and asking for business tips. More than one had commented on his self-made success despite his young age. Eli didn't think of himself as *self-made* any more than he thought of himself as young or old. He really didn't think of his age that often at all. At three months shy of twenty-seven, he understood that he was relatively young, but a number wasn't important.

The small crowd had been relentless in their pursuit of him, and he was only able to talk to James O'Conner during the brief formal introduction Nathan insisted on giving them. James apologized repeatedly, in case he had said anything about rich men that offended him, and Eli assured him that he was still the same regular guy he had talked to earlier. He promised to contact James soon.

There was one moment after the banquet when Eli insisted the donor crowd give him a moment of peace. A little girl holding onto a piece of paper came up to him and tugged on his jacket. She had drawn him a picture and seemed determined to put it into his hands personally. As he thought about that moment, he pulled the picture out of his pocket and looked at it again.

A woman dressed in a plain, colorless uniform caught up to her charge just as he glanced down to see who was tugging on him.

"Mr. Gardner, I am so sorry." The woman grabbed on to the girl's hand and gave it a solid yank.

He shook his head and stopped her. "That's okay, I'd like to talk to this girl." Ignoring the crowd, he went down on one knee, bringing himself to her level.

"Mr. Gard-*en*-er," she said, mispronouncing his name. "I drew you a picture."

The scar from her recent incision was still dark pink. It would soon fade, but her nose had a slightly crooked imperfection that gave her a uniquely satisfying appearance.

"Thank you," he said as he took the picture from her.

He looked at the pencil lines. Three figures drawn in the center of the paper were surrounded by small, round scribbles neatly lined up in several parallel rows which covered the entire page.

"Mr. Gardener, thank you for paying for my shurjury," she said with a slight lisp. Little tears glistened in the bottom of her eyes.

He smiled at her. "Are you Sarah?"

She nodded as the tears slipped down her round cheeks.

"Well, Sarah, you are *very* welcome," he said, blinking against his own tears. He turned her attention to the picture. "Is this you?" He pointed to the shortest figure in the center.

She nodded. "And this is you, and this is Mrs. Gardener," she said pointing to the other figures as she sniffled.

"And what are all of these?" he asked, indicating the small, round scribbles.

"Those are all your plants. The ones you take care of."

"My plants?" he asked quietly.

"Because you're a gardener, right? Don't you take care of all the plants? See, I'm helping you, because there are so many of them."

"Sarah." His voice was a low whisper. "I haven't found all my plants, yet."

"That's okay, Mr. Gardener. I can help you look for them. God will help us find them."

At that point, the woman looking after the girl said it was time to go and whisked her away before Eli could stop her. He remained on one knee, frozen in place, and watched her disappear through the door of the banquet hall.

As the carriage swayed down the street, he thought about the girl, and his eyes drifted up from the picture and rested on Ada. Despite being tired, her smile deepened as she peered at the newness of the city lights. Eli smiled at his wife and whispered the little girl's name in his mind.

Sarah. It felt right.

PART 4

Therefore if anyone cleanses himself from the latter, he will be a vessel of honor, sanctified and useful for the Master, prepared for every good work.

2 Timothy 2:21

Chapter 85

DAVID

David's office provided a warm sanctuary against the cold December air. Eli had arrived for their regular Friday lunch meeting and sat with a preoccupied expression opposite the banker. He and Ada had recently returned from Lambury where they had attended a banquet hosted by Nathan Keeler.

David wondered if the fancy event and modern city would tantalize the Gardners away from the small town of East Haven. But when he asked his friend about his time away, Eli had little to say of the experience: it was interesting, loud, even overwhelming, and he was thankful to be home. David was relieved to have an unaffected lunch partner—unaffected, that is, by the lavish lifestyle of the big city. Something, however, was exciting the young man that afternoon.

"You have a look on your face," David said as he watched him bounce his knee.

"A look? What kind of look?"

"One that tells me I'm going to have extra paperwork soon." David took another bite of his lunch as he waited for Eli to explain his next philanthropic endeavor.

"You're not really worried about more work, are you?" Eli asked with a laugh. "I figured now that Jacob is working for you—"

"Shall I put Jacob on your accounts, then?"

Eli shrugged as he drummed his fingers on the desk. "That's up to you. It doesn't really matter anymore. I'm pretty sure he knows I have money after last weekend." He glanced at the door. "And as a bank employee, isn't he bound by confidentiality anyway?"

David nodded. "Okay. I might put him on some of your projects then—if you're sure you don't mind. Now, you need to tell me what you have planned next before you wear a hole in my desk."

Eli moved his hand off the desktop. "Actually, I have something I think Jacob would be interested in." He pulled a card out of his pocket and handed it to David. "James O'Conner. I met him at Nathan's banquet. He and his wife provide children with prosthetic legs. I've written to him and asked for more information on his funding needs. He pays for most of the ministry himself, which means he can only do it part time. I know he wishes he could do more. I'd like to arrange something that will allow him to put all of his energy into it."

"All right, we can do that," David said. "Let me know when you hear from him, and we will get it all set up."

"And I'd like you to give Jacob some time off in April," Eli added. "James puts on an event every six months. It's a leg exchange for the children. I'm planning on being there, and I want Jacob to go with me."

"That's fine. I can spare him for a few days." David noticed the young man's leg still moving under the desk; he wasn't done. "What else do you have for me?"

Eli pulled a piece of paper out of his pocket. He unfolded it and smoothed it against his chest. As he looked at it, a grin spread over his face. He handed it over, and David studied it before shaking his head and looking up. Eli's eyes gleamed as his smile deepened.

"This." He tapped the paper in David's hand. "I want your help with this."

Chapter 86

ELI

Eli sat next to Ada, grasping her hand. He glanced at the plain white walls of the office before returning his gaze to Mr. Ackerman. He had sent this man a letter of inquiry in January. Upon receiving his reply, Eli brought it straight to David, unable to wait until their next lunch meeting. The letter included everything he needed to know. He could now move forward with the project he had asked David to help him with back in December. Mr. Ackerman's letter detailed all the information the couple would need to bring to him as well as the legal procedures they would need to follow. Travel plans were made immediately.

February proved to be mild, making their excursion to the big city easier. The couple had arrived in Stonewall three days ago. It was a seventeen-hour journey by train from White Falls, with a three-hour stop in Lambury. During the trip, both Eli and Ada lay awake in the sleeping car all night. The newness of the experience and the reason for their journey prevented them from being able to sleep. Instead, they tossed and turned, hoping they didn't disturb the other passengers when they occasionally whispered about their plans.

Once in town, they found their hotel, checked into their room, and spent the rest of the day exploring the trolley system and getting acquainted with the city. On the second day, they waited at the courthouse—but to no avail. On the third day, they finally stood before a judge. Eli presented him with their marriage certificate, some statements from David, a letter from Marcus, and a partially filled out form that Mr. Ackerman had sent.

The judge nodded; everything looked in order and their proceedings went quickly. He signed his consent on the form and sent the couple on their way. Now, they sat in Mr. Ackerman's office, nervous but eager. After handing him the paperwork, they waited quietly as he sifted through it.

"Well, this is going smoothly, Mr. Gardner," he said. "I just need to fill out the rest of the paperwork for our records, and we will be done here. Are you planning on leaving town today?"

"We leave tomorrow," Eli said. "I thought we might go to some of the shops in town. We don't get to experience a big city very often."

Mr. Ackerman nodded as he filled out the rest of the form.

"I hope you enjoy your stay." He pressed a stamp on the bottom of the paper. "That should do it. Congratulations, Mr. and Mrs. Gardner." He stood and shook their hands. "Please wait here."

He walked to the open door of his office and summoned a woman who worked behind a desk in the foyer. He whispered a few words to her, and she disappeared down a hallway. Mr. Ackerman sat down again.

"It will just be a moment," he said, smiling.

The couple turned their chairs and watched the door in anticipation. Eli's foot tapped lightly as he squeezed Ada's hand. She flashed a smile at him and squeezed back.

Chapter 87

SARAH

A lice put her finger up to her lip and pressed the center of it toward her nose. She crossed her eyes at Sarah and stuck out her tongue. Alice was a big, scary twelve-year-old. She was one of the oldest children at the orphanage, but everyone knew she wouldn't be around next year. The older children were usually "adopted" by someone who only required another worker they didn't have to pay. It was the fate of the unwanted, but no one liked to speak of it.

One day Sarah would be taken away also, but for now, she was safe. She was only seven, and she was small. But she wasn't pretty. Families who adopted a little girl as their very own only wanted the pretty ones. Even though Dr. Keeler had fixed her lip, she knew she would never look as nice as the girls who were adopted for real.

Sarah and the other orphans had just finished their morning lessons, and now they were required to spend an hour of quiet time at their desks. During that time, they could read, study, or practice their penmanship on their slates, but they were not allowed to talk. Sarah's intention was to make it through the entire hour without saying a word, but then Alice decided to make faces at her, and she wouldn't quit.

"You stop that, Alice Becker!" she hissed at the girl.

She tried to say it quietly, but all the others turned to stare at her. What made matters worse was that Miss Shelton walked into the room only one second before Sarah opened her mouth. She heard the outburst as well.

"Sarah," the woman said. "Come here at once."

Gleeful murmuring arose from the other children, which often happened when someone was being scolded. Sarah felt her face grow hot. She wanted to disappear as she put her book away and walked past the many gawking eyes.

Miss Shelton always wore a serious expression and had a mean way of speaking. She used sharp words that aimed right at the point of the matter. She never decorated her comments with anything calming or comforting. Miss Shelton made her feel as though she were always in trouble.

Sarah peered at her feet as she followed the woman down the hall, wondering if she would be led to the kitchen to work off her punishment. As they approached the director's office, she glanced up. Her heart skipped a beat. Forgetting herself, she grabbed the woman's arm.

"Miss Shelton, that's Mr. *Gardener*. Can I say hello to him? He helped me get my shurjury. May I please go into Mr. Ackmun's office to say hello?"

"You mean your *surgery*," the woman corrected. "And, yes. You may go into Mr. *Ackerman's* office," she said, correcting her again.

Sarah ran into the office with a huge grin on her face. "Mr. Gardener!"

She rushed toward the man. He stood up from his chair and stepped forward when he saw her. His smile was warm, and unlike Miss Shelton's stern gaze, his eyes danced as though they had a secret to share. He knelt down to meet her, and she grabbed onto his arms.

"Mr. Gardener," she whispered, "did you find any more of your plants?"

"A few of them. I get to help take care of them in April. I'm still looking for the others, but I found a very special one right here in Stonewall. I'm going to take her home with me."

"Is it a pretty plant... with a flower?"

He winked at his wife, who had moved closer to them. "I think my new plant is beautiful," he said.

"That's good." Sarah glanced around the office and noticed the papers in front of Mr. Ackerman. "Mr. Gardener, why are you here? Are you going to help one of the children again?"

"We're going to adopt one."

"Oh! That's the best kind of help," she said with a smile. "Are you getting a boy or a girl?"

"It's you, Sarah. We want to adopt you."

She took in a quick breath. Did she hear him right? She tried to ask, but her voice wouldn't work. She felt a fuzzy, distant ache within her heart that she had never allowed herself to feel before. Her eyes began to blur, and her throat tightened as she fought against the sobs that threatened to push their way out of her.

"Me?" she managed to say. "You want me?" Tears rolled down her face without her permission. "No one has ever wanted me before."

Sarah bit her lower lip and wiped at her eyes. She reached over and felt Mrs. Gardner's arm to see if she was real. This woman was going to be her mother?

"Well, we want you," Mr. Gardner said as his eyes blinked back their own tears. "And I'm so grateful God is allowing us to adopt you."

Sarah pressed her hand into her chest. She felt as though she might explode. Sobs finally burst out of her as she reached up and threw her arms around him in a tight hug. Was he really going to be her father?

He returned her hug, and the answer was an undeniable yes.

Chapter 88

ADA

As tired as she was, Ada could not pull her eyes away from the slumbering girl snuggled against her. Sarah lay in the sleeping car, tucked comfortably between her new parents while the train moved rhythmically over the tracks. The curtain was pulled closed, secluding the new family in a private envelope of bliss. Ada propped herself on her elbow and rested her cheek in her hand as she gazed at the little girl who was now her daughter.

After the adoption had been finalized, they helped Sarah pack. She didn't own much—a spare slip that was stiff and scratchy, a second pair of wool stockings, and a thin nightgown. Her most prized possession was a rag tied into something that might resemble a doll to someone with a good imagination. As they packed the girl's meager belongings, Ada caught Eli's eyes.

"Now I know why you want to go to the shops today," she whispered.

He smiled and winked.

Once in town, they walked down the street, peeking into shop windows until they found a store selling children's clothing. They bought Sarah some play clothes, a school outfit, a nice dress for church, and a few other personal essentials that Ada helped pick out while Eli waited at the store counter. He had their purchases packed into a crate, addressed to them, and sent to the back room with instructions to be delivered to the ten o'clock train heading for White Falls in the morning.

After the shopping trip, the new parents took their wide-eyed little girl to the hotel, where they decided to have supper sent to their room. They spread a blanket on the floor and ate their supper picnic-style. Sarah said she had never done such a silly thing and giggled throughout the entire meal. Her twittering was infectious, and soon all three were holding their sides, laughing so hard that they had to stop eating for several minutes.

After supper, it was time for bed, but Sarah was too excited to sleep. She asked question after question, trying to learn all she could about the new life awaiting her. Eventually, her inquiries were followed by long pauses until they stopped altogether. The young girl was finally asleep.

The next morning, they woke early, got dressed, and packed. They went into town to visit more shops before heading to the station. Once on board the train, they spent the long hours exploring the cars and playing games. Eli taught Sarah some of the hand clapping games Lily had shown him. She was a quick learner and was soon winning every round. As the sun fell behind the hills, they moved to the sleeping car and disappeared behind the curtains. Though still early, Sarah had no problem falling asleep, which was assisted by the rocking motion of the train. Because they didn't need to change trains in Lambury, they were able to stay in the sleeping car during their layover.

Ada reached over and gently pushed a strand of hair out of the girl's face. She caressed the small arm that rested against hers and looked at Eli as a tear slipped out of her eye.

"Thank you," she said quietly.

"We should thank God; it was His plan for us to have her."

"I have been," she told him. "I've been thanking God for Sarah ever since you first told me He whispered this idea into your heart. And I'm thanking you now because you listened."

Eli smiled and reached over to wipe Ada's cheek.

Chapter 89

JOHN

John shifted his weight as he listened to the pastor's closing prayer. He didn't really hear it; he was just waiting for Marcus to say his final amen so he could duck out of the sanctuary as quickly as possible. Earlier, he had been sitting with his family, but he stood up at the first appropriate pause and walked to the back. He leaned against the wall closest to the door and prepared himself for a swift escape.

For several months now, Sundays induced a certain amount of irritation for him; he had other things he could be doing. John was always busy with his farm work, even now in February, and that gave him an excuse to leave the church early when he had no good reason to stay. But lately, he felt resentment for having to be there at all. The service was just a bunch of feel-good sentiment, and he didn't have time for it. He was more comfortable in his fields or with his livestock.

He knew people didn't understand why he needed to leave so quickly, and he kept expecting someone to say something about it. When that happened, he would let that overly opinionated person know exactly why he had to leave when he did. He was doing something important; *he* was important, and he would make sure they knew it.

The prayer finally came to an end. Even before Pastor Duncan could finished saying amen, John turned, put on his hat, and walked out the door. He jogged down the steps and hurried over to where his horse was tied up. He hadn't bothered with the wagon this morning, nor did he bother dressing in his best clothes. His casual state would help ensure a speedy get away. He paused long enough to put his gloves on; that was a mistake.

"John!"

Even though he heard the pastor call, he refused to look up.

"Hey, John, hold up a minute!"

Marcus had somehow managed to run out of the building before any of his flock could bleat and bray at him. Of course, it helped that the pastor's favorite sheep wasn't even in town. But who could ever figure out what Eli Gardner did with himself these days? John tried not to think about that boy; he was still angry with him.

"Pastor, I need to get back to the farm." He avoided eye contact as he led his horse to the road.

"Yeah," Marcus said, "you're a hard man to pin down. I've been out to your place a few times, looking for you. You've been keeping busy. I saw how much of your land you've been preparing for the sowing season. It looks like a lot more than last year; you must be hoping for a big harvest."

"That's the plan," he said with a matter-of-fact tone. Whatever Marcus wanted to talk about, he didn't want to hear it. "Look, Pastor, we can talk later."

"When exactly is later, John? You've been dodging me for weeks. We need to talk now. It's been five months since you and Eli tried to take each other out, and you almost took the church building down with you—"

"That was Eli," John said, cutting him short. "And I saw how quickly you patched up that wall. We don't want to leave any evidence of his quick temper, now do we?"

"Well, the wall doesn't run off before the service is over," Marcus said bluntly. "John, I've watched you. You've never liked Eli, and I've seen you try to provoke him over and over again. I'd be hard-pressed to say he's the one with the quick temper."

John snorted contempt at the pastor's words, but Marcus continued to speak.

"You've always been angry with him. You've been passing judgment for over four years now. Why is that?"

John's pulse quickened. This was exactly what he didn't want to talk about. He glanced toward the church to see if anyone was walking out the door and then pressed his gloved finger into the pastor's chest, keeping his voice low.

"You don't understand, Marcus. You've had it too easy. Your life has been soft, and that makes you see too much good in everyone and everything."

John lowered his hand and shook his head. "I guess that can be seen as a kind of quality in a pastor, but it's just not practical. I used to think everyone was good too. It was a tough lesson when I found out how wrong I was. I figured out fairly young that my father wasn't what I thought he was, and I worked hard to make up for his faults. My life was difficult, and it wasn't fair, but I changed it for the better. I did that! I wasn't going to be pulled into that same lazy, pathetic, drunken lifestyle my father fell into. And God help me, I was *not* going to let him ruin my mother's life either."

John continued in a gruff voice. "I'm disgusted with people who won't do the work it takes to provide for their families. I don't understand how anyone can tolerate it." He took off his hat and wiped his forehead roughly. "I can't figure out why my ma was okay with it. I don't get why she couldn't see it. He was a bad father and a worse husband. And you know what? Here I am again! This town isn't any smarter than she was. I'm the only one who can see how bad that gypsy boy is, and no one is willing to hear me. None of you will listen to me any more than she would."

John shoved his hat back onto his head and grabbed the horn of his saddle. He put his foot in the stirrup and was about to pull himself up, but Marcus put a hand on his shoulder to stop him.

"John, your bitterness has blinded you. You think it's bad that I always see things in a positive light, but you can't see at all with the muck you're trying to look through. You've put Eli in a box of your own making. Explain to me how he doesn't provide for his family. They aren't starving. They own their home and the land it's on. They don't rent it; they own it. They've never once asked me or anyone else for help. You've made all kinds of assumptions about him based on your own resentments."

As Marcus spoke, John looked away and yanked out of his grasp.

"I know what I see, Pastor," he insisted. "Eli might know how to make himself look good, but I'm not going to be pulled in by his hypocrisy. I won't be fooled like that again." John pulled himself into his saddle and took the reins in both hands.

Marcus held onto the horse. "I'm going to challenge you, John. Let go of everything you think you know about Eli and try to see him through different eyes. Ask God to show you how to see him. You're not too busy to talk with God, are you? Ask Him to show you, and then take the time to get to know Eli. I bet you've never done that in all the years he's lived here."

John glared down at the town's peacekeeper; he just wouldn't stop.

"Fine. Have it your way, Pastor." He looked into the sky and lifted an arm to heaven. "Oh, God," he said, mockingly. "Show me the error of my ways! If I've misjudged Eli, then *please* give me a true understanding of who that gypsy boy really is, and I'll humbly bow down and eat the dirt below my feet. But if *I'm* right, then justify me to this stupid, oblivious town." He lowered his arm and looked into the pastor's disappointed face. "Marcus, I would be willing to bet every inch of my land that I am not wrong about him. Eli is a lazy, good-for-nothing, selfish man, and I plan to prove it."

He shook the reins and left the pastor standing in the road.

Chapter 90

ELI

Ada carried a tray into the sitting room and placed it on the small table in front of the sofa. There were three mugs of warm cocoa on it. She sat down next to Eli, and as he put his arm around her, she called to Sarah. The girl was engrossed in her evening playtime and hadn't noticed Ada bringing in the treat.

When she looked up from her toy, she smiled and rushed over to sit with her parents. Eli had been watching her play next to the fire with the doll that used to be on display in the hutch. He remembered carving the doll's head. He had wondered about the little girl who would own it. At the time, he had no idea it would be his own child.

Before he and Ada had left for Stonewall, he placed the doll on the bed in the back room. The Gardners' guest room would now be Sarah's room. Ada had bought some pink fabric and embroidered flowers on it before sewing it into a decorative pillow. She placed it on the bed next to the doll. When Evelyn heard of their plans to adopt the little girl, she brought over some paintings for the child's bedroom. They had once adorned the walls of one of her own daughter's rooms, but they had been stored away in the attic for many years. One of the paintings was of a kitten and the other was a lamb. They added a sweet, childlike feel to the room.

When Sarah first entered her new room, she gasped with delight as she took in every detail. She ran to the bed and swept the doll into her arms. Her eyes glistened with joy as she hugged it.

"What's her name? Is she mine?" Sarah asked as both parents laughed and nodded.

"You get to name her whatever you'd like," Ada said.

"I think she looks like a Clara," the girl mused.

"Then your names will rhyme," Ada pointed out.

Sarah smiled and said it was perfect. "Thank you, Mr. and Mrs. Gardener. I love her!" She gave the doll another big hug.

"Sarah," Eli said, kneeling down to look her in the eyes. "I don't think you should call us Mr. and Mrs. anymore. We're your parents now."

She brought her hand up to her face and pressed her cheek, as though her growing smile might start to ache.

"What should I call you?"

"What would you like to call us?"

She glanced back and forth between them.

"Would it be all right if I call you Mama and Papa?" She bit her lower lip.

Eli smiled and looked at Ada who was already nodding.

"That sounds *very* right," he said, turning back to her. She beamed and gave them each a hug.

They spent the next two days getting used to their new life and learning all they could about each other in the peaceful quiet of their home. During those days, a few visitors arrived to greet the newest member of the Gardner household. Evelyn came, as did the Webers and the Duncans. Sarah's eyes sparkled with each introduction.

She and Noah Weber got along quite well. Noah had just turned eight, and since Sarah wouldn't turn eight for seven and a half more months, he offered to walk her to school and show her the best way to get there. Hannah reminded him that the best route to school was the one avoiding rain puddles. Both children pouted slightly in their disappointment. Eli told Noah that he could walk her to school every day except for one; he flashed a proud grin at the boy and said, "Sarah's *papa* will take her to school on the first day."

That evening, Ada made the warm cocoa as a special treat to celebrate going to school in the morning. It was easy to see how nervous and excited Sarah was; she insisted she would be unable to sleep a wink. Ada patted the sofa cushion, and Sarah climbed into the spot between them. She leaned against her mama and sipped the warm drink.

Eli set his mug down; he had an idea. After going to his office, he returned with a pen, some ink, and their Bible. He smiled at them.

"When I was younger, my family's Bible had all our names written in it. That Bible originally belonged to my grandparents. Their names were inscribed at the top of the first page, followed by my father's name. My mother's was added when they married, and then my name was written down when I was born. I always wanted to add my family to the list as well, but that Bible is gone. Instead, we should write our names in the front of this one."

They both nodded as he sat down and placed the book on the table. He opened the front cover and wrote on the blank page. Sarah looked at the names closely.

"Sarah Gard-*ner*," she said carefully. "Not Gard-*en*-er? You're not really a gardener are you, Papa?"

Eli shook his head. "Not that kind of gardener."

"But you're looking for plants to take care of," she pointed out.

"The plants I'm looking for are actually children who need help, like you," he explained. "Do you still want to help me find them?"

Sarah smiled and nodded her head. "Yes!" She scrunched her face into a thoughtful expression. "But can we still plant some flowers in the spring?"

"Definitely," Eli said, laughing. He picked up his mug, and as he took a sip, he leaned back and put his arm around his family.

Chapter 91

JACOB

"You kinda walk funny, Mister," a boy said as Jacob walked back to the check-in table, holding more forms. He glanced at the boy's mother as he sat down.

"I'm sorry," she said. "You're too blunt, Billy. Apologize right now."

Jacob sighed; he was tired. James O'Conner's Leg Run was a larger event than he had thought it would be. He had never worked with so many people before. But this was a good tired; Jacob liked the rewarding feeling of helping others. He flashed a tolerant smile at the woman.

"Well, he's right. I do walk funny."

Billy leaned in toward him. "You got a new leg, didn't you?" he whispered.

Jacob lifted his pant cuff, revealing the prosthetic limb James had given him yesterday.

"How'd you know?"

"I remember what my first hinged ankle felt like. You're thinking too hard about how you walk, Mister. If you stop thinking about it, it'll get easier."

"That's a good idea, but how am I supposed to do that?"

"It's simple," Billy said. "Just think about something else. Pick something you really like. I think about a baseball card I saw in a shop window once. I want to be on one of those cards someday. Maybe it'll have to be a special team, but why not? It could happen."

Billy twisted the cap in his hand and shrugged his shoulders. "And anyway, it can't hurt to dream. Dreams get you to move forward." He grinned at his own poignant observation.

Jacob chuckled. "You're pretty smart, kid. How old are you?"

"Thirteen," he said proudly.

Jacob wrote the boy's age on his check-in form.

"I'm going to take your advice, Billy," he said as he continued to fill out the form. He handed the paper to the boy's mother and directed them to the next line.

As Jacob greeted the next family, he considered what he would think about when he tried to walk again. Baseball? Running around and playing ball was something he never thought he could do with Angel, but perhaps it wasn't such a crazy idea. He wouldn't be fast, but he already felt more stable on this new limb than he had with the wooden peg. He might not walk well yet, but at least he didn't need his cane anymore.

Regardless of whether he would ever run well enough to play ball or not, he knew what he would think about the next time he tried to walk. He would think about Laura and Angel. He hadn't seen them in three days, and it would be another three before he was home. He missed his family. Eli had invited them to go to Lambury to help with the Leg Run, but Laura stayed home with Angel. He would be turning two next month and was too young to be helpful at the event.

Jacob and the Gardners had left for Lambury on Wednesday. They spent all of Thursday with James and Sophia, training for their assigned tasks. The Leg Run was a two-day event, lasting eight hours on both Friday and Saturday. The work was constant, and there was little time for breaks, but Jacob enjoyed being involved in this event. He planned to help with the next one six months from now in October. He had a feeling he would continue to help James every year. When Angel was older, he and Laura could join him.

He glanced toward the waiting room at Ada and Sarah. The little girl was helping her mother take care of the families as they waited for their turn to be seen. The mother-daughter team made sure everyone had plenty of water and snacks. They answered questions and helped the families know where they needed to be. Sarah entertained the squirming children when they became bored with the long delay. Getting to know the Gardners' newly adopted little girl was delightful. They had brought her home two months ago and were proving to be good parents. Jacob always knew they would be, and he liked to finally see them in that role.

The Gardners were a humble and hard-working family; it was easy to forget about their wealth. When Dr. Keeler had invited the Martins to the banquet to tie leaves onto the tree, he said it was in honor of the help Eli had given. Jacob thought it was because Eli had set up the fundraising at the church. He thought the tree was going to represent all of the people who had been involved in the doctor's ministry. But when he realized that the tree only represented Eli's contribution, everything fell into place.

At first, he was confused by his mixed emotions. He wasn't sure if he was angry, embarrassed, or extremely grateful. But the more he thought about how Eli had handled the entire situation, including what had happened with Edgar, Jacob's respect for his friend overshadowed any prideful feelings he might have had.

Jacob was already thinking differently about money, especially now that he worked for Mr. Holden at the bank. Money—or the lack of it—didn't have as much of a hold on him as it used to. Having a moderate income didn't define him any more than being rich defined Eli. And being able to help others was more than just giving monetarily. There were a lot of ways to give to others, but no matter how a person helped, the most important aspect of giving was in the person's attitude: without any expectation of a return.

Jacob smiled as he greeted the next person in line. Even though he was tired, he knew he would still have energy later that evening. Nothing was going to stop him from practicing his walk. When he saw Laura, he wanted to stride into her arms without limping. James had made the limb as a thank-you for his help. It was a generous gift and Jacob appreciated it immensely, but he would've worked just as hard without it. The knowledge that he was making a difference in these children's lives was gratifying enough.

Though he would sleep well that night, he was glad to have another day of volunteering to look forward to. He had already shown his new leg to over half of the children who went through his line, and with each child, he felt a proud connection. But this pride was the good kind, and it was Eli who had helped him understand the difference.

Chapter 92

JOHN

A s John guided his wagon down the road, he glanced at the grey sky. The mild spring weather had brought just the right amount of rain, and the first hay harvest of the season had gone well. Now that it was the end of May, the soil was warm enough to plant corn. He made an early morning run to White Falls to pick up his seed. John had agreed to have it delivered to a Mr. Dixon, whom he had met less than a year ago. He began associating with him back in September. The man owned the White Falls bank and was, in fact, the one who had first introduced him to the Miracle Corn investment.

After John had shared the opportunity with the men at his meeting, it became obvious that Eli's little outburst had soured David Holden's opinion of the corn. He implied that the gypsy boy might actually be right. David believed that the corn was a bad investment and convinced the rest of the men likewise.

From that moment on, John decided to leave East Haven out of his plans. And since his account at the bank was handled by Daniel, it was possible for John to withdraw a large amount of assets with little explanation for his reasons. Daniel was not as experienced as his father and was not so bold as to ask the farmer what he planned to do with the money.

John took it to Dixon, who not only encouraged him to invest in the corn company but also offered to have the seed delivered to his own home in White Falls. He would wire the farmer as soon as it arrived. With Dixon's help, his investment moved forward without the overly cautious David Holden noticing. John bought the seed and invested half of his savings into the company. He also took out a loan from the White Falls bank, per Mr. Dixon's advice, and invested that into the Miracle Corn Company as well. When his money matured and his large, high-yielding crop was ready to harvest, everyone in East Haven would be sorry they hadn't listened to him. They would finally see how bad Eli was for that town.

He and his men would plant the corn this week. John had cleared twice as much ground than he had in previous years. He had prepared the west portion of his land; the maize fields would be conveniently butted up to the edge of Ray's property. His neighbor was also planting corn, and by mid-August, it would be apparent which crop was producing more grain per acre. He could hardly wait.

Upon his return from White Falls, John stopped at the mercantile to pick up a few items for Agnes. When finished with his errands, he guided his wagon around a bend in the road that headed away from town. As he rounded the corner, he noticed a group of children in the distance, standing by the edge of the lane. Two of the children were his own, Susie and Tommy. Their closest friends, Alberta Blake and little Eddie Johnson, were with them. The latter two lived in town but often came to the Miller house to play.

They had formed a circle around the smallest one in the group, a fifth child who did not look happy. They were pointing and laughing at the girl as they nudged her from one side of the circle to another. The target of their teasing was Sarah Gardner, the crooked nosed child Eli had adopted.

John was surprised when Eli had brought the child to church back in February, and he shook his head at the thought of the poor girl's new family situation. Well, maybe the wife could give her a better life than the orphanage, but John couldn't picture Eli as a family man. A good father placed the needs of his family above everything else and showed his children what a hard day of work looked like. A *good* father proved his love by working every day and sacrificing his own desires for their wellbeing.

Regardless of what he thought about Eli, he didn't think those kids should be picking on the girl, especially not two of his own. The children were too focused on Sarah to notice him pulling the wagon to a stop. Susie gave the Gardner girl a rough push and knocked her to the ground. The girl bumped her knee on a rock and started to cry as blood seeped from her wound. John jumped down from his seat and scolded the children.

"Hey, you kids leave that little girl alone. Susie! Tommy! You head home right now and stay in your rooms until I get there. And you two…"

He turned to Alberta and Eddie. "Get yourselves home as well. I'm going to have a talk with your folks."

The children scattered. John squatted down and looked at Sarah. He took his hat off and rested his forearms on his knees.

"Well now, that looks like it stings. Can you walk?"

She sniffled and shook her head. "I want my papa," she managed to say with a shaky voice.

"Hmm…" John sighed. He didn't want to offer her a ride, but he couldn't leave her there either. "I suppose I'd better take you home."

He put his hat back on, lifted the girl, and set her in the seat of his wagon. He climbed up, grabbed onto the reins, and coaxed the horses into motion. She continued to sniffle as she wiped her eyes. She tugged gingerly at the hole in her stocking and winced at her injury. John was afraid she might start to cry again, but instead she peered up at him.

"Thank you, Mr. Miller."

"You know who I am?" He was surprised she had addressed him by name, considering he himself had never taken the time to welcome her to East Haven, let alone given her much more than a quick glance.

"Yes, my papa told me about you."

"Yeah, I bet he did," John said under his breath. "I'm sure he had all kinds of good things to say about me."

"And he was right. I asked him why some of the kids at church call you 'Old Farmer Gruff' and papa said those kids just don't understand how hard it is to have a big farm like yours. He said you work real hard to have a pro… a pro…"

She scrunched up her face as her eyes drifted to the sky for a moment.

"…a *productive* farm, and that helps our town. Papa said you help people by giving them jobs, and since heroes help people, that makes you a hero. You helped me just now, so I know he was right about you."

John glanced at the girl. He couldn't think of anything to say. After a brief pause, her smile grew.

"My papa's a hero too. He helps children like me and Angel Martin— and the ones with all the legs!"

John didn't understand her comment about the legs, but he wasn't surprised that Eli made himself out to be a big hero to the Martin baby. And, of course, she would think of him as her hero because he adopted her. He decided not to say anything against Eli, at least not to Sarah. As she got older, she would see him through more realistic eyes. He didn't want to be the one who dashed her daddy-dreams. No matter what John thought of Eli, it really wouldn't be that horrible if Sarah continued to see him as a hero for her entire life; at least she would be happier in her ignorance. But he wasn't sure how to feel about what the girl claimed her "papa" said regarding him.

John pulled the wagon to a stop in front of the Gardners' gate. He jumped down and lifted Sarah from her seat. As he carried her toward the front door, Eli came out of the house with his arms crossed and his head tilted to one side.

"John…" he said, somewhere between a question and a greeting.

"Afternoon, Eli," he replied, cutting through the tension. "I came upon a group of children picking on your girl. Looks like they knocked her around a bit. She'll be okay, though, so you don't need to get all worked up over it."

He walked up the stairs and put the girl down on one of the porch chairs. Eli turned his attention to Sarah, and kneeling in front of her, he placed a hand under her knee. His demeanor completely changed as he ignored John to comfort his daughter.

"That looks like it hurts, Sarah. Are you okay?"

She nodded at him. "Those kids were saying mean things to me."

Eli was probably going to get angry and demand to know who the children were. When he found out some of them were Miller kids, John figured there would be hell to pay. Ada stepped out of the house and nodded a cool greeting to him. She walked up to Sarah and Eli, placing her hand on her husband's shoulder.

"It sounds like that made you feel bad," Eli said. "Why do you think they might have said those things to you?"

John was surprised to hear the calm sympathy in his voice.

The girl creased her nose as she thought about his question. "Maybe because I look different?" she suggested in a quieter tone.

"Maybe. But I think they might be sad. When people are happy, they tend to speak well of others. But sad people sometimes take their bad feelings out on those around them. What do you think we should do about it?"

Sarah glanced at both of her parents. "We can pray for them."

Eli nodded. "Often times that's all we *can* do."

"Can we pray right now?" she asked.

He nodded again, and the three of them closed their eyes.

"Dear Jesus," Sarah said quietly. "Please forgive those children for saying mean things and pushing me down. Also, please help me forgive them. Oh! And please give them something to be happy about so they won't be mean anymore—not to me or to any of the other kids at school. Amen."

They opened their eyes and Eli brought his face to hers. They touched the tips of their noses together. He squeezed her ankle and stood up. Ada scooped the girl into her arms and carried her into the house.

"Let's get that knee cleaned up," she said as she took her inside. Eli watched them go and then turned back to John. His demeanor shifted again, and his smile melted away.

"Eli, you probably ought to know that two of the children picking on your girl were mine," John stated.

"Okay," he said with a shrug.

"That's it? That's all you're going to say?"

"What were you expecting?"

John looked away. "I'll make sure she gets an apology." He lingered on the steps. "You know that girl thinks you're a hero."

Eli crossed his arms and shifted his weight. "That's good, I should be her hero. I hope your kids think of you that way too."

"She's a sweet girl," John said. "You better not disappoint her."

Eli stood in silence for a moment, shaking his head. "Goodbye, John." He moved toward his door. After stepping inside, he paused and turned back around. "Thanks for bringing her home," he said and shut the door.

Chapter 93

ADA

The early evening sun pushed long shadows across Evelyn's yard. The elderly woman was showing Sarah how to embroider a chain stitch as they sat on her front porch. Ada breathed in the warm air and watched her daughter concentrate on the needlework. She could have taught Sarah how to embroider, but she knew how much Evelyn enjoyed it.

"Do you have any grandchildren, Mrs. Russell?" Ada asked.

The woman glanced up from the lesson. "I have five," she said with a proud beam. "But I've only laid eyes on two of them. My oldest daughter still lived in town when her first was born, and I was able to meet her second child during their last visit. That was several months before you moved here. She had her third after that. The other two belong to my second daughter. I haven't met either of hers. My two youngest daughters don't have children yet, and my son isn't married."

Ada nodded with sympathy as Evelyn sighed.

"But I've heard so much about all of them," she added. "They write to me often. You know, my daughters all live very far away. It takes quite a while for their letters to get to me. And I have no desire to get on one of those loud, metal trains. Death traps!"

Evelyn patted Sarah on the cheek and sent her to sit on the porch steps while she practiced her chain stitch.

"I know it's hard to travel with young children," the woman said, making excuses for the oversight of her daughters. "I'm sure they'll come to visit again when my grandchildren are older."

"Well," Ada said, "until then, you can practice on Sarah."

She leaned forward, picked up the glass pitcher, and poured more water for Evelyn and herself. She glanced at the sky.

"I need to start preparing supper soon. Mrs. Russell, would you like to join us this evening?"

"Thank you for the invitation, but I think I will pass," the woman said. "I enjoy your family's company far too much, and I might stay longer than I should. I need to write to my son tonight. I want to send a letter off to him tomorrow."

"How is he doing? You mentioned he was working on a project. Has he finished it yet?"

"No," Evelyn said, shaking her head. "But he's learning a great deal about it. Unfortunately, it's taking longer than he thought. He has run into a few challenges and has to travel more than he had planned. I suspect he won't be able to visit for a while, but at least he has found a town to live in when he isn't traveling. Did I tell you he recently moved to Lambury?"

"Really? When was that?"

"Oh, let me see." Evelyn rubbed her chin. "Dear me! It was last June. He's been there for a year already."

"A year!" Ada exclaimed. "We were in Lambury back in December and then again in April. I wish we knew about it then; we would have looked him up for you. That's too bad." She took a sip of her water. "Is his project based in Lambury, or does it still require him to travel?"

"I think he moved there with the hopes that he could one day avoid much of the traveling. I hope he finds more success in that town; I want him to come home soon. I haven't seen him in nine years. I'm not sure I'll recognize him."

"Well, you can let him know that I, for one, am looking forward to meeting him." Ada smiled as she stood and walked toward the steps. "And I can't wait to hear about his project."

"I'll tell him, dear," Evelyn said. "If you'd like, Sarah can stay here while you make supper. I'll send her home shortly. We can get a lot of stitching done."

Ada nodded and placed a hand on her daughter's head. "That sounds perfect. Thank you, Mrs. Russell." She gave Sarah a kiss and went home to start their meal.

Chapter 94

JOHN

The leaf in John's hand was withered and streaked with yellowish-brown lesions. Mixed with the lesions were small, dark spots. He grabbed an ear of corn and pulled back the husk. The silk was dark and slimy, and the kernels were shriveled and grey. His eyes skimmed over his cornfield; this was the worst blight he had ever seen. Why was this happening?

When he first spotted the infection late yesterday afternoon, he gathered a handful of his men and ordered them onto the field. They worked for several hours, chopping down the worst of the stalks and placing them in a pile. When it was too dark to work, he sent them home. After another hour, he went home as well.

He didn't sleep at all that night. Early the next morning, he left a skeleton crew with his livestock and took the rest of his men back to the field. Several hours later, as he held the scarred leaf, he walked along the road to see how far the disease had spread.

Until a few days ago, the crop had been doing well, but this corn blight seemed to show up out of nowhere, and it was moving fast. His insides churned when he reached the fence. Ray's corn was just starting to show signs of small lesions. The blight had spread to his neighbor's field, and John wasn't sure he could control it.

He watched his men cut down stalk after stalk; it felt like they were hacking away at his gut. As he turned his gaze toward the road, he saw three figures on horseback riding toward him. He recognized them immediately, and a quick pulse of resentment shot through him. Ray Larson, Frank Stevens, and Eli Gardner dismounted their horses and scanned the cornfields.

"You've got corn blight! Are you kidding?" Ray yelled as he tied his horse to the fence. "When did you notice it?"

"Yesterday," John said. "We've been cutting it back as fast as we can, but this morning it's gotten worse."

"Why didn't you tell me? I could've had my men out here." Ray turned to the other two. "Frank, go back and round up as many men as you can. Tell them to grab as much digging equipment as they can carry and get back out here, quick. We need to dig up all the roots."

Eli grabbed onto Frank's arm and said a few words to him. Frank nodded and pulled himself into his saddle. John couldn't hear what was said, which made his anger burn hotter.

Ray adjusted his hat and looked at John. "Where did it start and how fast is it spreading?"

John pointed toward his land. "It started about a furlong that way. This morning it was about two hundred feet shy of your property, and now it's across the fence. I don't know what to tell you, Ray. It's moving fast."

Eli squinted as he scanned the corn rows. John wished his neighbor had sent that gypsy boy away instead of Frank.

"Is this going to spread to the wheat and barley?" Eli asked.

John scoffed at his question. "No, of course not. But neither of us can afford to lose our corn, so unless you have something useful to say, I suggest you get out there with the rest of the men and start pulling up the infected stalks."

"Ray, we need to get ahead of this," Eli said, ignoring him. "I think we should focus all our manpower—both yours and John's—on digging up a ten-foot strip down your field." He pointed at Ray's land. "Right there, about fifty feet in front of the disease line. Then burn it from that point toward John's land. If we work fast, it might not jump the strip, and we can save most of your crop."

"Burn it. All of it?" John yelled. "So, I don't get to save any of my corn. Is that what you're saying, boy?"

Eli turned to him and shook his head. "Look at your field. You've already lost your corn."

"I think he's right, John; blight lives in the kernels. Where did you get your seed this year?"

John crumpled the leaf in his hand and threw it on the ground. "We're wasting time." He brought his finger and thumb up to his mouth and whistled to his men.

❧

By the time Frank returned with a wagon full of workers, John's men had already moved onto Ray's field. Ray explained Eli's strategy to the newcomers, and they were soon making fast progress. After a while, more men from town showed up. Word had spread faster than the blight, and even the townsfolk not employed by the farmers came to help. Among them were Marcus and David, who looked out of place in their suit pants and nice shirts. Apparently, they didn't waste any time changing before heading over. John wasn't used to seeing them in the context of this kind of work.

Ray's wife Irene arrived with a wagon full of women. They had prepared a large amount of food and brought it to the edge of the fields, along with a barrel full of water. As they set up tables in the shade and laid out a hardy meal, Irene ordered the men off the field in shifts. She insisted they drink plenty of water and eat some food.

John was impressed with Irene's practical, take-charge attitude. She thought nothing of working alongside her husband whenever it was needed. She was well-suited for farm life, unlike Agnes. But he knew Agnes wasn't a farm girl when he married her. He never expected his wife to be like Irene Larson.

As the women served the food, John took a moment to check on the men's progress. The hot July sun beat down on the workers, and many of them had rolled up their sleeves or taken off their shirts altogether. His eyes landed on Eli. Like most of the men, he toiled in a short sleeved undershirt. His tattoos gave him the appearance that he had collected more dusty grime then the other men—as though his veins were magnetic, and the dirt was full of iron.

John watched the painted gypsy as he labored. He had never seen Eli working the land before. He was quick and steady, and he didn't seem to tire as easily as the others. As Eli pulled at a corn stalk, Irene came up behind him and placed a hand on his shoulder.

"You need some water," she said.

"I'll go in a minute."

"Go now, Eli. I know how hard you work; you won't stop if I don't make you. You're going to drop in this field right where you stand if you

313

work in this heat at the same pace you usually do. What good will you be to anyone then?"

As Eli moved to the next stalk and sank his shovel into the earth, Irene pointed to the barrel.

"Go drink some water so I don't have to explain to Ada how you worked yourself to death out here. You need to stand in that shade for ten minutes before coming back out here. No less than that, you hear me? I shouldn't have to remind you to take your breaks." She grabbed hold of his shovel; it was a firm gesture, but it was followed by a soft sigh. "I'd tell you to take a longer break if I thought you'd listen."

"Okay. I'm sorry, Irene." Eli released his grip on the shovel and wiped at his forehead. "Thank you."

As John watched their exchange, Eli's eyes swept across the field and landed on him. Irene tracked his gaze and pointed her finger at John.

"You too," she said. "Get over there and get some water. I'm not losing any of you men to this heat today."

John nodded and followed her orders without arguing.

The night glowed as the cornfield burned; dark smoke rose up and blotted out the moon. At least the summer wasn't too dry, John thought. But then he remembered that corn blight thrives in warm, damp weather, and he huffed an ironic laugh under his breath. If the season had been too dry to risk a fire, the blight wouldn't have been an issue.

After a strip of Ray's land had been cleared, Frank grabbed some torches from the wagon. John realized this was why Eli had pulled him aside earlier—to suggest that Frank bring them. Even before he mentioned the burn, Eli had already predicted what they were going to have to do. Half of the torches were taken to the cleared strip and half were taken to the far end of John's crop. The torches were lit and used to set a fire along the edges of the two fields. The flames crept toward the center, obliterating the diseased corn as they traveled to meet each other. There was nothing left to do but keep the fire from spreading beyond the boundaries of the corn.

A sour rage seared in John's gut as he watched his investment going up in flames. That rage was tinted with despair. He didn't see corn burning out in those fields; he saw all of his money, his hard work, and his hopes and plans diminished to ash. He had put everything into that corn. He was so sure it was going to be not only his validation but his vindication as well. He wanted to punch anything he could get his hands on. He wanted to curse. He wanted to sit down in the smoldering ashes and let it consume him, but this night was far from over.

The women left after all the food had been eaten and the sun had started to set. Ray and most of his men had gone home a few hours ago; the rest of *his* corn was safe. The barrel, still partially full of water, was set under a tree to hydrate the men who were staying overnight to monitor the burn. John placed a few of his workers at key locations along the perimeter of the field. The rest were sent home. It was going to be a long night.

Isaac was one of the men who stayed; Eli stayed as well. John insisted he go home, but Eli dismissed the order with a shake of his head and continued to work through the night, spreading dirt onto any flames that flared too close to the edge.

"You know I'm not going to pay you for staying," John said with no fight behind his words.

"I'm not expecting you to. That's not why I'm here."

"Why are you here, then?"

Eli leaned on his shovel and looked at him with surprise. "Because it's the right thing to do, John." He lifted his tool and continued to work the fire's edge.

Chapter 95

MARCUS

Marcus pushed the gate open and stepped into the yard as he thought about the meeting that had just taken place in his office. He had been concerned about John Miller's faith for several months, but after his crop had failed last week, Marcus was afraid the farmer would withdraw from God completely. He didn't come to church on Sunday, and it wasn't due to the controlled burn. The fire was completely quenched by Saturday morning. After a two-day burn, the farmer's field was drenched in a thunderstorm, displaying God's mercy even within the parameters of His discipline.

Of course, John's absence on Sunday may have been the result of his exhaustion. But Isaac Weber had monitored the burn for many of the same hours, and Eli never once left the field until the rain had finally stopped in the late afternoon. Both men were able to get themselves to church the next morning, though Marcus observed each nodding off during parts of his sermon.

John, however, seemed to be avoiding everyone, and Marcus was concerned that he might spiral further into his bitterness. He made room in his schedule to seek John out before the end of the week, hoping to help him navigate through this dark valley. But before he was able to do so, there was a knock on his door. John stood outside the pastor's office with his head held low and his hat in his hands. Marcus ushered him in and closed the door. After an uncertain moment, John started to talk, and once his words began, he told Marcus everything.

He was hurting. He was angry and embarrassed. He had lost a lot of money, but mostly, he was confused. He wanted Marcus to explain why this was happening and why God was being so unfair. Marcus was sympathetic but blunt. He pointed out John's pride and traced the consequences of his sin all the way to where the farmer now found himself.

They sat in the office and talked for several hours. Marcus explained how a person who is consumed with pride can be so focused on himself that his thoughts will move further from God. He showed John how far away from Christ he had grown over the years and how close to danger this brought him. He was able to help John understand why God chose to discipline him—not because He didn't love John, but because He didn't want to lose him. John's trials were not only the penalties of his own self-glorifying actions but a result of the Father's love and compassion as well. His plan was for John to be wholly restored; God desired their renewed relationship.

The most encouraging moment during their meeting was when John fully admitted to his sin and accepted that his pride had contributed to the trials he was now facing. He wept as he apologized for snooping in the pastor's office and for being blinded by his anger. And then he admitted how low his thoughts had actually sunk and how deeply in trouble he truly was. John confessed his utter shame, which threatened to drive him deeper within himself. He didn't know if he could escape its hold. He wanted to be released from life itself.

The pastor prayed with John for forty minutes. John humbled himself, joined in, and asked God to forgive him. He recommitted himself to the Lord and accepted the consequences he was facing. He asked Christ to free him from the bondage of his pride and to give him wisdom on how to protect his family from the destruction and ruin his sin had brought upon their lives.

As John was leaving the office, Marcus could see that he was transformed but still shattered. John told him his plan to relocate his family to White Falls, where he could look for work and try to build his life back up to whatever God would allow.

As the farmer walked away with slumped shoulders, Marcus closed up the church and headed to Eli's house. He pushed the gate open and nodded at his friend, who was relaxing on the porch with Ada. Sarah played quietly in the yard; Marcus waved at her as he walked up the steps and sat in the chair next to Eli.

"I just spent three hours with a very humbled John Miller," he stated.

Eli sat in silence. He crossed his arms and shook his head. "That was Miracle corn, wasn't it?"

317

Marcus sighed at his observation but didn't respond.

Eli frowned and said, "John invested in that company after all. I figured he wouldn't care about my opinion, but he should have listened to David."

"He made a bad choice," Marcus agreed, keeping his eyes locked on Eli.

Eli leaned forward in his chair. "You want me to bail him out, don't you? I can see it on your face, Marcus. I'm not sure that will help him in the long run. I can fix his problems now, but what is he going to learn from it?"

"I don't know, but his problems are bigger than you realize. He dug himself in deep. He's going to lose all of his land. The Miller farm will no longer exist, and he'll take his family away."

As Marcus explained the situation, Sarah came up the stairs.

"Papa, what's wrong with Mr. Miller? Why is his farm going away? Doesn't his farm help the families in town? What will happen to them if Mr. Miller moves away?"

The three adults turned toward the girl's question.

"I don't want you to worry about that, Sarah," Eli said.

"But Mr. Miller was nice to me. I don't want him to be sad. What if it turns him into a mean person, like those kids that pushed me down?"

"Sarah," Ada said, "why don't we go inside and let Papa and Pastor Duncan talk about this. It's time for your bath anyway." She took the girl's hand in hers and led her into the house, flashing a glance at her husband over their daughter's head.

"Sarah's right, you know," Marcus pointed out. "John and his family are not the only ones who will be affected by this. If East Haven loses the Miller farm, we're all going to feel it. A lot of men will be out of work when John leaves."

Eli sighed and peered at the pastor with resignation. "All right, Marcus. I'll talk with him. But I'm not sure he'll accept my help."

Chapter 96

JOHN

Isaac Webber had just left with the evening milk delivery. John sat in his barn as a heavy exhaustion ran through him. He leaned forward with forearms resting on his knees and stared at the straw dusted floor. He had sent most of his men home earlier, keeping a few on hand to check his other crops and keep them well irrigated. He almost expected those few men to return with news of another plague. He deserved it.

John moved numbly through the motions of the day. He felt as though he had been cut open and spread out, exposing all the ugliness inside. He didn't like what he saw, and he didn't like that others could see it too. He had a hard time understanding why God loved him, as hideously as he had acted. Even so, the idea that God *did* still love him filled his heart with a thirsty ache for his heavenly Father—and for a peace he hoped he might feel someday.

John rested his head in one of his hands, accepting the regret that would nag at his soul for a long time before any acceptance could begin to cover it. He prayed that joy would eventually replace that regret, but today he just felt weary.

As he sat on the hard, wooden bench, he heard someone walk into the barn. Looking up, he expected to see one of his workers, but his eyes met Eli Gardner. John closed them and hung his head again.

"You have every right to come in here and gloat, Eli. But I just don't think I can handle it today. Please," he begged. "Let me be."

"I didn't come here to gloat. I came to apologize."

"*You* want to apologize." John looked up again. "What for?"

Eli sat down on a milking stool that was across from him. "Because I'm a stubborn man who has a hard time trusting people," he admitted. "I kept a part of myself hidden away, and because of that, I didn't give you a chance to get to know me. If I had been more open, maybe you wouldn't have been forced to make your own conclusions about me. Maybe you would have believed me when I tried to tell you the corn was a bad investment. You might not be in this mess if I had been more honest."

"No, I did this to myself," John said. "I know when to take responsibility for my own foolishness. I wish I had listened to you—or at least to David. I had no reason to doubt him. I just had to do it my own way; I was so sure I was right."

He rubbed his brow and sighed deeply. "Listen, Eli. I was unfair to you from the beginning. I spent way too much time thinking poorly of you and judging you incorrectly. I said and did some horrible things. I'm sorry; I was wrong. I saw how hard you worked out on that field. Maybe you were just doing it for Ray, but thank you."

He peered at Eli for a moment. "Why don't you work like that every day? I know you have it in you. You could easily work your way up to Ray's lead man and give the other workers a run for their money. Don't you want to give your family more than you do now?"

Eli studied John for a few seconds. "What do you think I do when I'm not at Ray's?" he finally asked. "I don't work to help myself; I work to help others. When I'm not at the Larson farm, I'm helping someone else who needs it more than Ray does. I don't think you ever saw it because you never thought you needed help before. But now you do." He leaned forward. "Marcus told me you're thinking of moving to White Falls. John, you can't do that. Your farm is too important to this town. If you leave, a lot of men will be out of work. They won't be able to support their families. You need to stay."

John shook his head. "You don't get it. I don't even have enough to pay my men for the work they've already done this week. I have nothing to give Ray for his losses, nothing for my loan. I won't be able to pay for next year's crops—not even with what I might bring in with my wheat and squash. I doubt I can maintain my livestock through the winter, and I should probably give back all the hay I purchased from Ray in the spring. At least that could go toward what he will lose in his corn yield."

He let out a resigned sigh. "I don't have a future in East Haven. I appreciate how highly you think of my farm, but I am a ruined man, Eli."

320

"You're not ruined. Not if someone invests in your farm until it can stand on its own again."

"And who's going to do that?" John asked with a scoff.

"I will. But with some conditions."

John looked at him, confused. "You?" He searched the young man's face. Eli was serious; there was no mocking in his expression. "You..." John said slowly as realization dawned on him. "You can invest in my farm. That was you all this time. You helped the Webers... you did that. But what about the Martin baby? It doesn't make sense. You weren't on that list."

"You're right about the ledger, John; I wasn't on the list. But that doesn't mean I didn't help them."

"Wait... you paid for what the town couldn't raise." The puzzle pieces started falling into place.

"I told you I kept a part of myself hidden."

"Then, why did you say you couldn't help with the Webers' home? Why did you make us all think that?" John asked.

"I never said I couldn't contribute. You came to that conclusion on your own. I said that *you* couldn't tell the other men how much they had to give. It wasn't your place to decide what they could afford."

Eli paused for a moment as John tried to wrap his mind around the information he now had.

"Come on, John. Let me invest in your farm. I have the money; I could buy it outright. But I don't have the knowledge or the desire to run it. I want you to have it back someday. God has given you a talent for farming as much as He has given me a talent for investing."

"Investing..." John said with a self-critical chuckle. He thought back to when he had told the men about the corn investment. "...and what would you know about that?" he said, mocking his own words from that day. "So, these conditions of yours, what are they? I guess it's only fair that you get to tell me what to do after I tried to do that to you."

Eli laughed before taking on a more serious, business-like tone. "I'll cover all your losses this year and your expenses for next year, but you're going to have to become your own employee. Pay yourself what you pay your highest compensated worker; you'll have to learn to live on that. At the end of the year, any profit your farm makes above the cost of running it will be used toward paying off what I've invested. You'll do that for as many years as it takes to pay it back completely. After that, the farm is yours again. You can do whatever you want with your profits."

"So, I pay you back interest free? You won't make any money from this, you know. I guess that's more than fair. You're being too easy on me."

"Oh, you won't be paying me back," Eli explained. "You'll put those payments toward a charity, any one of your choosing."

"I suppose you're going to oversee that," John said.

"No, you can work with David on that; I don't need to hang over your shoulder. You'll be accountable to God, not me. After I give you the money and we set things up with David, our business is done."

"Why are you doing this?" John asked.

"Actually, you have Sarah to thank. She helped me realize something."

"Really? What's that?"

"She helped me recognize that investing in you feels right. People will always be a good investment." He reached out a hand to John. "If we have a deal, let's meet with David first thing."

John grabbed onto his hand and gave it a grateful shake. "I guess I'll see you at the bank in the morning. Hey listen…" He dropped his head and ran his fingers through his hair. "I know I don't deserve this, so..." He lifted his eyes and looked at Eli. "Thank you, friend."

Chapter 97

ELI

Sarah and Lily sat on the ground by the caravan's smokehouse, creating a miniature village out of sticks and rocks. They leaned twigs together to form houses and placed various sized rocks by them, insisting they were vardos. They traced roads and trails into the dirt. They picked flowers and weeds and placed them next to the tiny houses as a way of decorating their little yards. The mid-September sun kept the ground warm, and they created their town for hours. Eli enjoyed watching them play.

When he had told Sarah last month that they would be visiting the winter camp and spending six nights in the vardo, she was excited to finally meet her extended family. She knew the caravan had adopted her mama and papa just as her parents had with her. She loved listening to Eli talk about their time with the caravan and begged for a new story almost every night. After six months and many repeated stories, she said she felt as though she had known them her entire life. Come September, all those familiar characters would move from story to reality. She gleefully looked forward to what she called an adventure of a lifetime!

The following month, they enjoyed good weather during their two days of travel. Eli made a point of stopping for a meal in Clearwater. He told Sarah the story of how he met Dr. Keeler, which led to meeting her. Once they were back on the road, Ada made up thought provoking games to entertain the girl during the most tiresome stretches of their journey.

They arrived at the West Woods right before supper, and Sarah was delighted with the camp. She was greeted affectionately by everyone, and after Jed gave her a big bear hug, she traced his tattoos with her finger.

"You're just like my papa," she said with a smile.

When it was Rosa's turn to hug the little girl, Eli watched them instantly fall in love with each other.

Right after the adoption, Eli had written to Harold Ross and asked him to pass on a letter he had enclosed for the caravan. They received it in March, and after learning that the couple had adopted the girl, they looked forward to their next visit with great anticipation. When the small family finally arrived, Jed and Rosa doted on her and gave her the gifts they had been saving up since spring.

Though Lily was almost a year older than Sarah was, they got along well. Within the first day, the girls were inseparable. They alternated whose vardo they slept in and went for daily walks with Myra along Badger Creek. At twelve years old, Myra was like a little mother, playfully ordering the girls around. Sarah and Lily loved the attention and followed her orders without question.

Sam still lived in Tony's vardo, and for the most part, he ignored the young girls. He had grown almost as tall as his father and had similar coloring, but his features were more like Goldie's. Even so, Eli could see a bit of Ira around the boy's eyes.

"I can't believe how fast the kids are growing up," Eli commented to Jed as they sat by the fire. "I remember when Lily was born, and now she's almost nine. And Sam is practically a man. It's only been a year since I last saw them. What happened?"

"You know," Jed pointed out, "you married Ada at Sam's age. He just turned sixteen a few weeks ago."

"What! That can't be right."

Eli looked at Ada. She was laughing as she visited with the other women. Where did all the time go? So many things had changed.

"I'm sorry about Cobra," he said, glancing back at Jed. "I loved that dog too. That first night, if he hadn't sat on my feet, we probably would have sneaked out of the camp. I don't know what would have become of us." Eli chuckled. "You must have felt like you were taking on quite a handful when we ran into your vardo. But you changed our lives, Jed."

He smiled at Eli's words and lowered his eyes. "You seem like you've had a good year, son. You're in a better place than you were last fall."

"Yeah," Eli agreed. "Life is peaceful right now. I love being a father, and I've finally let go of a lot of things; I stopped fighting." He looked at the man who had helped him through his most difficult struggles. "Jed, I want to ask you something."

"Sure, what's going on?" He looked up from the fire.

"I want you and Rosa to come home with us. I want you to live in East Haven and be Sarah's grandparents."

Jed was silent.

"You don't have to decide now," Eli continued. "Talk with Rosa about it. You wouldn't have to worry about anything. We have room in the house, and we could always build onto it if we need to. Please consider it."

"What about the others?" he asked.

Eli would have invited them all to come if he thought they would agree. He understood why Jed mentioned them, he was asking him and Rosa to leave one part of their family for another. It wouldn't be an easy decision either way.

"Maybe they could change their summer market route and travel east instead of west," Eli suggested as he threw a stick onto the fire. "East Haven could be one of the towns on their new itinerary. I don't think God wants me to leave that place; I'm not done yet. Perhaps I'm just being selfish, but I miss having you around. I don't want our time together to be only one week out of the year. Tell me you'll at least think about it."

"I'll think about it," Jed promised as he leaned back in his chair and sighed.

Chapter 98

ADA

Ada set the candle on the small table by the bed and slipped under the covers, curling up to Eli. They had returned home yesterday evening with just enough time left in the day to give Sarah a bath. She had played hard all week and was at least two shades dustier because of it.

When it was time to leave the West Woods, she and Lily held onto each other as they cried over their impending separation. Sarah finally let go of her friend and made a tearful round of goodbye hugs. By the time she reached Rosa and Jed, the little girl could hardly speak as tears etched dark lines onto her dusty cheeks. They hugged her tightly and assured her that it would seem like hardly any time had passed before she saw them again.

Ada noticed an unspoken exchange in the glance between Jed and Eli. When Jed pulled him into an embrace, he whispered a few words to him. Eli nodded and clasped him on the arm before helping his family into the wagon.

The morning after their return, the little family went to church. All the way into town, Sarah talked about the worship time they had shared with the caravan. She wanted to know why her papa didn't play his guitar at their home church and why they couldn't sit around a fire during the services at East Haven.

Ada pointed out that it would have to be a much bigger circle, and the building wasn't large enough. She winked at Sarah and asked her to list all the things she liked about her Sundays with the town. The activity helped guide Sarah's mind back to the style of worship they would experience that day.

Ada loved visiting the winter camp; she missed everyone in the caravan throughout the year, but she also noticed how comfortable it was to come home to East Haven now. She loved both places; they each felt like home in a different way.

"Agnes Miller and I had a very agreeable conversation today," she said as the candlelight flickered shadows onto their ceiling.

"I'm glad to hear it," Eli said. "I don't know how much John has told her about what happened to his farm or my investment in it, but everyone can see the change in him. Maybe she's happier now that he's at peace. It's already affecting his workers. You should hear how highly Isaac speaks of him these days. Of course, I don't think I've ever met anyone as positive as Isaac. He was even optimistic after his house burned down. There isn't an ounce of pride in that man; he accepts help as graciously as he gives it. John and I could both learn a few things from him."

"I think you're too hard on yourself," she teased. Grinning, she poked him playfully in the side.

He grabbed onto her hand and turned toward her. "I asked Jed if he and Rosa would consider coming to East Haven to live with us."

Ada's heart skipped at the idea. "What did he say?"

"He said he would take a month to think about it and talk over the idea with Rosa. He'll write to us when they have an answer. We probably won't hear from him until after we get back from the Leg Run in October."

"Oh, speaking of that," Ada said, "did you know Mrs. Russell's son lives in Lambury? We could call on him while we're there. It would be nice to finally meet him."

"No, I didn't know. I'm not sure that will work out this time. You remember how busy we were in April. I've already purchased the train tickets, and I didn't allow for any extra days in the city." He reached up and brushed a lock of hair out of her face.

"Oh, well. Maybe next time." She sat up and leaned over the candle to blow it out.

As she laid back down, she rested her head on Eli's shoulder. It did feel good to be home. She closed her eyes and prayed that she would have a chance to share her love of the town with Jed and Rosa.

Chapter 99

ELI

Eli barely noticed when Ada walked into the sitting room, drying her hands on a towel. A few minutes earlier, Eli had come in through the front door and sat in one of the parlor chairs by the fire. He meant to let her know he was home, but the letter in his hand had distracted him.

On his way home from the post office, he sifted through a stack of mail; one of the letters was from Dr. Keeler. As he began to open it, he noticed the next one was from Jed, and he immediately abandoned the first. Eli had hoped to hear from him in October, but having to wait until mid-November for Jed's answer wasn't hard to understand. It was a big decision and he wouldn't make it lightly.

He went into the house, set the rest of the mail on the table by the sofa, and tore open Jed's letter as he sat down in one of the chairs. While his eyes skimmed over the paper, Ada came in and sat in the chair across from him.

"I didn't realize you were home," she said quietly. He continued to read for a few more seconds and then looked up with a smile.

"It's from Jed. Ada, they said yes."

She returned his smile as joyful tears pooled in her eyes.

"That was an answer worth waiting for," Eli added with a laugh.

"When?" she asked.

His smile relaxed the smallest amount. "Not for a while. They want to finish out the next market season. The earliest they could come is September. That's still ten months away."

328

A slight look of disappointment flashed over Ada's face, but she straightened her shoulders and broadened her smile.

"Well, it will go fast, and before we know it, they'll be here. We may want to wait to tell Sarah, though. Ten months may not be long for us, but it will seem like forever to her."

Eli nodded as he thought about how long ten months was going to feel to him.

"I think you're right," he said, attempting to be as positive as she was. "I'm going to write to them and suggest we visit earlier in September than we usually do. We can help them get ready for the move and travel back together. It'll be a snug fit, but they can stay in the house with us. I told Jed we could add on if we need to." He laughed. "That should make Mrs. Russell happy. Hasn't she been telling you for years that we need to do something with this place?"

"Yes," Ada said, giggling. "I'm sure she will have some very definite ideas on what we should do. You better consult her before you start." She winked at him. "I'm so happy they said yes. Thank you for asking them. Well, I guess I should finish the dishes." She stood and kissed him before disappearing into the kitchen.

Eli leaned back in his chair and thought about his talk with Jed last fall. What he had told Jed then was just as true now; he felt convicted that God wanted them to stay in East Haven. Even while having his most challenging conflicts with John and Edgar, he knew deep in his heart that he couldn't leave. It would have been easier to return to the winter camp, but easy wasn't what God required. Eli pushed through those difficult times, and now he felt a quiet peace.

In fact, everything in his life seemed to have calmed down. He and Edgar maintained a neutral acquaintance; neither spoke of their run-in with each other regarding Jacob's money. Eli, however, always brought Ada with him whenever he needed to go to the mercantile. He hoped her presence would make Edgar feel less apprehensive.

John, who had become a humble and contrite man, seemed to want a true friendship with Eli. When it was time to harvest his other crops, he shared with Eli how merciful God had been despite the corn failure. His other crops were remarkably healthy and had produced better than expected. During the harvest, when Eli wasn't at the winter camp in September or at the Leg Run in October, he worked on John's land for two days a week and on Ray's the other three.

After the harvest, John told Eli his plans for the next season. He promised to buy all his seed from a reputable source. He would need to rotate his fields because of the blight, and to be safe, he was considering not planting corn at all for the next two years. When he asked Eli's opinion, Eli reminded him that he was the expert and should trust himself to make the right decisions.

"You know, John," he said. "You really need a foreman or a manager. You have a big farm and I think you take on too much of the work yourself. No one doubts that your farm is well-run, but I think you would benefit if you had someone overseeing the work with you."

"I suppose you want the job," John said.

"No. I definitely do not want that job. You have a few workers who are better qualified. Isaac Weber has worked on your farm for quite a while now, hasn't he?"

John nodded. "Yeah... Isaac has always been a faithful worker."

As Eli thought about John's transformation, he couldn't help but realize how much it contributed to his own peace, which made it easier to wait on God's timing. He planned to enjoy the day-to-day existence of a tranquil life over the next several months. The only thing on his schedule until Jed and Rosa moved in was the next Leg Run in April. This, Eli thought, would be a nice change of pace.

Chapter 100

JAMES

James O'Conner surveyed the mess scattered around him. The Leg Run events always left his studio in disarray, but he was used to that. It would only take a few days to clean up. But he felt bad for the volunteers who had to work in such chaos. As untidy as the studio was, though, he had seen worse.

The last three events were much less stressful than the ones before. Of course, that was because of the same volunteers he was so worried about. He had more help over the past year than he ever had previously, and with Eli's funding, he was more prepared and had better supplies.

This was the third event in which the Gardners and Jacob Martin had volunteered to work. Last April was their first event, and it had gone well. They were brave enough to come back in October. Now it was April again. A full year had gone by, and they had plenty of experience; they seemed to be professionals during this Leg Run.

They remembered the children and made comments to each about how much they had grown since last seeing them. The families benefited from the extra help as much as James did. There were fewer questions and less confusion in the lines, and the waiting room seemed more pleasant because of that.

As James straightened the stack of papers in front of him, he made a mental note to file them away on Monday; he was too tired tonight. Eli tapped on his door and peeked into the private room used to fit the limbs onto the children during the event.

"We're heading over to the hotel now," he said. "We'll see you and Sophia at church in the morning, but we'll need to leave right after if we're going to make the afternoon train."

"Eli, wait." James scanned his desk for a paper he had put aside for the young man. "I wanted to tell you about the hospital's budget meeting. They hold a public assembly every August before their fiscal year ends. It's an open meeting for any current or prospective donors. Most of the meeting will detail the planned budget for the upcoming year. The board appeals to donors who are willing to contribute toward the hospital's funding needs. But they also set aside part of the meeting to listen to proposals from medical charities outside of the hospital. These charities are seeking to collaborate under their umbrella, but the board members are picky about who they work with. They want to keep their donors happy, so they won't take on any unpopular projects. I thought you might be interested in attending this year." James handed him the flyer.

Eli scanned the information. "In August," he clarified. "I think that might be interesting. Thank you, James. Will you be there?"

"Oh, no! I've tried that before. Needless to say, my presentation was a disaster, and the hospital wasn't interested in funding us. But then I met you—I think God's plan was better. Anyway, you never know what you might hear at the meeting."

James yawned and stretched as Eli folded the paper and put it in his pocket.

"You worked hard today," Eli said. "Get some sleep; I'll see you in the morning."

James nodded and waved after him as he left the room.

Chapter 101

ELI

Eli slipped into the hospital's budget meeting shortly after it had started. He had hoped he would have a few minutes to freshen up at the hotel, but his train had arrived in Lambury late that morning. By the time he checked into his room, he was only able to toss his bag onto the bed and smooth out his jacket before rushing out the door.

He took a trolley to the hospital, and after a quick search of the ground floor, he located the meeting in a large, crowded room. All of the seats in the conference room were taken, so he stood in the back with a few other men and soon realized he hadn't missed much.

A long table had been placed in the front of the room on a raised platform. Elderly men in glasses sat with stacks of papers in front of them. They wore high-quality business suits and droned on about budget figures and cost projections. They talked of their need to raise funds for public art on the hospital grounds as well as a plan to remodel the waiting rooms and cafeteria. They discussed staff wages, equipment, and their back stock of supplies. Eli began to tune out their words, wondering if this was a wasted trip.

He looked around at the other men in the room; most were dressed in business attire. He was underdressed in his rumpled travel clothes, but there wasn't much he could do about that. Eli missed much of what the monotone men in the front were saying; those closest to him were chatting a bit too loud. They told each other jokes and gossiped about this person or that; he wondered why these men had bothered to come at all.

Soon, the person who would speak next was being introduced. Eli didn't hear his name or what he would be discussing, but he could tell by the man's rough, informal manner that he wasn't a hospital board member. Maybe he should pay closer attention. As the guest speaker stepped up to the podium, the group of gentlemen next to Eli continued to talk and laugh; their volume seemed to increase.

"Oh, come on. This fella spoke at the last two meetings," one of them said to his companions. They snickered.

"You'd think he would get the hint," another said.

The man at the podium said a few words to the board member who had introduced him, but Eli was still unable to hear the exchange because of the disruptive chatter next to him. He decided to move to a new location halfway down the length of the conference room. Once there, he leaned against the wall and was able to hear the rest of the discussion.

"…you presented last year, did you not, sir?" the board leader asked.

"Yes, and the year before that," the man confirmed. "But I believe this year the hospital will truly understand the importance of this mission, especially if—"

"Yes, yes. Hold on a moment," a second board member said, holding up his hand. He had large front teeth, giving him a subtle chipmunk appearance that brought a grin to Eli's face. "If most of the other members recall your presentation, why don't you jump to the end and sum it up quickly. Just get to the main point, and state what you're asking the hospital to consider."

"Right… Of course," the man at the podium said, looking down at his hands. He shuffled the notecards he was holding and then, with a sigh, tucked them away in his jacket. "Well, as you know, I work with children who have been rescued from abduction."

Eli perked up at the man's words and took a few steps forward.

"Many of these children are taken at a young age with the intent to be sold into forced labor or physical exploitation. The few who are rescued come to us at various stages of their abduction. Our ultimate goal for these children is rehabilitation and reintegration. We hope to reunite them with their families or, when that isn't possible, to find suitable homes for them."

Mr. Chipmunk signaled the man to pause. "Sir, could you explain why you feel the hospital would be interested in a program involving these children? It seems as though you should be talking to law enforcement. Abduction and exploitation are legal matters, not medical issues."

The man nodded and ran his hands along his jacket. "Yes, the rescuing of the children *is* done by law enforcement, but we work with the children immediately after they've been rescued and processed. We are often their first contact with—"

"Excuse me," another board member interrupted, this one skinny with a large beaklike nose. "You aren't really answering the question. We don't understand why you are talking to us. Perhaps an orphanage would be better suited to take these children in."

"That's not actually correct," the man said, waving his hand in a negative gesture. "Orphanages are not prepared or equipped to work with the emotional and *medical* needs of these children. They are malnourished, injured, and abused—both physically and emotionally. They have illnesses and other physical traumas that need to be addressed immediately, sometimes over several weeks or even months. And I have barely touched on the mental and spiritual trauma these children face. They need a safe, long-term facility that is equipped to handle both the medical and emotional sides of their recovery. Perhaps a wing in the hospital dedicated to—"

"Ah, now we come to it," Mr. Beak-nose said. "How many of these children do you expect us to care for?"

The man at the podium folded his hands together. "Those of us who are currently working with these children commit to their long-term care. We can have up to six children at any given time, and the reintegration process can take from nine months to a year. Occasionally longer."

The board members shook their heads and murmured to each other, appearing to lose all interest. The man continued with more passion, holding up both hands and raising his voice to regain their attention.

"But we are not as organized as we could be if we had a localized facility, and I know that this would affect the—"

Once again he was interrupted by Mr. Chipmunk. "I'm sure you can appreciate that it is not practical for the hospital to dedicate an entire wing—or even a section of a wing—and its staff for just a few children per year who may or may not be able to reintegrate into society. Honestly, I doubt any of our donors would be pleased to see their money go to these kids who, quite frankly, would be viewed as damaged goods."

"But if you would just—"

"I'm sorry, sir, but we need to move on to the next presentation. I suggest you rethink speaking to us next year. I don't believe the hospital is the right partner for your project. Thank you; that will be all."

The man was ushered off the stage and shown to the side door. Eli stood in a daze throughout the entire presentation, but he soon realized that the speaker had left the room. Eli still had no idea what his name was. He jogged to the door and, slipping through it, entered a long hallway. The man was already at the far end of it, walking away with slumped shoulders. Eli called out to him.

"Excuse me, sir!"

The man turned and waited for him to catch up.

"I would really like to talk to you more about your ministry. I'm Eli; I didn't catch your name."

"My name is Charles…" he began. As he reached for Eli's hand, the door opened, and another man came running toward them.

"Wait! Please," he yelled. The new arrival was flushed with excitement. He stepped up to them and vigorously shook their hands as he spoke. "My name is Thomas Ives. I'm a physician, and you are exactly who I have been looking for. I'm certain I was supposed to meet you today. Please, let me explain."

Eli and Charles both nodded and mutually encouraged the interruption.

"Over the last year, I have been feeling convicted to work with children in need. I didn't understand to what capacity until hearing you speak just now. Please understand, I'm not concerned about my income." He shifted his eyes between them. "I just want to provide a service regardless of the wages. I came here today hoping I would find something to pursue along these lines. When you started speaking, I knew your ministry was the answer."

He looked at each of the men with an earnest expression. Charles was still nodding, and Eli couldn't suppress his grin.

"Oh, I'm sorry," Dr. Ives said, checking himself. "I jumped into your conversation. Are you colleagues?"

"Actually," Charles said, "Eli just introduced himself a few seconds before you came through the door. I would have to say, this day is turning out to be more productive than I thought it would be a few minutes ago. God has brought me a physician, and…" He turned to Eli. "I can't wait to learn about your interest in my work."

Eli continued to grin at the men. "Can I buy you both a coffee? I think you'll want to hear what I have to say."

Chapter 102

CHARLES

Charles sat across from the two men. Their table was shaded against the August sun by a large, two-toned umbrella. He chose this one, knowing it would be quieter out in the open air than inside the crowded coffee house. Eli took a sip of his drink before setting it on the table. He looked steadily at Charles and began to speak.

"I think your work with rescued children is extremely important, but I think the hospital board was right; they're not who you should be talking to. Even if they were willing to give you rooms and staff, it isn't the right environment for the kind of healing these children need."

As he spoke, Eli removed his coat. Even in the shade, the air was too warm. Charles noticed the tips of thick, dark lines peeking out from his cuffs. This man had tattoos.

"You sound like you have a better understanding of these children than most people," Charles said, removing his jacket as well.

"I do." A shadow passed over Eli's face. "You see, Charles, twelve years ago my wife and I were those children. Let me ask you something. The ones you work with, are they marked?"

Charles nodded. "Yeah, some of them." It was a detail he didn't often share.

Eli rolled up his sleeves, revealing more of his tattoos. "After we were abducted, we were able to escape a few days later. But not before we lost our families—and not before we were branded by the men who took us. We had our marks covered up, but that kind of scar doesn't ever go away."

He paused and rested his arms on the table. "Shortly after we escaped, we were taken in by a group of people that nurtured and loved us. They helped us heal by showing us the unconditional love of Christ. That's the kind of environment you need to create for the children you're helping."

"And you have an idea how I can do that," Charles said, leaning in toward Eli. His heart raced with the anticipation of moving closer to an answered prayer.

"I think you should build a transitional home and staff it with a physician," he said, indicating Dr. Ives, "as well as people who have a heart to minister to this type of trauma. I think it should be located in a small town far away from large cities."

Charles nodded. "I think you're right. Do you have any suggestions for me?"

Eli returned his nod as a large smile crept onto his face. "I own ten acres in a small town. I'd like to offer a portion of it as a possible site. How do you feel about relocating?"

"Well, I'm fine with that," Dr. Ives chimed in. "I'm not married; relocating would be easy."

Charles felt a rush of excitement in his gut. Was this really happening? This was the closest he had ever come to a fulfillment of his goals. A location, of course, was only the beginning; there was so much more that would need to be figured out, but it was a step in the right direction.

"You said you were married, Eli. How will your wife feel about this offer?"

"She'll be fine with it. She has a generous heart and loves kids. She understands what these children are going through, and she'll want to help."

"How far away is this town? Where do you live?"

Charles picked up his coffee and took a sip. He wanted to appear more composed than he felt, at least until he was certain this man's offer would work out.

"It's just a few hours by train. Are you familiar with East Haven?"

Charles almost spit his coffee out when he heard the town's name.

"East Haven!" He blinked a few times as he set his cup down. "You're from East Haven? I have family there."

"Really," Eli said. "What's your surname?"

"Russell. My mother lives in your town."

Eli started to chuckle. "Your mother is Evelyn Russell?"

Charles nodded as Eli laughed out loud.

"Mrs. Russell is my neighbor. You know the property I'm talking about, but I think you'll remember it as having belonged to the Colebrooks."

"Yes! Oh my goodness, I can't believe this. The Colebrook property would be perfect."

Charles was beside himself. A portion of land in his own hometown was being offered as a location for a transitional home. And the type of facility Eli was suggesting could help these desperate children far better than any situation he had thought to pray for in the past. God was amazing! He glanced at the two men who sat at the table, looking as excited as he felt.

"Well, what a day this has turned out to be. I now have a physician and a location. All we need now is some funding. We need to find someone who feels passionate about our cause *and* has money. I don't suppose you can introduce me to someone like that?"

A glint of excitement danced in Eli's eyes as he held out his hand in a greeting. "I'm Eli Gardner," he said. "I am *very* passionate about your cause, and I happen to have money."

Chapter 103

ELI

E li met Marcus at the station in White Falls. As he stepped off the train, he waved at the pastor. The men clasped hands and Marcus led him to his carriage.

"You look like you haven't slept in days."

"I haven't," Eli admitted.

The excitement from talking with Charles Russell and Thomas Ives was the only thing keeping him going. After meeting the men Wednesday afternoon, they spent the rest of that day and most of Thursday making plans for how to proceed with the transitional home. Eli would need to talk to David about cost analysis, while Charles looked into architects and discussed the new plan with his law enforcement contacts. Charles figured he would need a month to wrap up his affairs in Lambury. They looked at a calendar and decided on September nineteenth as a date for his arrival in East Haven.

That would work out perfectly. After Eli had received Jed's letter last November, he and Ada made plans to take Sarah to the winter camp early in September. During their visit, they would help Jed and Rosa prepare for the move to East Haven. When they returned, Eli would have plenty of time to meet Charles in White Falls by the middle of the month. Dr. Ives would arrive two months after Charles.

Eli asked if he should mention their encounter to Mrs. Russell or wait until Charles had a chance to write to her. The mischievous son smiled and suggested they surprise the woman. After all, it would only be a month later, and if he knew his mother, she would have prepared a room for him several years ago when he first considered moving back home with her. She had probably kept it ready for him all this time, praying for a visit someday.

Once Charles was settled in East Haven, he and Eli would begin to make more detailed plans for the transitional home. There were many things to consider, and the men estimated needing the entire winter for planning, which would allow for construction to begin in the spring. Realistically, the home's opening day would be sometime next fall.

During the year of planning and construction, any rescued children would have to continue with the minimal help provided by the volunteers Charles had worked with previously. Eli prayed for the protection and healing of those children who might miss the opportunity to stay at the transitional home. He longed to speed up the process, but it was important to take the necessary time to do this project right. Charles had already been working on it for four years; if he could still be patient, then so could Eli.

As he rode in the carriage with Marcus, Eli knew he would have to get some sleep; the exhaustion would hit him hard, but for now, his thoughts were racing. His mind kept going over what he had discussed with Charles and Dr. Ives. He made a mental list of everything that needed to be done before September nineteenth.

"Marcus, could you drop me off at the bank? I think I can still make it to my lunch appointment with David. I have a few things I need to ask him."

As Marcus nodded, Eli's foot began to tap lightly. He thought about what the next year would be like. This project felt so right! This was what God had brought him to East Haven to do. He had just found the rest of his plants, and because of God's provisions, he could stake up these weak, weather-beaten plants and give them the support and nourishment they needed to survive until the harvest. As impatient as he was to start working, he remembered to be still and praise God for His faithfulness.

Chapter 104

JED

Jed guided the wagon toward East Haven as Eli and Charles discussed their ministry project. Jed had first heard about it ten days ago when he and Eli spent a lazy afternoon fishing from the bank of Badger Creek. Eli had told him about Charles and the home for the rescued children, which he was not only going to build on his property but also fund and help run. Jed was used to Eli's enthusiastic drive; he had seen it before. But the passion in the young man's eyes for this particular project was stronger than ever; it was all he talked about, and his talking was constant.

When Jed and Rosa had finally made the decision to move to East Haven, they were motivated by their desire to be active grandparents. They wanted to be with Sarah every day and watch her grow up. But now that Jed knew about the children's home, he had yet another rewarding reason to look forward to their move. After the excited young couple told Rosa about the project, she was eager to offer her nursing skills to Dr. Ives. Naturally, it would be hard to leave the caravan, but Jed and Rosa wanted to keep themselves open to any path God placed in front of them. They felt as though a new season in their life was about to begin.

Before leaving the winter camp, Eli told the caravan about his plans. They were impressed, but the permanency of the children's home, coupled with the fact that Jed and Rosa were leaving with them, confirmed in their minds that Eli and Ada would never return to the winter camp for more than a quick annual visit. Ira said as much to Jed, but he assured him that even though the knowledge was bittersweet, the group accepted that these changes came from God.

After a long discussion with the caravan, Eli persuaded them to visit East Haven at the end of March before construction on the children's home began. He hoped they would bring his vardo with them and stay long enough to celebrate his twenty-ninth birthday. Sam could drive their vardo; he was now seventeen. After a two-week visit, the caravan could easily make it back to the winter camp with enough time to prepare for the start of the market season in May. Everyone, including Levi and Bea, agreed to come.

Soon, it was time for Jed and Rosa to say goodbye, and there wasn't a dry eye among them. The two vehicles set out on the road in the early morning. Eli drove his hitch wagon while Jed guided the horses that pulled his and Rosa's vardo. Sarah chose to ride with her grandparents, and together, the family of five traveled away from the West Woods, which had been Jed's home for over two decades.

Upon arriving at their new home, Jed parked the vardo next to Eli's horse stables. He and Rosa moved into the third bedroom but kept their wagon home set up as an extension of their living space. They could easily access it from the back door. Eli told them of his plans to add a second story to his house when construction on the children's home began. He wanted three more rooms: a permanent office for himself, a room for guests, and another child's bedroom. Perhaps they would adopt again in a year or two.

On the morning following their return, the Gardners rode to church, and the newest members of the family were greeted with a sincere welcome from many of Eli and Ada's closest friends. Even Laura's mother Edith acted civilly toward them, though she remained formal and reserved. Rosa and Grace had taken quite a liking to each other when the Duncans had visited the winter camp; Jed could tell, as he watched their reunion, that they would soon be close friends.

On Wednesday morning, Eli asked Jed to accompany him to White Falls when he picked up Charles. He explained on the way that Mrs. Russell was still unaware of her son's imminent return. The weather was warm, and the journey was uneventful; Eli and Charles were able to discuss their plans throughout the entire drive, and Jed smiled proudly as he listened.

Soon, the wagon pulled up to Evelyn's home where Ada, Rosa, and Sarah visited with the woman on her porch. She was giggling at whatever she was telling her guests, but as she turned toward the vehicle, her smile froze in place. Her hand moved to her mouth, and she tried to stifle her cry as she ran to the wagon.

"Oh, my child!" she said as Charles climbed down. She patted him along his shoulders and arms as though looking for reassurance that he was actually there. "Dear Lord! You have brought him back to me," she said with a quiver in her voice.

Charles reached his arms around her and pulled her into a wholehearted hug. When he finally let go of her, she asked, "How long will you be in town?"

"If you're willing to have me, I'll stay for good."

Evelyn nodded and hugged her tall, broad-shouldered son again. As mother and son sat on the porch and visited, Jed and Eli pulled his trunk out of the wagon bed and took it to the room that Evelyn had, indeed, prepared for Charles when she had first heard from his lawyer six years earlier.

After several minutes of thanking the men for bringing her son home, she was finally calm enough to listen to Charles speak of his plans for the children's home. He described the events leading up to his introduction to Eli and their decision to partner together on his project.

As Jed listened to Charles talk about Eli, he felt a deepening pride for the young man he had adopted, a pride that would have matched any birth father. Charles told Evelyn of Eli's offer to donate much of his land to the ministry and to completely fund their endeavor. Realization dawned on her face, and she turned to Eli and shook her head.

"I will be forever sorry that I misjudged you and Ada when you first moved here," she said, lowering her eyes. "But even though I would have never suspected any of this, I can't say I am surprised by it now that I truly know you."

"You're a good neighbor, Mrs. Russell," Eli replied. "You don't have to apologize. You've been a supportive friend to Ada, and we're both grateful for you. But it would be helpful if you could please keep our plans confidential for now. We'd like to wait until spring before we tell the rest of the town; we still have more details to figure out."

"Yes, of course," she said with a chuckle. "I can keep my mouth shut when I need to. I'm not so much a gossip as that." She smiled and glanced over at Jed. "You know, Mr. Gardner," she said, "I do think your tattoos suit you well. My boy has one also. I've never seen it, and it's been ten years too long for that!" She turned to her son. "Please, Charles. I'd really like to see it now. Would you be willing to show me?"

He smiled at his mother and nodded as he began to roll up his sleeve.

Chapter 105

ELI

Eli rounded the corner of the barn and found Ray repairing a fence post. The old farmer glanced up from his task and nodded a greeting as he stood up.

"Can we talk, Ray?" Eli asked as he stepped forward.

Ray removed his hat and leaned against the fence. He peered at Eli as though he knew where the conversation was headed. "Every time you ask for time off, you have a certain look on your face," he said. "It's a sympathetic look, and then I know you've found someone who needs your help more than I do."

"I'm sorry." Eli shifted his weight onto his other foot.

The farmer squinted as he continued to peer at him. "You know, I've suspected something for a while now. You don't really need to work for me, do you?"

"No," Eli replied, "not for the money. I would have worked for nothing, but I knew you wouldn't let me." He paused for a moment and lowered his eyes. "You're right, I do need to help someone again."

"There's something different in your voice." Ray wiped his forehcad and replaced his hat. "You won't be coming back to work, will you?"

Eli shook his head.

Even though he had only slept for a few hours, Eli felt wide awake when his eyes popped open. The brisk January morning was slowly gaining light, and there was much that needed to be done. Later that night, he and Ada were hosting a dinner meeting for a handful of guests who were either directly involved in the children's home project or knew something about it. With the help of David Holden, Eli and Charles would share the final details.

When Charles arrived back in September, he took a couple of weeks to settle in. During that time, he gave his undivided attention to his mother. However, by early October, he and Eli were hard at work. They began gathering information, writing up projected budgets, and consulting professionals. It consumed a good portion of their time, and Eli had to send an apology to James O'Conner via telegram; he would be unable to help at the Leg Run event that fall. Instead, Laura went with Jacob. Because Angel was only three years old, he was still too young to accompany his parents. His care was split between both sets of grandparents, who were more than happy to have the sweet boy stay with them; Angel was truly living up to his name.

In that same month, Sarah turned nine. Though Eli was busy planning the children's home, he dedicated the entire day to celebrate his daughter's birthday. Ada marked the molding around the kitchen door just above the girl's head; Sarah was thrilled to see that she had grown an entire inch that year. As she skipped and danced around the room, she bragged to Noah about her inch, even though he was already two inches taller than she was.

Halfway through November, Dr. Thomas Ives moved to East Haven and stayed in a spare room at the Johnsons' home. The townsfolk were pleased to finally have a local physician, and Edgar and Nora Johnson were especially proud to have him boarding with them. But Dr. Ives would only be renting a room until the following August, at which point other arrangements would be made. Charles and Eli had not yet announced their project, so the town didn't know that Dr. Ives would be moving into an apartment and office located in the north end of the children's home. Once he relocated, he would not only be tending to the medical needs of the town, but also to the needs of the children living at the home.

As the three men continued to plot out their mission, they spent many lunch hours in David's office. The undertaking perpetually energized Eli. When he wasn't meeting with the men or making quick overnight trips to Lambury to talk with architects and suppliers, he kept Ada awake late into the night, telling her about their latest progress.

As the January meeting approached, Eli brought a long list of preparations to her and Rosa; he needed their skillful hands in the kitchen. He was vaguely aware that his pace was too rushed for Ada; she often took short rests at the kitchen table. He understood her need for the occasional break. She was already busy with housework and taking care of Sarah, but as the gathering drew closer, he required her help more often. Ada doubled her efforts despite being worn out, and Eli made sure to tell her how much he appreciated it.

"I couldn't do this without you, Ada. Don't worry, things will calm down soon."

He slipped his arms around her waist as she mixed bread at the table. She turned to face him with a weary smile.

"I'm sorry I feel overwhelmed, there's just so much to do. I understand how important this is for you, Eli, but could we please try to find one day to spend together?"

"I would love that," he said, rubbing his thumb over her cheek. "Try to hang on a little longer, and after the meeting, I promise we can have some time."

That day, Rosa and Ada worked in the kitchen all morning. Sarah helped until it was time for her to go to the Webers' house. The women chopped vegetables and arranged platters full of tasty hors d'oeuvres. A light meal with easy finger foods would be a better use of time, allowing the guests to eat while the meeting was held in the front room.

Ten people would gather in the Gardners' parlor that evening, including Eli. It would be crowded, but he could make it work. As he lit a fire and set chairs around the room, Ada came up behind him and touched his elbow.

"The food is almost done. Could we sit down for a few minutes? We should take a moment to relax before everyone gets here."

He smiled and took her into his arms, giving her a long hug. "That's a great idea. You look exhausted. I'm sorry I've been pushing you so hard. Let's sit on the sofa until our guests arrive."

They sat down and he put an arm around her. As she sank into his shoulder, he sighed and looked at the crackling fire.

"Eli, I was hoping we could talk about something..."

A knock at the door interrupted her, and Eli jumped up.

"I'm sorry, Ada, they're already here. I promise we can talk later tonight." He jogged to the door and opened it. David walked in with a leather document folder in one arm and a large presentation board tucked under his other.

"Hello, Ada," he said as he looked around the room. "Good. I wanted to be the first one here." He turned his attention to Eli. "Let's go over some figures before the meeting. Is there a place we can spread these papers out?"

"Sure. How about over here?"

Eli ushered the banker to the dining room, and he smiled apologetically at Ada before his focus was drawn away.

Chapter 106

GRACE

Grace admired the beautiful display of food spread across the table; it must have taken several hours to prepare. On one end of the table, a stack of dishes towered next to finely embroidered napkins. The guests could serve themselves on the plates and carry their food with them. It was such a quaint and novel way to share a meal. Chairs were set in a large circle around the sitting room, adding to the casual feel of the evening.

A board draped in fabric was propped against an easel in the corner. The men hovered in a tight group around the board; Eli moved his arms in broad, sweeping gestures as they conversed. Six men stood in the Gardners' house, making the parlor feel smaller than it was. Eli and Jed, of course, were two of them. The other four were Marcus, David Holden, Thomas Ives, and Charles Russell. Evelyn stood next to her son, proudly hanging onto his every word.

Grace stood apart from the group, wondering if Ada and Rosa needed any help. She leaned toward the entry of the kitchen and peered in. The women stood close together, and as Ada spoke quietly, she held her head low. Grace decided to stay back and give them some privacy.

Ada looked tired. Rosa leaned in to hug her and whispered a few words in her ear. When she let go, she gently wiped under the young woman's eyes. Ada turned her head and saw Grace watching the exchange; she smiled and walked out to greet her.

"I didn't realize you had arrived," she said.

"We just got here," Grace assured her. She gestured toward the dining room table. "Ada, this looks beautiful. It must have taken you all day. No wonder you look so worn-out. Well, at least Eli has enough energy for the both of you. You should tell him not to keep it all for himself."

"I would, but I can't seem to pin him down long enough to say anything."

Grace noticed the quick glance Ada flashed at Rosa as they strolled into the parlor to join the men. Eli suggested everyone grab some food and have a seat. Grace sat next to Marcus and leaned toward Ada.

"Where is Sarah tonight?" she whispered.

"She's staying with the Webers for a few hours."

Eli glanced at the women. He shot a grin in their direction and winked at his wife before turning his attention to everyone in the room. He opened the evening with a prayer and asked Charles to say a few words. Charles talked at length about his ministry. He showed them floor plans and outlined a construction schedule. When he had finished explaining the physical and procedural aspects of the program, he opened up the meeting for questions. He was able to answer most of their queries, but when Marcus asked about the funding, Charles turned the discussion over to Eli.

Marcus restated his question. "Eli, I'm sure you know what you're doing, but this seems like a big endeavor. Are you certain you've thought of everything? What kind of budget does a project like this have?"

Eli smiled and uncovered the board resting on the easel. It charted expenses and plotted monthly budget projections. Grace's eyes glazed over as he pointed to figures and explained a trust fund yielding a yearly income that would cover the cost of running the home. She wasn't ignorant when it came to finances, but these numbers were staggering. Marcus had told her about Eli's money, but she had no idea he was this wealthy. She timidly raised her hand. Eli paused for her question.

"I find these figures astounding," she said. "But haven't you already committed to helping other children? What will happen with those ministries? Will this project prevent you from continuing to support them?"

Without blinking an eye, Eli shook his head. "No, Grace. The home's funding comes from a completely separate account. My commitment to Nathan and James won't end."

As Eli continued to go over the expenses, Grace studied David Holden's expression. He listened with an unaffected countenance; he seemed confident that Eli had more than enough assets to put toward the children's home. She turned to Marcus, who grinned at her with raised eyebrows. He leaned over and whispered in her ear.

"I guess Eli has decided that it's safe to let down his guard."

Grace refocused her attention on the young man's presentation. As he continued to speak, joy seemed to shine out of him and touch everyone who was present. He had finally accepted the role God had given him in a play that was written long before anyone in the room knew it even existed.

Chapter 107

ROSA

Rosa carried a tray into the parlor. Eli's meeting had gone well, and the evening was winding down. Charles escorted his mother home, while Dr. Ives walked back to the Johnsons' house. Jed strolled over to the Webers' to collect Sarah. David and Marcus stepped onto the porch to enjoy the cool winter air as they wrapped up their conversation, and Grace visited with Ada just inside the front door where it was warm.

Rosa could see how exhausted the young woman was and planned to send her to bed while *she* cleaned up the mess. As she picked up the dishes that were scattered around the room and placed them on the tray, she noticed Ada glancing at her husband.

Eli was still distracted. He scanned the papers charting out David's figures. Rosa stepped up next to him and placed a hand on his elbow. He looked at her with quick, preoccupied eyes as he put the papers in order, and then shifted his gaze back to the stack. Chewing on his thumb nail, he examined the numbers on the top sheet.

"Eli," she whispered. He continued to study the papers.

"Hmm…" he said.

She shook his arm until he looked up and set the papers down.

"This is quite a vision." She pointed at his paperwork. He grinned and opened his mouth to speak, but she gently hushed him. "For someone who can see all of this so clearly, you've missed something important." She tilted her head toward Ada.

Eli sighed. "I know I've neglected her these last couple of weeks; but I promise, things are going to calm down. It was just a big push to get everything done for tonight—" He stopped when Rosa shook her head.

"Ada has been trying to talk to you for several days. Eli, your wife is going to have a baby."

His face melted and his mouth slowly dropped open. He blinked several times as he looked at Ada.

"But I thought we—" He tried to speak but closed his mouth and swallowed. He shot a desperate look at Rosa. "Is it going to be like last time?"

"I can't tell you that, but you shouldn't assume it will be. Ada will need your encouragement."

Almost before Rosa was done speaking, Eli stepped across the room and grabbed onto his wife's hands.

"Ada." Looking at her as if no one else were in the room, he lifted her hands to his mouth and kissed them. "I'm so sorry. I didn't mean to ignore you. I should have taken the time to listen to you. I've been pushing you too hard. Are you okay?"

"I'm not feeling sick anymore," she said with a quiet laugh. "I'm just tired."

As he hugged her, Marcus came into the house to see what was delaying his wife. When he saw the couple crying in their embrace, he asked Grace and Rosa what had happened. Rosa smiled as she watched them continue to hold onto each other.

"Eli has just heard some good news, but it comes with a sad memory. We need to pray that the God of all comfort will bring them safely to the end of a full nine months."

Chapter 108

TONY

Tony wondered what the little town of East Haven thought of the vardo train when it arrived earlier that day. Eli was waiting in front of the bank when five wagon homes rolled along the main street of town. He swung into the seat of Ira's vardo, which was in the lead. After greeting them, he directed the caravan to his property. They set up camp in his back yard, and there was a warm reunion. Sarah and Lily met each other with happy squeals and ran into the house to explore Sarah's room. Tony figured he wouldn't see much of those girls for the rest of the visit.

The caravan would stay in town for the last two weeks of March, and during that time, Tony hoped to have a private talk with Eli. He liked their property; it was a nice place and well situated. He was looking forward to hearing more about Eli's plans for the children's home.

Sam asked where he should park Eli's vardo, and as they moved it into place, Tony joined them and helped unhitch the horses. With all the extra animals, Eli's stables were getting crowded. It was kind of his neighbors to lodge some of them in their barns. He was glad the young couple had good people living next to them.

That evening was clear, and the group ate their supper on the back lawn. Their conversation was joyful and animated, which quickly drew neighbors to their gathering. The number of guests increased, and the visit stretched on for several hours; but as the sky grew dim, their friends departed, and the travel-weary caravan members dispersed for the night. Tony lingered and motioned to Eli.

"You have a nice place here."

"Thank you. We've grown quite fond of it."

"Do you ever miss the markets?" Tony asked.

"No, not really," Eli admitted. "What I miss is spending time with all of you."

Tony hesitated. "Ever since my ma passed away, I just don't enjoy them as much as I used to." He sighed and crossed his arms. "I haven't told the others, but I'm sure they can tell."

Eli placed his hand on Tony's shoulder. "I'm sorry. I know how hard it is."

"I've been thinking about something." Tony said as he peered around the yard. "I'd like to stay here and help you with your children's home."

"Are you sure?" Eli asked.

Tony nodded; speaking the idea out loud confirmed it in his mind.

"Well, that would be great. I'd be honored to have you. But you should talk to the others soon and give them time to adjust to your plan."

Tony nodded again. "I thought Sam could have my vardo, and I could stay here in yours if you don't mind."

"I'd be fine with that," Eli said. "But we'll also have rooms for the staff and volunteers in the children's home."

"Either way; whatever is easiest," Tony said with a shrug.

"We can figure it out later. Until then, you can stay in my vardo. Get some sleep, Tony. We can talk with Charles tomorrow, and then I'll help you tell the others."

He patted Tony's shoulder and the two went into their respective homes for the night.

Chapter 109
ELI

The little church building at the end of town was crowded on this warm spring morning. Last fall, East Haven's population grew with the arrival of Jed, Rosa, Charles, and Dr. Ives. Many years had passed since the townsfolk had seen such a quick increase, and now the visiting caravan filled the church with another ten people.

As Eli skimmed the crowd, he caught sight of his radiant wife. Her glow was not just the result of her condition; there was a happiness spilling out of her that went beyond her quickly rounding belly. He strolled up to her, took her hand in his, and leaned toward her ear.

"Why is your smile so big?"

"This is an answered prayer," she said. Her eyes darted around the room filled with their friends and family fellowshipping together. "Ever since we moved here, I've wanted to bring these two communities together—if only for a short time."

"Well, if it's possible, I have some news that might make your smile even bigger. Marcus asked the caravan to sing a few songs today. Tony, Jed, and I brought our guitars. Jed's bringing them in now."

Ada's smile overflowed with delight. Eli understood her joy; he also looked forward to sharing the caravan's music. But there was a selfish motive underlying his feelings. Today's service was going to be difficult. Charles was telling the congregation about the children's home, and he wanted Eli to speak as well. Eli hoped the caravan's lively music would help calm his nerves.

The service soon began. After the congregation sang a few hymns led by the caravan, Marcus delivered a short sermon on a subject that was well chosen. It would segue nicely into the announcement about the children's home. Before Eli was ready, Marcus invited Charles to come to the front of the church and talk about their ministry. Eli's stomach twisted into a knot. He hadn't yet planned out what *he* was going to say; he prayed that the words would come to him.

As Charles walked to the front of the church, Eli turned to look at the congregation. Their faces were hard to read. Many of these people had strong opinions and were prone to making assumptions. When Charles stepped in front of all those piercing eyes, Eli's anxiety was momentarily displaced by his respect for the man. Charles willingly placed himself in that vulnerable position and opened up to those people.

He talked of the details around his imprisonment. Several years ago, he had attempted to protect a girl from abusive treatment. She had been abducted at a young age and forced into exploitation for the profit of the criminals who had taken her. When Charles fought the man who was mistreating her, he was taken to court. Out of fear for what might be done to her, the girl was unwilling to come forward in defense of his actions. Unable to prove his innocent intentions, he was charged and sentenced to two years.

While imprisoned, he learned more about the children who were being abducted. The boys were usually sold to dishonest ship captains and forced to do menial work on dangerous voyages. The girls had an even worse life, being used over and over for the greedy gain of money. As Charles was working off his sentence and learning about these dreadful criminals, he befriended the guards at the penitentiary. The guards, in turn, introduced him to some detectives who were attempting to track down the men that orchestrate this terrible crime.

Thus began his journey to put a system into place that would help the few who could be rescued. He told the congregation about his and Eli's plan to build a transitional home on the Gardners' property. He shared his hope to support the children through their emotional, spiritual, and physical healing as the home strived to reunite them with their families.

This was a delicate ministry that required discreet handling. It would be registered under the name Children's Garden Home and would be categorized as an orphanage rather than a home for rescued children. He asked the people to be mindful of the need for discretion and to be sensitive to the trauma these children would be dealing with.

"Our intention," Charles said, "is to help these young victims navigate through a reintegration process that focuses on the loving and healing nature of Jesus Christ. It is only through our redemption in Him that any of us can understand who we are meant to be—despite our past circumstances. I think Pastor Duncan's sermon from Second Timothy was divinely inspired this morning. In that letter, we are told to cleanse ourselves so that we can be honorable vessels, prepared by God for good and noble works.

"Every one of us is a vessel made by our Heavenly Father. Some are shiny, gold-plated vessels, while others are chipped and scratched. And still others are broken and waiting to be glued back together with God's love. Whatever may be on the outside of our vessels isn't what we should focus on. Instead, we should empty ourselves and ask God to fill us with His Spirit so that we can do great things for Him. This is what I hope to accomplish in these children. And it is truly a good work for *all* of us to help them cleanse themselves of their bitterness and pain.

"Eli will now come up and share his passion for this ministry. God has placed a burden on his heart for these children. He is a man who is truly being used in an honorable and noble way. His vessel has been long prepared for this exact purpose."

Charles gestured for him to come to the front. Eli took in a deep breath and thought, "Please, Lord, give me Your courage and strength." As he looked into the eyes of the people he had lived among for almost seven years, he realized that even those closest to him had not yet heard this part of his story. He swallowed and tried to steady his shaking hands.

"Many of you know that my parents—and Ada's parents—died a long time ago. On April sixth—just a few days from now—they will have been gone for thirteen years. They died shortly after I turned sixteen. But most of you don't know the circumstances around their passing."

He cleared his throat. "We were together when it happened. Our families were having supper at my house, and in the span of two minutes, Ada and I lost everything, including our freedom. That night, we were abducted just like the children who will be living in the Garden Home."

He paused and closed his eyes during the next part of his story. "Our parents were shot and killed by the men who took us, and in that moment, we witnessed the loss of everything and everyone we cared about."

When he opened his eyes, he found himself looking into Marcus' grieved face. The pastor pressed his mouth into a frown as he finally heard his friend's entire story.

"We were fortunate enough to escape before being sold, but we didn't escape the marks that these men inflicted on us. Our arms were branded with their symbols—and the price *they* decided the loss of our innocence was worth."

Eli took in a deep breath and proceeded to tell the congregation about their time in the cages, their escape, and their flight into the woods. His story flowed out of him, and with each word, Eli felt his heart lighten as the heavy burden of silence lifted from his soul. He didn't need to be ashamed of that part of his life anymore. He didn't care what they thought; he only cared that his testimony might help someone else who felt just as broken as he had. He told them of God's presence and mercy throughout their trials. He explained how God's plan had led them to a new family who took them in without hesitation.

"In much the same way as Charles mentioned, God used these amazing people to glue us back together and paint over our scars. They showed us an unconditional love that mirrored Christ's, and because of that, we learned how to trust Him again with our lives. We were able to move beyond our trauma and allow Christ to do His good work in our hearts."

Eli lowered his eyes, and as he glanced at his arms, his vision blurred out of focus.

"Their example has confirmed in my heart how greatly I desire to pass on the love that they showed us."

He cleared his throat again and wiped his eyes.

"And it is that same absolute acceptance that I'm asking you to show these children as well. Charles and I would like to invite you to be a part of our ministry. We hope you feel led to help us raise the children out of their previous circumstances and into a better understanding of God's plan for their lives. Please come and talk with us after the service; we will be happy to answer any of your questions. Thank you for your support and encouragement."

As Eli was about to step down from the pulpit, a voice spoke out. It was Edgar Johnson, asking a question in a tone he couldn't interpret.

"I assume you're asking us to help fund your ministry. Exactly how much are you trying to get from us?"

"No..." Eli was surprised by his query. "Our ministry is fully funded. We're asking for your help in other ways. First and foremost, the children could use your prayers. You can also pray for the staff and volunteers. Another way you can help is by simply encouraging them and accepting them into our community once they're emotionally healthy enough to come out in public. Please keep in mind what Charles said earlier: this ministry requires discretion and privacy. Of course, any of you are welcome to volunteer at the home, but there is required training for all volunteers.

"We estimate having no more than six to eight children living in the home at any given time, but there will be plenty of occasions to pour love into them. Are there any other questions?"

As he looked around the sanctuary, several hands rose. Charles joined him in answering the many questions asked that morning. After Edgar, however, the others only sought clarification on volunteering opportunities. As they continued to share with the church, Eli winked at Ada, who smiled proudly as she watched him.

Eli stared at the flickering and popping flames as he enjoyed the company of his family sitting around the fire with him. A peaceful feeling accompanied the cool March evening. It had been a long time since he was able to spend his birthday with all of them, and he realized he might not get the chance again. The group would be permanently splitting up in just under a week. Of course, he would still take Ada and Sarah to visit the winter camp every fall, and he was sure Jed, Rosa, and Tony would accompany them. But a melancholy mood nagged at his thoughts and threatened to disturb the tranquility of the evening.

Tony plucked gently on his guitar as the group sat in silence. Friends and neighbors had stopped by randomly throughout the day to wish Eli a happy birthday. Each small group stayed for several minutes at a time, and many of these visits overlapped. The day was full and social, but as the sun began to hover on the horizon, the guests slowly filtered home, and the caravan was left to their serene respite around the fire.

The silence was interrupted when Ira sighed and glanced around the circle. He nodded at Floyd before turning to Eli.

"It was really good to hear your testimony."

The others agreed with nods and mumbled affirmations.

"It meant a great deal to hear what you said about us," he continued. "We're all grateful that God chose us to be your family and trusted us to help you through those times. I think I'm speaking for everyone when I say that you and Ada have been a large blessing in our lives too."

Eli crossed his arms in front of his chest. "Then why do I feel like I'm causing the caravan to fall apart?" He glanced at Tony, who had stopped playing his instrument.

Ira shook his head. "God doesn't want us to be stagnant. He brought you into our lives to stir us up. Eli, what you're doing here is a good thing, and I am honored to think I might have had even a small part in helping you find your purpose. But I have a question about something you said. You mentioned that the rescued children may be too traumatized at first to go out in public. That comment brought back memories of our first summer with you. I remember how scared and untrusting you both were."

Ira peered at the young couple sitting across from him. "I was wondering what you plan to do for the children who are too scared to go to church on Sunday mornings."

Eli sighed. "Charles and I have talked about the possibility of holding a late afternoon service just for the kids. Or, maybe a Saturday night service. We haven't finalized those plans yet, and to be honest, we haven't asked Marcus about it."

"What if I led a small service every Sunday morning, right in the children's home?" Ira threw a quick smile at Goldie.

Eli studied the couple for a moment before his eyes traveled around the circle.

"Are you saying…?" He paused and leaned forward in his chair. He didn't know if he could voice the rest of his question. "Are you saying you want to stay?" he managed.

Ira nodded.

"We talked about it last night," Floyd added. "We all want to stay and help; *all* of us. What do you say? Will you have us?"

Ada covered her mouth as tears filled her eyes. Sarah wiggled her feet as she and Lily tried to hold in their squeals. Eli sniffed and cleared his throat as he pressed his lips together and nodded.

"Absolutely," he whispered.

Everyone stood and hugged each other. The caravan laughed through their tears, and the two little girls were finally able to let their giggles spill over. As the evening continued, their discussion focused on plans for the caravan's transition. Myra, Lily, and Sarah would stay in East Haven with Ada and Rosa while the rest of the caravan traveled back to the winter camp on the first of April. After informing Mrs. Perry of the move, they would dismantle the camp, pack up what they needed, and return by the end of the week. When these plans were agreed upon, everyone said goodnight and went their separate ways.

Once inside, Eli put out the lantern and pulled the blankets around them. He leaned toward Ada and rubbed her round belly. He could just make out her silhouette in the dark. She placed her head against him and sighed happily.

"You've had a good birthday," she said.

"Yes, and your prayer has been more than answered."

"Oh, Eli. Do you know how happy I am right now?"

He reached up and wiped away the joyful tears he knew he would find on her cheeks.

"Yeah, I think I do. Are you okay with me going to the winter camp? I don't have to go if you don't want me to."

"No, you should go. I'm sure they'll appreciate the help."

"Maybe I should stay. Everyone will understand if I don't go."

"What's wrong, Eli? Why are you changing your mind?"

He was quiet for a moment. He reached his arm around her and pulled her in close.

"You're almost as far along as you were when we lost Ruth Ann. And that also happened in April. Maybe I should stay."

She placed her hand on his chest. "Things already feel different this time, and I know how to rest when I need to. I feel God's peace; no matter what happens this time, I trust Him with everything. You can stay if you want, but I don't think you need to. And if you go, you can visit the willow tree one last time for both of us."

Eli kissed her on the forehead. "Okay," he said, closing his eyes. "I'll go."

Chapter 110

JOHN

John rode his horse onto the Gardners' property and went straight to the construction site, knowing that was where he would find Eli. He held two ropes in his free hand; each one pulled a cow behind him—his two best cows. Eli met him as he swung out of his saddle.

"John," he said, glancing at the animals. "I wasn't expecting to see you until tomorrow."

"Yeah well, I freed up my afternoon. Best thing I ever did was make Isaac my foreman. Should've done it sooner. I missed out on a lot of things."

"Well, I've certainly appreciated it," Eli said. "I'm not sure you realize how helpful you've been. You've volunteered a lot of your time to the children's home—and to helping me with the addition on my place."

John peered at the new construction as he took off his hat and wiped away the sweat on his brow. The mid-July sun was beating down hard and the ride to the Gardners' took longer due to pulling the cows.

"I've enjoyed it," he admitted. "Your architect has added some impressive features to both places. Your house is real modern now, and it didn't take too long to finish. I think I'd like to make some updates to my home. Agnes would like that. And now I know how to go about it."

John glanced at the ground and rubbed the back of his neck. "I think after this harvest, it should only take me two more seasons to pay everything off." He cleared his throat. "I'm gonna keep giving half my profits to charity. That should still allow for a couple of home improvements."

He tilted his head toward Eli and squinted. "I know you said I didn't have to tell you where I was giving the money, but I thought you might like to hear that I've been giving it to the orphanage where Sarah was living. I figure it must be a good institution if it produced a girl like her."

Eli smiled. "Thanks, John. That means a lot." After a pause, he pointed to the animals. "What's with the cows?"

"Oh, yeah. These are my two best milkers. I want to give them to the Home. All those children are going to need some dairy in their meals. I could show how to milk them and teach the kids how to make cheese and butter. What you don't use in the kitchen could be sold to help cover some of the cost of running the place. I know you've got that all figured out, Eli, but if those kids feel like they're contributing, it might help with their healing. I guess you would know best about that, though."

"I think it's a great idea," he said. "Thank you."

"Also," John continued, "I thought I could help the kids plant some corn—and maybe some other vegetables. I think you have enough land for a few small crops. I can show them how to work the land; it'll be good for them to learn that skill. Don't worry about what the cows are going to eat. I'll bring over some feed every week. You can put them in your stables until we build a barn for them. I'll help with that, too."

"John, that's really thoughtful. I can't thank you enough. If we get some chickens, we'll almost be self-sustaining." He laughed. "But seriously, this will make a big difference in our food budget. It means a lot. Why don't we put the animals inside before the sun gets too warm for them?"

As the men led John's horse and the cattle toward the stable, they decided on a time to meet with Charles to discuss building a small barn with a milking station. Once they got the animals situated, they stood in the cool shade of the outbuilding and peered out at the horizon.

"Ada seems to be doing well," John said. "It's getting close now, isn't it? You nervous?"

Eli chuckled. "Just a couple more weeks. Probably early August. I think I'm more relieved now than nervous. We didn't make it this far last time."

John shifted his eyes toward Eli; he didn't know that part of their past.

"But this one is going well." He grinned at John. "Of course, I'm sure I'll be a lot more nervous when her time comes."

"Nah, you'll be fine." John slapped him on the back. "Hey, isn't this home supposed to open in a couple of months? Let's get back to work; you've slacked off enough for today."

"Me? I've been here all morning. You're the one who just showed up."

John scratched behind his ear and put his hat back on, chuckling under his breath. "You know, I still want to punch you," he confessed.

Eli laughed and shook his head. "Yeah, but I'd still win."

"I don't know. You're starting to get old, *'boy.'* And I'm feeling pretty good these days."

The men continued their bantering as they walked back to the construction site.

Chapter 111

ELI

*"E*li, wake up…*"*

It was a hot night; Eli kicked off his blankets. In a half-sleep, he reached across the bed. Ada must feel miserable in this heat. As he patted along the mattress, he found her side empty. He sat up and rubbed at his eyes, trying to shake the heavy sleep from his thoughts. Did she call out to him? A voice echoed in his mind, but it seemed more like a memory than reality.

"Ada," he whispered.

There was only silence. He glanced at the bed to make sure it was empty and then pushed himself to a stand. As he walked down the hall, he regretted not taking the time to light the lantern. He saw Ada's silhouette standing motionless in the dining room.

"Why are you up?" he asked.

She didn't answer; she leaned forward and let out a long breath. He reached for her, and she gripped onto his arm.

"Get Rosa," she finally said in a shaky voice but wouldn't let go of him.

"Do you need me to take you back to the room first?"

She shook her head.

"Is it the baby? Why didn't you wake me?"

She kept holding onto him as if her hand had a mind of its own.

"Ada, I can't get Rosa if you're holding onto me. Are you going to be okay?"

She nodded, and glancing at her hand, she slowly let go of him. "I'll be fine."

Eli ran to Jed and Rosa's room. After the addition was finished, they moved Sarah into one of the upstairs rooms, but Jed and Rosa decided to stay on the main floor—at least until the baby was born. He tapped lightly on their door.

"Rosa?"

He could hear them stirring. When Jed opened the door, Rosa was tying her robe. She was more alert then her husband, who stood in the doorway rubbing his eyes. Eli looked past him.

"Rosa, Ada's asking for you. I think it's time." That statement seemed to perk Jed up.

"Is she in your room?" Rosa asked.

"No, the dining room."

Rosa went out to find her while Eli grabbed another lantern. When he caught up to them, Rosa was helping Ada into a chair.

"I thought there might be a knock on my door tonight," she said with an encouraging smile. "You had that look about you all day."

"What look?" Ada asked.

"There's a look women get when they're about to go into labor. I saw it yesterday. How long have you been having contractions?"

"They've been waking me up all night, but I've been able to sleep between them until now," she said.

And then, as if on cue, she went into another wave of pain that made her grip the chair. The pain faded as she breathed through it. Eli knelt in front of her and rubbed her arm.

"Can I do anything, Ada?" he asked.

She rolled into another contraction and shook her head as she concentrated on her breathing. Rosa put a hand on his shoulder.

"You can help me get her back to your room. I hope you're ready to meet your baby, Eli. Her pains are close together; it won't be long now.

367

Chapter 112

SARAH

Grandpa Jed woke Sarah while it was still dark. Mama just had her baby and they sat in the lantern light waiting for Grandma to come get them. This was supposed to be an exciting time, but she wasn't sure how she felt. Since Papa was happy, she tried to be as well. She wondered if it was a boy or a girl.

She picked up Clara, wrapped her in a small blanket, and cradled the doll in her arms just like she imagined Mama would hold the new baby. She tried to pretend it was a real baby, but Clara looked like a grownup; it wasn't the same.

"You look like a mama yourself," Grandpa said. "You'll be good at holding the baby even before you—"

The door opened, and Grandma peeked in. "Come on, Sarah. They're asking for you."

She followed her grandparents down the stairs to Mama and Papa's room. As she walked into the dimly lit space, Papa came to her with an elated grin. He held out his hand and led her to the bed where Mama was holding a wrapped bundle close to her. Mama's face was red and shiny, and even though she looked tired, she was wearing the prettiest smile Sarah had ever seen.

"Sarah," Papa said quietly, "We want you to meet William." She leaned toward Mama and peered down at the little baby boy.

"This is William Arthur," Mama whispered as she turned the bundle toward the girl and pushed aside the edge of the blanket. His little red fists were balled up and resting beside his ears. He stretched his tiny pink mouth into a large yawn and made a squeaking noise at the end of it. He was beautiful, and she couldn't help giving a piece of her heart to him.

Suddenly, a heavy weight pressed in on her chest; her eyes blurred, and tears trickled down her cheeks. Papa put his hand on her back and knelt down. That used to make him exactly her height, but she was taller now. She would be turning ten in a couple of months; the two and a half years she had lived with them had gone by so fast. Thinking about it made her cry even more.

"What's the matter?" he asked.

"Papa," she said, rubbing her eyes, "now that you have your own baby, are you going to send me back to the orphanage?" Once the words were spoken, she burst into sobs.

Papa put his arms around her and drew her into a big hug. "Of course not! You *are* my own, Sarah, just as much as William is. I could never send you back."

As he wiped away the tears on her cheeks, Mama reached over and took her hand.

"We love you, Sarah," she said. "You will always be our daughter, and now you're William's big sister. We hope you want the job."

Sarah looked at the baby in her mama's arms.

"Okay," she said, sniffling. She reached in and tickled his nose. "I can do that."

The little family laughed together, as two joyful grandparents stood in the doorway and watched.

Chapter 113
ELI

Eli stood on the back porch with Jed and Marcus. The frigid December air felt good despite its icy chill. Vardos were parked throughout his back yard, making it resemble—to a small extent—the winter camp. The difference, however, was that they were all dark and empty at the moment. From where the men leaned on the railings, they could look past the wagons and see the flickering lights coming from the Garden Home windows.

When the Garden Home first opened in September, Charles and his mother rode out to the White Falls train station to meet a detective and a woman with two young girls. The woman had been temporarily caring for the children until they could be relocated to the Home. She relinquished them into Evelyn's maternal care.

The girls were quiet and cautious when they arrived at the Home, but they seemed to relax when they were greeted by Hattie's good-natured smile. She and Floyd had chosen to live in the Home, along with Tony and a female staff member named Rita. Floyd and Hattie's room was located near the back of the building. Rita lived in the upstairs quarters that were designated for the female tenants; she would act as a sort of den mother to the girls. Tony stayed on the main floor in the section assigned to the boys.

Rosa, Bea and Goldie alternated the nights they stayed in the girls' ward to help Rita; while Jed, Levi, Ira, and Eli did likewise for Tony and the boys. Occasionally, other townsfolk would volunteer their nights to give the caravan a rest.

A few weeks after the Home had opened, two boys and another girl arrived. Currently, there were five children living there. Some had been rescued recently; others had been rescued months earlier but had to wait until construction was finished. Either way, by December Eli noticed a great change in all of them as they adjusted to the feeling of safety the Home provided.

The parents of one of the girls had already been found. They visited several times but chose to have her stay at the Home while they all went through the reintegration process together. They missed her dearly, but she had been stolen away two years ago. They were wise enough to know that it would take a long time for her to heal from the trauma she had suffered. While in town, they stayed in Eli's vardo.

Hoping more vardos would eventually be used for that purpose, Eli started working with Ira on a floor plan for a house. They would build it in the spring, and Ira's family could move in by late summer. Goldie was thrilled. She and her children had never lived in a house before, let alone one with a water closet and a copper to wash clothes.

Their home would have enough room for Levi and Bea, and they would always keep a room available for Sam, even though he said he would prefer to stay in his vardo. Now that he was eighteen, he wanted to make his own way in the world. He started working for John in the fall, and his parents suspected Sam's motivation had something to do with a pretty, young girl named Victoria Carlson.

As Eli watched the lights shimmer in the windows of the children's home, Marcus patted him on the shoulder.

"You and Charles have created quite a remarkable ministry."

Eli sighed. "We couldn't have done it without God. His hand was in every circumstance that led us here. He was even in the things we couldn't see."

The back door creaked as it opened, and the three men turned. Ada stood in the doorway, holding onto a plump four-month-old William.

"You men are going to freeze out here. Would you like me to make some coffee for when you come to your senses and realize how cold it is?"

Eli winked at her. "That would be great." He smiled and added, "We'll be in soon."

They turned again and looked across the property.

"You know, Marcus," Eli said, "you and David are the only people outside of my family who know where the money for this project came from. When I finally told you about it, I was afraid you would disapprove. But you said what better way to fund a ministry that saves children from bondage than with the money God took away from the very criminals who were perpetrating the crime. You said it reminded you of how God used the evil intentions of the brothers to put Joseph in a position to save them. And, Jed, you once told me that God is bigger than our problems and sees things we can't imagine."

He peered at the two men who had played such an important role in his life.

"You've both tried to tell me I was holding onto something that I needed to let go of. I wish it hadn't taken so long to figure out what it was. Even though I knew God wanted me to use the money for His glory, I didn't want to accept it in my heart. I hated having it, and I carried around a pointless guilt that kept me chained to a past I didn't want others to know about.

"For years, I tried to distance myself from the shame I thought that money represented. Back then, if God had offered me a choice between keeping it or giving us our old lives back, I would have chosen one unknown future for another, and in the process, I would have lost all of this."

"And what would you do if He offered you a choice now?" Marcus asked.

Eli looked over the railing at the ground below them.

"If God handed me a choice like that now," he said, "I would hand it right back and tell Him I could never be qualified to make a choice that was always—and *only*—His to make. I would ask Him to do His will, and I would praise Him for His wisdom, even when it hurt."

Eli shook his head as he continued. "I don't know why those men chose to steal us away. I don't know why our parents were killed or why our baby had to die. And I certainly don't know why He chose *me* for all of this. I used to think I needed to know the 'why' before I could trust Him.

"But now I understand that I don't need to know *why* to know that His plan is perfect. I may not even like His plan, but it will always be better than mine. God is sovereign, and He promises that our trials are small in comparison to the work He is doing in us. 'Our light affliction, which is but for a moment, works for us a far more exceeding and eternal weight of glory.' Sometimes we do get to understand things in hindsight, and it's always easy to acknowledge God after the work is done. But what God wants is our trust in the middle of the unseen. He wants our praises long before we ever know the 'why' of it all."

"Amen to that," Marcus said.

They stood in silence until Eli began to shiver.

"Ada is right. It's too cold out here. I bet that coffee is ready."

The men walked back into the warmth of the house, but Eli glanced back at the children's home one last time for the evening and praised God for all that had been—and all that was still to come.

Chapter 114

JAKE

Jake climbed out of the wagon seat and looked at the large house in front of him. This was supposed to be some great place that was going to make everything better? The people at this Garden Home were going to help him find his father? He didn't even know if his father was still alive.

He tugged at his sleeve. How did he know he could trust these people? Some lawman said he would be safe here... So what? That didn't mean anything. At best this was just some glorified orphan house with a bunch of sappy do-gooders, and at its worst... well, he didn't want to think about that.

As he and the detective entered the building, Jake glanced around the large entry, wondering if it would be better to hide out in the Garden Home for a while or run away that very night. Either way, he wasn't going to stay for long. As he tugged at his sleeve again, a rugged looking man walked up to him and held out his hand; Jake flinched back.

"I'm Eli," the man said. Instead of trying to shake his hand, he pointed at Jake's arm. "Don't worry; you can trust us here, even with that."

Jake put his arm behind his back and glared at the man. "I don't know what you're talking about."

The man smiled patiently and nodded. "Believe me, I know it's hard, but I promise you're safe with us. It's Jake, right? Did Detective Browning tell you anything about us?"

Jake shifted his eyes to the detective and shrugged. "Just that you might be able to find my dad, and you claim you can keep me safe. But why should I trust you? I don't know you. What makes you different?"

"Because I know what's on your arm. I know what it's doing to you, and I know how to get rid of it."

"I said I don't know what you're talking about," Jake insisted, dropping his eyes. "...and there is no way to get rid of it. I already tried."

Eli rolled up one of his shirtsleeves. "This is where my marks were," he said, showing Jake his arm. "I had mine covered by a man I didn't know at the time, but he proved that he could be trusted, and now he's like my father. What did you try?"

Jake reached over and grabbed the man's arm. He rubbed the dark vines that twisted into a cross and tried to imagine the marks that would have been there before. He felt the smallest flicker of hope regarding the man in front of him. Maybe he *could* trust him. Maybe this would be a good place to stay after all. Deciding to take a chance, Jake brought his arm forward and pushed up his sleeve...

THE STORY CONTINUES
IN BOOK TWO

FRACTURED VESSELS

Acknowledgments

Writing this book has been an incredible journey of growth. God has continually revealed Himself throughout a process that started in September, 2018. He has faithfully carried me through my unknowns, and I am in awe of Him daily! One of the most important things He has taught me is that a project like this is not a one person job. Several amazing people joined in the completion of this book, and I would like to take a moment to thank them.

My family has been a huge support and blessing. Many thanks to my husband Karl, my two beautiful daughters Emma and Rayna, my son-in-law Kaleb, and the three lovely young women I think of as my own: Megan, Grace, and Giana. They have all encouraged my writing and have willingly sacrificed some of their time with me. They have read several versions of my book and have given great input.

I have a gracious and talented group of people in my critique circle. Without my husband Karl, and my good friends, Jill W. and Rachael J., I would not be the writer I am today. They have pushed me and often asked me to take a close, critical look at my writing. Because of them, I learned to stretch myself, even when I didn't want to, and I am better for it. Thank you!

Thank you to Karl for writing my author's bio. What a relief it was to hand that over to the person who knows me best.

Editing was one of the areas that I most dreaded. So, it is with a truly grateful heart that I mention my editorial team: Donna, Jill, and Erin. I hope you realize how much your help has meant to me.

I am overjoyed with how professional looking my book is, both inside and out. Ghislain Viau at Creative Publishing Book Design has done an outstanding job designing my cover and formatting the interior. Thank you for patiently sifting through my scattered ideas and interpreting them into such a beautiful look.

Over the last two years, I have had some steadfast cheerleaders who have been with me through the highs and lows. I call them my biggest fans. Brandi and Anna, thank you for being close by to cheer me on!

Many friends and family have read through various rough drafts of my manuscript as I honed in on my style. I want to shout out a special thank you to all of my alpha readers who helped convince me that I really could see this all the way to the finish line: both of the Christina's, all of the Cindy's, Jenelle, Elizabeth, Alison, Betsy, Debbie, Patricia, Marian, Paul, Judy, Miriam, Anna, Maggie, Tracy, Lianne, Victoria, Katie, Danielle, several aunts and cousins, my dad, and many others. Thank you!

And finally, I have to mention an immense blessing that I did not expect: the many supportive and encouraging writers and book reviewers that I have met through social media. What an approachable and friendly group! I am so grateful for the people God has allowed me to meet. Thank you for your kindness!

About the Author

Gina Renee Freitag has been a professional seamstress in many capacities for over 30 years, from wedding dresses to outdoor clothing and gear repair and prototypes. She started in theatrical costume design and construction at Whitman College while earning her Bachelor of Arts in studio art, followed by a theater staff position at Pacific Lutheran University. She has also been a homeschool teacher for the last seventeen years. She was raised in the Seattle, Washington area, and her home remains there today with her husband and younger daughter. Her older daughter and son-in-law live close by as well.

Painted Vessels is her first novel, which started merely as an interesting story in her mind. As a class project, Gina encouraged her daughter to start writing down all of her stories and decided to take her own advice as well. Once she put the words to paper and was encouraged by supportive friends, she felt led to publish this narrative. And she hasn't stopped! The stories surrounding these beloved characters continue to form in her mind. She has plans for at least three more books in the Vessels Series.

Made in the USA
Middletown, DE
22 March 2021